'An uplifting story of hope and friendship, told with sensitivity and charm.'

—Kate Storey, author of *The Memory Library*

PRAISE FOR JO LEEVERS

'A brilliant, moving novel. Jo writes so beautifully about grief and our strongest emotions, but is also very funny.'

–Zoe Ball, BBC Radio 2 Book Club

'A pleasingly complex narrative, flecked with reflections on the healing properties of storytelling . . . This promising, poignant debut concludes with that vital ingredient: a well-crafted twist.'

–*The Observer*

'A compelling drama that would make a great book club read.'

–*Good Housekeeping*

'An engrossing mystery.'

–womanandhome.com

'A raw and moving tale about family, love and secrets.'

–*The Sun*

'This poignant mystery is beautifully written.'

–*Candis* magazine

'Immersive, compelling and beautifully written – I adored it.'

–Andrea Mara, author of *All Her Fault*

'All the momentum of a thriller and all the heart of a family coming to terms with its own messy truth. Jo Leevers is a master of forgiveness, that most divine of high wire human acts.'

–Catherine Newman, author of *Sandwich*

'A book about grief, family, friendship and ultimately hope, with two truly unforgettable characters at its heart. I loved it.'
—Jennie Godfrey, author of *The List of Suspicious Things*

'So beautiful and so human. A brilliant story that will stay with me.'
—Laura Pearson, author of *The Last List of Mabel Beaumont*

'A heartfelt exploration of how the secrets we carry shape our lives. The quirky, endearing characters and the mystery at its heart had me hooked.'
—Mikki Brammer, author of *The Collected Regrets of Clover*

'An incredible story of regret, grief and the gift of time.'
—Ashley Tate, author of *Twenty-Seven Minutes*

'A beautifully written story about the family ties that bind us. An absolute joy to read.'
—Carole Hailey, author of *The Silence Project*

'A gripping story about families — the secrets that drive them apart and the connections that bind them together.'
—Eleanor Ray, author of *Everything is Beautiful*

'Utterly riveting and heartbreakingly beautiful. Populated by characters so real I could almost reach out and touch them.'
—Emily Critchley, author of *One Puzzling Afternoon*

'A touching story of love, loss and what it means to be a mother. I devoured it in one sitting, but it will stay with me.'
—Imogen Clark, author of *In a Single Moment*

The
Museum
of
Second
Chances

ALSO BY JO LEEVERS

Tell Me How This Ends

The Last Time I Saw You

The Museum of Second Chances

JO LEEVERS

LAKE UNION PUBLISHING

Published by Lake Union Publishing, Seattle

www.apub.com

Amazon, the Amazon logo, and Lake Union Publishing are trademarks of Amazon.com, Inc., or its affiliates.

EU product safety contact:
Amazon Media EU S. à r.l.
38, avenue John F. Kennedy, L-1855 Luxembourg
amazonpublishing-gpsr@amazon.com

ISBN-13: 9781662540929
eISBN: 9781662540912

Cover design by Emma Rogers
Cover image: © lucky strokes © Daria Doroshchuk © Olga.And.Design © RoyalTraveler23 © Rawpixel.com © LadadikArt © ismail19797 / Shutterstock; © L Feddes © Irina Shmakova © The Nature Notes / Getty Images

Printed in the United States of America

For Kate, with love

Chapter One

Anyone passing by Portheast's town beach at dawn was guaranteed to see a tall woman dressed in brown and grey taking dainty steps along the shoreline. Her eyes remained fixed on the sand and if she saw something that glinted, fluttered or shone, she would dip down to pick it up, swift as an oystercatcher.

This was Evelyn Silver on her morning beachcomb and, as curator of the Portheast Museum of Maritime Curiosities, little escaped her attention, be it a colourful shard of sea glass, a silted-up watch or a discarded plastic bottle. Frustratingly, it was things like drinks bottles that tended to make up the bulk of her daily finds.

'This is why I carry two separate bags,' she would testily explain to anyone foolish enough to interrupt her first job of the day. 'One bag is for treasure,' she'd say, patting the worn leather satchel looped over her left shoulder. 'While this bag' – here, she'd indicate the larger fabric tote bag hanging off her right shoulder – 'is for common beach rubbish.'

'Treasure' was in the eye of the beholder, but the same could be said of Evelyn's museum, which was full to the rafters with random objects. Some were worthy of their museum status, like the cache of gold coins that had washed up from an 18th-century shipwreck, or a set of hand-tinted antiquarian maps. But most of the museum's cabinets were crammed with the flotsam and jetsam of daily life that Evelyn found either on her daily beach walks or from rummaging in car boot sales and charity shops.

This morning's haul, for example, included:

- A piece of broken china, blue and white, depicting a bird on a branch
- One pebble in the shape of a wonky heart
- One dog's lead, its leather hardened and salt stained.

She knew that not everyone would see the beauty in these things, and in fact many might have automatically consigned them to her rubbish bag. But Evelyn treasured these pieces and added them to her ramshackle museum, whether a piece of cracked pottery, a broken toy boat or an abandoned fisherman's glove. Because when Evelyn found such an object, she looked beyond its surface appearance. She would imagine the stories that might lie behind each lost item, stories of loss and longing and love, and then she acted as a guardian until their rightful owner came looking.

Unfortunately, as Evelyn reached the end of her beach clean that morning, her tote bag of trash far outweighed her satchel of treasure. It contained three plastic bottles, two large clumps of orange fishing line entangled in rubbery bladderwrack, assorted small fragments of blue plastic and several sweet wrappers. This disparity gave Evelyn a slightly lopsided appearance as she made her way up the slipway towards the quay and the museum where she had worked for as long as anyone in the Cornish fishing town of Portheast could remember.

Before she unlocked its heavy wooden door, Evelyn rolled her shoulders, breathed in the chill air and cast a last look back at the sea's horizon. A line of pale mist hovered over the silty mud of the harbour but, further out, darker squally patches were forming, telling her a storm was on its way. Through bitter experience, Evelyn had learned that the best thing to do at such times was hunker down and wait it out. She took the same approach with the dark moods that sometimes wrapped themselves around her, knowing that by and large, they too eventually passed.

Brushing the sheen of sea mist off her dark coat, Evelyn turned the heavy key in the lock and entered her museum, which had once been a 19th-century boat shed. Above the door, a hand-painted sign read **WELCOME TO PORTHEAST MUSEUM OF MARITIME CURIOSITIES, EST. 1988.**

Evelyn's father had made the sign and Evelyn had often wondered if he'd included the **WELCOME** as a daily reminder to her, because even in her youth Evelyn had not been famed for her outgoing nature.

These days, appreciative visitors to the museum were few and far between and Evelyn endured the more casual intrusions with a tight smile. Rainy days tended to be the worst, when whole families would crowd in, shaking rain off their umbrellas and calling out to each other in what Evelyn's parents used to call 'outdoor voices'. At first, their unruly children would dash from case to cabinet, leaving wet footprints and greasy fingermarks. Then their exclamations would become more muted as they realised the truth of the matter: this was not a place where fun was encouraged. If they didn't get the hint, Evelyn found that a hard stare could go a long way.

Even adults failed to see the point of Evelyn's collections, despite her meticulous labels. 'The most boring museum ever,' read one recent Google review. 'Full of old junk. Like a day out at the rubbish dump,' said another.

Yet Evelyn was undeterred. Her cabinets of what she called Miscellanea were her most precious, because one day someone could walk in and spot that special something they had lost, be it a stray earring, a forgotten photograph or a fishing float. In the meantime, Evelyn kept watch. 'You cherish everything, except yourself,' her mother Elsbeth once told her with a worried look in her eyes.

While these occasional visitors might not understand her ethos, they couldn't complain about the entry price, which had remained the same since her father cut the red ribbon to declare the museum open some thirty-eight years ago. His hand-painted sandwich board read: **ADMISSION 20P. CHILDREN FREE.**

Evelyn left her tote bag of rubbish by the recycling bins to sort out later and placed her leather satchel beside her desk. Assessing and cataloguing her day's finds was something Evelyn looked forward to, after her morning coffee.

But first, with 9 a.m. fast approaching, it was time to open up the museum. Back outside, she propped open the door with a heavy anchor, more rust than metal these days, and then, squinting into the mizzle, Evelyn took in the view that had remained unchanged for so many years. Several harbour boats were wedged in the claggy mud of low tide, some listing sideways with a sad, abandoned look. Further along the quay, shops and cafés were starting to open up.

She heard the scrape of wood on concrete as a blond man dragged a chalkboard menu outside his bakery. She had a feeling his name was Nils or something Nordic and he sold exotic buns laced with cinnamon and rye bread dense with seeds. Whenever she walked by, the smells made her mouth water, but she made sure to keep her head high and her eyes averted. Evelyn had a mistrust of anything new, no matter how delicious it smelled.

In the distance, where the slipway met the sea, she could see three elderly men sitting on a bench. Because they sat there cogitating so often, it had earned them the (generous, in Evelyn's view) nickname of the Three Wise Men. Nothing in this scene was out of the ordinary, but Evelyn couldn't shake a sense of dread that was growing inside her. It had begun during her beachcomb, and with each step of her morning routine, the ominous feeling had bedded in deeper.

'Hiya!' A loud call jolted Evelyn from her reverie and she looked up to see a figure ambling towards her. It was Della, who ran the ice cream parlour next door to the museum. Della walked with a rolling gait, as if she'd just dismounted a horse, and was wearing a patchwork jacket she'd bought in Kathmandu, a garment so garish it pained Evelyn to look at it for too long. But as she got closer, Evelyn noticed her neighbour was waving an official-looking brown envelope and the dread she'd been trying to stave off rose up, swift as nausea.

'Hiya,' Della repeated. Della was from Australia and, along with clothes she called her 'global style', she liked to dye her hair in bright colours. Her latest shade was a vivid purple, and several lurid tendrils clung to her pale cheeks, reminding Evelyn of the veiny jellyfish that sometimes washed up on the beach.

Della was looking at her in an odd way. 'Hey, I got my letter – did you?'

'Letter?' Evelyn replied faintly.

'Yep. From the council. I'm guessing you'll have one too.'

In that moment Evelyn realised why everything about the day had felt wrong: it was precisely a month since the men in suits had come to inspect their two boat sheds. They had carried clipboards and iPads and talked too fast about revenue and visitor numbers and the need to put Portheast on the map.

Opening her envelope, Della said the words Evelyn had been dreading. 'They want us gone, Evelyn. The council. They're kicking us out.'

Chapter Two

'No idea what I'll do,' Della said gloomily. 'I already had a quick look and there are no other cafés to rent.' The two of them sat on Evelyn's favourite bench, the one where the three old men had been earlier. It looked out to sea but also gave them a clear view of the boat sheds – 'Just in case we get a morning rush,' Della said with a wry smile.

The truth was, neither of their establishments was likely to be overrun with custom on a grey morning in February. Even in summer, Della's ice cream varieties were an acquired taste. Instead of offering customers old favourites such as vanilla and choc chip, she liked to make her own unique recipes. This morning, she had presented Evelyn with a scoop of her latest experiment, mint and burdock. 'The sugar will help with the shock,' she said kindly. Evelyn took small, polite licks, unable to decide which of the competing flavours was more unpleasant.

'In truth, this space is too big for me. I only need a little kiosk – just enough room for my freezer and a tea urn. Whereas you . . . Well, you'll need all the space you can get.' Della paused to taste her own ice cream, which had an unappetisingly grey hue. She scrunched up her face. 'Yeah, this one's liquorice and nettle. Might need a bit of refining,' she conceded.

Evelyn knew what Della was trying to say – that to the untutored eye, her museum was a big confusing muddle of stuff and a clear-out was long overdue.

'I just need to get on top of my cataloguing,' Evelyn said firmly. 'But it's all significant, every last scrap. All it takes is the right person to come along. One person's rubbish is another's treasure.'

Della gave a brief nod, having heard her excuses before. 'The letter says there's a period of review, but you know how these things go. It's a done deal: all worked out on the golf course before they bother consulting people like us.'

'But they can't just close us down, can they?' A coldness snaked through Evelyn's gut – and it wasn't Della's mint and burdock.

Della passed Evelyn her ice cream, smoothed out the letter and read out the highlights. 'Reassessing the needs of the community . . . Need to generate income . . . Cornish heritage will be preserved. Comments are welcome, blah blah . . . By the deadline: 7th of April.'

Evelyn let this sink in. 'That's in two months. Looks like they want our sheds back before the summer season.' She gazed forlornly down at the twin ice cream cones in her hands. Even in the February chill, they had begun to melt and drips were running onto her hands.

Della followed her gaze. 'Yeah. The texture might need refining too.' She nodded at a nearby bin. 'It's OK, you can ditch them.' With relief, Evelyn jettisoned both cones.

Della zipped up her multicoloured jacket and dipped her chin inside the collar. 'Yep. The council wants us out. And we both know who will be moving in.'

When the men came in the first week of January, all they said to Evelyn was that they were 'reassessing the property'. Thinking they might finally repair the hole in the roof, Evelyn gave them a polite welcome, but they didn't seem interested in the leak, each deftly sidestepping the bucket she'd placed under it.

The one in charge was called Mr Palmer. He had thinning hair and eyes as pale as a rabbit's and he asked to see all sorts of ludicrous things: a tally of visitor numbers, a health and safety policy and visitor feedback forms. When he saw the sign announcing the prices, he let out a bark of a laugh. 'That all you charge?' he asked. 'Well, that explains a lot.'

Evelyn knew it wasn't worth wasting her breath explaining the rationale – 'Enlightenment before profit,' her father Edwin Silver had announced to the modest crowd that had gathered for the opening ceremony – as the rabbit-eyed Mr Palmer was too young to remember how things used to be. So she said nothing and watched as he and his mute sidekicks went off to poke around Della's ice cream parlour next door.

After their visit, Della had headed straight to The Lugger pub, because if there was one thing that Portheast excelled at, it was gossip.

'It's all because of that celebrity chef, Rufus Rowan,' she'd reported back to Evelyn. 'Apparently, he's been sniffing around for a new restaurant to add to his empire. And our two "authentically Cornish boat sheds" are exactly what he's looking for. He's promised to put Portheast on the map.'

Evelyn was vaguely aware of this Rufus chap, a man with a bristling orange beard and an attitude to match. Already, he owned a string of restaurants in seaside towns, serving up fish and chips at four times the going rate. And now he wanted to take over Evelyn's museum.

Slowly, the two women walked back to their sheds. As Evelyn stepped inside, the calm darkness welcomed her back. With relief, she breathed in the briny smell, a saltiness that was woven into the coils of rope, the ragged nets and the myriad shells, stones and scraps of driftwood set under glass.

To her surprise, Della had followed her in and was bending down to look for something on the floor. 'Here you go.' Della brandished a brown envelope identical to her own. 'You must have missed it.'

Evelyn glanced at the pile of post that had accumulated behind the door: red pizza leaflets, a brochure for conservatories and what she strongly suspected was a final demand electricity bill. She accepted the brown envelope and walked over to her desk in the corner, where, after a moment's indecision, she added the council's letter to the tallest pile of paperwork.

As Della took in the scene of disarray that was Evelyn Silver's workspace, she mouthed a silent 'Wow'. Evelyn cleared her throat. 'Like I said, I just need to catch up on a bit of cataloguing.' But even she had to admit that her 'in-tray' had got a little out of hand.

Three sides of her desk were piled high with reference books and academic papers, then balanced on top of each pile were various objects. They included a rusty ship's lamp, a box of 1970s seaside postcards, a dry agapanthus seed head, three beach shoes (none matching) and a piece of driftwood that, to Evelyn's eye, resembled a rearing snake.

It was a good job Della couldn't see underneath the desk, which had become Evelyn's unofficial overflow space. There was a pile of mildewed books about fishing and several bin bags containing . . . well, she wasn't sure what was inside them. All she knew was those bags were starting to disintegrate and each time she sat down, small fragments of plastic floated around her ankles, like mournful black confetti.

But now, Evelyn needed to make a show of curatorial efficiency. She retrieved the morning's finds from her satchel and placed all three onto the green blotter in the centre of her desk: the broken shard of china, the pebble and the old dog's lead.

She picked up the pottery and began to dust sand from its edges. 'This fragment, for example, displays a hand-painted design that dates back to . . .' And then Evelyn stopped. With a flush of embarrassment, she realised her mistake: she'd recognised the pattern not from her book about the Cornish china clay industry, but from a shopping trip to St Austell last weekend. She'd popped into Asda for more bin bags, and a mug bearing that exact bird-on-a-branch motif had caught her eye, for the very reasonable price of £2.99.

Casually, Evelyn set aside the offending piece of pottery. 'I mean, not everything is going to be precious . . .' she blustered.

But Della wasn't bothered about the broken mug. She was staring at the old dog lead. This was a surprise to Evelyn, who had herself hesitated over which bag to put it in, unsure whether to classify it as treasure or trash.

Thoughtfully, Della ran a finger over the lead's ragged orange trim. 'Mind if I borrow this for a bit?'

'The dog lead?' Evelyn was itching to snatch it back because she wasn't used to people meddling with her treasures. 'I'm not sure. I mean, it's not useable. The leather is tough. It's been in the sea too long.' A note of alarm crept into her voice. 'More importantly, it's not catalogued yet.'

But Della was already making for the door. 'Don't worry, I'll bring it back,' she called out in her cheery antipodean accent. 'I've got a hunch.' And then Della was gone, leaving only the faint scent of patchouli oil in her wake.

Determined to put all thoughts of Della and the council out of her head, Evelyn resolved to make a dent in her cataloguing and labelling and remained hard at work for the rest of the morning. She did not pause to make her usual coffee and she definitely didn't let her eyes drift towards the stack of paperwork with the brown envelope on top. Evelyn liked the fact that once she was seated, the piles of books and papers around the perimeter of her desk served as a wall effectively hiding her from sight – not that anyone else ventured into the museum that blustery winter day. Outside, she could hear the spatter of rain on the paving stones and the slap of the sea against the quay as the tide crept in.

Where possible, Evelyn liked to make her museum labels using the manual typewriter her father had given her. Recently, the letter *E* key had stopped working, so the challenge was to describe each object without using that troublesome vowel.

Perhaps, she mused, it was a good thing that Della had taken the dog lead away – and not simply because the only viable alternative to 'lead' was 'leash'. Without knowing more about the object's history, she was unsure where to put it in the museum. Given its canine association, it could join the Natural History case, alongside the sun-bleached bones of seagulls, a fragile tern skull, and pink tellin shells, tiny as a baby's fingernails.

Realistically, the dog lead was probably destined for the catch-all Miscellanea cabinets. In Evelyn's view, this was where the museum's most interesting finds ended up. And inside the third Miscellanea cabinet lay Evelyn's most special object of all. For the past thirty-eight years, it had been her abiding hope that someone would walk into her museum and recognise it, but no visitor had ever shown even a passing interest in the item labelled:

One piece of fine Cornish lace, handmade. Found attached to a baby's blanket with a safety pin (now rusted), 3 December 1964

This fragment of cream lace, with its ragged edges and intricate motif of daisies, had been pinned to the blanket wrapped around the infant Evelyn when she had been abandoned. She had been a foundling, left with no note – only this piece of lace as an identifier.

Within the week, she'd had the good fortune to be adopted by Edwin and Elsbeth Silver of Portheast.

Evelyn supposed that meant she was the rightful owner of that piece of lace. But who made it, and why they had pinned it to their newborn baby's blanket yet never came back to claim her, had remained a mystery.

Finding its maker was one of the reasons why Edwin Silver had pulled strings to turn this abandoned boat shed into a museum. Handily, it also gave Evelyn a job at what had been a tricky time in her life, having recently returned from a failed traineeship in London that had ended in tears and disgrace. It was best if Evelyn remained closely anchored in Portheast, her father had said gravely, where she could catalogue facts rather than indulging in fanciful stories.

But with both her parents now gone, the true reason behind this museum had become clearer: her father had paved a way for the broken Evelyn to be made whole. It was a long-held hope that, if that lace remained on display, one day someone would walk into the Portheast Museum of Maritime Curiosities, recognise it and claim Evelyn as their own.

Having recently marked her sixty-first birthday, Evelyn knew the likelihood of anyone turning up and identifying the lace was becoming smaller. But if her museum disappeared, that slenderest hope would be gone for good.

Chapter Three

Although Della had run her ice cream parlour from the shed next door for almost six months, ordinarily the two women's paths rarely crossed. This was mostly down to Evelyn, who had become adept at ducking her head and doing a swift about-turn whenever she saw someone she had no desire to speak to. Handily, Portheast was a warren of thin cobbled lanes and alleys, which provided plenty of getaway routes. But at her desk, Evelyn was a sitting duck and even her fortress of stacked books could not hide her forever. As she saw the colourful shape of Della ambling towards her for the second time that day, she couldn't help feeling a little irked.

Her annoyance was swiftly replaced by alarm when she noticed that Della was not alone. Behind her, a figure lurked in the shadows and, for once, Evelyn regretted her rule of rarely turning on the electric lights.

'Hiya,' Della called, as if wandering in and out of Evelyn's museum was a daily occurrence. 'I've brought someone to see you.'

As Della stepped aside, Evelyn recognised Leonard, an elderly bachelor, who used to walk a stiff-legged spaniel along the quay every morning and evening. But now she thought about it, she hadn't seen him, or his dog, Jago, around for a while. His dog had been old and slow and had spent more time sniffing than walking. 'Come on, matey,' Leonard used to say, jollying the dog along.

'Hello, Leonard,' Evelyn said, getting to her feet. 'How are you keeping?'

The old man didn't reply. Instead, he held out his hands and, to Evelyn's horror, she saw he was holding the dog lead – the one with orange trim that she'd found that morning. Worse still, he was blinking back tears.

Had Evelyn inadvertently found the grim evidence that his beloved dog had drowned? Did he think she was somehow to blame? She cast a look of panic at Della.

But then Leonard spoke up. 'Thank you,' he managed. 'He's gone now, my Jago. Died a few months back and I scattered his ashes on the beach. Went down before anyone was up – even you,' he added.

'And that's his lead?' Evelyn asked, only half understanding.

'Yes.' Leonard ran his hands over the gnarly leather. 'That was my mistake, see. I scattered his ashes and then, in a fit of I don't know what, I threw his old collar and lead into the sea as well. At the time, it felt like the right gesture – setting him free or something.' He brought out a grubby handkerchief and blew his nose loudly.

'But as soon as I got home, I saw how stupid I'd been. I'd already got rid of his bed and blanket, given away my tins of dog food. And without his collar and lead, I had nothing to remember him by.'

He shook his head. 'I mean, that's nonsense because you never forget, do you? I still think he's with me, like I could turn around and he'd be trotting behind.'

Evelyn gave a quick nod. She knew that feeling of turning a corner and expecting to see the one you missed the most, or spotting the back of a familiar head in a crowd – and the awful hollowness as you realised your mistake.

'So, when young Della brought me Jago's lead . . .' Leonard paused, because he'd started to tear up again. 'It felt like a second chance. I know Jago's gone and he had a good life. But now, whenever I miss him, I can reach out for this.' Again, he ran his hands over the leather, which already seemed a little softer. 'It'll be a comfort.'

'Yes, I can understand that,' Evelyn said.

'Well, thank you for finding it.' Leonard began to shuffle off. 'I won't keep you.' Then he paused and glanced around the shed. 'Funny. Lived here all these years and I reckon this is the first time I've been in here.'

He paused at the cabinet labelled Seems Like Yesterday, in truth a place for all the things that didn't count as Miscellanea and weren't very nautical, like a wooden rolling pin, a battered tin miner's mug and a McDougalls flour bin from the 1970s. Shaking his head, he said, 'All of human life, right here. Who would have thought?'

The two women watched him go and, when Evelyn looked over, she was surprised to see Della had a gormless smile on her face.

'You did a good thing, Evelyn Silver,' Della said.

'Well, it was your doing, really.'

Della didn't answer. Instead, she absent-mindedly picked up a small brass snuffbox from the desk, one Evelyn had found at a boot fair several years ago but had not yet got around to cataloguing. Della turned the box over in her hands, as if weighing something up. 'The thing is, reuniting Leonard with that lead, well it's given me an idea for how we can save this museum. And my shed, while we're at it.'

Already, Evelyn had had more conversations today than in the past three months and she wasn't sure she could maintain her polite demeanour much longer. 'Go on,' she said with forced patience, dabbing at the tip of her long nose with a tissue.

'It's like Leonard said, "All of human life, right here." And, as you're always saying: "All it takes is the right person to come along."'

Evelyn sighed. She didn't need her *raison d'être* explained back to her. But it was like something had lit up inside Della and she was off, talking a mile a minute, gesticulating as she walked to the back of the museum and Evelyn's Miscellanea cabinets.

'All these bits in here, you found them locally, right?'

Evelyn nodded.

'Well, just like that dog lead meant something to Leonard, all these lost things could be linked to people who live right here, in Portheast.'

'Precisely,' said Evelyn tightly.

Della was still smiling, and nodding like one of those plastic toy dogs people used to put on the back shelf of their cars.

Evelyn frowned. 'And your point is?'

Della spoke slowly, as if to a child. 'So if we can prove this museum is relevant to local history and the community, doesn't that give us a better chance of saving it?'

There was a glimmer of logic in what Della was saying. But all that the men from the council had asked about was visitor numbers, which were embarrassingly low.

As if she could read Evelyn's thoughts, Della was talking again. 'You need to encourage people to come here, though. Because they can't spot things if they're too intimidated to set foot inside, can they?' Della looked around. 'I mean, turning on a few lights would be a start.' She reached for a cord and a fluorescent tube above them pinged and flickered into life. 'Come on, Evelyn, you could make this place amazing so it's actually a proper maritime museum, not just Evelyn's Shed of Weird and Unwanted Stuff.'

Evelyn bristled, and felt herself stand that little bit taller, as if to put a distance between herself and this enthusiastic antipodean. But then she thought of those men in suits and their barely concealed sneers as they had looked around her museum, and the high hopes she and her father had had for this place. 'It will be a fine enterprise,' he'd told her, a proud smile playing around his whiskery mouth.

Once Della finally left, the day was almost over. With all the toing and froing, Evelyn hadn't got far with her cataloguing. She'd only managed to classify and type up labels for:

Small painting of sailing ship, oil on wood. Circa 1930s, poss. attrib. A Wallis

and

Fishing bib, traditional. As worn for pilchard fishing, circa 1950

She congratulated herself on avoiding the errant *E* key for both labels, but gave up when it came to her next item, a framed print of an egret. It simply wasn't possible.

Her final task of the day was sweeping out the blown-in sand and it was always a satisfying one as it took her to the deepest recesses of the museum, where her second most precious exhibit resided.

For a brief period in the summer of 1991, the diorama entitled Cornish Life in Bygone Days had been a popular draw. It depicted a somewhat idealised scene, with two mannequins that had been donated by Debenhams in Truro that Evelyn had dressed in old-fashioned attire. The man stood by a range cooker, resting one rigid elbow on the mantelpiece and holding a long-dead pipe, and the woman was frozen in the act of carrying a tray of Cornish pasties to the table. Evelyn had made the pasties herself, using modelling clay and crimping the edges before adding several coats of varnish.

Assembling the kitchen items and dressing the mannequins in character had kept Evelyn busy in the aftermath of losing her mother, when Evelyn was twenty-eight. Naturally, she had grieved, but in truth her mother Elsbeth Silver had always been a vaporous presence in her life, a person who had drifted in and out of the house, only occasionally remembering to rustle up a meal or ask after her daughter. In contrast, her father had been much more solid: the rock to Elsbeth's fluctuating tides of affection.

He'd encouraged Evelyn to make the diorama, praising her creativity, and seemed flattered when she came looking for props and costumes. But that was decades ago. The display's heyday was long gone and, in recent years, Evelyn had heard sniggers of derision from visitors. Someone had stolen a pasty from the woman's tray. Another time, she discovered the man's wig had been pulled to one side, covering his eye. As she'd righted the stiff hairpiece and adjusted his metal-framed spectacles, Evelyn had whispered a quiet apology.

That day in February, as she swept her way past the diorama, she reached out and brushed her fingers against the hem of the woman's dress, a Laura Ashley design she'd found in her mother's wardrobe. Leonard was right: sometimes it was nice to reach out and touch something familiar. What would happen to Mr and Mrs Cornish Life and the rest of her collections if the museum closed? It didn't bear thinking about.

At that moment, Della's idea to get people through the doors seemed like a good one and perhaps her only chance to save her museum – and it might even bring Evelyn the answer to her own story she so craved. She stopped sweeping and stood a while, listening to the wind stirring the net floats that hung from the rafters. She should be filled with hope, excitement even. So why did she feel the steady creep of fear? It was as if someone unseen was starting to peel back the protective layers she'd folded around herself. And Evelyn did not like this feeling, not one bit.

Chapter Four

Evelyn's parents had been no-nonsense people: practical scientists by nature, they never concealed from Evelyn the fact that she had been a foundling. Whenever the subject arose, they discussed it with their usual direct approach.

'Your birth mother was unable to look after you,' her father would explain.

'Chances are, she was too young. Or unwed,' Elsbeth would add. 'But we'll never know.'

They hadn't even been worshippers at the church on the north coast where the infant Evelyn had been left, but a local doctor knew that the Silvers in Portheast were good people, ready to start a family, and a private adoption was set in motion. 'One day it was just the two of us – and then we were three. But we soon adjusted,' Elsbeth used to say with a vague smile.

In her teenage years, Evelyn saw how other mums and dads busily ferried her classmates to the cinema, play dates and sports tournaments and she realised how little impact her own presence had made on her parents' routines. She supposed they must have endured things like teething and chickenpox but, for the most part, the Silvers did parenting on their terms. Even the name they chose for their new baby felt a little half-hearted, as if Edwin and Elsbeth had started to thumb through a book of baby names but never got beyond the initial *E*.

As soon as the infant Evelyn was able to walk, weekends were spent on family field trips, as Edwin Silver specialised in the study of coastal flora and fauna, ably assisted by his wife, an accomplished watercolourist who painted the plants.

By the age of six, Evelyn knew how to identify milkwort, yarrow and eyebright; at ten, she was more familiar with the Latin names of plants than the Top Forty. In the school holidays, while her classmates jumped off the quay and learned to swim, Evelyn was far away, walking remote clifftop paths with her parents. In companionable silence, the three of them would comb through the clover and hardy grasses in search of perfect specimens.

The Silvers kept her warm, clothed and fed. They gave her a place in the world, albeit an unconventional one. The TV was only turned on for the news and she was frequently dressed in her mother's cast-offs: Marks & Spencer frocks and sensible cardigans. Her first bra was also a hand-me-down and she wore it with shame, crossing her arms over the too-large cups until the PE teacher had a quiet word with her mother.

At home, it was a tradition that on the first of each month, Evelyn was called into the kitchen to have her height measured. She stood with her back flat against the wall so that Elsbeth could mark a horizontal line above her head. At such moments, Evelyn felt like one of her parents' greenhouse plants: routinely tended and measured against some unstated ideal.

Her parents' lack of sentimentality meant that the words 'when we're dead and buried' had long been part of the family vocabulary. Still, it had been a shock when her mother went so early. It had happened on a clifftop ramble with Edwin, who described later how Elsbeth had sunk to her knees in a patch of sea-thrift, one of her favourites, before rolling onto her back to stare up at the perfect blue sky.

She had been forty-eight and had been felled by an undiagnosed heart condition, the ancient local doctor explained. 'A good thing your father still has you at home,' he added.

Her father had lived to the age of seventy-six, when he caught Covid. There was no time for last words, just his blurry image on her phone screen as an exhausted ICU nurse called Priscilla finally said, 'I'm very sorry, I have another patient in need. We need to say goodbye' and then the screen had gone black. Now only Evelyn remained to uphold the spirit of the museum. She had made sure its routines had remained unchallenged. Until now.

Evelyn locked up the museum and began the long walk up the hill to her home. Everyone had assumed the Silvers – and therefore Evelyn – were wealthy, but that had not been the case. After her father's death, it emerged that he had run up numerous debts, so after a hushed conversation with the solicitor, Mr Treffrey Junior, Evelyn agreed the contents of the house should be auctioned. The second surprise was that the Victorian home she assumed her parents owned was in fact a long-term rental from the Warburn estate, once the area's largest landowner. A peppercorn rent had been agreed when her parents first came to the town, but with them both dead, the tenancy was null and void.

With a doleful expression, Mr Treffrey Junior explained that Evelyn would need to adapt to being 'a woman of slender means'. Portheast now being awash with holiday lets and second homes, even a small cottage was beyond her. 'You will continue to be paid a small stipend in perpetuity, but if you wish to stay local, your best bet is Sunny Days,' he advised.

Sunny Days was a holiday park on the outskirts of town and not the sort of place the Silvers had ever frequented. But with little alternative, Evelyn was shown around the three static caravans that were available. She chose the one furthest from the clubhouse and beside a thin patch of woodland. Her new home was called The Mirage and it came with what the salesman called 'sea glimpses'.

She soon discovered that in summer, the place was overrun with children, dogs and Union Jack flags and in winter it became a quagmire of mud. The Mirage was one of the shabbiest models at Sunny Days, but what Evelyn liked most about it was its impermanence: the flimsy bounce of the plastic front door, the way that the bottled gas was always running out and her neighbours changed on a weekly basis. It was the opposite of what she'd grown up with: unquestioned traditions and furniture darkened by decades of wear. It fostered the illusion she might not always live this way.

The wind was picking up, dashing tiny grains of sand against her coat, which was not good news: if an easterly gale came in, her little home would be buffeted all night. She didn't mind it when the caravan rocked – it felt like a comfort of sorts – but Toots hated it.

Toots (short for Tutankhamun) was her cat and he'd appeared a few days after Evelyn had moved her meagre possessions into The Mirage. She'd returned from the on-site Spar shop to find a small black cat sitting on her top step, his tail neatly coiled around him. Then he'd slunk inside, given the caravan the once-over and settled onto the bobbly brown corner sofa. That evening, she'd shared her ready meal with him and this, it seemed, was reason enough for Toots to keep coming back.

As Evelyn warmed up her tin of soup, she left the caravan door ajar and it wasn't long before she felt the damp sleekness of Toots circling her ankles. He didn't always come – she suspected he had the run of several places – but it was nice when he did.

Later, Toots slept curled up at the foot of her narrow bed, but Evelyn couldn't settle. The wind whistled through the gaps in the plastic windows and the branches above her creaked and sighed, but she was used to that. No, it was the day's events playing on a reel in her head that kept her awake. The letter from the council, Della's slightly manic face and Leonard with his sad, rheumy eyes. Most of all, she was plagued by the thought of losing her beloved collections.

Unable to sleep, she got up and sat at the fold-out breakfast table. She opened up her mother's paintbox (one of the few things she'd kept from her childhood home) and she set to work. She had a few photographs of museum objects on her mobile phone (a necessary evil in this day and age), but she barely needed to look at them because the objects she wanted to draw were clear in her mind's eye.

By morning, she had finished and she stood up, stretched and admired her work. She had made a poster, which she would get photocopied.

At the top, bright red letters announced:

Calling all treasure hunters!

Below, she'd written a short paragraph:

Do you recognise these long-lost items? Come to a meeting at the Maritime Museum on Friday 6th February, 2 p.m. and you will find plenty of things like these that could relate to your family history. This museum is threatened with closure, but it is part of your Cornish heritage. Save Our Museum!

Then came the best bit: Evelyn had divided the rest of the page into four and drawn an object from the museum in each box. In the top left, she had chosen an old favourite, a neatly embroidered map of the Cornish coastline and a boat, worked in coloured thread on sailcloth. She'd found it in a jumble sale and always wondered about its origins.

Next to it was a newer addition, the painting she'd only just catalogued and that she secretly hoped was an Alfred Wallis. For the bottom left, she chose a pretty teacup she'd always loved. It definitely wasn't from Asda, but was in bone china and decorated with a design of golden lilies. The colours had faded and a hairline crack ran from the base to the rim, but otherwise it was perfect.

Finally, in the bottom right-hand corner, she had traced the familiar tiny knots and threads of her own piece of fine Cornish lace, its top speared with a rusted safety pin.

◆ ◆ ◆

Evelyn's morning beach scour was bleary-eyed and perfunctory, yielding one belt buckle, tarnished, one sock, black, and two pretty curlew feathers. In truth, she had half an eye on the time, because she knew that Potters Newsagents opened at 8.30 a.m. She remembered this shop from her childhood when it was piled high with comics, magazines and penny sweets. It was run by Mrs P and, each Sunday morning, Evelyn was allowed a quarter pound of pear drops. Mrs P would pour them onto the scales from a big glass jar in a cloud of icing sugar and, as the needle nudged the 4oz mark, she'd always toss in an extra one or two for Evelyn.

But Mrs P only did the odd afternoon shift these days and, as Evelyn looked around the shop, she was reminded of how much had changed. Shelves of cheap biscuits and tins of beans had long since replaced the magazines and a cold cabinet of beers stood where the penny sweets used to live. Only some slim piles of newspapers remained on the counter as a reminder of the shop's past life. But all Evelyn wanted was to use Potters' whizzy photocopier.

'I would like twenty copies of this poster please,' she told the young man who was slumped half-asleep at the till.

He raised his head and blinked twice. Evelyn wondered if, like her, he'd been up all night or was simply a bit dim. She tapped her fingernail on the counter. 'When you're ready?'

Scratching his uncombed hair, the boy leaned forward and looked at the poster more closely. 'Treasure, eh?'

'Well, possibly. Because I believe one person's rubbish is another's treasure.'

There was a pause as the boy blinked again. 'Colour or black and white?' he asked eventually.

Evelyn fixed him with the stare she reserved for people who sneaked in to use the museum toilet. 'Given that I stayed up half the night tinting each line drawing with watercolours, I would have thought that was obvious,' she replied.

He held the piece of cartridge paper up to the light. 'Seriously? You did these?'

She nodded and the boy scratched some more. Finally he said, 'How about we make the copies a bit bigger, eh? No extra charge.'

Turning his back, he pressed a series of buttons. Evelyn noticed that his sweater was on inside-out, the washing instructions label pointing upwards. Then there was a whirring, a bright flash of light and she watched as the machine churned out pieces of A3 paper. The boy patted them into a stack and laid them on the counter, still smelling of ink and warm to the touch.

He'd been right – the poster looked better in the bigger format. He'd done something to the colours too, made them slightly deeper, so they stood out more.

'Where are you planning to put them up?' he asked, as Evelyn looked for her purse.

She paused. 'Actually, I haven't really decided. I acted on a bit of an impulse. Noticeboards? Shop windows, I suppose?'

She felt a shadow of doubt, realising this would entail walking into the artsy gift shops, galleries and fancy bakeries that had sprung up in Portheast and having to explain her barmy idea to all those people. She looked down at the neat pile of posters and felt her enthusiasm cooling along with the inky sheaves of paper.

'I can help, if you like?' the boy said. 'I only work mornings. I know most of the other shopkeepers, see. And I can drive out to the library and the sports centre. The pub has a noticeboard too.'

Evelyn was about to say no, but then she imagined having to walk into the dark, beery fug of The Lugger and her mouth turned dry. It was not her favourite place. 'Well, that would be a great help,' she said, holding out her bank card.

'I don't suppose you remember me,' the boy said with a shy smile.

Evelyn studied his slim face, took in his wispy moustache and his light brown hair, which was shorn at the sides but with a long hank hanging over his collar. To all intents and purposes, this boy had a mullet. Strange, she thought, how even the ugliest fashions came around again. 'I'm sorry, I don't believe I do,' she confessed.

'Guess I've changed a bit.' He smiled, stroking his fledgling moustache, which seemed the source of some pride. 'I used to come into your museum in the school holidays, when I visited my grand-dad. I was obsessed with those gold coins – you know, the pirate treasure.'

'I do indeed. Eighteenth century. Presumed pillaged from a Spanish ship that sank in Cornish waters,' Evelyn replied. Then, a faint memory began to take shape: a boy who asked lots of questions in a posh, confident voice, accompanied by a genteel man who she'd recognised as Sir Jasper Warburn.

'Do you know, I think I might remember you.'

'I would have been about seven or eight years old,' the boy said. 'Anyway.' He held out his hand. 'I'm Jacob. And glad to help out.'

Outside the shop, seagulls shrieked and swooped and the sun broke through, making the damp flagstones on the quay glisten. And then, the past seemed to rush back in and she could picture the schoolboy Jacob and his grandfather more clearly. She saw a boy in shorts gazing into a cabinet. The silver-haired man standing beside him was very upright and proper but, as the boy talked, his hand came to rest gently on his grandson's shoulder. Did that ever happen, or had she imagined it?

'You are far too suggestible, Evelyn,' her father had told her often enough. 'You need to keep a grip on that imagination of yours.'

Evelyn shook her head. She was tired, overthinking things. She flipped up her hood and strode purposefully towards the museum.

Chapter Five

Jacob had been as good as his word and Evelyn started to see her posters appear in shop windows and on noticeboards all around the town, but each time she passed one, she felt a rush of embarrassment and bowed her head. By Friday, the day of the meeting, she was a bag of nerves. As 2 p.m. approached, Evelyn felt as if her insides were buzzing with insects, busy ones that jumped and fluttered against her stomach walls with trapped wings.

The floor of the boat shed was swept clean of sand, she'd set up a row of fold-out chairs and even given the glass fronts of the cabinets a rub with a duster.

By 2.05 p.m., the museum remained as silent and deserted as ever and Evelyn dared to feel relieved. It was clear no one was coming; not even Della, who was next door in her ice cream parlour. 'Might get a few sales off people coming for the meeting,' she'd said optimistically.

At 2.15 p.m., Evelyn let the weight of disappointment settle around her. She was cross with herself: it had been a stupid idea. No one in the town had stepped inside her museum for years; why would they start now?

But then she heard murmurings from next door, a muffled laugh and Della appeared with a slight young woman, wearing running gear. 'You know Alison from the sports centre, don't you?'

Evelyn nodded politely, as if games of squash and spin classes were second nature to her. Their arrival started some sort of trickle effect as next came Jacob (Evelyn suspected he'd been lurking outside but hadn't wanted to be the first one in). Then she recognised Sariah, who worked at the big hotel, and Jude and Kayla, teenage sisters who did shifts at their dad's pub, The Lugger.

Finally, George Rook sloped in and stood at the back, followed by a couple of fishermen, who had probably wandered in on their way to the pub. Everyone in town knew George, who dressed in a Barbour jacket and a flat cap but was no gentleman. He ran Portheast Antiques, and the rumour was that stolen goods and the odd forgery had passed through his hands.

George and his father had started out as 'knockers' – people who made house-to-house calls offering to buy old jewellery and silverware from the elderly in the days when an offer from a knocker tended to feel more like a threat. Before George's father retired, he'd earned the moniker 'Rook the Crook', now inherited along with the business by George.

It had been agreed in advance that Della would do the talking. 'Not my forte,' Evelyn explained unnecessarily.

'Right, welcome, everyone,' Della began in a booming voice that suggested that in a previous life she had been used to commanding attention. She explained how the council wanted to revoke the leases for both sheds and that a TV chef was sniffing around for waterside premises.

'Excuse me,' interrupted Kayla from the pub. 'But wouldn't a restaurant be good for local jobs?' She crossed her arms. 'I mean, your shop, this museum – no offence but you don't employ anyone else, do you? What about people like us? What we need in Portheast is new businesses.'

'But that's not the point of a museum.' Evelyn spoke up, as surprised as anyone to hear her own voice. 'It's not about making money. It's about preserving our history.'

Della gave her an encouraging nod, then continued. 'That's right. Do you think that chef Rufus cares about this town? He'll make his money, pay minimum wages and then be off. Same as he's done elsewhere.'

Kayla fell silent and glared back.

'Actually, I suspect Della's right,' said Jacob, who was sitting behind the sisters. 'My friend did a trial shift at his restaurant in Newquay and didn't even get paid. Word is, it's a regular pattern.'

'Is that the sort of business you want in Portheast?' Della asked. Without waiting for an answer, she gestured towards the cabinets. 'Like Evelyn said, this place isn't about profit. It's about preserving stories.' She paused. 'I mean, some of the things you see here might seem a bit random, but that's why Evelyn made the poster. To show there are some hidden gems.'

'Every object here has a link with Portheast,' Evelyn heard herself say, her hands clasped tightly in her lap. 'I've done my best to catalogue pieces, but you or your families might know more.' With relief, she looked down again.

Della took over. 'Right, take a look around. If you spot something you recognise, tell Evelyn. She can redo the label, adding your family's name and any new information. This will help us show the council that the museum preserves local history.'

Jacob stood up and spoke in his clear London voice. 'Yeah, so I just wanted to add that an object doesn't have to belong to you. I only moved to Portheast recently, but I used to visit this museum with my grandfather. Things like the gold coins – they feel like a part of my childhood.'

Sensing that the small crowd's attention was wavering, Della made a final rallying call. 'Remember, look for things that mean something to you. Oh, and if you fancy a drink or an ice cream afterwards, I need saving too!'

There was a scraping of chairs and Evelyn was dismayed to see several people heading straight for the door. 'Don't worry about them,' Della whispered. 'You won't please everyone.' She nodded towards the Fishing Life display, a mixture of driftwood, fishing attire and tangled nets. 'Those two are still here.'

Kayla and Jude were standing with their heads almost touching, as they conferred. Jude, the one with the eyebrow piercing, looked round, beckoned Evelyn over and pointed at a yellow garment, stained and worn. 'I remember my granddad's oilskin hanging up in the porch when we were really little,' she said. 'It was just like this one.'

Evelyn cleared her throat. 'These oilskins were worn by fishermen hauling pilchard drift nets from luggers. In the previous century, poorer people made do with overalls made from old flour sacks soaked in linseed,' she explained.

'Course he's dead now, our granddad. And he'd long given up fishing. No money in it.'

'Fishing is what made this town,' said Evelyn. 'It was famous for its pilchards, then crabs and lobsters.'

Wordlessly, the two sisters moved off, not exactly captivated by Evelyn's commentary, and she gently laid the oilskin back over a pile of broken driftwood.

Over at the cabinet with the pirate coins, Jacob was deep in conversation with sporty Alison, while at the Natural History cabinet, Bob, one of the older men, was pointing something out to Nils the baker. Perhaps Della was right – getting people through the museum doors could be a good thing.

Then, in the same way that Evelyn could always sense when rain was in the air, she felt a creeping unease. A low voice spoke into her ear: 'Few nice bits you have.' It was George Rook, a man she had always taken care to avoid. 'And then a lot of worthless tat,' he added.

Evelyn turned to face him and was pleased to discover she was a good couple of inches taller than him. For once, he wasn't wearing his flat cap and she noticed he'd had his hair cut short. She supposed he'd finally accepted that a ponytail was unsuitable for a sixtysomething, especially when combined with a comb-over.

Unbidden, a memory rose up of a school trip to visit some standing stones, when she'd ended up sitting next to the young George Rook on the coach. In their different ways, each of them had been outliers at school, excluded from the cool crowd. She could almost feel the fuzzy pelt of the seat upholstery, smell the stuffy air and hear the shouts of the other kids on the back seat. She and George had pointedly ignored each other but on the way back, in a rare act of camaraderie, he'd opened his bag of crisps and shared it with her.

But that was a long time ago and it was an acknowledged fact that the Rooks were a bad lot. George met Evelyn's gaze, then gave her a long wink. 'Course, now you've invited every Tom, Dick and Harry in here, you've got to be mindful of objects with, what shall we call it, uncertain provenance. Let me know if you ever need any help with identification.'

'That won't be necessary,' she replied primly, having no desire to associate her museum with a known con artist.

George got the hint. As he turned to go, she caught a whiff of his aftershave, which was oddly floral. All the more reason not to trust him.

An hour later, the museum was back to its empty, quiet self. 'I think it went pretty well,' said Della. 'You even did a bit of a speech, well done!'

'But do you think anyone spotted anything that could help our cause?' Evelyn asked. 'They probably thought it was a load of old rubbish.'

'I wouldn't be so sure,' added Jacob, who had stayed on to stack the chairs. 'Alison was having a good look around, and Sariah, from the hotel. Give it a bit of time and see what happens next.'

Evelyn watched them leave. It was kind of Jacob to be upbeat, but time was in short supply. It was only eight weeks until the council meeting to decide the fate of the boat sheds. Yes, people had come in for a gawp, but she didn't see how it helped their case. Gloomily, she wondered if Della would be better off pitching in with that dreadful chef Rufus, offering her ice creams as unique desserts to his overpriced fish and chips.

Outside, the easterly wind was back, spattering rain against the museum's small, dirt-clouded windows. That morning, sensing her jumpy mood, Toots had scarpered as soon as she'd opened the caravan door and Evelyn suspected he wouldn't be back until tomorrow. As the museum's closing time approached, Evelyn found herself yearning for a treat she rarely allowed herself these days. She tried to ration these occasions, knowing it wasn't healthy – and she would be mortified if anyone found out – but every now and then, she gave in.

At 5 p.m., she closed the museum door and locked it from the inside. Flicking off the electric lights, she retreated deeper into the recesses of the boat shed until she reached her beloved diorama, where Mr and Mrs Cornish Life were waiting. Unclipping the red rope that encircled the make-believe room, she stepped inside.

This season, the man was wearing her father's favourite weekend shirt, in cream and brown checked flannel. The woman wore her mother's dress, the hem trimmed with a white petticoat. It had always been a little loose on Elsbeth Silver, but was a perfect fit for Mrs Cornish Life. An Edwardian bonnet that fastened with a bow under her chin was the finishing touch.

Evelyn lit the candles on the table and let out a deep sigh. If she squinted, it was almost as if she was back home, with her mother serving the tea and her father about to take a puff on his pipe. Sometimes, she reminded herself, having a vivid imagination was a blessing rather than a curse.

Later, she would retire to the cot bed beside the range cooker, fold her too-long limbs into the tight space and pull up the mildew-scented eiderdown. But first, she would boil the kettle (an inauthentic modern one she kept well out of sight) and make herself a tomato cup-a-soup. Then she would tell her parents about the excitement of the day. She would leave out the bit about George Rook, but she would mention there had been an unusual hubbub about the place. She'd say that she'd kept watch on her Miscellanea cabinet, but, as usual, no one had paused to look at her piece of Cornish lace.

Her parents would remain as stiff and silent as ever, but that was OK because Evelyn liked to imagine their feelings. 'One day,' her father's painted-on sad eyes told her, 'the woman who made that piece of lace will come.'

Chapter Six

The Four Items

Item 1: One Bone China Teacup with golden lily design, circa 1948, with hairline crack.

Sariah Carnie was not a sentimental person, never had been. Efficient and organised, yes, which was why her job at the hotel suited her so well. She was a whiz with spreadsheets and had a knack for remembering guests' names and preferences. But the moment Jacob showed her the poster he wanted to put on the hotel noticeboard, her heart did a weird flip. She was probably mistaken. After all, there must have been hundreds if not thousands of teacups made like the one on the poster.

But one just like it used to belong in her grandmother's picnic hamper and the last time that hamper had been used was in 2009, when Sariah was thirteen, and very soon after that last picnic, all sorts of things changed in her family, for the worse.

It had been a family tradition that they all went to the beach on the May Day bank holiday and Grandma Karensa insisted on doing it in style, with proper food and her precious bone china. 'None of your paper cups and plastic plates,' she always said.

Except that year, her grandma had been complaining of dizzy spells, so Sariah's mum, Grace, and Auntie Rose took over doing the cooking, which really meant Grace had to do it all.

Nobody said it out loud, but her Auntie Rose had airs and graces. She didn't live locally, for a start; she'd moved to somewhere called Cheltenham and lost her accent. She talked like a BBC newsreader and, on the rare occasions when she did come home, Rose had a free pass from doing anything strenuous.

Rose sat around in a powder blue twinset and pink padded headband and leafed through a magazine while her older sister Grace cooked. She explained that she'd recently 'had her colours done' and pastels were her best shades. If Rose's colours were pink and blue, Grace's were black and red. Left alone to bake, whisk, roll and ice all the food for the May Day picnic, Sariah's mum got hotter and crosser, and Sariah kept out of her way.

On the day, Grandma Karensa got out her old picnic hamper, which used to belong to her own mother. It was made of wicker and inside there were brown leather straps to hold the china cups and plates in place. To Sariah and her younger brothers, that hamper had near magical qualities: when you heard the creak of it opening, you knew the picnic was about to start.

The family always sat in the same spot and used the same green and yellow checked blanket, its wool long-since stiffened with salty sand. Because she'd recently turned thirteen, Sariah had wanted to appear sophisticated, so she had stayed sitting on the itchy blanket while her brothers and her dad ran down the beach, black silhouettes against the dazzle of the sea. It wasn't long before Sariah regretted her decision because there was nothing to do except wait for the boys to get hungry and come back. Finally, Jamie and Liam ran up the beach like excited puppies, kicking up sand and dripping seawater everywhere. They didn't get told off. Unlike Sariah, Jamie and Liam could do no wrong.

Out came the food: warm bread rolls, hard-boiled eggs with salt in a twist of paper and shiny slices of ham that made Sariah's stomach turn. Then came the good stuff: scones with cream and jam (jam first!), shortbread and a big simnel cake with marzipan and icing. Then Grandpa Luke and her dad slept and the women drank tea from a flask. She noticed that Auntie Rose stuck her baby finger out to one side when she held her teacup, and so, hoping to appear sophisticated, Sariah asked for a cup too. Yes, she insisted, she would like the taste. But when she took her first sip, she had to turn her face away. Grandma Karensa had been right: it was horribly bitter.

Sariah waited until all the grown-ups were asleep and the boys had run off before she carefully carried her cup over to the big rock in the middle of the beach. She liked to imagine that, from afar, she would look alluring, sipping her tea and looking out to sea – the sort of girl a handsome stranger might find irresistible.

The accident happened in an instant. One minute, she'd set the teacup on a flat nook in the rock; the next it was tumbling. She wanted to wind back time, rerun the day so it spooled out differently, with her running down to the sea with her brothers, drinking orange squash instead of tea and staying away from the jagged rock.

Horrified, she looked down. Tea had turned a patch of the grey stone black and the empty cup lay on the sand. Praying it wasn't broken, she jumped down. But there it was – a long crack, from base to rim – and she knew her fate was sealed.

Over at the picnic blanket, the grown-ups dozed on, but even in sleep, her mother Grace's face looked clenched and angry. Sariah held the cup and thought of all the times she'd been told off for far less serious misdemeanours. Panic began to bloom. She would be in such trouble.

Then she heard an unfamiliar voice beside her. It was Rose, carrying the picnic hamper. 'Here,' she said, holding out her hand. 'Give it to me.' Rose took the cup and placed it back in the basket, turned at an angle so that the crack didn't show. Then she fastened the leather straps around the stacks of plates, cups and saucers and closed the lid. 'There, all packed up. And when we get back, I'll make sure I do the washing up.' She gave Sariah a wink. 'No one needs to know.'

'Thanks,' Sariah whispered. Then they sat together, listening to the calls of seagulls and the rush of the waves until the air cooled and the boys came running back up the beach.

'Makes a change, you doing something useful,' her mother said when she saw Auntie Rose already carrying the basket, and Rose gave a polite shrug. In Sariah's mind, the broken cup wouldn't reappear until next May – a whole year away.

But next spring, there was no picnic and the family had bigger problems to think about. Grandma Karensa's dizziness had got worse and she'd had a fall, breaking her hip. She languished in hospital, where they diagnosed other unmentionable ailments. Grace sent Sariah round with cottage pies, stews and soups for Grandpa Luke.

The last time Sariah saw her grandmother, she had held a drink of water (sadly in a paper cup, the only sort available) to the old woman's lips, but she was too weak to sip. Sariah wished she could get that image out of her head.

After the funeral, Grandpa Luke got a place in an ex-Armed Forces home, a nice one-bed unit with a red emergency cord hanging in the bathroom and a wipe-clean armchair. Down in the lounge there was bingo on Thursdays and singalong Saturdays. Auntie Rose came back for the funeral, but only on a day-return ticket. A month later, the council wanted her grandparents' house back, so it was down to Sariah's mum and dad to clear it out.

Perhaps the cracked teacup was discovered and discarded at that point, or the hamper was dispatched, unopened, to a charity shop; Sariah had no idea. Because, after Grandma Karensa's funeral, things at home went from bad to worse, with arguments and slammed doors. Sariah started staying over with friends whenever possible and when she was fifteen, she left home for good. She had barely spoken to her mother since, but the last she heard, she was still in Redruth, while her father was long gone.

Seeing the cup on the poster, Sariah could pretend it was a strange coincidence. But when she'd seen it for real in the museum, there was no doubt it was the same one: that jagged crack was etched in her memory. Quite how that lone cup had ended up behind glass in the local museum was a mystery, but one Sariah had no intention of solving. That cup was a painful reminder of how Sariah felt as a child: always in the wrong or about to get told off.

As she walked away from the chaotic museum, Sariah vowed never to set foot in the place again. In her view, Evelyn Silver was wrong. Objects might come with stories, but not all of them needed to be shared.

Now aged thirty, Sariah had no plans to have a family. But if she ever did, she would do things differently. She would draw her child towards her, rather than letting them drift away. And she would make them feel loved – no matter how many cups they broke or mistakes they made.

ITEM 2: HAND-EMBROIDERED PICTURE OF A BOAT AT SEA, WITH A SECTION OF THE CORNWALL COAST. COLOURED SILK THREAD ON SAILCLOTH. DATE UNKNOWN.

Alison Blake was bone-tired. She'd been up since 6 a.m., sliding out of bed quietly so as not to wake Roy. Before heading to the sports centre for her shift, she'd made their son, Will, his packed lunch to take to nursery and put on a load of laundry. Once at work, she updated the rota and left a message with the plumber because the women's changing rooms had flooded again. She made herself wait until 8 a.m. before texting Roy.

Forgot to say, he now hates Rice Krispies. Cheerios only!

She hoped the exclamation mark looked jokey rather than shouty. It was tricky, sometimes, to get the tone right.

She watched the blink of grey dots on her phone screen, picked at the skin around her nails and wondered if she'd gone too far. She didn't want to imply Roy couldn't work these things out on his own. 'Micromanaging' he called it.

The dots disappeared and Alison supposed she'd find out later if she'd overstepped the line. She'd come to sense the mood of the house as she stepped through the front door; it was like dipping your toe in the water before a swim, that split second you had to decide if it was freezing cold or bearable. But either way, you had to jump in.

The sports centre's office was busy all morning, so she couldn't really afford to take a lunch break, but she kept glancing over at that poster some guy called Jacob had put up, the one about a meeting at the museum. It was illustrated with four intricate drawings, which was kind of weird – who even drew pictures these days? But everything about that so-called museum was weird, including the woman who ran the place. As a child, Alison had been scared of that tall stick of a woman who walked alone on the beach. To be completely honest, Alison was still a little scared of her.

But, somehow, at 1.50 p.m. that Friday, Alison found herself standing up and asking Ollie to mind the phone. 'Just popping out, I'll be as quick as I can,' she said. All she wanted to do was take a closer look at that piece of embroidered sailcloth that had appeared on the poster, because a very similar picture hung over the mantelpiece in her dad's cottage. It was the closest thing they had to a family heirloom and it had been made by her Grandpa

Fred when he'd done his national service in the navy. 'A keepsake for your Grannie Helena, waiting at home,' her dad, Keith, had explained with pride. 'Lovebirds those two, never had a cross word.'

Alison had always liked that story. She'd pictured Grandpa Fred lying in his bunk, stitching and dreaming of Grannie Helena back in Cornwall, while his mates played cards or passed round a girlie magazine and their ship dipped and rolled on an ocean far from home.

Fred Blake had presented that piece of embroidery to his fiancée in 1956 and Alison could only imagine how treasured it must have been. It depicted a map of Cornwall, a boat at sea, and the words *Sailing home to you, my lovely bride* were picked out in tiny white stitches. Finally, beside the boat he'd stitched the red initials *FB*, for Frederick Blake, and then, marking the spot where his fiancée waited in Portheast, he'd stitched *HB* in red, for his soon-to-be wife Helena Blake.

That framed piece of embroidery had come to represent true love to Alison and, as a teenager, she'd gaze at it in the hope that one day she would find a love as pure as theirs. Yes, she was a romantic at heart, but what was wrong with that? She didn't get why everyone was so introspective these days, raking over every unhappy moment and squeezing out every last drop of despair. Alison had what her father called a sunny disposition and it had helped them both get through losing her mum when Alison was a teenager.

In Alison's view, you had a choice: dwell on the negative or look for the positive. For instance, Roy wasn't a bad person – he just found it difficult to express his emotions. He was easily frustrated, so his feelings came out in words and deeds that didn't always feel like love. But he was always sorry afterwards.

So, that Friday she'd gone to the town museum in search of a reminder that true love did exist in the shape of this second piece of embroidery that looked to be by her grandpa's hand. How it had ended up in the museum was a mystery, but she hoped it was more proof of the thread of love between her grandparents.

When she found it in a glass cabinet at the back of the boat shed, Alison let out a small gasp of joy. It most definitely was by her grandpa, she was sure of it, and if anything, this picture was even more beautiful than the first one, as if his love had grown stronger.

She knew she and Roy were going through 'a blip'. That wasn't unusual after having a baby, was it? But seeing that keepsake was the reminder she needed: she and Roy would find their way back to each other. Their own thread wasn't broken, just a little frayed.

Alison leaned in for a last, long look at her grandfather's work. And then she frowned. For all its beauty, something was wrong with this picture. Just like the one hanging on her dad's wall, it showed a boat sailing on the waves off Cornwall, with Fred's initials, *FB*, above the boat. But where the initials *HB* for Helena Blake should be, marking Portheast, there was nothing but green stitches, signifying land. But an inch or so to the west were two red dots, so small you could easily miss them. But when she squinted, Alison could make them out. And they didn't say *HB*, but *SW*.

It was as if Alison was falling backwards, into a darkness with no end. She blinked, looked again, to make sure she hadn't imagined it. No, they definitely said *SW*. Then she realised that the larger words that danced over the waves were also different: *Wish we could sail away together, my true love.*

She turned and walked smartly out of the museum, breaking into a jog as she reached the hill and, with each slap of her trainers on the ground, she chastised herself. *Stupid, stupid, stupid.*

She shouldn't have let that Jacob put up that poster in the sports centre and she definitely shouldn't have gone to the museum. Then she'd never have seen that her grandfather Frederick Blake had been a cheat, saving his best work for someone else. Someone with the initials SW.

But the run helped, because once she was showered and back at her desk, Alison felt much better. She shook her head and almost laughed at how silly she'd been, because SW could mean anything – a place, a pet, a best friend. It could even be SW for south-west, his beloved corner of Cornwall. Already, that block of hurt inside her was starting to dissipate and as she issued tickets, booked gym sessions and answered the phone, she could feel it leaving her body and dispersing into the chlorinated air. Problems were a bit like a toothache: the temptation to prod it with your tongue was always there, but you also had the choice to not go poking around.

To be on the safe side, she formed a plan. Before she'd become a mum and taken this part-time job, she'd worked in public relations. This was a situation that required what her old boss had called 'damage limitation'. He said the first thing to do in the face of bad news was to act quickly and gather all the information possible. Then, you needed to assemble a committee of efficient people, to help you.

Alison flicked through a mental Rolodex of the people she'd seen at the museum meeting in search of an efficient ally. There was really only one contender. Picking up the phone, she rang the Warburn Spa hotel. 'Hello? Yes, please could I speak to Sariah Carnie, your manager. Yes, I'll wait.'

ITEM 3: SMALL PAINTING OF SAILING SHIP, OIL ON WOOD. CIRCA 1930s, POSS. ATTRIB. A WALLIS.

George Rook noticed that she'd hedged her bets on the label, indicating it was 'possibly attributed' to Wallis. That was one way of putting it, but in 1987 this unsigned painting had indeed sold as an early Alfred Wallis, and for a good price.

Interest in the self-taught St Ives painter had been at a high and people were falling over themselves to exclaim about his 'expressive naivety'. George thought that was a load of rubbish. In his view, the best thing about Wallis's naive style was that it was very easy to copy.

He'd only done a couple of Wallis tributes – he preferred that word to 'forgery', which was so judgemental. It was never good to flood the market with discoveries, or people started to get twitchy. Realistically, there was a limit to the number of Alfred Wallises that could be found languishing in lofts. But this one had been his favourite. It was done on plywood and George had achieved a perfect shade of blue for the sea (using boat paint, just as Wallis had), while the clouds had a fluffy charm.

And now it had been put on a poster, summoning him through the museum doors. Once inside, it didn't take long to locate the painting and he was pleased it was still in good nick – barely a scratch on it. Still in its original frame too, bought from Woolworths in St Austell. He and his father had given it their special ageing treatment: a quick rubdown followed by a wipe over with nail polish remover and, voilà, an authentically aged frame. For anything 19th century, they tended to leave the nail polish remover on for an extra fifteen minutes.

The painting had been sold to an anonymous client, but George knew it was Sir Jasper Warburn who, at the time, owned half the land around Portheast as well as Warburn Hall. Rumour had it he'd been sowing his wild oats again and had bought it as a gift to placate a disgruntled Lady Catherine Warburn.

These days, the much-diminished Warburn family still owned a smattering of tied cottages, but the Hall had been sold off and converted into an exclusive spa hotel. When the place was gutted, the contractors sent plenty of fittings George's way, with late-night deliveries of chandeliers, a marble fireplace and some garden statuary, but, sadly, that little painting never reappeared.

Someone else must have whisked it away – or maybe its beauty went unnoticed and it ended up in a car boot sale, the sort George still frequented. In fact, he often saw Evelyn Silver at them too, rooting around in boxes of bric-a-brac. When George did a boot fair, he looked for a different sort of junk, the type he could resell for an inflated sum. In the old days, this meant inlay cabinets, silver candlesticks and costume jewellery, but these days anything with a whiff of rustic sold well: chests of drawers he could repaint and rub down with wire wool, pig benches and wobbly milking stools. 'Authentic' was a word he used a lot, along with 'charming', and holidaymakers lapped it up.

As for the locals, George knew most didn't hold him in high regard. Some of that dated back to his father's era, because old Mr Rook didn't care who he cheated, double-crossed or lied to. The forgeries had been his father's idea, too.

When George's high school teacher asked his dad to come up to the school, they both thought he was in trouble. But instead, Miss Mackay wanted to congratulate him on his son's artistic skills. 'This boy has real talent,' she said, all dewy-eyed, as if she'd discovered a star in the gutter. 'I think you should consider A levels and then art school for George.'

Miss Mackay thought she was doing George a favour, giving him a route out of Portheast to Falmouth, Bristol or London, where he could set the art world on fire. But, instead, her words gave old Mr Rook a different idea.

The next weekend, George's dad beckoned him into the back room of the shop. 'Got a present for you, lad,' he said. It was an easel and a stack of fresh white canvases and George could hardly believe his luck. 'For me, really?' he said. Then his dad gave him the second part of his present: a big book called *Great British Artists*. 'We'll start with something easy,' he said, breaking the spine and laying it open at a Ben Nicholson. 'See how you get on.'

It only took George a few months to get the hang of Nicholson's style with its chalky finish and deceptively simple geometric shapes. *Composition, Portheast* sold for a record sum to a private dealer and George's future was sealed.

By the time Damien Hirst and Tracey Emin were making waves in London, George was turning out near-perfect versions of existing Great British Artists, from Lowry to Hockney. Soon, he was in too deep, enmeshed in a network of dealers and buyers keen to hide their money in art. The Portheast Antiques shop ticked over fine, but it was only the tip of a deep and rather grubby iceberg.

He'd seen a real Alfred Wallis once, when the new Tate in St Ives opened, and it had taken his breath away. The way the man had painted each tiny window of the boat and captured the movement of the sea was marvellous. But above all, his deceptively simple painting was full of emotion and at last George understood what all the fuss was about. Wallis had been a genius.

So when George found his own version hanging in Portheast's museum, it was a sobering experience. He gazed at it for a long time, seeing it for what it was: a lifeless fake. He watched a few other people pause, look at it and move on and, after a while, a deeply troubling thought came into his head. By advertising the painting on her poster, was Evelyn Silver sending him a message? Was she trying to flush him out and expose his fakery? He hadn't stayed under the radar this long to be shopped by Evelyn Silver, so if she wanted to send him a message, he would send one back.

George watched Evelyn for a while, and when she'd finished talking to the sisters from the pub, he nipped in. He just wanted to drop a hint, remind her that he too was familiar with the 'provenance' of some of the pieces in her museum, but Evelyn put on her respectable schoolmarm act and looked down her nose at him like she had no idea what he was talking about. She was nothing like her father, Edwin Silver – a far more straightforward man.

George Rook left the museum fuming. Clearly it pleased neither of them, but he and Evelyn Silver had unfinished business.

ITEM 4: ONE PIECE OF FINE CORNISH LACE, HANDMADE. FOUND ATTACHED TO A BABY'S BLANKET WITH A SAFETY PIN (NOW RUSTED), 3 DECEMBER 1964.

I saw the drawing on the poster, but I had to be sure. It was the first time I'd been inside the museum and I'm glad I went because I found it quite moving, seeing that missing fragment of lace. I've kept the other half folded away, safe and sound.

Evelyn. It's an unusual choice of name, isn't it? Quite formal. But that was the Silvers, I suppose. I'd thought she might have been called Daisy, to match the chain of flowers worked into the lacework pattern. Perhaps the Silvers didn't notice the daisies, or they chose to ignore that small hint from her birth mother.

Anyway, Evelyn is a woman now, tall and a little stern, as if she's grown into her name. But that's what we all do, isn't it? Adapt our behaviour to the situation and make the best of it. We face things we never thought we'd get over. Days pass, they become months, which become years and finally you reach a point where it's hard to imagine how things could have turned out.

Had circumstances been different, would Evelyn have become a different person? If she'd been called Daisy, for example. Or if she'd been able to stay with her birth family.

I see her walking on the beach and even when she's alone she stands so stiffly, as if she's holding something tightly inside herself.

I'd like to say a comforting word or two, but it's too late for that now. It would be too confusing.

But when I saw she'd put that piece of lace on the poster, it meant a lot. It was a sign that she recognised it for what it was: a token of a mother's love.

She's an educated woman – she must know about the foundling tradition. When a baby was left, the mother tucked something into their blanket to identify them. It might have been a scrap of cloth, a silver locket or half a sixpence. Then, if the mother was ever able to return and claim her baby, she had proof it was hers. The torn piece of fabric could be made whole; two halves of a coin could be joined together. Of course, reuniting the two fragments of lace wasn't possible. But I hope she knows she was never forgotten.

Chapter Seven

When she woke, Evelyn was momentarily confused by the darkness and sense of space all around her. But then she realised she wasn't in her caravan, she was under the rafters of the museum. As she lay there, the early morning light began to peep through the gaps in the slate tiles and then came the distinctive thunk of a seagull landing on the roof. It was time to get up.

An ache had taken hold in her knees, her neck and her shoulders and she vowed that it was the last time she would sleep here. She was too old for such childishness and the diorama was a museum piece, not a substitute for home. Honestly, a psychologist would have a field day, she told herself. She stood, shook out the eiderdown, plumped the tiny pillow and tidied away her cup. Smoothing down her hair, Evelyn made her way to the museum's door, collecting her satchel and sack on the way.

Outside, the harbourside was wrapped in a soft silence and, after the hubbub of yesterday, Evelyn appreciated the calm as she headed to the beach for her morning duties. The tide was high, so there was less sand to cover than usual, but each small step along the shoreline soothed her. This, she reminded herself, instead of sleeping in a child-sized bed, was a healthier way to regulate her emotions.

That was the term the doctor had used all those years ago. 'Hysteria tends to stem from an accumulation of unprocessed feelings,' he explained to her. 'An outburst is the body's way of expelling them. What you need to do is find a better way to regulate your emotions.' He'd recommended long country walks. 'Or if you don't like going out, you could try aerobics. They show it on the TV.'

Evelyn had watched one session of the Green Goddess on Breakfast TV and was horrified by the woman's crotch-hugging Lycra and boundless enthusiasm. Long walks, accompanied by her mother, seemed the safer option. Every now and then, they would stop to admire an outcrop of wild thyme or remark on how the blackberries were ripening late this year. Her mother began to bring her art materials and they would sit together, quietly sketching the nature around them. As they packed up, her mother might ask, 'Feeling better?' and Evelyn would reply, 'Much.' And that was as far as their discussions went, regarding Evelyn's state of mind and her return home from the regrettable business in London.

Her morning haul was disappointing. The storm had blown in plenty of interesting driftwood, but this was outweighed by plastic bottles and a single diver's fin.

In truth, she'd found yesterday's events a little overwhelming. Of course she wanted to save her museum – she was its curator and, without it, she would be nothing. But it had been her private sanctuary for so long that seeing people milling around inside had felt like an intrusion.

So when Evelyn made her lopsided way back along the quay, she was perturbed to see a small huddle of people gathered outside her museum. She didn't know if she could cope with yet more visitors but, as she got closer, Evelyn realised with relief that they were outside Della's, drinking from mugs. Evelyn hoped for their sakes that Della's coffee was better than her ice creams.

She recognised Alison, her tiny frame bound tightly by running gear, Jacob, who had helped with the poster, and of course Della, who was regaling them with a long-winded story about backpacking in Thailand. As Evelyn dumped her sand-heavy bag of rubbish on the flagstones, she caught the end of Della's anecdote: ' . . . and it turned out, we'd taken the wrong path!' Even to Evelyn, no master of the bon mot, it seemed a punchline that lacked oomph.

'There you are,' Jacob exclaimed, as if happy for the interruption.

'Indeed I am,' Evelyn replied and turned away to fumble for her key. As she pushed open the heavy door, she was surprised to feel it swing inwards with ease until she realised Jacob had reached over her head and was holding the door for her. What's more, he proceeded to follow her inside, with Alison and Della close behind.

Evelyn drew herself up to her full height. 'Can I help you?' She looked at the trio of expectant faces and understood she might have been a little rude. 'Sorry, but I'm not open until 9 a.m., which is fifteen minutes away. I mean, I haven't even had breakfast yet . . .'

'All sorted,' said Della, pushing to the front and brandishing a paper bag. 'Homemade rock cakes. I'm thinking of adding a section to the menu: Della-icious Bites.'

Evelyn thought she saw Jacob give the briefest shake of his head, but it was too late; she had already accepted the paper bag. 'Thanks,' she said. 'But did we have an appointment?'

'Not as such,' Della replied. 'But the three of us thought it would be good to have a chat. Alison got in touch with Sariah, who got in touch with me and I called up Jacob. We thought you could do with a museum committee,' she added brightly. 'I'll add you to the WhatsApp group. But, first, let's debrief.'

'Debrief?'

'Yeah, discuss what we achieved in yesterday's initial meeting and our next steps. But we need to get a move on – Alison has to get back to work.'

Jacob stepped forward. 'How about you sit down, Evelyn,' he said kindly. Obediently, she slipped behind her desk where, protected by her wall of books and papers, the invasion felt a little less, well, invasive. She watched Jacob unfold three of the chairs that were still stacked against the wall and arrange them to face her desk.

Alison produced a notebook and clicked the end of her pen. 'So,' she began. 'Present: Evelyn Silver, Alison Blake, Jacob Warburn and Della . . . ?'

'Dayvon,' Della volunteered.

'Devon?' Alison did a double take.

Della narrowed her eyes. 'No. Dayvon. Spelled D-A-Y-V-O-N.'

Without another word, Alison raised an eyebrow and made a small mark in her notebook. 'Apologies sent by Sariah Carnie. She's on board, but Saturday mornings are hectic at the hotel.'

It had been a long time since Evelyn had been present at a meeting where minutes were taken and apologies were noted, yet here she was in her own museum, hearing phrases from another lifetime. Absent-mindedly, she reached into the paper bag on her lap, broke off a piece of rock cake and popped it into her mouth.

First, it was the claggy, doughy texture she noticed, followed by an unexpected saltiness. Then came the unmistakable tang of charred raisins. She chewed hard and swallowed.

'Good, eh?' Della grinned.

She took care not to catch Jacob's eye.

Thankfully, Alison announced, 'To business.'

It turned out that Alison used to work in PR in Truro. 'I mean, I didn't run any campaigns myself, but you learn a lot when you do the admin. And I've written loads of press releases. Believe me, if I can make power tools sound exciting, getting coverage for a Save Our Museum campaign will be easy.

'I suggest we offer the media some human-interest stories: local people who recognise an item in the museum and can relate it to their own family life. My old boss would say, "Always look for the hook."'

Alison looked around expectantly. 'Did anyone get good feedback from our visitors yesterday?'

Evelyn thought of Kayla and Jude's lukewarm interest in a battered old fishing bib, then the way Rook the Crook had sidled up to her, talking in insinuating tones.

'Um, nothing very significant, I'm afraid,' she said.

'Anyone else?' Alison looked around.

'As I mentioned already, I've always been fascinated by those gold coins,' Jacob said in a clear voice that demonstrated he was comfortable with public speaking. 'But they don't have any link to me or my family.'

There was a disappointed lull. Then Della piped up, 'Obviously, I'm no local, but I did see Sariah looking at something in one of the cabinets. I mean, looking *hard*. Transfixed, I'd call it. Might be worth checking in with her?'

Alison made a note.

'But what about you, Alison?' Della continued. 'Didn't you see anything? You're Portheast born and bred.'

Alison abruptly crossed her legs, which sent her notebook slithering from her lap to the floor. Jacob lunged forward to get it, at exactly the same time as Alison bent down. There was a flurry of 'Sorry' and 'No, I'm sorry' and by the time Alison sat back up, her face was quite pink. She opened her notebook at a fresh page. 'Possibly,' she said lightly. 'But my research is ongoing.'

Evelyn's stomach gave a hungry growl, which seemed to remind everyone that time was passing and they had places to be. Alison said, 'Right, to sum up, I'll start putting out feelers with the local press. Flag up that the museum is in danger and we'll have some human-interest stories for them very soon. Someone is bound to come forward – yesterday was just the beginning, Evelyn.'

'Great stuff.' Jacob clapped his hands together, which everyone took as a signal to stand up. As he'd done yesterday, Jacob started folding away the chairs. He waited until Alison and Della had left before he sidled over to Evelyn. 'Sorry about the rock cake,' he said. 'I did try and warn you.'

'Oh, she means well,' Evelyn replied, privately wondering what had brought Della all the way from Australia to Portheast, and to go into catering of all things. 'But I really am very hungry.'

'Nils does a good cinnamon bun,' Jacob said. 'I'm walking that way if you want to come?'

Evelyn didn't want to admit that sniffing the sugary air was the closest she'd got to visiting the new Swedish bakery. 'OK,' she said firmly. 'I accept your offer.'

They must have looked an unusual couple, walking the length of the quay: Evelyn in her unofficial uniform of a long brown skirt and grey cardigan and Jacob in his trainers, baggy jeans and over-sized sweatshirt.

She noticed that he'd done something to his hair so that it stuck up more than usual. 'You know, I remember your haircut being cool first time around. All the rage with blokes who wore denim waistcoats and drank in The Lugger in the late seventies.'

Jacob laughed. 'Yeah, you're right. I probably could have got the old barber on Fore Street to do me a mullet for a fraction of the price it cost me in Soho.'

Evelyn remembered glimpses of Soho: pubs crowded as a Tube train carriage, the vegetable mulch of Berwick Street Market, stall-holders shouting out, flogging their wares, and seedy shops that advertised SEX in big neon letters. She'd walked through those streets on weekends, too scared to stop but secretly thrilled that all this was going on in broad daylight, almost on her doorstep.

'So, did you grow up in London?' she asked.

'Well, the quieter outskirts. Chiswick.'

'Hmm, I think you mean posher outskirts,' she said. 'I spent some time in London in my twenties and I doubt it's changed that much.'

'Ah, you got me.'

'So what brought you here, Jacob?'

'Well, I always had a soft spot for this place. Memories of holidays staying with my grandparents, I suppose. After my parents split up, it felt more like a haven than ever.'

'I'm sorry to hear that,' Evelyn said. 'About your parents.'

'That's OK. Long time ago. We've all moved on.'

'And then you heard the siren call of Potters Newsagents.'

Jacob gave a rueful smile. 'Not exactly. It was the only job going. Not much demand for archaeology graduates in Portheast, you see. Especially ones who didn't actually graduate.'

Evelyn sensed he wanted to say more.

'Girlfriend trouble,' he explained as they headed towards Nils' bakery. 'Dumped just before my finals and I didn't cope well. So I came to Portheast to lick my wounds. At first, I was worried about living on my own, but it's done me the world of good.'

Evelyn felt her chest tighten. He wasn't the first person to come back to Portheast to mend a broken heart.

'And where is it you live?' she asked.

'Attic room over the newsagents. Only a bedsit, but it suits me.' Jacob nodded towards the hills behind the town. 'Plus, it gives me a view of Warburn Hall. Or Warburn Spa, as it's called these days.'

'That must be strange,' she replied. 'It being the old family seat.'

'To be honest, I hate the idea. It was a stupidly big place – turrets and everything. My grandfather only lived in a couple of rooms by the end. But even before that, the house always felt a bit dark and unloved. My best memories are of doing things outside: playing on the beach, walking around the town with my grandfather. And, of course, visiting the museum. Anyway, here we are.'

They had reached the bakery, its window showing rows of glistening buns swirled with icing, puffy croissants and flaky slices filled with custard.

'I'll get a couple of buns, shall I?' Jacob asked and Evelyn gratefully accepted, but only because she wouldn't have been quite sure what to ask for or how to pronounce it. *Kanelbulle*, the label said.

'Thank you,' she said, taking her second baked gift of the day. 'And for your help with the poster.'

'Honestly, it's a pleasure. The job at Potters is only part-time and it's hardly taxing. It's good for me to keep busy.'

'It can help,' she said with a weak smile.

'So Alison's very, um, organised,' he said, biting into his sugary bun.

'That she is.' Evelyn hadn't yet made up her mind about the tiny dynamo that was Alison Blake. On the surface, she was all appeasing smiles and efficient notetaking, but she sensed a fragility underneath.

Jacob continued: 'I hope you didn't feel like the three of us were, you know, moving too fast. But her idea about finding people who spotted something special in your museum – it's a good one. In fact . . .' He rubbed his palm over his chin and she heard the soft rasp of his stubble. 'Weird thing is – and I didn't want to mention this in front of the others – at yesterday's meeting I did see something I recognised.'

'The coins?'

'No. Something else. A painting. A small one of a boat. In fact, it was the one you put on the poster. But it was only when I saw it for real that I realised.'

'Small painting of sailing ship, oil on wood. Circa 1930s,' Evelyn recited. Then, looking left and right to make sure no one was listening, she whispered, 'I'm not certain, but I have a hunch it might be an Alfred Wallis. Which would be very good news indeed.'

Jacob fixed his blue eyes on hers. 'Well, that was exactly what my grandmother was told. It used to hang in her bedroom, you see. It was a gift from my grandfather. Whoever cleared out Warburn Hall missed a trick, but their loss could be your gain. And the museum's.' With that, Jacob raised his hand in farewell and strolled off, leaving a scattering of cinnamon sugar in his wake.

Evelyn stood for a moment, thinking. She could remember where and when she'd acquired most of the things in her museum and she'd picked up that little painting at a jumble sale in 2019. She remembered the timing, because it was one of the last she'd attended before the lockdowns. It had been inside a cardboard box of nautical art which had cost her £5 and she was ashamed to admit that the box had sat, untouched, under her desk until very recently. The odd thing was that jumble sale had been held before Warburn Hall and its contents had gone up for sale.

But that barely mattered. If she and Jacob were right, the museum's future was suddenly looking far brighter. She knew how the wheels of the council were oiled: if she had an Alfred Wallis on her hands, she would have enough money to persuade the powers that be that the two old boat sheds on Portheast quay were wholly unsuitable for Rufus Rowan's fish and chip empire.

Chapter Eight

For her job at the hotel, Sariah was required to wear a crisp white blouse, a gold name badge and a big smile. The Warburn Spa had what head office called a discerning clientele, which, in Sariah's opinion, translated to 'entitled stuck-up idiots who think money means more than manners'.

No one would have guessed that the manager of the Warburn Spa had left home at fifteen with barely a GCSE to her name. She'd started out cleaning holiday cottages and guest houses, then got a job on reception at a small hotel in Newquay before moving to the new hotel in Portheast and working her way up. Now, each time she pinned on her badge, Sariah experienced a small frisson of satisfaction because this was more than anyone ever thought Sariah Carnie of Redruth would ever amount to.

She was the public face of the Warburn Spa, which meant that by the end of a shift her face ached from smiling, which widened into a rictus when faced with a particularly tricky customer. That morning, a couple from Cheshire had forgotten to book their spa treatments, but insisted they needed relaxing massages before lunch. 'I have over eighty thousand followers and I don't think they would be impressed by your customer service,' the woman said in a threatening tone. Mr Cheshire, clearly familiar with this performance, sneaked off to have a quiet vape on the front steps until the deal was done.

Sariah persuaded another (far nicer) couple to move to a later slot, with the promise of a free afternoon tea. 'My pleasure,' she said to Ms Cheshire through gritted teeth.

Mostly it was fun at the hotel: the staff were a laugh and some of the guests, too. But there was something jarring about meeting people who thought nothing of spending £200 on dinner when Sariah knew some of the junior staff lived off kitchen leftovers and McDonald's kids' meals.

Mind you, those high-paying guests didn't see what went on behind the scenes: the flit of grey mice across the kitchen floor, the hair-matted gunk that lurked in the water pipes beneath the spa, barely kept at bay by industrial-strength unblocker. 'Yes, madam, all our cleaning products are natural and phosphate free,' she would recite, turning on that winning smile.

After she'd escorted the Cheshires to the massage suite, Sariah checked in three more couples and then, oh joy, a hen party. Already, the bride was a little queasy (Pimm's all the way down from Paddington) and her sister was looking daggers at the maid of honour. They were booked in for the bottomless Prosecco brunch and Sariah predicted tears – and the mop-up bucket – before 4 p.m.

It wasn't until lunchtime that Sariah had a chance to look at her phone. Somehow, since going to yesterday's meeting at the museum, Alison had talked her into joining a WhatsApp group and it appeared there had been a debrief. Skimming the morning's messages, Sariah sighed. Wasn't everyone getting a bit carried away?

Alison was planning a media campaign and wanted to find human-interest stories linked to the museum's collections. In Sariah's view, Alison's time would be better spent sorting out her own life rather than meddling in other people's. She had seen the lairy way her partner, Roy, acted in The Lugger and heard about fistfights after last orders. She hoped he was nicer at home.

Jacob was in the group too. He had the same hearty confidence and perfect teeth as some of their guests. But there was no telling how a family's fortunes could change, because here was Sariah with keys to all the rooms of the Warburn family pile while Jacob was working in Potters Newsagents.

Then there was Della – honestly, hadn't she heard of fashion? – and of course the town's biggest weirdo, Evelyn Silver. This group really wasn't Sariah's thing at all.

Another message from Alison pinged in: *@Sariah Hey, Della thought a museum exhibit caught your eye. Fancy telling me its story for the press release?*

Sariah sighed and left her on read. Of course she'd seen Grandma Karensa's teacup, but what would she say? 'Yes, I saw a broken cup that's somehow ended up in the big jumble sale that passes for Portheast Museum. It reminded me how I lived in fear of it being discovered because then I'd get what for . . .'

Oh, there was a story attached to that cup, but it wasn't one for sharing.

Unconsciously, Sariah lifted her fingers to her scalp, worried at the tiny patch above her left ear, the bare skin that felt both sore and pleasingly soft. It was an easily hidden flaw in her otherwise perfectly groomed appearance: hair tied up, the same sweeps of make-up each day to highlight her cheeks, eyes and that winning smile.

Her phone pinged again and this time it was Jacob.

@Sariah Hey, I've had a bit of a brainwave re the Save Our Museum campaign. Thought we could create a website, but I don't know how. Do you? Just need a simple one.

Yes, I bloody well do, she thought.

Sariah worked best when she was fired up by anger and determined to prove people wrong. It was how she'd made her own way in the world because she hadn't been to private school or university like Jacob or had the money to go travelling around the world and open up an ice cream parlour on a whim, like Della. And she was certainly more capable than that oddball Evelyn.

Sariah's own mother had said, among other put-downs, that she was 'nothing but trouble', that she was 'as thick as two short planks' and that she 'ate them out of house and home'. For a long time, Sariah would retaliate, shouting awful, ugly things at her mother. But then she learned a different way of coping: she held those painful words inside, turning them over until they became a hot ball of resentment. It was that heat that kept her going: working double shifts, smiling harder to prove that Sariah Carnie was someone to be reckoned with.

Yes, sure, I can build websites. It's pretty easy really she typed back. Even better, Sariah realised that if she was in charge of the website, she could decide what objects appeared on it – and she was going to make sure that cracked teacup was never seen again. There was only a tiny chance that someone in her family would see it, but it wasn't one Sariah wanted to take.

Chapter Nine

Evelyn was beginning to feel like a sheep, one that had been herded into a pen by a very enthusiastic sheepdog, and that sheepdog was called Alison. For whatever reason, Alison was so inspired by the campaign that she'd come down to the museum in her lunch break to update her. 'Combined it with a jog,' she said, running on the spot to prove her point.

She explained that she was planning a press release, but she needed more stories. 'I feel like there are lots of connections out there. We just need to winkle them all out.'

Then Alison started talking about some idea of Jacob's to make a website. 'We could show off the most interesting objects – take the appeal wider,' Alison said.

Evelyn was no fan of technology, but it dawned on her that this could be beneficial. If there was a website, people could just stay at home and look at the pictures online rather than tramping through her museum, stealing her varnished Cornish pasties and complaining about her oddly worded labels, born out of the necessity of thinking up descriptions without using the letter *E*.

'That sounds interesting,' she replied.

Alison said Sariah was a bit of a tech whiz and asked if she could come and take some photos for the website. 'I mean, your drawings were lovely, but we want lots and lots of pictures. Which would be a bit time-consuming for you.'

Alison had a diplomatic way about her, as if she was used to placating people. She said Sariah and Evelyn could pick out some more objects together. 'But be sure to include the original four items from your poster, won't you?' she added, as she started limbering up for the run back to work.

'The lace, the painting, the cup and the embroidery.' Evelyn ticked them off on her fingers.

'Yes. Definitely the embroidery,' Alison said and then she was gone, running up the quay. Watching her go, Evelyn found she was warming to Alison's quiet persistence, and it was nice that she had recognised the beauty in the embroidered sailcloth. Like her own hand-worked lace, that keepsake had clearly been made with love.

However, when Sariah Carnie arrived at her museum some days later, Evelyn wished she'd never said yes. Where Alison had been gently insistent, Sariah was plain spiky. From the jut of her chin to the way she jabbed at her laptop, everything about her was hard-edged – even her smile, which she turned on and off like a switch being flicked.

'Right, first thing I'll need is the catalogue of your collections,' she said, narrowing her eyes as she looked around the museum.

Evelyn faltered. 'Oh, I don't have any catalogue. I mean, it's ongoing.' She mustered a smile. 'I thought we could just have a look round and see what we like.'

Impatience radiated off Sariah.

'But we could start with the four objects I put on the poster,' Evelyn said and led her towards the case containing her small fragment of lace, keen to ensure it made it onto the website.

'Mm, yes, very pretty,' Sariah said in a perfunctory way and snapped it on her phone. 'Next?'

Evelyn led Sariah to the framed piece of embroidery, then the little painting and finally to the cracked teacup.

'I don't think we'll bother with that,' Sariah said with a forced laugh. 'Let's stick to museum-quality objects. Not broken old crockery.'

Evelyn had had enough of Sariah's rudeness. She took a deep breath and had every intention of giving this uptight woman short shrift, when they were interrupted by a knocking sound.

'Hiya, anyone home?' Della was standing in the museum doorway. 'Is this a good time?'

'It's a very good time,' Evelyn said. 'Come in. We need your help.'

In the end, Evelyn left the two of them to it. 'Just choose things that look suitable,' she said. 'I've made my selection – even if one of them has been rather rudely vetoed.'

Sariah looked away, suddenly absorbed in a display of seagull and goose feathers. 'Well I never. These were used to clean windows in the olden days,' she said with fake enthusiasm.

Evelyn frowned. 'Just show me your selection before you go,' she said and retreated to her office area, where she added another couple of hardbacks to the fortress of books that encircled her desk.

The two women took their time and, now and then, Evelyn heard them talking and the odd burst of laughter. But it wasn't the unkind sort of laughter she'd heard from other visitors. It sounded like they were having fun. When Sariah and Della had finished, they came and stood in front of her desk, nudging each other like naughty schoolgirls.

Sariah started swiping through photos on her phone. 'Here's the pictures we took. I got shots of your labels too, so I can include the correct information.' She sounded more conciliatory than before.

'It was surprisingly hard to whittle things down,' Della added. 'Once you start looking, there's an awful lot of interesting stuff here, you know.'

Evelyn did know, but it was nice to hear it confirmed. Then she and Della stood either side of Sariah to look through the photographs and, as Evelyn saw them on the tiny screen, she couldn't help feeling a small swell of pride. The first three items were her lace, the embroidered boat at sea and the pretty little painting. Then came Sariah and Della's own choices, which included:

- A baby's high chair, oak, circa 1930–40
- A ceramic chamber pot, decorated with a poppy and leaf design, 1950s
- A wristwatch, stopped at 11.21, donated by Mrs Brown of Rattle Street
- A pair of children's slippers, felt and lambswool, 1920s
- A handmade doll, carved from driftwood and dressed in silk and cotton, circa 1900
- A green porcelain vase with crackle glaze, date unknown
- A framed display of fishermen's knots
- A necklace of faience and gold beads
- A brass tin, presented to sailors upon the occasion of Christmas 1914 by Princess Mary, containing tobacco and a tinder lighter (unused).

'I took more pictures, but these are the ones we liked the best,' Sariah said.

Evelyn nodded her approval because the women had chosen objects that spoke of forgotten lives. She'd often wondered about the family of children that had each taken a turn on the old-fashioned high chair, gradually wearing the wood on the arms smooth, or which wartime sailor had resisted smoking his tin of tobacco because it felt too precious.

Then Sariah opened up her laptop, did some clicking and a page sprang to life. At the top it said *Portheast Museum of Maritime Curiosities*, then underneath, *Save Our Museum*.

'I've already got a template in place, so all I need to do is add the copy and images,' Sariah said. 'Alison is getting the local media to cover the website launch and I'll include a *Get In Touch* page so people can email us their memories.' She snapped her laptop shut. 'All we need to do now is wait for those stories to come in.'

Della, who had been surprisingly quiet, said, 'You know what would be really good?'

Evelyn raised an eyebrow, humouring her.

'Once you get some interesting stories, you could hold an exhibition.'

'An exhibition?' Evelyn repeated dumbly.

'Yeah, I know it's a pretty radical idea, having an exhibition in a museum.' Della laughed at her own joke. 'But give it some thought, hey?'

Chapter Ten

Toots the cat made it very clear that Evelyn had been neglecting him and he was not best pleased. He rejected her first peace offering, a tin of sardines, and sat with his back to her, every now and then giving his tail a twitch. Finally, he relented when she got out the hard stuff: a packet of Dreamies treats.

It was good to see him again but she wouldn't have blamed him if he'd stayed away. Something about the new busyness to her days meant she could see her caravan through fresh eyes: there were several stains on the brown corner sofa, in reality a thin layer of foam that she should have replaced long ago, and the windows needed a good clean. Then there was the sour smell that had bothered her for some time, but had no discernible source.

Still, it was the best place for her to sit and let the events of the past few days settle. A week ago, her life had been ticking along at its regular pace. Since Della had appeared waving that letter from the council, her days had been an endless series of disturbances. People who had been near strangers were now calling her by her first name and wandering into her museum, suggesting meetings and websites and, now, an exhibition.

It was odd, she thought, how in a small town, you could absorb a superficial knowledge of people, yet never dig any deeper. For instance, she knew that Della was from Australia, but she had no idea why she'd come to Portheast or how long she intended to stay. She'd noticed a young woman called Alison who had been pregnant and then reappeared with a tiny baby in a sling and Roy, one of the Pinlow brothers, by her side.

Years ago, standing in the queue at the post office, she had overheard a woman she now knew was Sariah asking for a form to redirect her post from an old address to the staff accommodation at the new hotel. And, like everyone in town, she knew that Jacob was a down-on-his-luck Warburn and that George Rook was not to be trusted.

Yes, in a town like Portheast you could be surrounded by people that you recognised, or who recognised you, but still feel a deep, gnawing loneliness. She was her own worst enemy, of course. Since childhood, her habit had been to put her head down and rush past anyone who attempted conversation.

'Say hello, Evelyn,' her mother would urge her on trips to town, pressing a hand between her daughter's shoulder blades. Evelyn would do as she was told, but she was far happier when she could return to her own private world: the doll's house in her bedroom or the various secret camps she had made in the overgrown bushes of their garden, hiding behind waxy leaves of camellia and laurel.

Part of her reticence came from the fact that everyone in the town already knew more about Evelyn Silver's circumstances than she would like. It was common knowledge that she had been adopted by the Silvers, a special delivery from the north coast. Although only a short drive away, that part of Cornwall had always felt like another country to her – a place overshadowed by tall engine houses from its mining past and craggy drops into the sea. The grassy cliffs and curved bays of Portheast seemed gentle by comparison.

With people already knowing so much about her past, Evelyn tried to guard what little she could. She would angle her arm around her exercise book at school so no one could copy her answers and politely declined rare invitations to playdates. She grew accustomed to eating her packed lunch on her own, dutifully working her way through oatcakes and grapes and a single bruised banana ('Full of potassium, good for growing bones') packed by her mother, while her classmates tucked into Ski yoghurts, Wagon Wheels and bags of Wotsits.

She was bright, but it was decided that university would not suit her temperament, not even one that was relatively close by such as Exeter. Instead, she did an Open University degree in Classics and then took up the unofficial position of proofreader for her father, who was writing up a lifetime's knowledge in a book he'd catchily titled *Coastal Grasses, Mosses and Ferns of South Cornwall*.

So it was a surprise when, one Monday morning, she was summoned to her father's study and presented with an advertisement in the jobs pages of *The Guardian*. 'It's a trainee curatorship,' her father explained, smoothing out the newspaper. 'And I have a few strings I can pull.'

'But it's in London,' she'd stumbled.

'Well, it's the British Museum.' He laughed. 'So, yes, it is.'

Her mother wasn't sure Evelyn was robust enough to cope with life in the big city, let alone the rigours of a nine-to-five position. But Edwin seemed keen for his daughter to spread her wings. And, as each dull day passed in a fog of proofreading, watching the *Six O'Clock News* over tea and then Horlicks before bed, Evelyn began to wonder if there was more to life.

So she went ahead and applied and was accepted onto the scheme. Her father even helped arrange her accommodation: a curator in the East Asian Antiquities department had a spare room in her flat in a redbrick mansion block near Goodge Street. On sunny days, Evelyn and her landlady, Frances Parfait, strolled to work together through the backstreets of Bloomsbury. Frances wore brogues with a tweed skirt suit and was a chain-smoker, and liked to complain that the museum wasn't the institution it used to be. 'Back in the day, curators were Oxbridge only,' she said, dropping her cigarette onto the museum steps and grinding it out with her sturdy lace-up.

Gradually, what Evelyn came to love most about those walks and London in general was that nobody knew who she was. She'd thought the busyness and the anonymity would be terrifying, but in fact it was a liberation. As she started to explore beyond her small patch of WC1, she revelled in it. Unlike Portheast, nobody knew Evelyn Silver's sad past and, for a while, it felt as if life was opening up into a series of larger vistas and possibilities.

She even loved the antiquated routines of the museum, the way all the curators and the small cohort of trainees had to queue up at the porter's window behind a pillar in the foyer each morning for their keys. You had to be ready to recite your key number quickly, so as not to hold up the line. 'Nine-three-one,' she'd say clearly and the porter would hand over her weighty key on a chain.

It hung around her neck and made her feel important as she made her way through the galleries to whichever department she was assigned to that month. Her first placement had been in Maps, accessed through a secret door that was set into a run of bookcases: a keyhole in the woodwork beside *The Cartography of Ancient Greece* was the spot to look for.

Next, she shadowed a curator in Egyptology, where she got used to the musty smell of long-preserved bones and was told never to touch anything with her bare hands. This was followed by a stint with her landlady in East Asian Antiquities. Frances was more easy-going and actually encouraged Evelyn to handle the collections. She also took frequent smoking breaks, leaving Evelyn alone to admire the ceramics laid out for cataloguing.

Then she met Asa Lingard, a fellow trainee curator, who had a passion for Greece and Rome. He'd been on a dig in Rome in his final year at university and waxed lyrical about it to Evelyn. 'The evidence is all there, right in the middle of the city: ancient columns and slabs of rock that were carved thousands of years ago.' He had long, gangly arms and they wheeled around in the air as he got excited. 'The Colosseum is mind-blowing – you must go. All that gore and debauchery.'

Asa had grown up in Edinburgh with academics as parents and he was almost as cripplingly shy as Evelyn. But somehow, when they were alone together, their mutual awkwardness evaporated, as if two negatives made a positive. At the weekends, they often met at a cinema in Bloomsbury, where, finally, during an afternoon showing of *A Room with a View*, Asa dared to lay a clammy hand over Evelyn's. Within months, they were spending every spare moment together and exchanging longing looks across a table of the British Museum canteen. After lunch, Asa would walk her back to whichever department she was working in. With his curly hair and strong nose, Evelyn dared to tell Asa he was as handsome as the Roman statues they passed by. He, in turn, said she was as rare and precious as the ancient Egyptian jewels she was finally allowed to dust with a tiny brush.

Yes, as she told her parents over the phone, life in London was pretty wonderful. Until it all came crashing down.

Chapter Eleven

George Rook was on his fortnightly visit to St Austell library when he heard about the museum's new website. 'You should take a look,' remarked the librarian as she checked out his next Colin Dexter novel with a sharp beep. 'Imagine, all those things, hidden away for so long.'

'Is that so?' he replied thoughtfully. He decided it would be wise to take a look straightaway and so logged onto the public computer.

The first two things that caught his professional eye were a nice-looking watch, which was probably worth a bit, and one of those WWI tobacco tins that people always thought were worth a fortune, but sadly were not. And then he saw something far more worrying – that blasted painting, with Evelyn's description reproduced word for word.

Anxiously, he clicked back to the homepage and scrolled down to see what else that infuriating woman had put up. And then he stopped scrolling because what he'd found was far more worrying than that little Wallis tribute. What was Evelyn Silver thinking?

When Minnie Fraser, St Austell's longest-serving librarian, came back to check how George was getting on, she found he'd disappeared without so much as a thank you. The chair had been pushed back and when Minnie jiggled the mouse, he'd left a page from the museum's website still open.

She remembered the place from a school trip long ago: dusty cabinets and an overwhelming reek of fish. The item George had left on his screen was rather lovely, but not something she remembered seeing there. But then, she reasoned, there was probably stuff squirrelled away in the dark corners of that shed that even Evelyn Silver didn't know about.

Chapter Twelve

Initially, it seemed that only cranks were interested in emailing the website address Sariah had set up: stories@portheastmuseum.org. In the first week, a man in Newquay wrote asking for love (although in rather more graphic terms) and someone in Roche claimed that the ceramic chamber pot belonged to his Uncle Graham and the museum would be hearing from his solicitors. He later emailed to apologise. *It's safe and sound under his bed. But let me know if you'd like to purchase it.*

Each member of the committee – Evelyn, Della, Sariah, Alison and Jacob – had access to the email account and Evelyn tended to check it in the evening. The second week after it went live, there was a short article in the *St Austell Bugle* and the site started getting lots of 'hits', which, according to Sariah, was a good thing.

Hi all. We've got an interesting email, Alison put on the WhatsApp chat one Tuesday afternoon. Evelyn logged in and saw it was from a man in nearby Fowey.

Dydh da – Hello there. I don't have any family connection to these objects, but I do recognise the fishing knots in the frame, he wrote. *My father taught me a couple and I'm proud to say I can still do them. I would be happy to talk further about this.*

Meur Ras – Thank you, Michael Bower.

Happy to chase this up, Alison added to the chat. Then she wrote, *@Evelyn New email just come in. Best you to deal with directly.*

Intrigued, Evelyn checked the inbox on her phone and saw the next message was from *George@PortheastAntiques*. With a sinking feeling, she opened it. The message managed to be both cryptic and to the point:

Dear Evelyn, it would be best if you removed some items from the website. It will only stir up trouble for us. Best, George Rook.

'Us'? There was no 'us'. He was probably hoping to piggyback on any media attention and get publicity for his shop. Without delay, she sent a reply:

Mr Rook, please cease and desist from contacting us. I have no association with Portheast Antiques, nor do I wish there to be any. Sincerely, Evelyn Silver.

As I tried to mention discreetly, it's a matter of provenance, came the reply.

Staring at the phone in her hand, Evelyn had a strong urge to throw it at the wall. To distract herself, she began to rearrange the books on her desk. Then she bashed out a label for an item on her typewriter: *Walking stick, oak, with fish carving atop.* Then, in a rare fit of efficiency, she carried the newly catalogued walking stick over to the Traditional Attire area and propped it up. 'There,' she said to no one in particular.

George could not tell her what to do. 'Nothing but a knocker,' her father had said, each time they passed by the window of the antiques shop. These days, Portheast Antiques didn't even deserve its name, specialising in twee tat that George Rook should be ashamed of.

At the end of the day, Evelyn was doing her last walk around the museum when she heard footsteps. 'I'm about to close,' she called out. And then she didn't say another word, because George

Rook had closed the door behind himself and deftly turned the key in the lock.

'I think it's time you and I had a chat,' he said gravely.

She still had her phone in her pocket, so she could dial 999. Or she could WhatsApp the group. Failing that she could shout out, because Della might still be next door. But Evelyn did none of those things, because a low knot of dread told her that, on some level, she knew why George Rook had come.

'So,' she said. 'Take a seat.'

She nodded at the fold-out chairs and sat back down at her desk.

'How can I help?' she said in what she thought of as her 'kindly curator voice'.

On the occasions when Evelyn had observed George Rook in his shop, she'd seen him putting on quite the performance: strolling back and forth like a puffed-up pigeon, gesticulating and talking up whatever piece he was trying to flog. As an affectation, he kept a magnifying loupe tucked into his top pocket and, when he got the scent of a sale, he would whip it out and make a show of inspecting a supposedly rare postcard or piece of costume jewellery. But now, there was none of that bluster.

'Well, I'm afraid there are several things. First of all, it's the painting,' he said. 'When I saw it on the poster, I thought, well, no harm done. It's only going to be seen in Portheast. But now you've gone and put it on a website, haven't you?'

'Yes. Sariah made the website. And Alison is doing publicity,' she said, trying to sound authoritative. 'The campaign seems to have struck a nerve. Finally, people are seeing that local history is important.'

George gave a sigh. 'And you think that's a good idea – putting it all on a website?'

'Well, we have to do something. Otherwise I'll lose the museum.'

'I understand that, Evelyn. But let's start with that Alfred Wallis painting. It's not what you think it is.'

Deep down, Evelyn had suspected as much. The composition had a feeling of constraint, as if the artist was trying a little too hard, and it had none of the unfettered joy of Wallis's other work.

'I see,' she said flatly. Her dream of presenting an undiscovered gem to the world and getting a windfall that could save her museum was fading before her eyes. 'Are you sure? I mean, Jacob thought it had belonged to his grandmother.'

'Well, that much is true,' George said forlornly. 'It was painted to order, you see. It was my dad's idea – he approached Sir Jasper and said he might have a pretty little collectible painting coming up, but it had to be on the QT. Back then, must have been in 1987, Sir Jasper was in a pickle: his wife had caught him up to his old tricks again and he was on a final warning. This was a peace offering to her.' George raised his eyes.

'So you – you painted it?' Evelyn could barely keep the anger out of her voice.

'Afraid so.' A shy smile crept over George's face. 'Do you like it?'

'Like it? It's an abomination. You should be ashamed of yourself. How many other fakes have you done, that unsuspecting people have bought thinking they've got the real thing?'

'Oh, a few Nicholsons; I went through a Pre-Raphaelite stage, but they were a bit fiddly. Did a few Hockney swimming pools. Oh, and plenty of Bridget Rileys – op art was a gift to us,' he said.

He ran his hand over his shorn head. 'In my defence, our customers weren't exactly innocent art lovers. These paintings appealed to the sort of people who didn't want to buy on the open market or leave a paper trail. They had an excess of cash and saw these black market paintings as a way of hiding it, with no questions asked and, more to the point, no tax.'

'So how did that fake Wallis end up in a jumble sale in Roche in 2019?' Evelyn asked.

'No idea. I was as surprised as you when I saw it again.'

Evelyn let her gaze slide over to the spot where the offending artwork was displayed, hung between a rusty scythe and a rattan carpet beater. 'Poor Jacob. He must never know. To him, it has sentimental value,' she said.

'Well, I'm not about to broadcast it,' said George. 'But you might do well to take it off the website.'

'Right. Yes.' Evelyn felt the disappointment sink in, heavy as wet sand. To her horror, she felt the swell of a sob. 'Oh, I'm sorry,' she said. 'It's been a difficult time. What with the council wanting to close me down and then all this . . . fuss.' She gestured around the boat shed. 'All these people. They mean well but, you know. It's all a bit overwhelming. After so long.'

George, who had seemed on the verge of saying something else, nodded. 'It's been your little hideaway, hasn't it?'

Evelyn did not want to be pitied, least of all by this odious man. She gave a sniff and gathered herself. 'So, you said there were several things you wanted to talk about.'

'I did?'

'Yes. And you said, "firstly". What else are you going to tell me? That you, the appointed expert, have decided that the rest of my collection is worthless?' Evelyn stood and began walking around the display cabinets. 'What about this?' She pointed at a faded Cornish flag, handstitched and allegedly waved during the D-Day celebrations. 'Is this a fake?'

'No. Evelyn. I'm sorry, I didn't mean to upset you.'

But Evelyn wasn't listening. 'And this – are you going to rubbish this as well?' She snatched a tablecloth off a pile of fabrics and shook it out with a billow of dust.

George was taken aback: this wasn't the mousy Evelyn Silver he knew. 'No. Actually, that looks like rather good Victorian linen.'

'And this?' She'd come to a stop by the Miscellanea cabinet. 'What about this – is this fake – do you want me to take this off the website so nobody sees it?' she asked, her breath coming in short, tight gasps and her hand resting on the glass above her own piece of Cornish lace, the one speared with a rusted safety pin.

George looked down at the floor. 'No,' he said. 'I'm sure that's genuine. And I swear, if I knew anything more about it, I'd tell you.'

There was a long silence. He averted his eyes so that Evelyn could blink away the dampness that was blurring her vision.

George brushed the dust from the tablecloth off his trousers. 'I suppose it's only a little website, isn't it?' he said eventually. 'Unlikely to get much attention.'

'It's just so that we can get a few human-interest stories,' Evelyn explained, calmer now.

'So the website won't stay up for long?' he asked.

She shook her head. 'Once a few people have come forward, we could take it down. We've already had one promising email, from a chap in Fowey. It shouldn't take long to get a few more.'

'Ah, I suppose it's not like anyone beyond Cornwall will be looking at it.' George tugged at his collar and fiddled with the top button, a gesture that put Evelyn in mind of the boy he'd once been, long before he'd joined the family business: a boy who sat on his own on the school bus, who preferred drawing to football and had once shared a bag of crisps with her.

'Perhaps I overreacted,' he said with a rueful smile. 'One little website can't do much damage, can it?'

Chapter Thirteen

Once she had started something, Alison liked to see it through and that was how she found herself loitering outside Potters Newsagents on a Wednesday lunchtime instead of taking Will home for his nap.

When she'd first suggested forming a Save Our Museum committee to Sariah, she hadn't been totally honest about her reasons. She'd talked up the community aspect, but neglected to mention it was also a way for her to keep tabs on that wretched embroidered picture of a boat to see if this SW person came forward.

But then she'd been surprised by how much she had enjoyed the meeting. She'd felt the old thrill of starting a publicity campaign – and it had been a long time since Alison had had fun or felt excited about her work. Finding stories, writing press releases and working together for a good cause were a far cry from unblocking the toilets at the sports centre.

What had started out as her personal damage limitation strategy had grown into something bigger. She genuinely wanted to follow up on the first proper email that had come in, the one from Michael in Fowey about old-fashioned fishing knots. His story struck a chord with her because it was about the simple pleasures of growing up by the sea and she had emailed him back to say she'd like to visit and hear more.

But the problem was, Alison didn't have a car anymore – Roy needed it to drive to the repair garage he ran with his two brothers – and taking Will and his buggy on the bus would be a hassle.

However, she happened to know that, like her, Jacob only worked mornings. She also knew that he drove a souped-up Mini, the kind of car a rich kid might get as a 21st birthday present, and so she pushed open the door to Potters Newsagents and wheeled the buggy inside.

She watched as Jacob looked up in surprise and two pink dots appeared on his cheeks. A magazine lay open on the counter and he rolled it up swiftly, but not before she saw its title. It was a copy of *History Today*, hardly saucy reading material.

'I've come to ask you a favour.' The words were barely out of her mouth before he said a trip to Fowey sounded great. 'Sometimes the afternoons drag,' he admitted. That wasn't the case for Alison, who felt like there was never enough time to get the house straight and dinner cooked and Will fed before Roy got home.

'It won't take long,' she said as Jacob strapped in Will's car seat and pretended not to notice the shower of breadstick crumbs her son was already spreading over the upholstery.

Michael lived in a bungalow on the outskirts of Fowey and when they rang his bell, a dog set up a furious yapping, which was followed by a long pause.

'Saw you had the baby, so I've shut the pup in the kitchen,' Michael explained when he came to the door. He was a sprightly man, all sinew and sun-wrinkled skin and he smiled down at Will in his car seat. 'He's a cute chap. But my puppy, Max, can be a bit bouncy and we don't want to scare him, do we?'

Michael was easy company, happy to tell them his memories of fishing trips with his dad, Brian. 'Seeing that display of knots on your website, well it took me right back to those quiet times, in the days long before kids were glued to screens. Be a different world, by the time your little one's grown up.' He nodded towards Will, who had fallen asleep on the journey, but was starting to stir and rub his eyes.

Alison took a photograph as Michael demonstrated one of the easier knots. 'My fingers aren't as nimble as they used to be, but I can still do the reliable Blood Loop.' He smiled, twisting and flicking a line into its shapes. 'Course, we were only weekend amateurs, but we both enjoyed the peace, looking out to sea and chatting when we felt the urge. And if we landed a mackerel for tea, all the better. So when I saw these knots, all those memories came back.' He held his fist to his chest. 'I don't mind saying, they gave a tug at my heart.'

Michael tried to show Jacob how to do a simple knot and Alison unbuckled a now wide-awake Will, who made straight for a stray dog biscuit he'd spotted under the table. Subtly, she tried to prise it out of his chubby fingers and swap it for a healthy rice cake, but Will was having none of it. 'Sorry, we'd better make a move,' she said.

'I'll offer your story to the press, but we're also thinking of holding an exhibition. Can we include your words in that, too?' she asked as they said their goodbyes.

'I'd be flattered,' Michael replied.

Alison could already envisage the exhibition's launch: Della could do hot drinks, Nils could do small bites and maybe Sariah could get them a deal on wine and beer. As Jacob drove the winding roads back to Portheast, her mind was buzzing with ideas. 'This could be so good,' she told him. 'We can invite the media. Reel them in with all the little human-interest stories and then, boom, break the bigger news story that the council wants to shut down the museum.'

She hadn't felt this buzz since she'd worked for the PR company in Truro and she told Jacob about the last campaign she'd worked on, which had involved taking journalists on a tour of a Cornish gin distillery. 'They all got roaring drunk and said they wanted to go clubbing. All these posh London journos ended up in Jangles, dancing to Nineties hits. Can you imagine?'

'Jangles?'

She'd forgotten Jacob wasn't a proper local.

'It's a Truro institution,' she explained. 'Back in my youth it was the place to be seen – think Bacardi Breezers and Ed Sheeran on repeat. And it hadn't changed a bit.'

Jacob gave her a smile. 'Ed Sheeran aside, it sounds like you enjoyed your job.'

'Yeah. I did.' Alison trailed off, then swivelled round to check on Will in his car seat. 'But then along came this little one.' She stroked Will's cheek. 'I wasn't planning on becoming a mum at twenty-one, but life is full of surprises, hey. Anyway, PR isn't a job that keeps family hours, so I gave it up. For now, the sports centre makes more sense: mornings only and I can pick him up from nursery.' But even talking about the sports centre made her feel trapped, as if she was already back in the windowless office with the sharp smell of chlorine, the endless complaints and Ollie's lame jokes.

'Plus, I get a discount at the sportswear concession,' she said brightly, holding out her arms to show off one of her many zip-up running tops.

She got Jacob to drop her at the crossroads, explaining that it was better if she walked up to the housing estate from there. 'Keeps me fit,' she said with a smile. As she slotted Will's car seat into the buggy frame, he made a lunge for her hair and she was grateful she'd had it cut short recently – it meant there was less to grab hold of.

'Right, got to get going,' she said. 'Thanks for the lift.' She started walking as fast as she could up the hill and didn't look back. She'd be lucky if she made it back before 5 p.m., when Roy would be revving their knackered Toyota Corolla up their drive. Already, she could feel her chest tightening.

◆ ◆ ◆

'Tell me again,' Roy said, chewing hard. 'You took our son, where?'

'It's for the Save Our Museum campaign,' Alison repeated. 'A guy called Michael over in Fowey does those old-fashioned fishing knots and there's a framed set of knots in the museum. We're linking items in the museum with ordinary people's stories to show they are still relevant and this . . .'

She heard it before she felt it, the crack of his slap. Then came a feeling that was akin to relief, because she now could stop wondering when he'd next explode. The waiting had become the background hum to her life and the not knowing was almost the worst part.

Like a driver whose hands slipped into position on a steering wheel, Roy's reached for her arms and held them until his fingers found old bruises. Alison counted to twenty and kept her eyes fixed on Will, who was looking down at his plate of cold peas and pasta. She reached twenty-two before Roy let go.

'So, you took my fifteen-month-old son to see a complete stranger – a man who could be a rapist, a child abuser or who knows what?'

He was just a man who made nice knots, she wanted to say. Who wanted to talk about his dad and had a dog but had shut him in the kitchen because he didn't want to scare Will who, at that moment, was absorbed in ferrying a row of peas from one side of the plate to the other. Michael in Fowey couldn't have known that there were scarier things in her son's life than a bouncy puppy with a wet nose.

She too kept her head down as Roy talked, telling her the things she'd heard before – how he was out all day, working his fingers to the bone, providing for his family. 'The whole point is that you can spend your afternoons looking after Will,' he said. 'Not go chasing all over the place on your own. Visiting men.'

'He was a pensioner, Roy,' she blurted out. 'He was just an old boy. And besides, I wasn't . . .' Too late, she realised her mistake.

Sometimes, she swore Roy could read her mind. It was as if he'd crawled inside, poked around with his grimy mechanic's fingers and scooped out all the good bits, the parts that were about having fun or laughing or thinking up ideas, and he was gradually replacing them with something thick and grey, much like the foamy scum she cleaned from the sink each evening.

'You weren't what? On your own?'

She could say she was with Sariah, or Della or even Evelyn. But it wasn't worth it because somehow Roy would be able to tell she was lying and then he'd find out that she'd been in a car with another man, Jacob, a soft posh boy who wouldn't stand a chance against Roy.

'Upstairs, now,' Roy said.

She knew not to argue. As she went, she deftly lifted Will out of his high chair and put him in his playpen. Then she wound up the clockwork toy that sang nursery rhymes and placed it beside him. The songs didn't last very long, but she hoped the sound would be a distraction for her son, once Roy had followed her upstairs.

Every other Sunday, Alison took Will to see her dad, Keith, but even that gap felt too long at the moment, because Will was changing by the day, learning something new and brilliant. Only yesterday, he'd picked up a leaf, holding its stalk between his thumb and forefinger. She knew this was an excellent demonstration of his motor skills, which made her proud, but she also wished she could slow down this gallop through his toddler milestones, turn back time and enjoy every milky, tired moment of his baby days all over again. There were other ways in which she wanted to turn back time as well.

'Look, his walking is getting steadier,' her dad said as they both watched Will cruise his way around the living room.

'I'd say he's got the family swagger,' Keith added. 'The Blake walk, that is. Not those Pinlow boys.'

When she'd left the house, the Pinlow brothers had been spreading themselves around Alison and Roy's living room, warming up for an afternoon of rugby on the TV. As she closed the front door, she heard the tinny crunch of a beer can in someone's fist and knew it was the first of many.

Changing the subject, Alison told her dad about how she'd been to Fowey to interview a man. 'It's for a campaign to save the museum,' she said. 'You know, the one down by the harbour.'

Will was careering straight towards the sharp edges of the coffee table, so she stood up and guided him back to the wooden puzzle her dad had laid out on the carpet. Then, as casually as she could, she said, 'Funny thing is, there's a picture in that museum that looks a little bit like our one.' She indicated towards the embroidered picture over the fireplace. 'But Grandpa Fred wouldn't have made another, would he?' She passed Will a puzzle piece and watched him slot it into place.

Keith looked up at the picture and gave a gruff laugh. 'No, one in a million, that picture. Just like your Grandma Helena.'

'That's what I thought,' Alison said firmly. 'Must have been the fashion back then for lots of sailors at sea. Gave them something wholesome to do.' No one had come forward yet with any information on the other embroidered picture and, logically, there was a good chance SW was long dead and buried. But if anyone did come out of the woodwork, Alison would be the first to know.

'Weird old place, that museum,' her dad said after a while. 'Can't say I've ever felt any urge to go in there.'

'You're right,' Alison agreed quickly. 'Not your sort of place.' She didn't want her dad wandering in and getting a nasty surprise. Suddenly, everything was starting to feel very stuffy in this small front room, so she stood up. 'Will, fancy a go on your swing?'

In truth, it was a bit cold outside, but it was always nice to see the garden. The terraced house had been her grandma and grandpa's before it became her dad's and the garden was unchanged, with areas set aside for growing flowers and vegetables. That afternoon, the earth was still dark and loamy, but Alison knew that come spring there would be potatoes and runner beans to eat, and sweet peas and azaleas for her to take home.

She and her dad took turns pushing Will in the bucket swing and she loved the way her son's blond hairs caught in the breeze.

'How's things?' her dad asked. 'At home.'

She knew what he meant, but her dad was already too hard on Roy, always on at him about fixing up their own garden or laying off the beer and it didn't help, not one bit.

'Fine,' she said lightly, in another act of damage limitation.

But Alison knew her father wasn't fooled.

'He's trying,' she said, toeing a bald patch on the soggy lawn. 'He took Will out in the buggy the other day without me even asking.'

Keith didn't reply. He'd brought Alison up on his own from when she was eleven and this fell far short of what he thought made a decent father. She tugged her sleeves down so that they covered her wrists.

'Too cold?' her father asked.

'It has turned a bit chilly.' She stopped pushing Will and together they watched the swing slow, its arc growing smaller until it was almost at a standstill and she shivered because their visit had gone so quickly. It was almost time to go home.

Chapter Fourteen

Traffic to the website is up 60% this week – @Sariah

Some interesting looking emails too – @Della

Let's meet up re the exhibition – @Alison

Evelyn scanned the day's group messages with a mixture of pleasure and horror. This rise in visitors to the website was a good thing and the sooner the site had done its job, the sooner she could ask for it to be taken down. Because since her unsettling chat with George, she wasn't sure that showing off the museum's collections was such a good idea.

She'd assured George that it was unlikely anyone outside Cornwall would find the website, but it was becoming clear that had been wishful thinking – it was called the World Wide Web for a reason. And now everyone was getting increasingly excited about the exhibition idea. In fact, the messages between these young people never stopped – her phone was pinging more than it ever had in its small plastic-cased life.

Hereby convening a Save Our Museum committee meeting, Friday 5pm? Pub afterwards? – @Jacob

Within minutes, there were four thumbs up. Evelyn's finger hovered over her screen and then, with resignation, she added a fifth.

Given that Alison had been so keen, Evelyn was surprised that she wasn't the first to arrive on Friday. Instead, it was Jacob, who assumed his usual job of putting out the chairs, followed by Della with Sariah, who had popped into her ice cream shed on the way. 'I brought coffee. And Anzac biscuits!' Della announced.

'We're her taste-testers,' Sariah added swiftly, which served as a coded warning to those in the know.

Although the chairs were set facing Evelyn's desk, it was clear that Sariah intended to take charge. Alison didn't arrive until 5.15 p.m., when she steered the baby buggy in. 'Sorry, last-minute change of plan. I've brought Will, but he'll soon be asleep.'

'No worries,' said Sariah. 'I'll start, shall I? While you get sorted.'

Alison kept her head bowed as she wrestled her way out of her bulky jacket and went through her bag for her phone, which she promptly dropped on the floor. 'Sorry,' she said again, embarrassed. 'I'm all fingers and thumbs.'

'Alison?' Sariah had her eyebrows raised. 'You must be getting better weather than the rest of us.'

Evelyn frowned, then saw what she meant: Alison was wearing a pair of sunglasses.

'Oh.' Alison reached up to take them off but then seemed to change her mind. 'Yeah, right. Conjunctivitis. Not a pretty sight.' She waved at them to continue. 'Go ahead, ignore me.'

'Right, to business,' Sariah said decisively. 'I've done a spreadsheet of the objects that are on the website. Where people have been in touch, their details are listed in the next column. I suggest we follow up and interview these people, making sure they are happy to have their words included in articles and an exhibition. As you do so, please mark the item with an asterisk so we don't double up. It's a shared document online, but here's a hard copy.'

She passed around sets of stapled papers. Evelyn ran her eye down the left-hand column, which listed each item. It continued onto a second page, with some less familiar items.

'Yes, I added a few more bits to the website,' Sariah explained smoothly. 'I had the extra photos so it seemed a shame to waste them.'

Evelyn scanned the additions and saw things like *pendant, captain's cap, stone sculpture* and *Roberts radio*.

'Well, I suppose that's OK,' she said, a little huffily.

They discussed exhibition dates and Della suggested the 19th of March. 'It's a couple of weeks before the council's decision day and it's a Thursday – always a good day for a schmooze.' Then Sariah asked, 'Any suggestions for what we call the exhibition?'

Jacob raised his hand, like an overeager schoolboy. 'Portheast Rediscovered?'

Sariah shook her head. 'Too boring. Next?'

'Cornwall Through the Ages?' Della offered.

'Even worse.'

'Well, you think of something then.' Della crossed her arms.

There was a silence.

'Let's move on to publicity,' Sariah said. 'Alison, over to you.'

Alison looked uncharacteristically flustered. 'Ah, OK.' She started looking in her bag again, fishing out a nappy, then a soft toy in the shape of a banana that let out a squeak. 'Sorry, forgot my notebook,' she said.

Sariah gave Alison a sharp look, one probably used on guests who tried to make off with the hotel bathrobes.

'How about I wait until more stories are in, then pick the best ones for the press release?' Alison suggested.

'Biscuit? Anyone?' Della said, trying to break the tension. 'Anyone, anyone?' She put the plate back down. 'Speaking of publicity,' she ventured, 'I might have a few UK contacts.'

Sariah bristled. 'But Alison is media, Della, you're . . . hot drinks.'

Della lifted her hands in the air and brought them down on her thighs with a slap so loud it made Alison jump. 'Fine. I was only offering. I could have called up some TV faces: Lorraine, for example. Or Dermot. But by all means ignore me.'

There was a stunned silence. 'Really? You have contacts like that?' Alison asked.

'Well, I haven't seen Dermot since his birthday bash, but yeah. It's a small world, TV.'

They all looked at Della, in her dungarees, Doc Marten boots and box-dyed hair. 'Really?' Evelyn repeated.

'What can I say. I had a career change. Used to run a newsroom in Sydney but got a bad case of burnout. Well, a breakdown, to be more accurate. Then they gave me a daytime chat show, said it would be less pressure, but it wasn't me, you know? So I jacked it in, went travelling and ended up here, in the mother country.'

Jacob, who had been scrolling on his phone, nudged Alison and showed her the screen. Alison passed the phone on to Evelyn, who saw an image of a woman in full make-up, with a big blond blowout. She was wearing a low-cut red dress and rested a mani-cured finger gently on her chin. *Daytime With Della* it said under-neath. *Australia's TV Darling*.

Evelyn looked from the screen to the woman in front of her and back again. Despite the traveller clothes and the purple hair, the TV star was recognisably their Della. Della, who had pitched up in Portheast six months ago and opened an ice cream parlour, despite what seemed to be minimal catering skills.

Della leaned over. 'Cripes, I've not seen that press shot in a while. What was I thinking – all that make-up!'

'You never mentioned you were such a high-flyer,' Evelyn remarked.

'Hmm, maybe I didn't. But that was the point of coming here – to do something completely different. Really, I was heading for Penzance, but the train terminated early. So I looked at the map, googled hotels and got a taxi to the Warburn Spa for the night. I woke up the next morning and the sun was shining. I came down to the harbour, saw the To Let sign and thought, "Why not?"'

Della's voice turned more serious. 'I admit, it's taking a while to build up the business, but I'm loving this chance to rethink my priorities. Not sure how long I'll stay, especially with the council's plans, but I'll always be grateful that Portheast gave me this second chance.'

'It's that kind of place,' Jacob said softly.

'That's it!' Sariah blurted out.

This time it was Evelyn who jumped in alarm.

Sariah waved her hands around in excitement. 'The exhibition: we could call it Second Chances. Because Evelyn finds these lost and broken things and gives them a second chance. And then we're finding people who have a link to them, which gives the objects a whole new meaning.'

She sat back with a big smile, a warm and genuine one that changed her whole face and was nothing like the one she flashed at hotel guests.

'I like it,' Alison said and everyone nodded their agreement.

'Glad to be of service,' Della said. Then she stood up and offered around the still full plate of biscuits. 'No takers?'

With Della revealing her past career, she was charged with the job of inviting the council to the exhibition's opening night. 'I'll suggest that, ahead of their discussion on the leases, they might like to see the role the museum plays in the community, etc.,' she said. 'But I might not mention the media will be there too. Keep it as a surprise.' She gave a long, deliberate wink. 'Then the journos can put them on the spot about the threatened closure.'

'Excellent plan,' said Alison.

'Good work, guys.' Sariah stood, stretching her arms up, and for an awful moment Evelyn thought she was about to start high-fiveing everyone.

Then Jacob said, 'Alison, everyone, quick pint in the pub?'

But Alison was already doing up her coat. 'What? Oh, no, I've got to get straight home.' She looked away. 'Actually, it's good news that we've got Della on board for publicity because I'd better scale back my contribution.'

'What?' Sariah said.

'It's all too much, really. The job, looking after Will. I never should have volunteered, really, it was silly of me.'

She sounded close to tears but, without waiting for a reply, Alison steered the buggy out of the door. By the time Evelyn and the others stepped out, there was nothing to see but the single lamppost and the gleam it cast onto the damp stone. For Alison to have reached the corner that quickly, she must have been running.

Chapter Fifteen

After Alison's disappearing act, enthusiasm for going to the pub seemed to wane. Evelyn was the first to bow out, saying she needed to lock up, and she stayed at her desk moving things around with no real purpose until she judged it was safe to emerge. Evelyn Silver might be slowly coming out of her shell, but there was still only so much conversation she could take in one day.

Before leaving, she unfolded the stapled spreadsheet again to take a closer look and found herself staring at the listing for her fragment of lace, as if a note or email address might magically appear beside it.

As Evelyn walked along the quay, she saw a shapeless silhouette heading towards her. She paused, because behind her lay only Della's ice cream parlour, her museum and the slipway, so she couldn't imagine where this person was going.

As they drew level, the stranger also stopped and Evelyn could make out the lumpen shape was a woman, who was wheezing and holding a hand to her chest.

'Is this the way to the museum?' she asked, her words coming between gasps.

Evelyn took in a bulky coat, plimsols too flimsy for the season and then a face that was as worn as her clothes: a starburst of lines around her lips gave her away as a smoker and her dark hair was threaded with white.

'It is, but I've just closed up for the day,' Evelyn replied.

'There wasn't a phone number, so I had to come in person,' the woman said. 'But then the bus was late – always is – and then I had to walk from the main road.'

Evelyn had been looking forward to getting back to her caravan for an evening on her foam sofa with Toots and did not welcome (a) yet more conversation or (b) an update on the state of the local bus service.

'I'm sorry if you've come a long way, but we open again tomorrow: 9 a.m. sharp.'

The woman swore and raked her hair angrily. 'Seriously?' she said. 'I've come from Redruth, which means two buses, changing at St Austell. Then, like I say, the evening route doesn't come down into town.'

'Well, I'm sorry . . .' Evelyn began.

'I came about the lost things,' the woman said. 'The stuff that's ended up in the museum.'

Evelyn felt a softening. Wasn't this what they wanted – local people connecting with objects from the past?

'Ah, you saw the website,' she said more kindly. 'In that case, the best thing to do is go to the *Get In Touch* page and send us an email. Tell us which item is relevant to you and please include as much detail as you can. We're planning an exhibition,' she added brightly.

'I don't know anything about a website,' the woman replied grumpily. She pulled a piece of paper out of her bag, which was a big black thing with metallic chains as shoulder straps. As she unfolded the paper under the yellow lamplight, Evelyn recognised her own handiwork: it was one of the posters Jacob had photocopied.

'I saw it in the library,' the woman said.

Evelyn noticed a pinhole and a small tear in each corner of the poster, as if it had been ripped from a noticeboard.

'It said to come. So I have. About this,' she said, jabbing angrily at the bottom left corner. The woman was pointing at the cracked teacup, the one with a golden lily design. 'It's mine, see. Or rather, it was my mother's and her mother's before that. It was a complete set, except one went missing, didn't it? Just the cup.'

Evelyn took a step back. This wasn't the heart-warming scenario she had imagined, of lovingly reuniting people with their long-lost objects.

'It's mine,' the woman growled. 'And if you've got it, I want it back.'

Eventually, Evelyn persuaded her to write down her details. 'I'll add your name to the spreadsheet and one of the team will be in touch presently,' she said, liking how efficient this sounded. 'But this is a project to gather stories. Not a lost property service.'

She wasn't sure the woman was listening because she was looking around, clutching her bag to herself. 'How am I supposed to get back to Redruth now? You got a car?'

'I'm afraid not,' Evelyn said firmly, for once glad that her parents' Volvo had been sold for scrap. That seemed to do the trick and the woman started to walk off.

'As I say, we'll be in touch. And if you have any memories associated with that particular item, you're welcome to write a statement for the exhibition,' Evelyn called out optimistically.

She didn't quite catch the woman's reply, but it sounded like 'No chance.'

At home, as she and Toots settled into their usual places on the corner sofa, Evelyn fired up her laptop. It took her a while but she worked out how to access the online spreadsheet and scanned the list for the cracked cup with the golden lily design. When she couldn't see it, she scrolled down the list again, more slowly this time. But it wasn't there. She checked on the paper printout, but it wasn't there either.

And then Evelyn remembered: the woman had seen the poster. Which was a bit of luck, because when Sariah made the website, she had decided not to include that cup. 'Broken old crockery,' she'd said in a sneery voice.

Unable to add any notes to a non-existent listing, and not adept enough with spreadsheets to add a further row, she decided to put the details on the WhatsApp chat.

Woman came to museum re Golden Lily china cup. Rather abrasive, but I feel there's a story there. No email, only a mobile number. Then Evelyn added: *Her name is Grace.*

She watched the group chat, but nobody replied and she supposed they all had better things to do on a Friday night.

As she listened to the pattering of rain on her caravan roof, Evelyn thought about how Della had provided them with the perfect name for the exhibition. For all these years, Evelyn had been picking up objects that had ended up on the beach or been consigned to junk boxes and giving them a second chance. She knew that an object's meaning never stopped with its first owner or maker – that was only the start of its story, which could continue like ripples from a skimmed stone.

Now, some of those ripples were returning to their source and, not for the first time, Evelyn began to doubt the wisdom of this project. Having lived in Cornwall most of her life, she was familiar with people who believed in auras and good and bad vibes. Thanks to her thoroughly scientific upbringing, Evelyn didn't hold with such notions, but that woman she'd met on the quay made her think twice. Unhappiness had radiated off her like an overpowering perfume and Evelyn had a feeling that not all of the stories they might unearth would be happy ones.

Chapter Sixteen

Sariah stared at the group messages, trying to take in what Evelyn had posted, but it made no sense. When she'd built the website, she had deliberately left off the cracked teacup to avoid something like this. And yet, somehow, her mother had found out. The family past she'd tried to outrun was rushing in like a rip tide, ready to drag her back down.

She had a rare Friday night off, but wished she was downstairs working because it would be a welcome distraction. She would be kept busy with the usual complaints about faulty TV remotes, pillows deemed insufficiently plump or the peculiar smell in Room Six's carpet that seemed impervious to Febreze.

Even dealing with the ongoing feud between the two Italian waiters or giving the chef a final warning about his whisky habit would be preferable to the task in hand: facing the fact that her mother had come to see Evelyn.

Sariah typed several draft messages before settling on: *What did she say?*

Evelyn's reply read: *She seemed to want the cup back.*

Well, that sounds about right, thought Sariah. Her mother Grace had always felt short-changed by life. Whether the house was a mess, rain was forecast or the milk had gone sour, she'd look for someone to blame – and Sariah had always been first in the firing line.

Next was her dad, Clint, but he had shipped out not long after Sariah left. Her brothers, Jamie and Liam, were the golden boys, but eventually they too had flown the nest, moving to Penzance where they had their own roofing business. She followed their company's page on Facebook, so she'd seen glimpses of her brothers growing older and caught the odd snippet of family news.

Jamie had married Shona, a woman who everyone described as 'bubbly'. Liam soon followed, marrying a Jenny and going on honeymoon in Ibiza. In the past few years, Sariah had noticed that both brothers were starting to sport a small paunch apiece. They were only in their late twenties while she, somehow, was thirty.

She hadn't spotted their mother in any of the wedding snaps, which mostly focused on the happy couples: Jamie and Shona cutting the cake; Liam and Jenny embracing under a magnolia tree, the sky behind them retouched an unlikely blue.

Sariah had coped with so much during the past fifteen years and there had been plenty of times when she had wished for a mother to turn to, even hard-as-nails Grace. But now, Grace had come to Portheast searching not for Sariah but for that cracked cup, of all things.

How pathetic was that? But her mother had always prided herself on never giving an inch. Occasionally, Grace's rage at the world meant standing up for Sariah, like when she'd let rip during a school parents' evening: 'What do you mean she's "easily distracted"?' she'd bellowed across the desk at Sariah's form teacher. The school hall had fallen silent and heads turned. 'If my daughter is messing about, you lot need to teach better,' her mother had said.

It became a catchphrase for a while, other kids shouting out in class: 'You lot need to teach better!' Sariah had laughed along, but it would have been nice if she, and her mother, had stood out for different reasons.

There was no way she was going to put any of this on the WhatsApp for the others to read: Jacob, who would always be cushioned by his family name and a trust fund; Della with her secret stellar career; and Alison with her perfect little estate house and baby.

But maybe she could talk to Evelyn, whose foundling past was common knowledge in Portheast. She was curious, too, to hear what her mother looked like these days. Did she still dye her hair that fearsome shade of black and smoke like a chimney? Most of all, she wondered if Evelyn had detected the smallest hint of regret in her mother's eyes.

The next morning, Sariah's work schedule included a meeting with a wedding planner, chasing a late laundry delivery and talking to a cleaner who was never on time. But all the while, she kept flicking back to the WhatsApp chat, wondering how her mother had come to hear about the museum campaign. By lunchtime, she couldn't wait any longer.

@Evelyn How's things with you? she messaged. Evelyn replied with the spurt of water and wind emojis, probably thinking it a weather report. Sariah would need to have a word; older people and emojis were a lethal combination.

@Evelyn I am coming down, she replied.

Evelyn had been right, though, the quay was windy and wet and the museum was as quiet as ever. As she walked into the cavernous dark shed, Sariah could barely see the top of Evelyn's head behind her wall of books. As she got closer she saw Evelyn was absorbed in a guide to nautical flags.

'Recent acquisition?' Sariah asked.

Evelyn snapped the book shut. 'Unfortunately not. Several years old, but I'm trying to make a dent in my cataloguing backlog.'

Sariah surveyed the piles of objects and boxes that surrounded Evelyn's desk and wondered if it was humanly possible to finish the task. 'Just out of interest, where do you pick all these things up?' she asked.

'Well, aside from the beach, I have been going to charity shops, jumble sales and the odd country auction for years,' Evelyn replied.

'How do you keep track? I mean, it must be hard to remember where you found every single thing.'

Evelyn frowned. 'There are some that test my memory. But I can remember most of them.' She picked up the book of flags. 'This, for example, was from an RNLI book stall.'

Sariah tried to make her next question sound casual. 'So, that cracked cup, for instance, the one that woman Grace came about. Do you remember where you found that?'

'Indeed I do. It was in a school jumble sale a few years ago. I searched for a saucer, but there wasn't one. Even though it was cracked, the pretty design caught my eye.'

Evelyn closed her volume on nautical warning flags and looked up. 'Was there any particular reason why you decided to leave that cup off the website?' she ventured.

Sariah hadn't been intending to say why, but once she started talking the words kept coming and she realised she'd been holding them in for far too long. 'I'm pretty sure that cup belonged to my grandmother,' she said. Then she explained about the last time she'd seen it, the awful moment when it had slipped and her fear of it being discovered. 'So you didn't see any other cups like it at that jumble sale? Or a big wicker picnic hamper?'

'No, it was just that one, among a box of unwanted crockery. But none of it was as nice as that teacup.'

Evelyn reached for another hardback book from her pile and opened it at its title page. Presently, she asked, 'So the woman I met yesterday, any idea who she was?'

'I think you had the pleasure of meeting my mother, Grace. I haven't seen her in fifteen years, but it sounds like she hasn't changed. Sorry if she was rude.'

'Ah,' said Evelyn. 'No apology needed. Well, not from you, anyway.'

Sariah picked up a shell from Evelyn's desk, then put it down again. 'How did she seem?'

'Well, a little grumpy. She'd come a fair distance and hadn't really understood the point of the poster. But underneath all her moaning, she seemed . . . troubled.'

'Ha, that's one way of putting it,' Sariah said bitterly. 'My mother was always at war with the world, as if she was put upon and everyone else was to blame.'

Evelyn set aside her book and reached for another object, a pewter tankard engraved with a ship. 'So, tell me about your grandmother, the one who owned the cup – was she any easier to get along with?'

'Yes and no,' Sariah said carefully. 'She was a proper matriarch, so you did as you were told. But Mum always said that Grandma Karensa had lost some of her bite, so maybe it ran in the family. That hardness.' But even as she said it, she remembered a softer love from her grandma, times when she'd let Sariah stand on a kitchen stool to help make scones; rubbing the butter into the flour and then patting out the dough, her grandma pretending not to see when she popped scraps into her mouth. In fact, those baking afternoons had been a little escape for all of them, with her mum and even Auntie Rose joining in with the quiet, methodical work of rolling and mixing.

'So, would you like to be the one that calls Grace to follow this up?' Evelyn asked.

Sariah shook her head. 'I don't think so. In fact, I doubt she has any intention of giving us a story for the museum. All she wants is to get it back. I mean, what's she going to do with a broken cup? My mum just hates the idea of missing out on something.'

She sat down on one of the fold-out chairs. 'One summer, I must have been about fourteen, she took me and my brothers out for the day. We came to Portheast, in fact, and there was a woman swimming off the quay. "See her," my mum said. "Living her best life. Free as a bird. And here's me, lumbered with you lot."'

'I think plenty of mothers must feel like that at one time or another,' Evelyn said. 'It's just that your mum said it out loud.'

Then Sariah felt a pang of guilt, because here she was moaning when Evelyn's own mother was dead and buried and her birth mother remained unknown.

'Well, personally, I think you should give her a call,' Evelyn said. 'Why not see what she has to say – or what you want to say to her?' She fixed her gaze on Sariah. 'Because you have been given a chance to get back in contact with your mother. And you shouldn't let it go.'

Sariah nodded. 'Thanks, I'll have a think.'

Back at the hotel Sariah typed out a message:

Hi Mum, Sariah here. Evelyn at the museum gave me your number – I'm helping the Save Our Museum campaign. I saw the cup too and also wondered if it was Grandma Karensa's. Funny seeing it again. Evelyn said you wanted it back. Shall I bring it over?

After she'd pressed Send, Sariah sent a second message.

@Evelyn Thanks for the chat. Waiting to hear if she wants to meet up. If she does, would you come with me? Seeing as you've already met her. Could do with the moral support, but no worries if not.

Chapter Seventeen

Alison was pushing the baby's buggy along the long, straight road out of town when the Warburn Spa minibus passed her by. She spotted Sariah driving and was about to raise her hand to give her a wave, when two things stopped her. First of all, Sariah's face was fixed in a weird sort of grimace and, secondly, if Alison lifted her right arm too high, it triggered a sharp pain in her shoulder.

She was puzzled to see Evelyn Silver sitting in the passenger seat – where on earth could the two of them be going together? This train of thought must have made Alison slow her pace because suddenly Will was awake, rearing forward in the buggy and pushing against the plastic rain cover and she knew she'd missed the small window of opportunity for his afternoon nap.

A month ago, walking along this smooth stretch of pavement had been guaranteed to lull Will into a sleep, but these days he fought that urge, rubbing his eyes and straining at the safety harness in case he missed out on anything.

Please sleep, she thought. Please make it easier. Because she knew that if Will skipped his nap, he'd be cranky all afternoon. Worst-case scenario, he'd end up having a meltdown at teatime, just as his dad got home. Which would be bad news for everyone.

So Alison kept walking at a steady pace, hoping the swish of tyres on damp tarmac and the warm fug inside the buggy's rain cover might still work.

Roy didn't need the extra stress of a whingy toddler right now. The Pinlows' garage wasn't doing well; people had started taking their cars up to the new place on the industrial estate that offered discounts, a jug of coffee and mini packs of Biscoff biscuits. 'No sense of loyalty these days,' Roy had said, thumping his hand on the table for emphasis. Roy was a very physical person, it was how he expressed himself.

For instance, his favourite thing to do with their son was toss him up in the air and catch him. 'Woo-hoo, how's my boy?' he'd shout and Will would giggle, but soon his laughter would change, hovering on the edge of hysteria, and Alison's stress levels would rise because it didn't sound like fun anymore. 'Please, he's just had his tea,' she might say, but even that was interfering.

'He's a boy' was Roy's stock reply. 'He can take a bit of rough and tumble.'

She knew it was Roy's way of showing his love. She just wished he'd try something else as well, like reading Will his bedtime story or doing bath-time or playing with the cars or bricks or bits of train track that ended up strewn around the living room by the end of the day. 'Place is a tip,' Roy often said, like it was her who had upended the toybox five minutes earlier.

Yes, Roy showed his love in physical ways, and it was also how he showed his frustration. Which was why Alison had decided to stop helping out with the museum campaign.

Last Friday she'd run to the meeting and back with the buggy, betting on the fact Roy always went straight to the pub on Friday and wouldn't be home until late. What she hadn't bargained for was Roy's mate, Clem, spotting her as she dashed back home.

Roy calmed down a bit when she explained she'd only gone to the museum to say she couldn't continue helping out. Anyway, what was she thinking, pretending she could do the PR? Once Della revealed she was the true media star, Alison realised how stupid she'd been.

Temptation was out of her way now because Roy had taken her phone. Thankfully, he'd let her send one last email, which had drawn a line under the whole museum nonsense. And now she was free to get on with her real job: looking after their son.

As the rain started to come down harder, Alison gave up on the idea of getting Will to sleep and turned the buggy around. Sensing the change, Will kicked the rain cover harder and Alison watched from above as two little leather shoes beat out a rhythm all the way home.

Chapter Eighteen

They were only ten minutes into the journey when Sariah began to wonder if bringing Evelyn along had been such a good idea. She'd said such sensible, non-judgemental things the last time they met, but as Sariah negotiated the narrow roads that took them closer to the town where she'd grown up, an uncomfortable silence fell.

Evelyn was not the world's best conversationalist and Sariah's own gambits – the weather, pointing out Alison and her baby as they left town, the ongoing roadworks – were short-lived. Her nervousness increased with each passing mile.

Sariah and her mother had exchanged a total of five texts, none of them effusive given that they had barely spoken in fifteen years. All these years later, Sariah still felt as if she was about to get a telling-off.

Evelyn had brought along a cardboard box containing the cracked cup. It was swaddled in layers of bubble wrap and sat in the footwell and Sariah kept stealing glances at it. 'I told your mother that the museum isn't a lost and found service, but then I had a think and I decided it was the right thing to do,' Evelyn had said. 'It's not like I don't have hundreds of other cups. And it did seem important to her.' Now that cup was leading Sariah back to her family and she still wasn't sure if that was a good or a bad thing.

'This is it,' Sariah announced as they turned into a street of near identical terraced houses. She pulled up the handbrake and peered at the house she'd grown up in. It had barely changed: still the same grey pebble-dashed front, peeling paint on the windowsills and a stingy front garden where only weeds survived. Everything about the place felt cramped and mean: even the front path was too narrow for them to stand side by side.

The door opened almost immediately, as if Grace had been waiting.

'Here we are,' Sariah announced in a fake jolly voice and, as they walked into the dark hallway, she felt Evelyn give her a reassuring pat on the shoulder. There was a lot of clattering and fuss about making a pot of tea and Sariah resisted the urge to make a wisecrack about how they'd brought their own cup. Instead, she behaved herself, saying 'Great' at the right moments as her mum updated her on how well the boys were doing, what with the business taking off and Jamie and Shona trying for a baby.

All the while, Sariah was taking in her surroundings. The pine kitchen cabinets were the same, their round handles dark with use. The red and green splashback was furred with dust. The kettle had been updated, but she knew without looking that its insides would be thick with limescale.

But mostly she sneaked glances at her mother and she was shocked by how old she looked. She was only fifty – younger than Evelyn – but everything about her seemed worn out, from her skin to her saggy leggings.

Be nice, she reminded herself and she tried to muster the smile that she could produce instantly for strangers but not, it seemed, for her own mother.

As they passed back through the small hallway, she noted the same ugly yellow carpet and the long scuffs on the wallpaper where her brothers used to prop up their bikes. From the tiny front room she heard Evelyn saying polite things about a framed print on the wall and she felt a wash of shame.

Here was the proof that for all her striding around in her hotel uniform with her nose in the air, Sariah Carnie had grown up poor, and not poor and proud, but poor and grubby. She accepted a mug of tea and stared into it, scraping at the old tannin stains with her fingernail. Then, without meaning to, her hand crept up to that spot behind her ear so she could worry at the sore, bare skin that lay there, which always used to calm her. She forced her hand down.

'So, we brought the cup,' she began. 'Seeing as you were so keen to have it back.' She placed the box on the cheap Ikea coffee table, between an ashtray and the local free paper.

'Evelyn bought it at a jumble sale. So, it seemed odd to me that all of a sudden you want it. Especially as it must have been you that cleared out Grandma's house in the first place.'

'Of course it was me. No one else was going to do it, were they?'

Sariah looked towards the bay windows, foggy with dirt. Her mother was an embarrassment, and she really wished she hadn't brought Evelyn along to witness this sorry scene.

'Always the martyr.' Sariah dared to meet her mother's eye.

'I didn't choose that role,' Grace replied plainly. 'It was given to me.' She started to unwrap the cup, peeling back the layers of bubble wrap with a surprising tenderness.

'Ah and there it is.' She blinked away a glistening in her eyes.

'I hope you're happy,' Sariah said, already reaching for the bubble wrap and trying to fold it into a neat square.

'Oh, but it's not for me,' Grace said, quite calmly.

'Sorry?'

'No, it's for your Auntie Rose. She'll be so pleased.'

It was a surprise to hear her name because she hadn't thought about her upwardly mobile aunt in years, but it made sense that she would lay claim to that tea set, the only tasteful thing her grandparents had owned. She supposed it might be worth some money too, even with that sixth cracked cup.

'It was all she wanted when I cleared the house out. She was very insistent,' Grace added.

'Well, bully for her.' Sariah must have been squeezing the bubble wrap too hard because she heard a muffled pop. 'I hope she enjoys using it for her Women's Institute tea parties or whatever she does these days.'

'Oh, *Sariah*,' Grace said in exasperation, reminding Sariah that her mother had never allowed back-chat – and she definitely never let anyone speak ill of her little sister.

'Rose is still teaching, but she's back in Cornwall now, has been for about six years,' Grace continued. 'The boys keep in touch and I visit when I can.' She paused. 'You could come with us next time, if you like?'

'And why would I want to do that?' Sariah shot back.

'Well, she's family. And you might find you have things in common, with your fancy job and all.'

Then Sariah felt bad because Rose had been kind to her. She remembered that day on the beach and Auntie Rose coming down to help her, packing away the cracked cup and telling her not to worry. The gulls had wheeled above, the sea had sparkled and Sariah had felt the warmth of knowing she had someone on her side.

'Maybe that cup reminded her of the last time we were all together.'

'Yes, she said something like that.' Grace looked thoughtful.

Sariah felt the fight seep out of her. She gave up trying to fold the bubble wrap and laid it down on the table where it unfurled in slow motion. She wasn't sure how they had reached this point. She'd envisaged handing over the cup, some polite chit-chat and then she and Evelyn would drive back to Portheast, duty done. If she was honest, she'd hoped she might finally get an apology from her mother for all the times she'd been hard on Sariah, while her brothers got away with blue murder. But somehow, it had twisted round to it being Sariah's fault for not keeping in touch.

'Anyway, more tea?' Grace asked brightly.

Annoyingly, Evelyn, who had been sitting quietly in the corner, said 'Yes please' and Grace bustled off to make another pot of undrinkable bitter tea. This stuffy, dusty room was getting to Sariah so she stood, stretched and walked the short distance from her armchair to the sideboard. Photographs were arranged on it: two each of Jamie and Liam when they were little, and one of Sariah playing in a paddling pool in a friend's garden. There was one of Grandma Karensa and there was her parents' wedding photo, everyone dressed up in Nineties suits and frocks.

Next door, she heard the kettle come to a furious boil and click off.

Her mum had gone full meringue for her wedding dress, wearing the best that Bridal Belles of Truro could offer, with puff sleeves and acres of synthetic silk. Meanwhile her dad's suit was so boxy he resembled a sheet of card with arms and legs. As for the bridesmaids, they were a motley bunch, all different heights and sizes trussed up in pink, and Sariah didn't recognise any of them.

She put down the photograph as her mother came back in. 'Where was Auntie Rose?' she asked. 'Why wasn't she at your wedding?'

Grace busied herself with the cups, offering Evelyn a plate laid with custard cream biscuits, like they were a rare delicacy. 'Oh, don't be asking me about that. I don't want to think of that man ever again. I only keep the photo out of respect to my parents. Paid for that wedding, every last penny.' Her mother bit into a custard cream. 'And I did love that dress.'

'Yes, yes.' Sariah felt frustrated. 'But if it was such a big day, why wasn't Rose there?'

It was as if something in the air between them altered, the silence broken only by the sound of Evelyn stirring sugar into her tea.

'She was away,' Grace replied and Sariah knew that no more would be said on the subject. On the way out, she sneaked a last look at the wedding photo. It *was* a nice dress, albeit in a full-on Nineties way, with a nipped-in waist and a sweetheart neckline. Her mother also wore a rare smile. Behind, Grandma Karensa looked stout and proud beside a more serious Grandpa Luke (probably already mentally calculating the cost of the bar tab).

'We need to go now,' Sariah said firmly. 'Pass my regards to Jamie and Liam. And I hope Auntie Rose likes the cup.'

Chapter Nineteen

On the journey back to Portheast, Evelyn found herself at a loss for anything to say. She'd been flattered that Sariah had asked her along, but she'd ended up feeling like a spare part, watching Sariah and her mother exchanging sharp words, locked in a battle of wills.

'Sorry for dragging you into my family mess,' Sariah said when she dropped her off at the crossroads. 'Must rate as the worst day trip ever.'

'Well, it was good that you went. At least you're talking again,' Evelyn said, trying to be upbeat. Then she watched the minibus disappear off in the direction of Warburn Hall. From where she stood, Evelyn had two choices: turn towards the caravan site or walk down to the quay to check on her museum.

But Evelyn felt disinclined to take either route. Instead, she continued walking uphill, leaving the town behind. Passing through the kissing gate, Evelyn remembered the walks along these cliffs with her parents. 'It's a good place to think through a worry. I often come up here alone,' her mother had told her. At the time, Evelyn couldn't imagine what worries they might be, because her mother's days did not seem that arduous. They were spent painting flowers and drifting through the rooms of their Victorian home, stroking furniture and looking out at the distant sea.

Unlike Sariah, who seemed to freely admit that her childhood had been a disaster, Evelyn had always believed that growing up in the Silver family made her the luckiest girl in the world. She lived in a lovely house and, at weekends, the surrounding countryside was their garden: when coastal path walkers passed them by, the Silvers must have made a perfect picture. Elsbeth worked on her watercolours, intent on capturing the exact yellow of the common bird's-foot trefoil, while Edwin pottered among the wildflowers with their young daughter.

Evelyn could almost hear the bright ting-ting of her mother's brush on the side of her enamel water cup, or her father's voice as he explained which plants not to touch. 'Sea campion has the nickname witches' thimbles, so we don't pick that one,' she remembered him saying. 'The flowers are bad luck – harbingers of death.'

As Evelyn reached the worn trail of the coastal path, she turned her face to the wind and its force felt like a comfort, a constant in her life. Around her she saw still-snug buds of gorse, briars threaded with brown ferns and, beyond that, the blues of the open sea. Her mother had been right: this was a good place to pause and take stock, except Evelyn felt more confused than ever.

She was starting to question the whole Save Our Museum enterprise, because what good had it done so far? It had reopened deep wounds for Sariah and it had revealed that the seemingly chipper Della had washed up in Portheast after a breakdown. It was becoming clear that Alison was finding motherhood hard and could no longer spare the time to help out, and soon she would have to break the news to Jacob that the painting he fondly remembered was a fake. And Evelyn's vain hope that someone would recognise her piece of lace was fading fast. All these meetings and chats and photos and the website had come to nothing.

Perhaps the sensible thing would be to give up their boat shed leases and let the council do its worst. Like those girls from the pub had said, at least there would be jobs for Portheast.

The next morning, she was woken by a drilling sound in her ear: Toots demanding his breakfast. It was a good job he was so insistent, because Evelyn felt a yearning to stay in bed. Even with its duvet dusted with cat hair, it was the safest place to be when one of her low moods rolled in, stealthy as sea mist.

Over breakfast, Evelyn opened the stories@portheastmuseum. org emails and saw, to her surprise, that the first email was from Alison, filing an interview she'd done with a man called Michael about a framed set of fisherman's knots. It was a short but lovely paragraph, but her eyes flicked to the bottom, where Alison had signed off: *As mentioned, I must regretfully step back from the project, but I wish you every success and will be cheering you on from the sidelines.*

Alison was only confirming what she'd said already, but Evelyn felt the disappointment sink in like a smooth, dark pebble. Having a toddler and a part-time job must be hard work, but this sudden departure didn't feel right. When Alison had chaired that first meeting, it was like seeing her come to life: she was capable and enthusiastic and had good ideas for how to get the museum into the news. She was wasted at the sports centre. Evelyn wished there was something she could do to help her out.

Evelyn's dark mood lingered all morning as she sat at her museum desk, listening to the plink-plink of rainwater coming in through the hole in the roof. When the door opened at lunchtime, she let out an exasperated tut, and looked up, expecting to see Della. But it was a man in a jacket bearing a supermarket logo. 'Wrong address,' she called out to save him the bother of coming inside.

Taken aback, he got out his phone and read aloud: 'Please email us or come to the museum during opening hours.' He looked around. 'This is the museum, right?'

'It is indeed. My mistake.'

'I'm on my break, see,' the man said and held out his hand. She took in his handlebar moustache and hair tied back in a scrappy knot. 'I've come about my watch.'

She braced herself to explain yet again that this wasn't a lost property office, but the man was flicking back to the website on his phone. 'This one,' he said and showed her the picture of a wristwatch, stopped at 11.21. 'My mum donated it, she's Mrs Brown, and I'm Carl Brown. When the watch broke, I said chuck it out, but she said, no, it was of maritime interest.'

Evelyn invited him to sit and, heart thumping, readied herself to hear her first proper story. Carl explained that while these days he delivered groceries, for many years he'd been a volunteer with the RNLI and it was after one of his first callouts that his watch had stopped working.

'This was in the winter of 1997, so I was barely twenty,' he said. 'I was half expecting the call as I could see for myself that the sea was getting really rough – waves as high as houses and they were relentless. Times like that, it's as if the water is at war with itself.'

Evelyn nodded because there had been times when she'd stood at a safe distance and witnessed the power of the sea.

'We got word that a rogue surfer had gone out and run into trouble. She'd lost her board and was being tumbled by the waves, pounded with each fresh one. The terrible thing was, we could see her coming to the surface for a few seconds and then she'd get dragged under again. By the time we reached her, she had started to drift out in a rip tide and her strength was all but gone.'

Evelyn discovered that she was sitting on the edge of her chair, keen to hear more.

'She had barely any breath left in her. It wasn't far back to shore, but when we all reached dry land, the relief was incredible. It wasn't until I got home that I noticed my watch glass had cracked.

It was meant to be top of the range, waterproof and all the rest. It didn't survive that rescue, but our crew did and so did the surfer.'

Carl gave a small cough and she knew he'd already chosen his words for this last bit. 'I'm glad my mum donated the watch to this museum. I hope it stays here forever, stuck at 11.21 as a reminder of the immense power of the sea – and the lifesaving work RNLI volunteers do.'

Evelyn felt a rare swell of hope. If they could get more stories like this, her museum might just be saved. 'Thank you so much,' she said because Carl was already standing up.

'Got to get back to work – deliveries to make,' he explained.

'Right, of course,' she said to his retreating back, then called out, 'Do come to the exhibition.'

It took her a while to decipher her scribbled notes and then type them up, using her laptop rather than her key-deficient typewriter, but when she'd finished, she scrolled through the text, her heart beating fast.

Looking around, she realised she felt a desire to share this moment with someone and proudly carried her computer the short distance next door. Della tossed down the cloth she'd been using to wipe the counter for her non-existent customers and squinted at the document on the screen.

'Mate, this is the business.' She grinned at Evelyn. 'This is a great story for the press. And if we can get enough like this for the exhibition, there's no way the council can refuse to renew our leases.'

Evelyn smiled back. 'It is rather good, isn't it?' she ventured. On returning to her far darker boat shed, she realised what a novel pleasure it had been to share good news with someone who wasn't feline or an ex-department store mannequin.

In a further fit of efficiency, she opened up the online spreadsheet and added a big fat asterisk beside the listing for the watch, to signify it had a story. Then she pulled up the emails, proud to be juggling not one but two documents on screen at the same time. Yes, she was definitely getting into the swing of this system Sariah had set up.

In fact, she could see a new email had just arrived, which no one else had read yet. It was about the embroidered picture on sailcloth, the one she'd seen Alison admiring, and an idea began to take shape.

Without hesitating, Evelyn composed a reply and her fingers flew over the keyboard with a new-found enthusiasm.

Dear S. West,

Thank you for contacting us to let us know that you recognise this piece of embroidery. It is a very fine piece of work, which I have long admired without knowing its origins. If you are able to shed light on this matter, please email back or drop in at the museum, between 9 a.m. and 5 p.m. We are collating stories for a forthcoming exhibition on 19th March. It is called Second Chances and the aim is to save the Portheast Museum of Maritime Curiosities.

Sincerely,
Ms Evelyn Silver,
Curator

The glum mood of the morning was forgotten because Evelyn could already envisage the grand opening of the exhibition: there would be a ribbon to cut, she would wear her smart wool dress and there would be cheering. The assembled media would look on, rapt, while council officials hung their heads in shame, realising the error of their avaricious ways.

Then the imaginary cheers faded and the memory of another exhibition opening elbowed its way in, one so disastrous that it had ended her career. Evelyn could still feel the sensation of falling and hear the crack of ancient pottery hitting the tiled floor. It was a sound she would never forget, nor the collective gasp of horror.

She shook the memory away. No, it would be nothing like that. Yesterday, she'd witnessed Sariah bravely confronting her past and now Evelyn also needed to be bold. With a frisson of anticipation, Evelyn gave her email a final skim and pressed Send.

Chapter Twenty

Della Dayvon wiped down the immaculate counter for the umpteenth time that morning. It was important to open up each day and keep the place looking spick and span, even if it was the middle of winter and Portheast had yet to develop a taste for her ice creams, drinks and new range of Della-icious Bites. The only person she'd seen all morning was Evelyn, but she didn't count as a customer. Especially as, even when they were free, she never seemed very taken with Della's offerings.

Still, the story about the watch that Evelyn had shown her was a good one – perfect, in fact, for the press campaign Della now appeared to be in charge of since Alison had stepped back. Della really should have kept her big mouth shut at that meeting.

When she had arrived in Portheast, she'd decided to leave the media life behind. Della Dayvon might be a big name in Australian TV, but here she liked being just another visitor, albeit one with a surname that made some Cornish folk frown.

Except she'd blown it by telling the museum committee about her old job and now she would have to go back to her old ways, glad-handing and smiling until her cheeks hurt. That Della Dayvon felt like a different person, one who wore plunging necklines, spray tan and three different kinds of foundation – *plus* concealer and highlighter. When the cameras rolled and the lights came on, she had sprung to life, enthusing about the latest film premiere, laughing at her co-host's jokes or furrowing her brow in faux concern (as much as was possible with Botox) to coax confessions from guests.

Daytime With Della was a big hit, but nighttime Della increasingly felt empty and alone. One morning, when her 4 a.m. alarm went off, she couldn't move. It was as if she was wrapped in a fog that nothing could penetrate – not even her producer screaming threats down the phone.

Once she'd scraped herself up off the floor and made it into work, she looked so grim they immediately put her on a fortnight's sick leave. The company paid for an emergency stay at a luxury clinic that promised to deliver the nation's favourite presenter back to the studio in time for the Melbourne Cup special. But that chirpy Della was never to be seen again.

Instead, en route to the clinic she'd bribed the cab driver to make a detour to the airport, where she got the first of several flights that whisked her far away from her old life to Bali, Thailand and Nepal, where she failed to achieve spiritual enlightenment but did pick up a nasty case of giardia. Then, she limped on towards Europe, becoming well acquainted with the bathrooms of Florence, Rome and Paris before ending up in London. Her father had been a Brit – she had dual nationality – so it was only right to visit the old country. She'd spent a couple of weeks drinking pints in Earl's Court and went to see a blue door in Notting Hill that turned out to be much like a blue door anywhere. Then she remembered she hated that film anyway and admitted to herself that she missed home.

Then, the week before she was due to head back to Sydney, she saw a picture of an outdoor theatre that seemed to be cut into the rock, overlooking the sea. It was called the Minack and it was in Cornwall, so she'd splashed out on a ticket to Penzance, but never made it to the theatre and ended up in Portheast. She still hadn't been to that theatre.

She much preferred the new Della, a person with no past who could change her hair shade at will and wear clothes in any pattern, without being told they 'didn't read well on camera'. Today Della was wearing yellow and black striped dungarees that she'd picked up in Kathmandu. Granted they weren't ideal for late February in Cornwall, so she was wearing her thermals underneath and a black bobble hat on her head, which made her look like a very large bumble bee. Not that Evelyn noticed. She was an odd fish and the two of them had barely spoken before those council letters came, but Della was starting to appreciate her peculiarities.

Della put her cleaning cloth away and got out her iPad. It was time to make a list of all the people she could call up to come to the exhibition launch and the jobs that needed doing.

Bless Evelyn's quirky little typewritten museum labels, but they would need to print up the new, longer descriptions for each item and organise the exhibition pieces in some way. She'd spot-ted a sign outside a bungalow, advertising homemade wooden benches and planters – maybe that person could knock up some plinths for them.

Then there was the small matter of the clutter that filled every spare inch of the museum. As Australia's TV Darling, Della Dayvon had persuaded a footballer to confess his affairs and a politician to perform in a panto, but she sensed getting Evelyn to have a sort-out might be beyond even her powers.

A sharp rap on her counter distracted Della from her to-do list. It was Sariah, looking more dishevelled than usual, easing herself onto a bar stool.

'Looks like you could do with my favourite hangover cure. It's coffee, but not as you know it,' Della said.

'Worth a try,' Sariah replied. 'I came down to see Evelyn, but she wasn't at her desk. So I thought I'd pop in here.'

'She's probably fossicking around at the back – I mean, you could get lost in that place,' Della said. She leaned in and confided, 'You know, I reckon she might have a little snooze in there sometimes.'

Della reached for her stove-top coffee pot and poured Sariah what she called her Espresso Magnifico, adding a savoury nibble on the side of the saucer. 'Mini cheese scone. On the house,' she said proudly.

'Ooh, yes, perfect,' Sariah said, shaking out a sachet of sugar and pouring it into her coffee. 'I wanted to apologise to Evelyn, really. She got dragged into some family business yesterday.'

She took a sip, winced and reached for a second sugar sachet.

Della beamed. 'And that's why I call it rocket fuel!'

Then she flipped her iPad round so Sariah could see it. 'Look, I've been making a list of what we need to do ahead of the exhibition.'

Sariah ran a finger down the list, making the odd nod. 'Yep, there's a designer in Truro who would do a good job of printing the labels. Yes, I can get us a crate of wine at cost and the hotel can loan us the glasses.'

She took a bite of the cheesy morsel and chewed hard, watched closely by Della.

'Good, eh?'

Sariah chewed some more and nodded. 'Mm. I can't quite place the flavour?'

'Doritos,' Della said triumphantly. 'You crush 'em up and mix them into the dough. Tangy Cheese variety, obviously.'

'Lovely. Saving it for later,' she said, tucking the morsel into a napkin. Then Sariah slid off the bar stool, brushed some crumbs off her front and set her hotel name tag straight.

'I'm needed back at work,' she said. 'And I've changed my mind about talking to Evelyn, so no need to mention I came by. Frankly, yesterday was embarrassing and I'd prefer to forget about it.'

Della was confused. 'Got it. I won't say anything about that thing I don't know about.'

Sariah gave her the stern look her staff had come to fear. 'Don't forget to add caterers to your list. You'll be very busy as our MC, so I suppose we could try Nils' bakery?'

Della was about to explain that the beauty of her party bites was that they could all be frozen in advance, except the giant cranberry cheese ball, but Sariah had already disappeared, leaving a half-drunk cup of coffee on the counter.

Chapter Twenty-One

As the date of the Second Chances exhibition crept ever closer, Evelyn's dreams became populated with fast-moving vehicles that she couldn't control. Sometimes she was driving a car but couldn't reach the pedals and woke with her feet frantically tapping the end of her short bed. Other times, she was freewheeling down a hill on a bike with no brakes, and she awoke breathless and sweaty, Toots eyeing her with irritation.

She found herself in a strange limbo, where she and her museum were the focus of plans, schedules and unexpected deliveries, yet she was not in control.

She kept reminding herself that she should be grateful: Sariah, Della and Jacob were all pitching in to save the boat sheds and her livelihood. But she couldn't help feeling that the original spirit had been subsumed by the rapid back and forth on the group chat.

Will deliver flyers explaining campaign and exhibition asap – @ Jacob

Great! Drink is on order – @Sariah

Press release finalised, as attached. Comments? – @Della

How about some 'My Favourite Item' forms, so people can add more stories? – @Jacob

Evelyn's own contributions dwindled to the odd thumbs up, while Alison never seemed to come online.

When the exhibition launch was a week away, Evelyn was shocked to see they had made the front page of the local newspaper. This was because a short time ago Della had appeared unannounced at Evelyn's desk, chewed on her pen and asked: 'So, would you say, Evelyn, that the museum is a home for forgotten objects that are relevant to Cornwall?'

'Um . . .' she'd begun, trying to gather her thoughts.

'I'll take that as a yes,' Della said.

Which, she supposed, was why the headline on the front page of the *St Austell Bugle* read: *Museum is home for forgotten objects relevant to Cornwall.* Clearly, as a journalist, Della had been a fan of the leading question.

Della and Sariah had become thick as thieves in the past few weeks and it was not uncommon for Evelyn's days to be interrupted by chatter and peals of laughter coming from the shed next door. Conversely, Jacob seemed a little lost and lonely. 'I hope Alison still comes to the exhibition,' he said to Evelyn one afternoon as he was unloading a set of wooden display stands that Della had persuaded a carpenter to make at cost.

'I'm sure she'll try,' Evelyn told him, although she wasn't optimistic. The last time she'd seen Alison, she'd been pushing her little boy's buggy along in the drizzle, but since then, she seemed to have vanished. 'She must be busy at work.'

'Well, that's the thing,' replied Jacob. 'I swung by the sports centre and she hasn't been in for a while. Off sick – shingles, apparently.'

'But that's awful. Is her partner looking after her? And what about the baby?'

Jacob gave a small shrug, but she saw the worry in his eyes.

'Leave it with me,' she said. 'I'll see if I can find something out.'

Evelyn sometimes saw Alison's father, Keith, on her way back from her morning beachcomb, because he was one of the so-called Three Wise Men who took up residence on the bench facing her shed, along with Leonard, of the recently departed dog, and Bob, the fisherman who got seasickness.

The next morning, she saw the three men were in situ. Dropping her tote bag outside the museum, Evelyn tried to affect a casual saunter as she headed towards them, carrying several flyers about the Second Chances exhibition.

'Good morning,' she said, as if interrupting their morning cogitations was part of her routine. Three weather-beaten faces looked up at her, but only Leonard replied. 'Morning. Catch anything tasty down on the beach this morning?'

Evelyn decided to ignore his effort at a joke and thrust a flyer into Keith's hands. 'Do come,' she said. 'And remind Alison as well.'

'I'll try, but she's been laid low for over a week and doesn't want to spread it.'

'Spread it?' Evelyn was puzzled because she didn't think that was how shingles worked.

'Yeah, bad case of flu. Can't visit, in case I catch it. Might have to step in myself and represent the family,' Keith mused.

Odd, she thought, that Alison's father had got the wrong end of the stick – that was usually her forte.

Back at her desk, Evelyn checked her emails and was rewarded with a reply she'd been waiting for. It was from S. West and it told the story behind the embroidered boat on sailcloth. As she read it, a smile spread across Evelyn's face. Yes, it might raise a few eyebrows, but underpinning those words was a genuine love. What was it Alison had said about a good story – look for the hook? Evelyn thought Alison would be proud of her work.

◆　◆　◆

As the date of the exhibition crept closer, Jacob volunteered to help Evelyn set up the displays, and although she was quite capable of doing the job solo, he was pleasant enough company. He didn't interfere, just made a few suggestions like 'I wonder if that little pair of slippers would look nice next to the embroidery?' or 'How about we move the framed knots closer to the little painting?'

In this way, the two of them mounted the objects on wooden stands and arranged them in a large semicircle in the middle of the museum. It had been hard to narrow them down to ten, which Della suggested was a good number. 'Enough to get the public's attention, but not so many that they'll lose interest,' she said.

The final edit was:

1. A small painting in the style of Alfred Wallis, with text by Jacob Warburn, who remembered it hanging in Warburn Hall

2. A framed set of fishing knots, accompanied by the memories of Michael Bower of Fowey

3. A pair of felt and lambswool slippers, worn by three generations of the Haywick family, as explained by Ella Haywick

4. A handmade sailor doll, as remembered by Alice Fleet, aged eighty-two

5. A wristwatch, stopped at 11.21, remembered by RNLI volunteer Carl Brown

6. A boat at sea, embroidered on sailcloth, with text by S. West of St Mawes

7. A captain's cap, with words by Mrs Potter, the captain's great-niece

8. Eighteenth-century gold coins, with words on pirates and shipwrecks from Arnold Stubbs, landlord of The Lugger

9. A green porcelain vase, with librarian Minnie Fraser's comments
10. A piece of lace, with safety pin attached.

She had misgivings about including the 'Wallis' painting, but she'd amended the label and Jacob looked so happy seeing it on display with his own words underneath that she didn't have the heart to withdraw it. Soon she would tell him the painting's sorry tale, but with excitement and nerves mounting, now didn't feel the right time. At least, she reminded herself, Jacob's memory of seeing it in his grandparents' home seemed a happy one and his words were correctly spelled and punctuated. Sadly, not all the statements were as eloquent as Jacob's, and some were decidedly sketchy on historic detail. Arnold the landlord's, for instance, had the ring of a late-night chat in the pub:

Hundreds of years ago, pirates ruled the waves. There are still ship-wrecks off our shores, but exactly where remains a closely guarded secret. These gold coins are booty from one such wreck.

She could almost picture him leaning over the bar and giving the side of his nose a tap to imply he knew more. Meanwhile, Minnie the librarian's admiration for the green ceramic vase had more to do with interior décor than Cornish heritage: *I love this vase because its colour matches my dining room wallpaper exactly and I think it would look lovely on my table,* she'd submitted.

Nevertheless, each item's story was authentic and when all the pieces of printed card were fixed to the stands, the effect was impressive. As she looked around, Evelyn realised that only the description for her lace remained unchanged, because she had no more information to add. Its brevity felt like a fresh humiliation.

She must have been staring at it for a while because Jacob came over and said, 'You never know – the exhibition could be the perfect opportunity for someone to recognise it.'

She supposed he'd have heard about her lace a while ago, because a small town thrives on gossip, no matter how scant the facts.

'That's sweet of you to say,' she replied, 'but I'm not holding my breath.'

Chapter
Twenty-Two

Deciding what to wear for the grand opening of the Second Chances exhibition was an easy task for Evelyn. Since moving to her caravan, she had whittled down her clothes to the few items that would fit inside the slim wardrobe that was designed for holidays and short stays. As a result, she had three sets of work clothes in shades of brown, grey and taupe, a pair of waterproof trousers for walks and three dresses 'for special'. The one she chose for the exhibition was in beige wool with buttons at the neck, which she'd bought in Hobbs in Covent Garden in the spring of 1987.

As she pulled the dress over her head and smoothed it down, Evelyn noticed that she'd lost weight since its last outing, which had been Christmas carols on the harbourside, and that a small hole had appeared under one arm. It didn't matter really, because all eyes would be on Della, who was the MC, introducing the exhibition at 6 p.m. sharp.

Under duress, Evelyn had agreed that she would be on hand in case Della needed to field any questions her way. 'We each need to play to our strengths, apparently,' Della had said pointedly and Evelyn sensed she was still sore that Nils was supplying nibbles.

Turning left and right to see herself in the unreasonably short mirror (Evelyn's appearance below the knees had been a mystery for the past five years), she tried to quell her rising panic. The only thing that made the prospect of the exhibition bearable was reminding herself that by the end of the day it would all be over and Evelyn Silver could return to her quiet life, hopefully with the museum's future looking rosier.

As the event got under way, everything seemed to be going exceptionally smoothly. The exhibits looked perfect. The first people to admire them were members of the press, and they seemed to be enjoying what Della called 'a private preview' and Evelyn called 'letting the journalists in early'. True to her word, Della had rallied the local media and the big guns from London, thanks in part to Sariah laying on complimentary overnight stays at the Warburn Spa.

'Yet to meet a journo who turns down free booze and a night in a hotel,' Della said. Sadly, neither Dermot nor Lorraine could make it (early starts the next morning) but each had sent one of their people. As it got busier, the journalists gathered beside what Della referred to as her podium, but was in fact a tea chest turned upside down and draped in a white sheet.

Standing in a huddle on the other side of the podium stood three representatives from the council. Each held grimly on to his beer glass, taking it in turns to cast surreptitious glances around the shed, as if measuring it up. Evelyn was gratified to see Mr Palmer's rabbity eyes dart nervously over towards the journalists. 'Well, Evelyn, quite a show you've put on here,' he remarked, making it sound like she'd done something disreputable. 'The press have already been asking me some tricky questions.'

'The community values its museum,' she said. It was a line Della had coached her to say and she liked it very much, along with her next one: 'The exhibition is a celebration of our shared heritage.' Having run out of pithy phrases, she glided serenely away from Mr Palmer and his colleagues.

As the 6 p.m. official start time crept closer, Evelyn took her assigned place behind Della and looked out at the sea of faces. She recognised Jude and Kayla from The Lugger and old Mrs Moran, in her green cloche hat and with three dachshunds in tow. She was generally acknowledged to be the oracle about anything that went on in Portheast. Towards the back, a shifty-looking George Rook stood shoulder to shoulder with Leonard and Bob, who had taken time out of their busy bench-sitting schedule. Jacob was at the door handing out flyers, and Sariah was doing the rounds with two wine bottles, seamlessly weaving her way through the crowd and topping up drinks.

Evelyn's usually quiet museum was a hubbub of voices and she took a moment to take in this fact. At the museum's opening ceremony thirty-eight years ago, it had been a smaller gathering, almost as if people were there out of obligation rather than free will. 'Your father has called in a lot of favours to make sure it's a big success,' her mother had confirmed, nodding at the mayor and several councillors in grey suits and slip-on loafers. When Edwin Silver cut the ribbon to declare the museum open, there had been a smattering of polite applause, but now, as Della stepped up onto her podium, there was loud clapping and a few whoops.

She cut an impressive figure, dressed in an electric blue jump-suit she had found in a St Austell charity shop, the low 'V' of her neckline secured with a vintage brooch. In a commanding voice, Della began: 'Thank you, people of Portheast and beyond, for com-ing today. As you'll hear from my accent, I'm not a local, but I do know that this town has a proud history. It's also lucky enough to have its heritage preserved through the objects you see in this museum. Your curator, Evelyn Silver, has been quietly cataloguing items that tell Portheast's story for many years. The time has come to celebrate her work and rediscover this museum's significance.

'This exhibition is called Second Chances, because all these items could easily be overlooked, but they hold the key to the history of Cornwall and its people.

'Please join me in wishing Portheast's museum a long and happy future and thanking Mr Palmer and his team for their unstinting support.'

At the sound of his name, Mr Palmer gave a sickly smile and raised his glass, prompting several camera flashes from the media's corner.

'However,' Della's voice boomed and then she paused for effect. 'What you may not know is that the museum's lease is up for review. In order for our paid council representatives to make an informed decision, please express your opinions, as explained in the flyer. The same goes for my ice cream parlour next door, also under threat.'

Mr Palmer seemed to develop a sudden interest in the museum floor.

'Now, replenish your glasses, grab some snacks, as kindly provided by Nils' bakery, and enjoy the exhibition.'

With the formal bit out of the way, Evelyn felt a warm rush of relief – and she hadn't had to say a word. In celebration, she availed herself of a second glass of wine and began making her way through the exhibition wearing what she hoped was a benign smile and dispensing regal nods. In the distance, Sariah was deep in conversation with someone Evelyn couldn't quite see, while in the doorway Jacob was talking to Alison's dad, Keith, who had just arrived. Sadly, there was no sign of Alison herself.

Further towards the back of the museum, she noted that George Rook had barely moved from his position in front of a cabinet, which made her wonder if he was equally ill at ease at this kind of occasion.

An hour later, the crowd had thinned out a little and, telling herself it would soon be over, Evelyn made the rash decision to accept a third glass of wine. She was pleased to see several people reading their flyers, which told them how to contact Mr Palmer. Some had also picked up Jacob's *My Favourite Item* forms and she looked around to congratulate him on his initiative.

In the aftermath of what happened next, Evelyn found it hard to recall the exact sequence of events. What she remembered most of all was a feeling of inevitability, as if underneath the superficially professional veneer of the event, chaos had always been waiting to spill over.

She could see the top of Jacob's head and hear his unmistakable Radio 4 voice, but it was impossible to reach him. Blocking her way were Leonard, who was discussing dog treats with Mrs Moran, and Arnold from The Lugger, who was taking one of the council men to task over parking fines.

Just out of her reach, Jacob was demanding, 'Why isn't she here?' With horror, Evelyn realised that the person Jacob was talking to was Alison's partner, Roy Pinlow, and she knew that with each word he said, Jacob was making a bigger mistake. 'She should be here, it's not fair,' he continued.

She could only watch helplessly as Roy reached out to grab Jacob by the shoulder, pulled him in close and whispered something in his ear. Jacob instinctively raised his arm to push Roy away and that simple action changed everything. First came a punch and then, as Jacob fell to the ground, Evelyn heard the crack of a boot on bone. She gasped and her hand came up to cover her mouth. She tried to get closer but then, with an ease that suggested this wasn't his first rodeo, Roy's older brother pushed through, twisted Roy's arm behind his back and marched him out, while the younger brother brought up the rear, steering a baby buggy.

A shocked silence fell, one that seemed to suck all the joy from the room. She heard an embarrassed cough; then the sound of someone slowly zipping up their jacket, no doubt getting ready to leave. The silence was excruciating but worse was to come because, unbelievably, she could hear more raised voices and this time they came from further inside her museum.

Whipping round, she saw the source: it was George Rook and he was standing with one arm on top of a display cabinet. His chin was raised in an arrogant tilt and he was telling one of the VIP journalists that, no, he wasn't going to move out of the way. 'It's my town and I'll stand where I like,' he barked at a young man in a blazer. In return the journalist shouted back, 'I can hardly write about this exhibition if I can't see it, can I?'

No, no, no: everything was spiralling horribly out of control. If only she could get to George and the man in the blazer, Evelyn felt sure she could smooth things over. But her legs felt heavy, as in a dream, and before she could act, someone roughly pushed past her, heading for the door. It was Keith, Alison's dad, his face red with emotion, and she caught his words: 'No right to do that'.

As she wondered what Keith could mean, she realised that his push — not to mention three glasses of house white — meant she was faltering, losing her balance and then falling backwards. She had a sickening flashback to a similarly catastrophic incident many years ago, but this time there was no sound of breaking pottery — instead, she felt a firm grip on her elbow and with a lurch she was righted again. It was Mrs Moran who had come to her rescue, still holding her three dogs' leads in her other hand. 'You nearly went flying there, Evelyn,' she said. 'That Keith Blake needs to mind his manners.'

Queasy with shock, Evelyn realised several things at once: she was drunk, she was tired and she would really like all these people to go away. Mumbling her thanks, she decided it was time to step outside for some fresh air. Then maybe the world would stop spinning and men would stop behaving badly. Why was it, she wondered, that when women drank, they ended up laughing or crying, but men ended up fighting?

Taking deliberately careful steps, she made her way past the exhibits, which, miraculously, were still safe and sound. And then she stopped, because someone was standing at the plinth closest to the door, the one displaying her own ragged piece of lace. It was a woman she didn't recognise and she was peering at the lace, rapt, holding on to the stand with both hands, as if to steady herself. She turned to Evelyn, her eyes wide with disbelief.

'This lace,' she said in a voice full of emotion. 'I can't believe it. I feel like I know its story.'

Evelyn tried to steady her breathing. In all these years, this was the first time anyone had stopped to look at her lace, let alone said anything about it, and although Evelyn had imagined this moment for so long, she found herself lost for words. Suddenly feeling stone-cold sober, she took in this woman. She estimated she was probably in her late twenties; her expression was without guile and her neat features and soft curls put Evelyn in mind of a Renaissance painting.

The woman blinked and said, 'I take it you are Evelyn Silver. Is there somewhere private we can talk?'

Chapter
Twenty-Three

She couldn't believe it had finally happened – did this woman hold the clue to Evelyn's birth story? Had she come to the museum to see the lace and to tell Evelyn everything?

'Please, come inside and have a seat,' Evelyn said, aware her words sounded too high and tight. She touched the woman's sleeve, almost afraid she might disappear if she let go. Her mind was racing: this young woman clearly wasn't her birth mother, but she'd recognised the lace. Might she be another relative?

Not taking her eyes off the woman sitting at her desk, she rushed over to Della. 'Please, can you take everyone into your shed?' Della took one look at Evelyn's face and sprang into action. Holding the last two bottles of wine above her head, she called out, 'OK guys, let's take the party next door. My shed needs saving too!'

In minutes, the museum was empty. There were smeary glasses set on windowsills, and pastry crumbs and creased flyers littered the floor, but Evelyn barely noticed as she rushed back to the mystery woman at her desk.

'I don't even know your name,' she said breathily.

'I'm Edie,' the woman replied and Evelyn felt excitement welling up. Such similar names – surely this was a good sign? She scanned Edie's face, looking for echoes of her own features and wondered if, yes, there was something familiar about her mouth. In fact, the more she looked, she saw that Edie's eyes were also a little like her own, despite being a flinty blue to her brown.

'Well, as you know, I'm Evelyn.'

'It's so good to have this chance to talk.' The woman's expression turned serious as she held out her hand. In a daze Evelyn shook it, although what she longed to do was pull this woman to her, hold her and never let her go.

Evelyn gathered herself. 'So, let's start with the lace. As you can imagine, I've always treasured it.' She looked down at the floor, worried her emotions were about to get the better of her. 'In a way, this museum has been one huge cabinet for it, keeping it safe until someone came.'

'It must be very special to you,' Edie replied.

'Well, of course. It's my most precious thing.' Evelyn balled her hands together in her lap, trying to regain some control. But she couldn't wait any longer. 'So please, Edie. Tell me everything you know.'

'Well, a lot is under wraps for now, but we're all very excited.'

'All?' Evelyn gasped at the thought of not just one relative but a whole family waiting to meet her. 'Yes, I understand. Introductions should be done slowly,' she said. 'But if you could give me a name – well, that would be wonderful.'

A tiny crease formed between Edie's eyebrows and she began to flick through her smart shoulder bag. 'I have documents here that will answer all your questions.'

Evelyn watched as she retrieved a glossy white folder. On the front was an artist's drawing of a black timber-clad building that looked very much like her own museum, but above it a large sign read CORNISH FISH & CHIPS BY RUFUS ROWAN®.

'All the relevant proposals are in here,' Edie continued. 'As for the name, it's on-brand with the other outlets but of course with a local angle.' She gave a bright smile.

Evelyn was hit by a dizziness, as if she was teetering on the edge of a carefully constructed edifice that was collapsing inwards. She had made a terrible mistake.

'But, the lace – you said you knew its story . . .' she stumbled.

Edie wrinkled her nose. 'Hmm, I think I said I *felt* like I knew its story. I mean, isn't that the point of the exhibition? To convey the story of each object?'

Things began to feel very far away and as if through a tunnel Evelyn heard herself say, 'You were just being polite, then. This is about my shed and you've come to butter me up.'

'That's not a phrase that I would use,' Edie replied smartly, zipping up her bag. 'My role as local liaison manager is to forge links between the company and the community.' She gave a sniff. 'I was expressing an interest. Because Rufus Rowan Holdings finds that if we establish common ground with locals at an early stage, future negotiations tend to be smoother.'

Already, this Edie woman was standing up, keen to get away. She cast a final look around the museum. 'Wonderful high ceilings,' she said. 'So authentic.'

Evelyn kept her voice calm and low. 'Out. Now,' she said and pointed to the door. She listened until the tip-tap of Edie's heels walking down the quay had faded and then double locked the door and turned off the lights: the mess could wait until the morning.

The sounds of laughter and music drifted in from the shed next door, noises from a parallel world that was continuing unaware of her pain. There had been many occasions in Evelyn Silver's life when she'd got the wrong end of the stick and then felt a crushing shame at her mistake. But this had to be the worst.

In a daze, she walked to the diorama at the back of the museum. It would provide a warped sort of comfort, but in that moment, it felt fitting. She had no expectation of sleep as she folded herself into the small single bed and gazed up at the familiar outlines of Mr and Mrs Cornish Life beside her. She imagined what her parents might say if they were still alive. 'Oh, Evelyn, you silly goose,' Edwin would have said with a shake of his head, while her mother Elsbeth would have sounded softer: 'Oh, dear me. What a fix.'

Her mother had said something equally anodyne when Evelyn arrived home from London, after 'the incident'. Evelyn's inability to judge a situation correctly had been the problem then, too.

'You can't go accusing men of things that simply never happened,' her father had said, his face rigid with anger.

Separately, Elsbeth had soothed: 'You made a mistake, it happens.'

But now, as she lay gazing up at the faint outlines of the rafters, Evelyn went back over the evening's events, separating them into strands and then smoothing them out so each incident was laid in a row and she realised something. Yes, she had jumped to conclusions when she saw Edie, but at the same time, the woman had deliberately misled Evelyn for her own gain.

Through her shame, Evelyn was struck by the revelatory thought that two things could simultaneously be true: she had been mistaken, but that didn't cancel out the fact that the other person was lying. And she began to consider if that might also have been the case thirty-nine years ago.

Chapter
Twenty-Four

All through the wonderful year that was 1987, she and Asa were getting closer. Their relationship had progressed from cinema dates and earnest late-night discussions about the ethics of the Elgin Marbles to him staying over in her room in Bloomsbury. Asa lived with three postgraduate students in a basement flat in Stockwell, so her place was the better option, especially as her landlady, Frances Parfait, spent the occasional night away.

Those times when they had the flat to themselves, Evelyn savoured every small moment. She would stand in the galley kitchen watching people scurrying by on the street below and marvel that they were unaware how, three floors above, Evelyn Silver was falling in love. Often, she would make a cafetière of coffee and take it back to bed, where Asa lay in the rumpled sheets. Then, together they would set off for the short walk to the British Museum, passing under plane trees and peeking through railings at secret garden squares. As they got closer to work, they would kiss and then Asa would drop back to ensure they didn't arrive together, the museum being a terrible place for gossip. In later years, she looked back on those days as the happiest she'd known.

'I'm thinking of moving out of my flat,' Asa said as they walked to work one morning. It was starting to rain, so they were sharing her large umbrella and every now and then her hip bumped against his.

'Oh?' she replied, her heart thudding harder.

'I thought we could discuss, um, future options,' he said. 'Over lunch.'

She looked down at the glossy London pavement, where his suede desert boots and her red ballet pumps were both already darkening with the rain, and felt a shudder of pleasure.

'I would love that,' she replied. 'It's a date.'

He'd chosen an oddly stuffy restaurant, Rules in Covent Garden, but she took this as a sign that a proposal of sorts was on the cards. 'I will be back at the museum by three, won't I?' she asked a little anxiously. She was back in Egyptology and that day, at 3 p.m., there was a special event. 'All the curators and a few members of the press will be there,' she reminded Asa.

Several recently restored pieces, including a set of ceramic pots and a canopic jar with a stopper in the shape of a jackal, were ready to join the Egyptian collections. Evelyn felt a special affection for the jackal head, as she'd been permitted to dust its fragile surface. Her supervisor, Dr Marianne Guest, had explained the role this canopic jar played in ancient burial rites: it was to hold the person's stomach, while other internal organs were put into separate jars. Only the heart was left inside the mummified body, which had made perfect sense to Evelyn now in her throes of love.

'I'm sure we'll be done in good time,' Asa replied. 'The service here is excellent.'

Rules was a place of dark red velvet banquettes and gilt picture frames and it had a similarly old-fashioned clientele, which was probably why they were shown to an inconspicuous corner table, which was hidden behind a stained-glass divider.

'Is this place OK?' Asa then asked nervously. 'My father always books it for special occasions.'

Evelyn reassured him it was lovely and opened her menu. She wasn't officially vegetarian, but was privately horrified by the array of venison, rabbit and milk-fed lamb that scampered across her menu. Having spent much of her childhood in clifftop meadows, she'd grown familiar with these animals, learned to read the meaning of a twitching nose or the flick of a tail. They felt like old companions.

Against the waiter's advice, Asa ordered port and Evelyn suspected he'd got confused.

'A bottle, sir? Are we quite sure?' A smile tugged at the waiter's lips. 'Very good, sir.'

They had booked an early slot to avoid the rush, but what with the port and her indecision over the menu (so many childhood friends, sliced, diced and roasted), their orders got backed up and soon Evelyn was rather the worse for wear.

'Such silly small glasses!' Asa laughed, topping her up again. 'Here's to silly old us.'

By the time they reached dessert, Evelyn felt quite queasy. She'd ordered poussin, mistakenly thinking it was fish, and picking meat off the bones of a baby bird, on top of all the port, had been challenging. It was unfortunate that Evelyn realised she urgently needed the toilet at precisely the moment Asa began his speech.

'So, Evelyn, I expect you are wondering why we are here today,' Asa began, slurring a little. 'I want to ask you a very important question. It concerns our future.'

But it was no good, she couldn't wait. 'Asa, just wait a sec, I need a wee.'

As she began to make her wobbly way to the bathroom, Evelyn felt a flurry of joy, anticipating what Asa was about to say. She would say yes, she'd love to move in together and then they could look for a little flat, a bedsit even. She thought of suggesting Finsbury Park or Crouch End, because both areas were within reach of the Piccadilly Line for work. She would buy bright curtain fabric in Berwick Street Market and they would ask the landlord if they could paint their walls in sunshine colours. If they didn't have a garden, she would buy window boxes and plant geraniums, or herbs for cooking. Those were the thoughts running through Evelyn's head as she walked between the tables towards the toilet. And then she came to a standstill.

Ahead, sitting in a booth, was her father. He was clinking glasses with his companion, who was dressed in a tweed suit and brogues exactly like those worn by Evelyn's landlady, Frances Parfait. Evelyn was about to say hello when two things happened. The first was that her father reached out over the table, grabbed Frances Parfait's hand (for it was her) and pulled it to his whiskery lips where he repeatedly kissed it. The second thing was that Evelyn's bladder awoke from its temporary state of shock and reminded her she really did need to go, right now.

After relieving herself, Evelyn stood at the sink and tried to regain her composure. Her reflection in the mirror showed lips stained dark and an unnervingly wild look in her eyes. She needed to calm down. The obvious explanation was that it was a case of mistaken identity – after all, she really was very drunk. Except she could clearly picture the way that her father's soft, pliable lips had rubbed their way across Frances's hand, like an overeager dog.

Pushing open the door, she half expected to see strangers sitting at the table – confirmation that her imagination had gone into overdrive – but there was no mistaking the fact that it was her father and her landlady, engaged in an illicit lunch date. Worse still, from her new vantage point Evelyn could see that, beneath the table, Ms Parfait's tweed skirt had been inelegantly pushed up her thigh by her father's other hand. She recognised the edge of the nylon slip as one that was rinsed out each Sunday night and hung over the bath to dry.

Her stomach roiled, a bitter nausea rose up and Evelyn knew she had to leave immediately. She pushed aside a waiter and opened the door. She felt awful for abandoning Asa, but telling him what she'd seen would have made it real and all she wanted to do was run. Outside, the streets of Covent Garden were rammed and she had to sidestep tourists reading maps and ladies with shopping bags hanging off their arms. She hopped on and off the kerb to make her way through because it felt imperative that she get back to the safety of the museum, where the galleries would be cool and orderly and nobody would know what she'd seen.

She made it through the museum gates, scattering grey pigeons as she ran up the steps. At last, she was inside and the soft echoey atmosphere of the entrance hall wrapped around her. People were studying the museum's floor plan and a guard nodded to her. She was back in a world where calm decorum reigned.

It was almost 3 p.m. and, as if on automatic pilot, Evelyn navigated her way to the Egyptian Gallery, just in time for the ceremony to present the new exhibits to the world. She used her hefty key to open the tall wooden door and slipped in just as her supervisor began her speech. Evelyn sat attentively, trying to ignore the sheen of sweat that seemed to be forming on her face. She had a raging thirst and, when she bent her head to try and discreetly wriggle out of her hot mackintosh, a wave of nausea reared up to meet her.

A few feet away, Dr Marianne Guest was explaining the significance of the pieces, which had been so carefully restored. She extended her thanks to her curator team and then Evelyn felt a jolt of horror as she heard her own name mentioned. 'Our trainee, Evelyn Silver, has also been a great asset.'

Marianne Guest, a warm and inspiring woman, looked out at the crowd. 'Evelyn, are you here?'

Evelyn feared that if she made any sudden movements, she might be sick, or faint, or both, but she risked raising her hand.

'You should be up here with the rest of us, come on,' Marianne said warmly.

Evelyn had no choice. In a daze, she rose and made her way to the front of the gallery. She told herself that if she kept breathing and didn't move her head too fast, all would be well.

'Yes, up you come!' encouraged Marianne, who was standing behind a table where the newly restored pots were laid out. 'Evelyn has a promising future here,' she added and, wordlessly, Evelyn watched as Marianne's hand reached for her own. And then Marianne began to shake Evelyn's hand up and down, like she would never let go, and the vibration seemed to pass through her, jiggling her stomach, her intestines and her throat, where a thick, hot lump was growing.

The bitter bolus continued to swell in her throat and Evelyn could only look down mutely at Marianne's hand. In her mind, she saw another hand and the way her father's damp lips had dragged across it and she imagined all the other places his lips and hands had been and then the world was closing in, dark and muffled, and she had to escape before her lunch of port and baby bird came back up.

But she wasn't quick enough. A torrent of pink liquid forced its way out of her and she was heaving and reaching, blindly, for something to steady herself. Her eyes and ears seemed sealed shut but she gripped what must be the edge of a table and then her body jerked again, desperate to get rid of its last swill of port, and as it did she felt the table shift under her.

There was an unusual sound of something sliding, then a loud crash, followed by another slightly smaller crack. She was on her knees and her eyes were open again, except she wished they weren't because the floor was splattered with wet pink fragments. And the fragments weren't poussin, but pottery – precious, ancient Egyptian pottery. She could even make out the unmistakable pointed ear of a jackal.

Arms hoisted her up to standing and someone brusquely wiped the vomit from her face with a hard paper towel and then two security guards escorted her from the scene of devastation. She remembered sitting in a plain white room, the guard's arms crossed and him refusing to meet her eyes. A set of keys hung from his belt and she knew that her own key on its chain, and the status it signified, would never be returned.

Later it was confirmed that a total of three precious pieces of pottery had been tipped onto the floor when Evelyn Silver had knocked over a table. A further item, a grain jar, survived, but it had been the least rare and valuable of them all.

When Evelyn's father came to collect her, her shame was complete. Her belongings would be packed up and sent on later, he told her. 'Frances is very upset too – she put herself out for you. We all did.' Then he telephoned her mother: 'Drunk, in the museum . . . The damage, inconceivable . . . May press charges. Getting the next train home.'

She was given the window seat on the train, not as a treat but because she couldn't be trusted. 'Might go wandering off in search of more drink,' her father said darkly. The outskirts of London passed in a blur. Later, she saw drab fields and then the sea, confirming that she was leaving the life she'd glimpsed so briefly: the new life she could have begun with Asa.

She only spoke of it once, the thing that had set those terrible events in motion. It was on that train journey home, somewhere between Exeter and Newton Abbot, by which point she'd lost hope.

'I thought I saw you,' she said lightly. 'At Rules restaurant.'

Her father's head jerked up.

'Yes, with Frances Parfait,' she continued and then a word came to mind, one she could not remember ever using before. 'Canoodling.'

Her father slammed his hand down on the train table. 'What rubbish,' he said, eyes wide. 'Do not speak of this nonsense again.'

Shortly afterwards, an elderly lady in a purple coat sat opposite them, so Evelyn and her father remained silent until they rose, together, as the train pulled into their station. Only then did he say in a low voice, 'You can't go accusing men of things that simply never happened. You were mistaken, plain and simple.'

It was all Evelyn could do to nod. She had just banjaxed her career and lost the love of her life – not to mention causing untold damage to the field of Egyptology. Adding drunken ramblings to her list of crimes was small fry.

Once back home, she retreated to her childhood bedroom and refused to come out. She accepted the simple meals her mother left on a tray outside her door, but declined to come to the phone when Asa called. Weeks passed and still she could not face the outside world. Wrapped in her duvet and with the curtains closed, flashes of that day came back to her, sharp as electric shocks. But they were disjointed, as if the day was too monstrous to tackle as a whole. It was a huge and slimy rock she could not climb, or a wild animal she was afraid to approach. So eventually she decided to stop trying. As her own memories became hazier, her father's words acquired a sharper focus. Evelyn had been drunk and disorderly, so what she needed was a more orderly life.

When her father first mentioned establishing a local museum, she understood this was an act of charity, because Evelyn would never find work in any other institution.

'A mind like yours needs to be kept busy,' her father said.

'Routine can be good,' her mother added nervously.

In that way, Evelyn's fate was sealed and she never felt the urge to leave Cornwall again. Asa wrote her a long letter, expressing his thoughts across several pages. First, he was puzzled: *Did I offend you in some way?* and then shocked: *What on earth happened back at the museum?* Finally, he declared himself heartbroken.

She didn't know where to begin answering his questions, so the simplest thing was to ignore them. Asa and that world soon became a distant memory, as unimaginable as life on the moon. Her mother offered her sympathy in a hand-wringing, ineffectual sort of way, but Evelyn couldn't explain herself. It was so much simpler to say nothing and a silence settled between them, heavy as fog.

One evening her father announced it was time for him to resume his trips to London and Evelyn had looked up, confused. 'Academics to visit, auctions to attend,' he added genially and she gave a quick nod, feeling guilty for thinking otherwise.

Tonight, Edie had wrinkled her neat little nose and implied Evelyn had been a fool for imagining Edie had come about the lace. But really, Edie had tricked Evelyn.

And the truth was, her father had done the same almost forty years ago. He'd made Evelyn feel so small and wrong that she'd doubted her own instincts. He'd lied to her and, wracked with guilt at her own mistake, Evelyn had accepted it.

As she lay awake, Evelyn wondered what else in her life she'd accepted at face value, particularly where her father was concerned. She'd always assumed that the piece of lace was evidence of her Cornish birth story, made by a local woman who was too young or poor to keep her baby.

But what if Evelyn had been looking in all the wrong places? Her mother might not have been Cornish at all, but someone her father had known for decades, and continued to visit throughout his marriage: an unassuming woman in a tweed suit called Frances Parfait who had worked at the British Museum.

Chapter
Twenty-Five

For the first time in many years, Evelyn did not feel like doing her morning beachcomb. Easing herself out of the diorama's tiny cot bed, she felt old and broken and her mouth was sour. Passing by Mr Cornish Life, she resisted the temptation to knock his pompous little pipe out of his hand. Then she gazed into the blank painted eyes of Mrs Cornish Life. Had Elsbeth known about her husband's philandering? Or had she, like Evelyn, been deceived – told over and over that she was imagining things?

Her mother's funeral had been as small and unobtrusive as Elsbeth Silver had remained throughout her life. After abandoning her degree to marry Edwin and move to Cornwall, she'd fallen out with most of her family. Only an aunt and an uncle had stayed in touch and come to the funeral. 'Still don't understand why she moved here,' the uncle had said, biting into a sausage roll. 'It's the ends of the earth.' The aunt, musty in mothballed black, said that to her knowledge, the only heart problem Elsbeth had suffered from was when she fell for Edwin Silver.

And what of Frances Parfait? When they had been introduced at Frances's Bloomsbury flat, Frances had remained entirely professional, briefing Evelyn on the workings of the hot water tank and advising her of the times when she could use the kitchen. Some evenings, they watched television together – they both loved *Inspector Morse* – but their chats rarely ventured beyond their mutual admiration for the fictional detective. All Evelyn remembered about their walks to work was her landlady's deep love of cigarettes and a disdain for the museum's falling standards. Frances Parfait had joined the museum from Oxford in the 1960s and had since risen up the ranks to become one of the first female curators. Certainly that profession would have been incompatible with motherhood, particularly the unmarried kind.

With a satisfying crack, Evelyn shook out a black plastic bin bag and began to fill it with the detritus of yesterday's event. The wine glasses she stacked in their crates, to be returned to the hotel. When she found several forgotten triangles of Nils' pumpernickel bread topped with herby cream cheese, she popped them in her mouth for her breakfast.

She had no intention of opening the museum today, but at 9.30 a.m., someone began knocking on the door, quite insistently.

'Hey, it's me. Sariah.'

Evelyn stood very still. She felt bad that she hadn't caught up with Sariah since their trip to see her mother, Grace, but she was in no fit state to receive visitors.

'Evelyn? You in there?' There was a pause. 'I need a bit of a chat, really. I've brought you a cup of tea.'

Evelyn reluctantly unlocked the door and opened it so that Sariah could slip in.

'Tea, you say?'

She needn't have worried about her dishevelled appearance because Sariah barely glanced at Evelyn as she handed her a takeaway cup. 'It's OK, it's from Nils' place. Della's still sleeping off a hangover,' she said, pacing the sticky museum floor. 'Just wondered how you thought last night went?'

Evelyn eased the lid off the cup and took several sips. 'Well, a mixed bag,' she said.

Sariah continued pacing. 'I think the council's running scared – I saw Kayla on my way here and she and her sister have already emailed, saying they want you to stay. More to the point, they said their dad has too, and people round here tend to listen to him.'

'That's good,' Evelyn offered, but she could tell Sariah was working up to something.

'Did anyone keep a tally of who came? Because Jacob said that old boy over in Fowey who wrote about fishing knots didn't make it. And no sign of Alison. Just her bloke,' Sariah added darkly.

'Yes, although I wish he hadn't. Is Jacob OK?' Evelyn asked.

'He's fine, but he's got a black eye. I mean, it's not fine, what Roy did. But that's Roy.'

'We should check on Alison,' Evelyn said.

'I know. I did drive up there and knock on her door and there was no answer. But you're right, I should go back.' Then Sariah stopped pacing. 'Thing was, last night I had a surprise visitor.'

You and me both, Evelyn wanted to say, but she kept quiet.

'My mum came,' Sariah said.

'Ah. How did that go?'

'She was different, actually. Sort of softer.' Sariah gave a rueful smile. 'Threw me a bit, to be honest.'

'Well, that sounds like good progress.'

'Yeah, I suppose. I mean, I wasn't planning to keep in touch. I thought it would be easier to forget about the lot of them.'

Evelyn drained her tea and began to crush the paper cup for her recycling bin. 'Except pushing things to the back of your mind never really works,' she said, taking care to find the right words. 'And you never stop wondering how and why things happened.'

'That's true,' Sariah said.

Evelyn resumed peeling damp flyers off the floor and stacking glasses. She took a breath. 'Actually, I had a surprise visitor too.'

Sariah let out a small gasp. 'Who? Was it about your lace – did someone come forward?'

Evelyn frowned: was there anybody in this town that didn't know her story? 'Well, I thought so at first, but it was a false alarm.'

'Oh, Evelyn, I'm so sorry.' Sariah came closer. 'Can I give you a hug?'

Evelyn saw women doing this sort of thing all the time: hugging each other when they hadn't been apart five minutes, shouting 'Love you!' down the phone for no particular reason. She shrugged and gave in to the unfamiliar sensation of another body pressed to hers. She caught a whiff of almond shampoo and the fake fur trim on Sariah's hood tickled her nose. She pulled away, grateful for Sariah's understanding.

'The thing is,' Evelyn said, 'my visitor did me a favour. She helped me see things more clearly and I think I've been looking for my birth mother in all the wrong places. I've been sitting here in Portheast, but I've started to wonder if I should look further afield. In London, for example.'

'London? Is that what you heard last night?'

'Not exactly. But this woman I met, she made me realise how I always take people at their word. When the truth might lie elsewhere.' Evelyn reached for the broom and began to sweep. 'Sorry, back to your mum. How did you leave it?'

'She suggested we meet up again. Talk things through.' Sariah moved a crate of wine glasses over to the door.

'Sounds promising.'

Sariah fetched a second crate and the glasses gave a merry tinkle as she put it down on top of the first. 'Funny, isn't it?' she said.

'What?'

'A couple of months ago, the two of us hadn't ever spoken and now look at us – chatting like old friends.'

◆ ◆ ◆

It was mid-morning before Evelyn began trying to trace Frances Parfait. She realised that, when it came down to it, all she knew about the woman was that she'd loved ancient East Asian artefacts, Benson & Hedges cigarettes, *Inspector Morse* – and possibly her father, Edwin Silver.

A short trawl through the British Museum's website showed that, unsurprisingly, she was no longer working there – she would be in her eighties by now – but neither was she mentioned as a visiting speaker or as an author of any of their specialist publications. However, it turned out that Frances Parfait hadn't bothered taking down her LinkedIn profile, even after her retirement. It seemed she had officially stepped down in 2009. Since then, there had been no further updates.

Once, she'd known Frances's landline number off by heart, a relic from the days before mobile phones, but now only the number for Asa's old flatshare lived on, uselessly, in the recesses of her mind.

Just once, she thought she'd seen Asa. In the summer of 1991, she'd been in the queue for the till at B&Q, buying a trellis for her mother, who was concerned her jasmine was wilting rather than climbing. She'd noticed a tall man two people ahead of her in the queue and something about the way he tilted his head to one side rang a bell of recognition. She'd stood on tiptoe and noted that he was buying two disposable barbecues and a set of tongs, and standing beside him was a small fair-haired boy.

It being August, Cornwall was full of visitors, so it was not beyond the realms of possibility that Asa Lingard had brought his family here on holiday. Her heart thumped so hard she feared she might be sick. But then the cashier asked him a question and she saw him turn and look behind him. He was miming something, holding up his hand and asking, 'Bag?' It was almost as if he was looking directly at Evelyn and, unthinkingly, she felt her face break into a smile.

Then, from behind Evelyn, a voice piped up: 'No, darling, I've got loads' and a woman breezed past, adding another item to the conveyor belt: a pink blow-up beach chair.

It hadn't been Asa at all. As he packed his barbecue goods into a reusable carrier bag, she realised this man's chin was too weak, his stance was all wrong and his accent was more Essex than Edinburgh. But it had shaken her, the thought that it could have been. It was a reminder that the real Asa Lingard must be out there somewhere, possibly also lighting a beach barbecue, making sand-castles with a son and pumping up a plastic chair for a wife who was too fancy to sit on the sand.

But largely, Evelyn had banned herself from thinking about Asa or wondering what he was doing. Naturally, she stayed away from London and the British Museum, but she also took care to avoid any reminders of him. If she caught a glimpse of a magazine article about ancient Rome, she turned the page. She officially became a vegetarian (the sight of meat reminding her of their final meal) and she refrained from watching *University Challenge*, which had been his favourite programme. She even swore off Penguin biscuits, their tea break snack of choice. So by the time the internet arrived, she had trained her mind not to slip down any dangerous rabbit holes and she had resisted even googling his name.

Now, however, she opened her laptop, returned to the British Museum website and checked every department's staff list with mounting excitement. Yet she could find no trace of Asa Lingard. She did some more straightforward searches, but still couldn't find any record of him.

Had he become a conspiracy theorist, fastidious about leaving no digital footprint? Worse still, had he died before the internet gobbled up everyone's names, birthdays, jobs and funny cat videos and shared them with the world? She hoped it was the former and that he was living a life of obscure academia, his thoughts unsullied by the internet, barbecue tongs and, ideally, a wife.

Evelyn shook her head at how easily – and ludicrously – she'd been sidetracked. This was about Frances Parfait, she reminded herself. There was no record of her on 192.com, but she struck Evelyn as the sort of woman who might enjoy being a thorn in the side of residents' committees and the like, so she searched Frances's name combined with 'Bloomsbury', 'Fitzrovia' and 'London', but yielded nothing. She contemplated ringing the museum, or the handful of smaller establishments devoted to East Asian antiquities, but she knew they were unlikely to give out any information. After a few hours of dead-ends she began to think that there was no option but to return to the flat in Bloomsbury.

Chapter Twenty-Six

Back at her caravan, Evelyn fed Toots and took a quick shower. This was more arduous than it might sound as she had to assume a hunched position and keep one hand pressed against the shower door at all times to ensure water did not escape from the cubicle.

After her tepid dousing she got dressed and selected her third best dress for the day ahead. Having slept in the wool one, it was in no fit state. She rejected her navy blue number with a sailor collar as too fancy and settled on a brown linen one she'd bought at a jumble sale. It was from a shop that specialised in maternity wear, which explained why the bust area came with two liftable flaps (initially, she'd assumed it was an outré fashion statement). Still, it passed muster with a belt.

As the train pulled into Paddington, Evelyn felt like she was in a dream – albeit one where she was tired, hungry and nervous. But she had been waiting passively for too many years. It was time to know the truth.

Returning to London, the faces she saw were marked by woe: on the concourse, a lonely man picked half a sandwich out of a bin and in the Ladies', a young woman with bad teeth asked her for spare change.

Ignorant as a tourist, she followed the stream of people down the steps to the Tube, where she held on tight to her bag and watched what everyone else did. Nobody bought a cardboard ticket anymore; instead they tapped their bank cards at the turnstile, so Evelyn did the same. The first train due was the brown line – the Bakerloo – so she got that.

The smell of hot dust and the roaring sounds remained unchanged, but inside the carriage the adverts no longer promoted shampoos to cure baldness or courses to learn Pitman's shorthand. Instead she read about dating apps, food delivery services and AI assistants. When she got off at Oxford Circus, the platform was so crammed with people that Evelyn had a moment of panic, imagining a dreadful accident had occurred. But no one else seemed in the least bit perturbed and eventually the crowd began to move and she continued up steps and along tunnels until she emerged onto the street.

The first things she noticed was that Topshop had disappeared, which felt like some sort of sacrilege, particularly as she'd purchased her beloved sailor-collar dress there all those years ago. In Topshop's place stood an Ikea. People walking in looked reasonably normal, but those leaving looked like ragged survivors of some catastrophe, wearing dazed expressions and clutching huge blue bags.

But then muscle memory took over and she found herself walking a once familiar route through Fitzrovia's backstreets towards Frances's flat. She passed a pub where she and Asa had drunk Grolsch beer until neither of them could see straight, but fancy coffee shops and juice bars had replaced the old corner shops and video rental stores.

She was so close to her goal, yet Evelyn felt oddly detached from what might unfold. It was as if she was on a day trip, come to revisit a different version of herself – the Evelyn who could have stayed in London, gaining in confidence and knowledge – and as she walked, she dared to imagine how things might have turned out.

Almost certainly, she would have moved into a flat in north London with Asa. They would have celebrated with a bottle of cava, then cherished small acts of domesticity like cooking their first meal together and sticking up their art gallery posters with Blu Tack. A year or two later, they might have bought their first house, moving to Hackney, which would have seemed expensive at the time but they would later realise had been a steal. She would have dined on masala dosas, pad Thai, falafel and vine leaves instead of her mother's egg salads and hotpots.

She would have visited basement bars where the bass beat was so strong you felt it in your gut, drunk rum and had questionable haircuts. She might have dressed in Lycra and oversized shoulder pads, crop tops and, for a brief period, stonewashed denim. Over the years, she and Asa would have progressed from LPs to CDs to downloads and then back to LPs, in an ironic sort of way.

Gradually, Evelyn's weekend trips back to see her parents in Portheast would have become less frequent. She would say the train fare was too expensive, but really it was because every time she visited she felt lonely and wrong, and eventually Asa would point out that your family wasn't meant to make you feel like that.

She would agree and then, when they started thinking about starting a family of their own, that version of Evelyn might have gone to see a counsellor and talked about how she felt, knowing so little about her own birth story. After each session, she would have told Asa that the talking helped. She might have said it felt like sloughing off a thick layer of skin, one that was heavy and grey and had weighed her down for too long. Sometimes that process felt raw, but mostly it felt like she was getting a second chance.

But none of that had happened.

Evelyn turned a corner and there was the redbrick mansion building where she'd spent nine months of her life in 1987. The building had been spruced up, with shiny door furniture and an intercom. Fearing that if she didn't act fast she'd find an excuse to walk away, Evelyn reached out her finger and pressed the bell beside the number 12a.

'Hello?' It was a man's voice – young and with a hint of an accent she couldn't place.

'Hi. This is going to sound weird, but does Frances Parfait still live here? Or do you have a forwarding address?'

In the silence that followed, she wondered if this was where her journey ended, discovering that Frances had moved out long ago or had died.

'Hello?' She wondered if the man was still there.

There was a crackle and his voice came back on: 'Who is this?'

'My name is Evelyn Silver. I knew Frances many years ago. I lived here, in fact.'

His reply was curt: 'Wait there.'

Through the glass doors, Evelyn saw a man approaching, dressed in a uniform, and as he opened the door she saw it was a nurse's tunic. He spoke quietly, as if he didn't want to disturb anyone, and she wondered if this had always been his way or was an acquired habit.

'How can I help?' he asked.

'Sorry, this is a bit out of the blue, but I was in the area.' She gave a nervous laugh and watched as the man's face shut down.

'Miss Parfait is unwell,' he said. 'She's not able to accept visitors who are just "in the area".'

Evelyn felt the pressure of the past twenty-four hours pressing in on her and realised she was close to tears. This was her only chance. 'Sorry, I don't know why I laughed. None of this is funny and I wasn't just passing. I have come all the way from Cornwall to see Frances, but I didn't know she was ill. Is it serious?'

The man jiggled the keys in his hand impatiently and she knew her time was up.

'Please, can you tell her I'm here? Say I've come to talk about the past.'

'I already told her your name,' the man said. 'She's asked you to come up.'

The nurse was called Samuel and as he led the way through the chequer-tiled foyer, he explained how he had to protect his client and make sure she didn't get too tired. They stepped inside the small old-fashioned lift and as he pulled the zigzag metal gate across with a clank, Evelyn was sliding back in time, remembering the smallness of this lift, how embarrassing it had been when you shared it with a stranger; how much fun it had been with Asa. She caught sight of herself in the lift's mirror – a vision of drabness – and looked away. How had she become so old?

'She sleeps a lot, but she still has all her faculties,' Samuel said.

Entering the flat, everything felt smaller than she remembered and as if the colours had faded. In the hall, the reds and blues of the Persian carpet were sun-bleached and the edges of the phone table were chipped. But the smell was still the same: a mixture of furniture polish and tinned soup.

Evelyn braced herself, expecting to be led into Frances's bedroom. She envisaged a hospital bed, a discreet bedpan and the fug of illness. But she was shown into the living room, where a stick-thin woman sat at the window. Most surprisingly, she was dressed in a royal blue velour tracksuit.

'Excuse my appearance,' said Frances Parfait. 'Loose clothing works better these days. Gentler on my skin.'

Instinctively, Evelyn sat in what had been 'her' place on the left-hand side of the sofa. 'I'm sorry, I didn't know you were ill,' she began.

'Oh?' Frances said archly. 'I thought good news always travelled fast. Which is how your father probably views my impending demise.'

Evelyn was thrown. 'Oh, he died,' she stumbled. 'Five years ago, during Covid.'

'Well, how about that.' Frances raised a hand in the air, then let it fall back into her lap. 'And all this time I thought he'd "ghosted" me. Isn't that what they call it these days?'

The veins on her hands were raised, the loose skin dotted with dark spots.

'I don't know,' Evelyn said. 'I'm sorry, if you weren't told.'

Frances leaned forward. 'Evelyn Silver. You always were a shy thing. But you still say "sorry" and "I don't know" an awful lot.'

It was becoming clear that Frances Parfait had long since stopped caring about manners.

'Well, you've got to the heart of it,' Evelyn replied, because she too had had enough of being polite. 'My life has been full of apologising and not understanding what was going on – like what exactly went on between yourself and my father.'

'Really?' Frances sounded incredulous. 'Why do you say that? I mean, you saw us carrying on that day in the restaurant. Most embarrassing.'

'Yes, I suppose I did. But I didn't comprehend, not properly.'

Frances looked sceptical, as if she didn't believe a woman of twenty-two could have been so naive.

'All OK, Miss Parfait?' Samuel the nurse stood in the doorway.

Frances raised her eyebrows and replied, 'Yes, fine. Still dying' and Samuel walked away, shaking his head.

Evelyn unbuttoned her coat and pushed her hair back from her forehead, which was clammy with sweat. If Frances liked people being direct, she could oblige.

'OK, so you clearly had a relationship with my father. I need to ask, are you my . . .' No, actually, she couldn't say the word. 'Did you give birth to me?'

Frances had been gazing out of the window, seemingly absorbed by the slow-moving traffic and the office workers heading home. When she replied, her acidic tones had softened. 'Oh, Evelyn. Whatever gave you that idea?'

'Because you and my father, well, you clearly had a long affair. And then, when I was twenty-two, you gave me a home. I suppose I jumped to conclusions.' She felt her hope drain away, like water circling down a plughole.

'Oh, Evelyn.' Frances sounded grave as she turned to face her. 'Edwin was never honest with me, but I had hoped he was a different man at home.'

'I don't know what to believe anymore.' Evelyn felt like a soft toy that had been thrown from person to person in some cruel game and then suddenly dropped to the ground.

'There you go again with your don't knows.'

Evelyn's hands were two tight fists. 'So tell me, Frances,' she almost shouted. 'Tell me the truth.'

Chapter
Twenty-Seven

Samuel placed a twiddly side table between the two women, then set down two cups of tea and a plate of biscuits. 'He doesn't do this for everyone,' Frances remarked. 'Likes to remind me he's a nurse, not a waiter, so he must approve of you.'

'Ten minutes maximum,' Samuel warned. 'Then it's time for a nap.'

'What do you want to know?' Frances asked.

'About the affair? Whether my mother Elsbeth knew. But most of all, whether my father told you anything about my birth story.'

'Quite the wish list.' Frances took a sip of tea, then set the cup down with care. 'Well, Edwin and I first met properly in the British Museum in the Seventies. I was walking through the East Asian ceramics gallery and, at the time, it felt like fate. But now I know there was no element of chance about it: he'd been waiting for me, or someone like me, to come along for quite a while.

'We'd overlapped briefly at Oxford, but he didn't make much of an impression. And then he left early, as did your mother, Elsbeth. She and I weren't friends, but I'd heard of her – this exceptional young woman who had thrown away her education, got married and run off to some remote corner of Cornwall.'

'So you recognised him, when you met again?' Evelyn prompted.

'Indeed. Looking very dapper, briefcase in hand.' Frances gave a wry smile. 'At first, Edwin and I kept things professional. Our first conversation was about methods of dating ancient lacquerware.'

'Maybe he was in London for a meeting,' Evelyn said, clinging on to the things she'd been told. 'He liked to keep up to date with the latest research: visiting galleries, archivists and so on.'

Frances sighed. 'My dear, your father was a hobbyist, at best. He was a failed undergraduate, sent down with a basic knowledge of history and archaeology – barely enough to hold his own in dinner party chit-chat. Put him among true experts and he was lost.' She shook her head. 'Your mother was more talented, but for whatever reason, opted to keep that hidden.'

'But all his books, his collections – it was his whole world. You must be wrong. He was writing a book . . .'

Frances had a faraway look in her eyes. 'I've often wondered if that's what motivated his forays into the museum – his lack of knowledge rather than any great passion. He was a fraud, compensating for his ignorance. Being more generous, he was a magpie, briefly obsessed with whatever caught his eye until he spotted the next bright, shiny object.'

Evelyn pictured her father's study: framed pressed flowers hanging on the walls, cabinets full of botanical samples and shelves lined with leather-bound books. She herself had been given the job of proofreading his great work, pages upon pages of tightly typed words that had made her sleepy with boredom, but she assumed that was due to her own lack of expertise. But *Coastal Grasses, Mosses and Ferns of South Cornwall* had never found a publisher.

'Well, you must have liked him well enough,' she said sharply. 'You had an affair with him – and for a long time.'

'Such a tawdry word, but I suppose if the cap fits.' Frances sighed. 'Yes, it was a long-drawn-out thing, but intermittent. He'd be around for a while and then disappear for a few years. Then, just when I'd given up hope, he'd reappear, telling me he'd been on a top-secret field trip to Morocco, or seconded to a university library in Washington. He was very convincing.'

Evelyn remembered the stories that she had accepted as the truth. 'He told me he had to leave Oxford because he was ahead of his time. The dons trumped up some case against him, because he outsmarted them in every lecture.'

'Is that so?' Frances said. 'I heard a different version, that he was done for plagiarism. But the odd thing was, Edwin didn't leave Oxford. He stayed on in digs in the city, strode around with books under his arm like he was still one of us. It seemed to impress Elsbeth and off they went, to a house he'd found in Cornwall.'

'He always said they didn't need pieces of paper to confirm their intelligence.'

'Yes, that sounds like Edwin.' Frances gave a rueful smile. 'But I think he did need confirmation – all the time. He was horribly insecure. And that was why he decided to charm me. He explained that he and Elsbeth had a child, but now she was at school, he was free to return to academia. He wanted to pick my brains about current research so he could perform well when he got an interview.'

Evelyn sat forward. 'What did he tell you about me? Did he say where I came from?'

'He didn't say much. Just that he and Elsbeth had been approached to adopt a foundling. Being good people, they agreed it was the right thing to do.'

'Did he say who my mother was?'

'Oh, Evelyn, to be honest, it didn't interest me. And then, as Edwin and I became closer, I wasn't minded to ask. It would have been rubbing salt in my own wounds. Besides, Edwin also preferred to keep things separate. He became very adept at that over the years.'

It was then that a new thought slid in, cold as ice, and Evelyn forced herself to ask, 'Do you think he had another girlfriend all along, before he got married? That way, Edwin might still have been my father, but with another woman?'

'It wouldn't surprise me if he had other women on the go over the years.' Frances reached for her teacup and drained it. 'But that he had a baby with one? I doubt that very much.'

Evelyn remained silent.

'Later, we tried, you see, Edwin and I, because I so wanted a child. But it never happened. I assumed it was me, but when I got myself checked out there was no problem. Privately, I think he was firing blanks. I take it you don't have any siblings?'

Evelyn shook her head. This felt unnecessarily vindictive – was Frances just throwing her off the scent? 'If all you're saying is true, why was my father so keen for me to live with you?'

'I have no idea. At the time, I said, "Edwin, isn't it a bit late for us to be playing mummies and daddies?" and he laughed and said never mind all that – he had big plans for Evelyn Silver.'

'Big plans?'

'Oh yes. He'd scraped all he could from me by then, so your traineeship was perfect. You were rotated through all the departments, weren't you?'

'Yes.' Evelyn didn't see where this was going.

'Let me guess, he was so proud of your progress, he'd come and visit you at lunchtime.'

'He did. He'd get the early train and come straight to the museum.'

Frances put a gnarled finger to her chin. 'And, let me guess, during those lunches your father often developed a raging thirst or a deep desire for a ham sandwich and he'd dispatch you to the canteen.'

'Well, I was hardly going to let him starve.'

Evelyn had loved those visits, the admiration in her father's eyes as she'd talked about an interesting fact she'd learned about ancient Egyptian embalming techniques or Chinese glazes.

'My dear, I'm not blaming you. It was a long time before I realised what he was up to.'

'Up to?'

'When you trotted off to the canteen – which was a good twenty-minute round trip – I dare say you left him alone at the cataloguing desk with the trays of recent acquisitions.'

'He was my father. And he was an expert, practically one of us,' Evelyn protested.

'Except he wasn't. But he was smart enough to know that if something disappeared from the acquisitions tray, there was little record of it ever existing. Boxes of, say, "ceramics, 14th century" were logged, but individual items had not yet been catalogued.'

'No, you're wrong. My father was a good man,' Evelyn stumbled.

'Is that so?' Frances said in a low voice that chilled Evelyn to her core.

Then, as if by some invisible cue, Samuel appeared with a blanket that he tucked around Frances. 'I'll show you out,' he said.

Frances looked up with tired, watery eyes. 'I wish I'd been nicer to you back then – more welcoming. But it was a difficult time for me professionally. I'd let Edwin get greedy. My supervisor had his suspicions and there was talk of an investigation. But then came the big hoo-ha with the Egyptian department breakages – which you know all about.'

Evelyn felt a flood of shame.

'Not great for you, but personally I was glad because it took the heat off me. Suddenly, every department was in a tailspin about display protocols. And of course, with you leaving, Edwin went to ground. There were no more disappearances and the museum was happy to sweep that troubling episode under the carpet. Except my reputation never recovered. For all my hard work, a cloud of suspicion hung over me until the day I retired. Now, I have nothing but disdain for the lot of them.'

As Samuel escorted Evelyn down in the lift, she stared ahead and asked, 'Cancer?'

He nodded.

'How long does she have?'

'Weeks rather than months,' he replied.

Evelyn wrote her phone number on a paper napkin she found in her bag. 'I doubt she'll want to talk to me again, but just in case,' she said.

She couldn't face the noise and crowds of the Tube, so Evelyn decided to walk back to Paddington station. The cold air came as a relief and she steadily put one foot in front of the other, barely aware of her surroundings. At a pedestrian crossing in Marylebone, she heard the blare of a car horn and a man put out his arm to stop her from walking into the oncoming traffic.

She'd gone to London in search of a mother, but suffered another loss: Edwin Silver was not the father she thought he was. If Frances was to be believed, he was a con man who had used Frances and then secured Evelyn's traineeship so he could continue plundering the museum. She blinked back tears as this betrayal sank in. None of it made sense, though, because everyone knew Edwin Silver was a decent man. And if he'd sold these stolen pieces, where had all the money gone? Certainly neither her mother nor Evelyn had seen any of it and hers had been a childhood of hand-me-downs and no holidays.

On board the train back to Cornwall, she averted her eyes from the dark windows that reflected back her own tired face, with its slightly too large nose, heavy eyebrows and long chin. She'd always wondered who she'd inherited these features from and, this morning, she'd hoped she was close to finding the answer. But now she was travelling home more confused than ever.

Three hours into the journey, she purchased a limp cheese and pickle sandwich and sent a message to Sariah:

Hope your day better than mine. Went to London, but was a wild goose chase.

Sariah swiftly replied: *Sorry, that's hard. Call if you need a chat S x*

It was kind of her, but Evelyn was all talked out. She was about to put her phone away when a new message appeared, from an Unknown Number.

Frances here. Samuel has bought me a diddy little phone so I can send texts. I remembered two things. He said your birth mother was young. And I feel sure he mentioned the name Agnes. A local might know more? Good luck.

Chapter Twenty-Eight

Agnes. It was a simple name, but it ran on a loop tape in Evelyn's head as she lay in her wind-rocked caravan that night. She barely slept as she repeated it to herself, trying to imagine who it might belong to.

In the morning, she dared to say the name out loud, quietly at first as if trying it on for size. 'I'm looking for Agnes,' she murmured as she made breakfast.

'Hello, Agnes, I'm Evelyn,' she whispered to herself as she faced down an easterly wind on her beachcomb.

Back in the museum, she tipped out the single item weighing down her tote bag, a sand-encrusted rubber doormat, and then reached deep into her satchel, which contained a hairgrip in the shape of a butterfly and a soggy shopping list. 'Today's everyday is tomorrow's history' had been one of her father's sayings, but she doubted whether this list – *Crisps, beer, pie (chicken?), verruca ointment* – would enlighten the historians of the future.

It seemed that the WhatsApp group was fizzing and pinging with activity, but she could barely focus on it. The latest messages read:

Great news! – @Della

Fantastic progress! – @Jacob

Whoop! – @Sariah

Clearly, she had some catching up to do. Scrolling back, she discovered that late yesterday afternoon, while she had been running around London, Mr Palmer had asked if Evelyn and 'her committee' could attend an interim meeting first thing on Monday morning. The council needed more time to make 'an informed decision' about the boat sheds.

Good news she added to the chat, forgetting to add the now standard exclamation mark. In her heart, she wasn't sure it was, because didn't the council have ample information already? She was worried they planned to put her on the spot by demanding non-existent visitor satisfaction forms and business plans. But in truth, the real reason she couldn't summon any enthusiasm was because her mind was on other things. All she could think about was the name Agnes.

Frances's idea to talk to the older people in the town was a reasonable one. Someone would be able to remember when a young newlywed couple called the Silvers arrived in town and were soon joined by a newborn baby. But no one obvious sprang to mind.

The fact was, her parents had rarely socialised with the local people. Her father only had useful acquaintances, while her mother seemed happiest when she was on her own, up on the clifftops. Oh, she dutifully baked a cake for the school summer fair and bought raffle tickets, but Evelyn could not remember any other mothers crossing their threshold. Not even a neighbour.

Undeterred, she decided to make an initial list of the town's elders who might remember the events of 1964. On it she put:

- Mrs Moran (surely aged over eighty)
- Arnold, landlord of The Lugger (only in his fifties, but knows everything)

- The Three Wise Men: Leonard, Bob and Keith (indeterminate ages).

Naturally, there were plenty of other people that Evelyn knew by sight but had never exchanged more than a few words with, but broaching this delicate matter felt slightly easier if she started with people who had come to the exhibition.

She knew for a fact that Mrs Moran walked her three dachshunds on the beach each lunchtime, so Evelyn resolved to stretch her legs around then in the hope of bumping into her. She loitered self-consciously at the top of the slipway from twelve midday until 1.15 p.m., becoming increasingly disgruntled and cold. She gave directions to a visiting couple from Chicago and returned a brown McDonald's bag to a van driver who had parked up for lunch and 'accidentally' dropped it out of his side window. Finally, she saw the solid figure of Mrs Moran ambling towards her.

'Oh, hello!' Evelyn called out, giving a little wave. Mrs Moran, who was busy depositing three bright pink dog poo bags in the bin, ignored her until she was good and ready.

'Hello, Miss Silver,' she said with a frown. 'What brings you down here at this hour?'

'Oh, just taking a walk.'

Mrs Moran, who was trying to untangle a spaghetti of dog leads, ignored her reply.

'Yes, taking a walk. Ruminating. The way we all do,' Evelyn added breezily.

One of the dogs stopped to dig a hole, forcing Mrs Moran to slow down.

'Yes, ruminating,' Evelyn continued, ignoring the shower of sand being kicked at her legs. 'About the old days.'

'I liked your exhibition,' Mrs Moran said. 'Shame some men can't take their drink, though. I always thought better of Keith

Blake.' She tugged her green felt hat down, so her eyes were almost hidden and only the tip of her nose peeped out.

The dog stopped digging and Evelyn plucked up her courage. 'Mrs Moran,' she said. 'Do you remember when I was a baby? Back in 1964.'

Mrs Moran tilted her chin up and eyed her warily.

'I do,' Mrs Moran conceded.

'And what do you remember about me arriving? Like, who brought me and what did my parents tell people?'

'It's not my place to say,' Mrs Moran said primly.

Evelyn tried again. 'Well, my parents told me no more than the bare bones, you see. And now they are gone.'

'Didn't Elsbeth explain?' Mrs Moran asked. She took off her hat, revealing a helmet of grey hair that was almost exactly the same shape as her cloche.

'Not really. She just said cheery things like "And then we were three" and that my birth mother was unable to look after me. Nothing more specific.'

'Well, I don't like to talk out of turn,' Mrs Moran stalled, but Evelyn was losing patience.

'Naturally. But if you had to tell me, what would you say?'

'I'd say that your mother told you all she could.'

'Do you mean my father knew more?'

There was a fraction of a pause, then Mrs Moran pressed her lips together and set off down the beach, her heels kicking up small puffs of sand. Her parting words carried on the wind: 'Don't drag it all up, Evelyn. It's too late.'

Frustration rushed in because Evelyn knew that Mrs Moran was never happier than when she had a tasty bit of information to pass on. If you wanted to know if the nudists were back on the secret beach, or who had been given a parking ticket or if the sheep were on the farm lane again, Mrs Moran was your woman. So why was she being so tight-lipped? Back in 1964, Mrs Moran would have been in her twenties, but Evelyn wagered that she knew all the gossip then too.

Back on the quay, Evelyn looked for her next targets. An hour ago, all Three Wise Men had been on their bench, but now it was just Bob and Leonard. She had the feeling that since Keith blundered out of the exhibition, he had been avoiding her. Was he embarrassed by his drunkenness? She wished she could reassure him that she was the last person to be judgemental about inebriated blunderings.

Approaching the bench, she put on her jolliest voice. 'Hello, gentlemen.'

Leonard's eyes briefly flicked in her direction, then returned to the choppy sea. 'Lumpy out there today.'

'No good for fishing,' agreed Bob, also staring straight ahead.

'Thank you for coming to the exhibition,' she said.

'S'alright,' Leonard replied.

Bob looked up and everything about his face looked shrunken from years of weather-watching, from his stubby nose to his scrunched eyes. 'Did it do the job?'

'No idea. The council's dragging out their decision,' Evelyn replied. 'But I've discovered that when you start unravelling stories, there are inevitably loose threads.'

'Threads, eh?' Leonard said, tapping his walking stick on the ground.

'Ah. Threads,' Bob added gravely, as if he was well acquainted with such problems.

Evelyn ploughed on. 'For me, for instance. The threads of my story,' she tried.

The two men continued gazing out at the horizon, but Evelyn sensed that, swift as an undercurrent, the mood had shifted.

Leonard leaned to one side, so he could see around Evelyn: 'Size of those waves.'

Bob nodded. 'Wind's getting up.'

'So I thought I'd try asking around. See if anyone had any memories from when I was little. Or if anyone remembered a woman called Agnes.'

It was almost as if she was no longer there. Looking straight ahead, Leonard used his walking stick to point out to sea and nudged Bob. 'You reckon those buoys fixed good enough?'

'Have to see,' Bob replied, stroking his chin.

Evelyn stared at them. 'Seriously, is that all you have to say?'

'Suppose time will tell. Let's see if those buoys are still there in the morning.' Leonard tapped his stick again. 'Don't let us keep you, Evelyn.'

She knew she had been dismissed, but she didn't understand why.

Although she walked past The Lugger pub twice a day, Evelyn had not stepped over the threshold for a number of years and she preferred not to dwell on the reason why. But once inside, she discovered it was unchanged: there was still that hoppy smell of beer, a slight tackiness underfoot and rock ballads playing on a loop. The embers of a fire glowed in the grate and several old-timers were nursing lunchtime pints. In a corner, the two tourists from Chicago she'd seen before were digging into sticky toffee puddings. At the bar, Jude greeted her.

'We sent our emails to the council,' she said. 'Dad did too.'

'Good, good, thank you,' Evelyn said, all the while trying to peer into the gloomy doorway behind the bar.

'What can I get you?'

'Actually, it was your father I was hoping to catch.'

'Dad? Sorry, he's down the cash and carry.' Jude nodded a welcome to someone behind Evelyn and began pulling a pint. 'Want to wait? Or shall I give him a message?'

'It's not easy to put into words,' Evelyn admitted, confidence in her mission waning.

An arm reached around her for their freshly pulled beer and a voice said, 'Cheers.' She turned to see George Rook and, as he took his first sip, his eyes didn't move from her face.

A hotness prickled at Evelyn's hairline because she suspected he was thinking the same thing as her, that the last time she'd set foot in this pub was on New Year's Eve in 2019 and something unexpected had occurred on the stroke of midnight. She remembered a cover band singing 'Mr Brightside' and how George had said it was good to see her after all these years and then someone started counting down from ten, nine, eight . . .

Her father had been at a Rotary event in Truro. 'Go out, have fun for a change,' he'd said and, surprising herself as well as the regulars at The Lugger, Evelyn had followed his advice. It had taken a day to recover from the hangover, but far longer to put behind her the intense embarrassment of behaving so wantonly.

Come to think of it, their embrace had probably occurred on this very spot.

'George,' she said stiffly.

'Can I get you something?' He waited a beat. 'G and T, wasn't that your tipple?'

Evelyn gave him her sternest look.

'Something soft then – elderflower – and crisps?'

Evelyn's stomach betrayed her, letting out a low growl.

At a table in the corner, Evelyn ripped open the bag of crisps and as she savoured the first sharp tang of salt and vinegar she told him she'd only accepted his offer because she was hungry.

'Naturally,' George said. 'Anyway, were you pleased with how the exhibition went the other night?'

Evelyn ate two more crisps, then took a sip of her sugary drink. 'I don't know that pleased is quite the right word. Afterwards, I felt quite . . . confused.'

'But it was a success, wasn't it? Surely the council bods were impressed? And everyone's been sending in their forms and emails. It's the talk of the town.'

'Well, if by some miracle they do let me stay, it'll be no thanks to you.'

'Me?' George looked affronted.

'Yes, I saw you. Refusing to move out of the way for that London journalist. Quite uncalled for. We want to attract visitors, not scare them off.'

George wiped a line of foam from his lip. 'I was trying to protect you, actually. And your museum. I did try and warn you, but you went ahead anyway.'

'I have no idea what you mean.'

'Evelyn, I tried to do it subtly, suggesting you might not want to attract too much attention. I mentioned the issues of provenance. But you didn't want to know.' George moved his head a little closer. 'You still haven't taken down the website. Evelyn, it's there, for anyone to see.'

She waved him away, like an annoying fly. 'I changed the label on the painting. Nobody was interested in your feeble attempts at fakery, George Rook.'

'Not even Jacob?'

She fell silent. 'Well, I haven't quite worked out how to tell him,' she confessed. 'I think he's more fragile than people realise. Not your average Warburn.'

George leaned forward and Evelyn reared back in alarm, but he was only after the last of the crisps. 'Your father established your museum with a very specific purpose,' he said quietly.

'Yes, to give me a job for life.' Then, remembering her lace, she added, 'And to give me hope.'

George looked down at a wet circle his beer glass had left on the table and ran his finger through it. 'I'm sure that was part of it. But it also served Edwin Silver's purposes.'

All at once, she didn't want to hear any more because his words were slotting into place with the things Frances Parfait had said about her father in the worst possible way.

'No,' she pleaded. Putting her hands over her ears and closing her eyes, Evelyn felt a particular sort of shame, the sort that came from a lifetime of seeing the world in one way and then realising she was in a minority. And now she was being forced to shift her viewpoint, inch by inch.

When she opened her eyes again, George was looking at her with a sad expression. 'Your father and mine had a long-standing arrangement,' he began. 'It started with the odd museum-grade piece that Edwin came by via his contacts. Meanwhile, my father knew people with money who fancied having a pharaoh's scarab or a Roman mosaic in their Marbella villa. They also liked the idea of being art lovers, which, as I told you, was where I came in.'

'Museum grade,' Evelyn repeated to herself. Then, to George, she said, 'I think I might have an idea of who his "contacts" might have been.'

George gave a long, slow nod as if he had an inkling too, but she didn't dare say more.

'The thing is, my dad's customers are starting to die off and a few unsuspecting relatives have tried to get valuations for probate. My dad covered his tracks pretty well, but I've had to field the odd tricky question. All it needs is some fancy journalist to remark how odd it is that a small, out-of-the-way museum has not only a painting 'possibly attributed to' Alfred Wallis, but a 14th-century East Asian green porcelain vase and an ancient Egyptian gold and faience bead necklace and people will start to wonder why. And then, they will start to question what else you might have tucked away in the dark corners of your museum.'

Evelyn thought of the stacks of sealed-up cardboard boxes at the back of the shed, some of which reached the highest rafters. Then there were the multiple carrier bags hidden under the bed in the Cornish Life diorama and a few items her father had locked inside the display cabinets.

'There are boxes I've never opened,' she admitted. 'You see, once I started collecting things myself, I almost forgot all his stuff was there. He said it was donations from fellow botany enthusiasts. And, frankly, the last thing I needed was more pressed flowers.'

'The stuff my dad took off his hands – well, it wasn't pressed flowers,' George said soberly. They locked eyes, each beginning to comprehend the scale of the problem.

'Boxes and boxes,' Evelyn whispered, wondering if it was too late to add a double gin to her elderflower.

'What I don't get is why he did it,' said George. 'Was he creating a nest egg for you to discover one day?'

Evelyn considered this. 'I'm not sure. Someone I met in London thought he was more like a magpie, a compulsive collector who took things because he could. My mother and I certainly never saw any money. It makes no sense.'

For so long, her museum had been her place of safety, its clutter acting as a barrier between her and the outside world. But now she felt as if that old boat shed was full of hidden dangers, traps that were lying in wait.

Chapter Twenty-Nine

Alison wasn't sure how many days had passed since she'd left the house. She could remember picking Will up from nursery and pushing the buggy in the rain and getting home wet and cold. But after that, the shape of her days had become less clear, all blending into one long round of cleaning and making herself presentable and waiting for Roy to come home.

In the end, she decided it was probably twelve days, which was a nice even number.

Before this stretch of twelve days, she'd been to see a man called Michael in Fowey who had a puppy. He'd shut it in the kitchen to keep Will safe and, in a way, she felt like she was doing something similar. Shutting herself in, to keep everyone safe.

When Roy got like this, the best thing to do was to wait it out and keep life as calm as possible. Before long, and with little warning, his mood would lift. Very soon, he'd give Alison her phone back and they would both act like nothing had happened. Surely, it couldn't be long, now. He'd rung the sports centre and said she was off sick, but she had a feeling they might sack her this time.

Because she was 'sick', Roy took Will to nursery each morning and picked him up at lunchtime too. She imagined what the nursery staff would be saying: 'Alison still not well? You're a star, Roy. Wish my husband was as well trained as you!'

He didn't bring Will straight home, though, and Alison worried about her son being at the garage all afternoon: it was a dangerous place, full of heavy machinery and noise. The best thing she could do was make the house as nice as possible for their return at the end of the day.

Some people made do with a quick hoover and a wave of the duster, but not Alison. She washed the floors and windows, wiped down the skirting boards and put an extension brush on the vacuum cleaner to get into all the little corners and crevices. The bathroom was scrubbed and bleached, the taps buffed to a shine and every door handle disinfected. Will's toys were tidied away and she'd done the laundry. Everything was ironed, right down to the socks and tea towels.

Aside from Roy and Will, the only person she saw was the Tesco delivery driver. She didn't know if he was a mate of Roy's or if it was her lank-haired appearance, but he kept his distance, just stacked the crates up outside the front door and waited in silence for her to unload each one.

Sariah came by once. Alison heard her knocking and she sat in her spot under the front window until she went away again. It would only drag things out if someone else got involved.

But then, Roy came home in a good mood, and she dared to think it was over. He slammed the front door and called out, 'Hello, love' as if nothing had happened and Alison sprang into action, doing what she always did best: she soothed and coaxed and asked him if he'd had a busy day and she got Will's tea ready and then cooked Roy steak and chips, his favourite.

'Great stuff, cheers,' he said, pushing his plate away. 'Just heading up for a shower.' Alison cleared the table, scraped the cold scraps of fat and a smear of ketchup into the food recycling bin and stacked the dishwasher. Then she wiped Will's face and sat down to read him a story before bath-time. She heard Roy's feet galloping down the stairs and smelled his aftershave a second before he appeared in the doorway.

'Right, best be off,' Roy said. Then he looked puzzled. 'Don't you want to change him? He's been in those dungarees all day.'

'Change?' Alison didn't understand.

'No time now,' Roy continued in a jolly voice and held out his arms. 'Come on, little man, time we were off. Free drinks tonight!'

Will obediently slid off her lap so Roy could scoop him up.

'Where are you going?' Alison felt a jolt of fear that she'd forgotten something vital.

'The exhibition, silly.' Roy let out a laugh. 'Starts any minute.'

'Oh.' She stood, feeling stupid. Had she been out of the loop that long? How could she have forgotten the date? Alison looked down at her shapeless top and jeans and remembered that her hair needed a wash.

'Give me two minutes,' she said and turned to run up the stairs. She was halfway up when she felt the rush of cold air as he opened the front door.

'Don't think that's a good idea: you still look peaky. But don't worry, we'll tell you all about it when we get back,' Roy said and the door slammed behind them.

She remained standing on the stairs long after she'd heard the car driving away.

The hours ticked by and she worried about Will and how tired he'd be in the morning. She made sure everything was spick and span and lit a scented candle that promised Serenity, but it seemed a big ask of a small candle. By 10 p.m., she knew the exhibition must be long finished and that Roy must have taken Will to the pub.

At 10.30 p.m., she heard the car's motor and positioned herself casually on the sofa with a magazine, as if she had been relaxing.

Roy carried Will in, asleep in his car seat, and set him on the hall-way floor. She took in her son's flushed cheeks, a scattering of crisps in his lap and his swollen nappy. 'I'll take him up,' she whispered.

But Roy ignored her and walked into the kitchen. She heard the fridge open and close, then the crack of the ring pull on a can of beer. 'Fun and games tonight,' he called out too loudly and she knew the happy drunk stage was long gone and they were heading into belligerent drunk.

She left Will sleeping and followed Roy into the kitchen, blinking in the sudden glare of the lights.

'Oh yes, fun and games.' Roy set his can down and wiped his mouth. 'Had to give the Warburn boy a bit of a smack,' he said. 'Remind him what's what.'

Roy did a poor imitation of a whiney posh voice: 'Erm, excuse me old chap, but where is Alison? She should be here.'

A fist-thud on the table made Alison jump.

'Nobody tells me what to do.'

'He's just a kid,' Alison tried to soothe. 'He's nothing.'

But then Roy started talking about her dad and she froze. He wouldn't hurt him, would he? Not her dad.

'Yeah, your poor old dad,' she heard. 'Quite upset.'

'What did you do?' she demanded, forgetting to use her soft voice.

'Me? I didn't do anything. Was you and your stupid exhibition that did it. Bent your dad right out of shape.' Roy let out his stupid drunk giggle, the one that meant he probably wouldn't remember anything the next morning.

'Roy, please. What happened?'

'No idea, love. Something got him worked up, though – stormed out, effing and blinding.'

She didn't believe him. He must have said something, because no one else would want to upset her dad, the kindest man she knew.

Her jaw tight with unspoken words, Alison began making up a bottle for Will. She carried it and the car seat upstairs and then, as gently as she could, she changed Will's nappy and got him ready for bed. As she gave Will his milk he looked up at her with wide eyes. Usually, this was her favourite part of the day, a quiet moment of trust and love. But looking down, all she saw in her son's eyes was confusion and she knew this couldn't go on.

Chapter Thirty

When Alison had first met Roy, he'd given her butterflies, little flutterings of excitement whenever she saw him playing pool in the pub. But now she realised she'd misread the signs. Her body had been sending her a warning message and they hadn't been the stirrings of love, but fear.

In the aftermath of Roy coming back from the exhibition, she'd started to see things more clearly. All weekend she'd behaved herself, biding her time, and then last night she'd lain awake until she was sure Roy was out for the count. With slow, steady movements, she'd got up and knelt down beside the chair where he'd slung his clothes. Without taking her eyes off Roy, she'd felt inside his pockets until she touched the smooth surface of her own mobile phone.

Then she'd backed out of the room and locked herself in the bathroom. Even so, she'd made sure to flick the phone to silent before turning it on and watching the screen fill with icons, missed calls and unread messages.

She had a horrible feeling she could guess what had upset her dad at the exhibition, but she needed to check. She opened up the Save Our Museum committee spreadsheet and there, beside the listing for her grandfather's embroidered picture was a big fat asterisk. Just as she'd feared, someone else had followed up on this SW's story and written it up for her poor dad to see. She'd tried so hard to control things, find out who SW was and limit the damage, but she'd failed.

Then, this morning, when Roy got up, showered and held out his hand for Will's packed lunch, signalling he was still in charge, she realised she was also failing her son.

The problem was, Alison didn't know what to do next. For now, she had her phone back, but who could she call? And how could she put into words what was happening? It wasn't as if Roy had expressly forbidden her from going out; it was just an unspoken understanding that she wouldn't until his say-so.

She walked from room to room and settled in her usual spot on the living-room floor, her back to the wall under the front window. This was a good place to wait: it meant she could hear the first rumble of the car engine and, if she looked up and to the right, she could see anyone who came to the front door. Every part of her body felt poised and ready to run, adrenaline pulsing through her veins, and yet she felt immobilised with fear. What if she left? But what if she stayed?

Alison watched the rectangle of pale sunshine move slowly across the cream carpet and she sat very still, unable to choose.

Chapter Thirty-One

It was the day of the interim meeting with the council. Sariah sensed that Conference Room Three at the council offices had seen better days. There was a whiteboard, on which someone had written *Aims and Objectives* in red marker pen before realising it was not wipe-off ink. There was a flipchart that had run out of paper, a water cooler with no cups and the corner of a carpet tile was stuck down with brown parcel tape. Della clocked it too. 'Not sure what Health and Safety would have to say about that,' she remarked, but no one replied.

Despite the unimpressive setting, there was a nervous excitement in the air. Evelyn was wearing a curious brown dress with two flaps over the bust but, more worryingly, she had barely said a word since Sariah had picked her up. She supposed Evelyn was nervous about the fate of her museum, but then she remembered her saying she'd been on a 'wild goose chase' to London and Sariah resolved to sit down and have a good chat with her – once all this council stuff was out of the way.

'You OK, Evelyn?' she asked.

'Sorry, I am a little tired. Overwhelmed, you could say.'

Jacob didn't look much better: his black eye had turned an alarming shade of green and he kept making sad spaniel eyes at the door, no doubt hoping Alison would put in a last-minute appearance. But Alison hadn't answered any of their messages and Sariah didn't have high hopes.

If she was honest, Sariah also felt on edge, as if she'd been called into the headteacher's office. This had been such a regular feature of her schooldays that she had to quell the urge to slide down in her chair, chew gum and say, 'Yeah, what of it?'

Only Della seemed composed and confident. She'd eschewed her usual trippy traveller clothes for a black polo-neck sweater and jeans and tied her hair back in a tight bun, which meant you could see more of her dark blond roots and less of the crazy purple. She sat with her shoulders back, a folder and a laptop placed on the table in front of her.

It was Della who had made sure they were all there on time and had asked (i.e. instructed) Sariah to drive them here. Now, Mr Palmer and his colleagues were precisely three minutes late for their 9 a.m. meeting.

At 9.05 the door opened and three men and a woman entered, wearing uniformly uninspiring grey suits that Sariah guessed were from the office wear section of Primark. 'Sorry, sorry,' bumbled Mr Palmer, offering a damp hand to each of them. Sariah noticed that Della did not stand up. As another power move, she had taken a chair at the head of the table and they all watched as Mr Palmer hesitated, then took his place at the other end, next to the unemptied bin and the sticky-taped carpet tile.

As introductions were made, Sariah couldn't help looking at the empty chair between Jacob and Evelyn and she wished Alison was here too. An officer called Leanne Cobb read out from a pre-prepared document, talking at length about budgets and visitor numbers and how Portheast offered scope for growth.

'Hence our need for a few more questions,' Mr Palmer interjected.

'Not a problem,' Della said, leaning back in her chair and crossing her arms. 'In fact, I've taken the liberty of preparing a short promo. To help you envisage our full potential.' Then she flipped open her laptop and turned it around so the screen faced the officials. Mr Palmer started to say something, but it was too late; Della had already clicked the Play arrow and loud, rousing music drowned out his words.

A booming classical composition accompanied a video of the boat sheds, beginning with a drone shot of the quay. It hovered above a few boats that bobbed prettily, then swooped down towards the sheds. A series of still images flipped and whooshed across the screen: customers queuing at Della's ice cream parlour (Who? Had she paid them? Sariah wondered) and then photos taken at the Second Chances exhibition.

There was a shot of Sariah laughing with Jacob, another of Evelyn looking shyly proud and one of Roy and his brothers gathered around the free drinks tray. Mrs Moran and her dogs struck a pose with Jude and Kayla, while Alison's dad, Keith, and old Bob, the fisherman who got seasick, were pictured peering at the exhibits.

As the music rose to a crescendo, Sariah was embarrassed to feel the prickle of tears: chord changes got her every time. A voice intoned: 'Portheast – celebrating our past, looking to the future' and the screen faded to black.

'Well, that was . . . unexpected,' Mr Palmer managed.

'Furthermore, Evelyn and I are considering linking the two boat sheds, so people are taken on a retail journey from museum to café. We may add a small gift shop, with a tasteful selection of replica items,' Della said breezily. 'For many museums, this accounts for a large proportion of their revenue stream.'

'We are?' Evelyn, who had been doodling on a pad, looked up.

Della ignored her. 'Discussions are ongoing,' she said firmly.

An impassive Mr Palmer smoothed down his tie and said it would be good to see some figures. 'Projections for visitor numbers, revenue and so on.'

'Not a problem,' Della replied and got to her feet, indicating the meeting was over. The two of them shook hands again, each seeming intent on gripping the other's hand more tightly. The handshake went on for some time.

'I'd like to extend our decision date by a further six weeks,' Mr Palmer added. 'Shall we say, the nineteenth of May?'

Was this good or bad news? Sariah wasn't sure. Meekly, they all followed Della out of the meeting room and into the council car park, where they were greeted by the unedifying sight of two seagulls scrapping over an empty chip wrapper.

'Well, you are full of surprises,' Evelyn said to Della.

'Got to keep them on their toes,' Della replied. 'And just as well I am, because you kind of checked out in that meeting, hey?'

'Sorry. Lots on my mind,' Evelyn replied.

Sariah put the minibus in gear and set off towards the quay, where she dropped off Della and Evelyn. Next, she pulled up outside the newsagents. Turning off the ignition, she faced Jacob and asked, 'Did Evelyn seem a bit odd to you? I mean not the usual Evelyn oddness, something else?'

'Well, it's her world, that museum.'

'True. Anyway, how's your eye?'

'Better than it looks,' Jacob replied. 'Just feel a bit of an idiot.'

'Roy Pinlow is the idiot, always has been.'

Jacob undid his seatbelt, but didn't move. 'Hey, do you think Alison's OK? I'm worried. But I'm probably not the best person to go and check on her,' he said.

The easy option would be to say that she was sure Alison was fine and that she'd soon be back at work, but Sariah had a bad feeling about Alison and Roy and what went on behind the shiny green door of their house up on the estate.

Before she could change her mind, she said, 'How about we both head up and see?'

It was a relief when they pulled up outside the house and saw that the red Toyota Corolla was gone from the drive: unless Roy came home for lunch, they would be able to talk to Alison without him interfering.

As before, Sariah knocked on the door, but there was no sound of anyone stirring inside and when she pushed open the letterbox all she could see was a shoe rack holding two sets of trainers and a small shelf for keys. Above it, a white wooden sign read LOVE LIVES HERE, but Sariah had her doubts. 'Alison,' she shouted through in her loudest voice, the one she used to call last orders in the hotel bar. 'Are you in?'

When she pressed her face up to the letterbox a second time, Sariah smelled the trapped odours of furniture polish, bleach and laundry detergent. The smells reminded her of the holiday homes she used to clean: empty and perfectly impersonal, ready for the next guests to imprint their personalities on the place. But Alison and Roy had lived here for almost two years.

'You don't need to come outside. Just let us know you're OK,' she called out.

Then she straightened up and began to walk back, so she could take another look at the house. All the curtains were open, but the windows were dark. She thought she saw a flicker of movement at the living-room window, but she couldn't be sure.

'What do we do now?' Jacob said, both hands pushed into the front pockets of his jeans. He couldn't look more uncomfortable if he tried. 'Police?'

'Maybe,' said Sariah, but she had a feeling that rather than putting a stop to whatever was going on, that could be the touchpaper to ignite something far worse.

'Let's wait for a bit,' she said. The two of them climbed back into the minibus and for the next hour they did just that, alert for any sign or sound. She watched two starlings flit from one stunted bush to another, then the wind sent a scrap of paper spinning along the newly tarmacked pavement. But at number 12b Pinewood Crescent, nothing moved.

Chapter Thirty-Two

When she heard Sariah call her name through the letterbox, Alison held her breath. Then came the lower rumble of a male voice and her heart gave a lurch before she realised it wasn't him, it was Jacob. She looked down at her stained tracksuit bottoms, raised her hand to feel her claggy, unwashed hair and decided to stay right where she was sitting. How could she begin to explain what had been happening?

After a while, she heard their steps recede and the slam of two car doors, but, although she strained to hear, the engine did not start up. All she heard was faint birdsong and the gentle swish of leaves. Alison got out her phone and started to type a message to Sariah, telling her she was still ill, but she didn't get further than a fake-jolly *Hi!* before she put it down again.

As she sat there, it was tempting to close her eyes and let her thoughts drift – she'd barely slept the night before. But then she heard an engine start up. Heart racing, she peeped out of the window and saw the Warburn Spa minibus was parked at the end of their drive, with Sariah and Jacob in the front seats.

She hoped they would drive off soon, just in case Roy came home unexpectedly. Already, he would have taken off his jacket to change into his overalls. As he did, he might have given his inside jacket pocket a reassuring pat, feeling for Alison's phone, and realise it was gone. Any second now, the little red Corolla might come zooming up the road and onto their drive. Then his key would be in the door and she would be here waiting, a sitting duck. And she didn't need an audience for that.

From outside, she heard the blast of a car radio and someone flicking through the stations. She heard a snatch of a morning phone-in, then music. It was an old song, a favourite of hers, and Jacob or Sariah must like it too, because it got turned up a few notches. It reminded Alison of driving to her old job at the PR company, the journey just long enough to blast out a few disco classics from her playlist. She used to turn the volume right up for this one because she loved it. Just like she'd loved her job.

She stood up, her legs a little wobbly. She held on to the windowsill and saw that at last they were going – Sariah was doing a three-point turn. Jacob had his window wound down and she could hear Candi Staton singing about being a lost and lonely wife and a long-buried memory came to her, one she hadn't let in for a long time. Her memories of her mum were so precious that she was irrationally scared that if she took them out too often, they might fade and lose their colour, like old photographs.

She could picture her mum dancing to that song in the kitchen, shimmying her way towards Alison, pointing and singing along, telling her that young hearts should run free. Sometimes her dad joined in too and her parents would join hands, with Alison in the middle. 'Alison sandwich!' her mum would say. Times like that, she had felt so loved.

Alison found herself walking towards the front door, but she must have moved too fast because the dizziness almost felled her. As she opened the door she realised that it was too late, because the minibus was starting to move. There was a grind of gears changing and its left indicator started flashing. In a few seconds they would be gone.

In her thin socks, Alison began to run down the drive and onto the gritty road and she raised her arms in the air. She waved like her life depended on it, like one of the Railway Children. Her heart thumped and her right shoulder screamed in pain but it was working – the minibus came to a jerky halt. Both doors opened at the same time and Sariah and Jacob were running back towards the house.

It was Sariah who got to her first, wrapped her arms around her and said, 'It's OK, we've got you.'

◆　◆　◆

Alison didn't want to take much with her. She packed a few of Will's toys and clothes, a stack of nappies and his favourite blanket. For herself, she just took a change of clothes and her phone charger, which she found in Roy's bedside table.

Walking around the house with Sariah by her side, she saw her belongings through different eyes. Her supermarket-bought clothes, the battered paperback beside her bed, her pink plastic hairbrush – it all looked so cheap and tawdry and she didn't want to put any of it in the carrier bag that Sariah held out. Not even her running kit. She'd done so much running, but the problem was that she'd kept coming back to this miserable little house with its mean rules and its atmosphere of fear.

Their first stop was the nursery, all the while keeping an eye out for a red Corolla. 'Taking him out early today,' she explained to the staff. They looked unsure, but they had to let Will go with her. Then Sariah drove to Alison's dad's. That was the worst part: seeing the pleasure on his face when he opened the door – 'Hello, love.

Are you better?' – and then how his face had crumpled when he realised why she'd come.

Sitting on her dad's sofa with Will cuddled up beside her, Alison started to feel the tension leaving her body and it was as if Will also knew something fundamental had changed. He still had the packed lunch she'd made him this morning and she watched him studiously transfer raisins from a tiny cardboard box into his mouth, then pop the lid off a plastic tub of carrot sticks. She'd packed his food a few hours ago, but already it felt like another lifetime.

She looked into the kitchen, where her dad was making them beans on toast. When she saw him raise his big paw of a hand and give his cheek a brisk wipe, she went into the kitchen and closed the door.

'He kept saying you were ill,' her dad said tightly. 'I shouldn't have believed him.' He didn't look round, but continued stirring the saucepan furiously. 'I should have checked in on you.'

'Not your fault, Dad.'

She went over to the bread bin, pulled out a bag of white sliced and fed two into the toaster. It was coming up to 12.30 p.m., which meant Roy would be pulling up outside the nursery to pick up Will. Would his good-guy demeanour slip as they explained he was too late, or would he wait until he was back home before he let his true feelings show? She imagined his rage when he discovered she'd gone and taken Will too, the inanimate objects that would get kicked, thrown and pummelled in the absence of her softer body.

'And it wasn't my fault either,' she said firmly and set about buttering the toast.

She began to lay the table. Life would go on. They would survive, to misquote another of her and her mum's favourite disco anthems. This morning she'd felt so alone, but now she didn't: she had her dad and she had friends, good people like Sariah and Jacob.

For the next few days she wrapped Will in love, read him all her old baby books and played with the toys her dad kept in a big trunk. She told her son they were having a little holiday with Grandpa, but she sent Roy a very different message. Now she had her phone back, she had access to the record of incidents that she had been keeping for the past year, knowing that this time would come.

They were listed in a document she'd called *Sports Centre Cleaner Rota*, in case Roy went looking. She'd taken photos too, of the bruises, and noted the dates. She told Roy about her document and said he needed to stay away from her and Will, but she was happy to work out an access agreement, once he was calmer.

Looking at the photos she'd taken in the brutally bright light of the bathroom, she felt sick at how bad things had got. There was no way she wanted her dad to know those details, but, one evening, as they stood side by side at the sink, he surprised her.

'It's like the frog in boiling water,' he said, out of nowhere.

'Sorry?' she replied.

'If you put a frog in a pan of boiling water, it'll jump right out. But put it in cold water, then slowly increase the heat underneath and it'll stay put. Until it's boiled alive.'

Alison ran the tea towel around a plate, couldn't look him in the eye.

'But you jumped out in time. And that's what matters.' He patted her on the back, which, from her dad, was a major show of affection.

She still needed to talk to him about what had happened on the night of the exhibition opening, but that could wait. Right now, her priority was to make sure Will felt safe and loved – the way she did, with her dad by her side.

Chapter
Thirty-Three

After four days at her dad's, Alison felt it was time to get Will back into his routines, and as she passed people on the short walk to his nursery, she kept her head held high. She noticed Mrs Moran do a double take, the cogs turning in her head as she worked out that Alison was coming from her dad's house rather than the new housing estate, and Alison knew that the news would soon spread.

At the nursery, she explained as briefly as she could what had happened. She said she needed to talk to a lawyer, but in the meantime, she didn't want Roy picking Will up from nursery. She'd expected the manager to bridle at this, but instead she pulled Alison in for a hug. 'I knew something wasn't right,' she said. 'People get ill, of course they do, but there was something about his manner. You know when you just get a vibe?' Alison nodded. Her own instincts had been way off for a while, but she was learning to trust them again.

Her next task of the day was to pay a visit to Evelyn's museum, because one thing her instincts had managed to tell her was that her dad's outburst at the exhibition and that embroidered picture were inextricably connected.

Down at the quay, she sneaked past Della's ice cream parlour and stepped into the musty museum. By some miracle, Evelyn wasn't at her desk and Alison found herself alone, standing in front of an array of wooden stands for the Second Chances exhibition. It looked good and she felt a pang of regret that she hadn't been around to help.

She looked at Evelyn's piece of lace, a small painting and the framed fishing knots with Michael's words printed below, which gave her a swell of pride. And then she saw it – the embroidered picture of a ship at sea.

As she took in the words printed beneath it, her first concern was for her father and how he might have felt, reading them with his friends and neighbours milling around. It revealed a betrayal by her grandfather, there was no doubt about that, but Alison was surprised that reading them herself she felt no anger. Maybe it was because she'd had her fill of rage for a while, or maybe it was because the words she read spoke only of sadness and love.

A BOAT AT SEA, EMBROIDERED ON SAILCLOTH, WITH TEXT SUBMITTED BY S. WEST

I lost track of this beautiful piece of embroidery around thirty years ago after a house move, when my daughter threw it out. It is wonderful to see that it has been rescued.

It was sewn in 1968 by Frederick Blake of Portheast. Frederick and I loved each other, but we were both married and we couldn't be together. I am 'SW', which is stitched in initials almost too tiny to see, marking the spot where I lived. Freddie made me this picture as a token of his love. The fact I could only gaze at it in secret made it all the more

As Alison turned to leave, she saw that Evelyn was back at her usual place behind her desk.

'Good to see you,' Evelyn said warmly. 'I heard you've moved to your dad's. Sariah told me – I hope you don't mind.'

'Yes, I'd prefer people to know,' Alison said. 'I should have left ages ago. But you adapt, don't you? To awful situations.'

'This is true,' Evelyn replied.

Alison knew all about Evelyn and her piece of lace, but this made her wonder what other secrets had kept this woman hidden in this dark museum for so long. She gestured to the exhibition. 'Looks like it all came together really well.'

'Yes, it did,' Evelyn replied. 'Thank you for your help.'

'Oh, I got all fired up at the start, but then I kind of fell out of the loop.' Alison summoned her courage. 'And, if I'm being totally honest, my motives for getting involved weren't very admirable. Mostly, I wanted to keep tabs on that embroidered picture and see who this SW was.' She nodded towards the framed piece of sail-cloth. 'But then I started to enjoy being part of the committee. It felt important.'

'And you were good at it,' Evelyn said.

'Until I stepped back. Went AWOL.'

Evelyn give her a rare smile. 'That was why I took matters into my own hands,' she said proudly. 'I saw you admiring that embroidery and I followed it up on your behalf.'

Alison's mouth dropped. She wasn't sure Evelyn grasped the consequences of her actions. 'Well, I think it gave my dad a bit of a shock, seeing those words in black and white for all the world to see. Not necessarily something you want to announce to the whole town in one go, that your father was in love with someone else all through his marriage. And another man at that.'

She watched Evelyn's face change, turning from pride to horror.

'Oh, no,' she said. 'Oh, no.' She began to back away, as if she could distance herself from what she'd done. 'Blake,' Evelyn mouthed. 'Keith Blake, Alison Blake . . .' and with each word she smacked her palm against her own head. 'How could I not realise?'

'Yep. Frederick Blake was my grandfather.'

'I didn't make the connection.' Evelyn's words came in gasps. 'I thought I was helping, that you'd taken a shine to that embroidery. Oh, I'm such an idiot. I had to go meddling, didn't I?' She smacked her head again. 'Idiot, idiot.'

Alison reached out and pulled Evelyn's hand from her face. She let go of her own frustration, feeling it deflate like air from a sliced tyre. 'No, you're not. I should have said it was by my grandpa at the start, instead of trying to be sneaky.'

'I'm so sorry. Please, tell your dad. I didn't mean to embarrass him.'

'I'll explain.' Alison said. 'It seems so ridiculous now – the way they couldn't be together.' She began to zip up her jacket, an all-weather number she'd borrowed from her dad. She glanced at Evelyn, whose arms were still wrapped around her long body.

'I'm very sorry,' Evelyn repeated.

'Worse things happen at sea,' Alison said with a thin smile.

'For what it's worth, Steven West seems like a lovely man,' Evelyn said. 'He's a retired accountant, still lives in St Mawes.'

Then Alison had an idea. 'Do you think he might like it back? The embroidery. Perhaps that's a solution. It's probably what my Grandpa Fred would have wanted.'

Evelyn walked her to the door. 'I wish I'd never started this whole Second Chances thing,' she said wretchedly. 'I mean, I really appreciate how everyone pitched in to help. But now, the stories we've unearthed have revealed far more than we bargained for. I mean, secrets have been exposed. I've disrupted lives.'

She began counting on her outstretched fingers. 'I've upset you and your dad. Then there's Sariah, whose mum got in touch after fifteen years, which can't be easy. Someone got my hopes up, looking at my lace, but it's come to nothing. Even that little painting that belonged to Jacob's grandmother is problematic in more ways than one. Not even accounting for the other things in here which are of dubious provenance.' She cast a nervous look towards the dark recesses of the shed. 'And I still don't have a clue what to do with them. Honestly, I wish we'd never started this.'

The old Alison would have soothed Evelyn with words of sympathy, but she was done with keeping the peace. 'I disagree,' she said. 'It's hard when secrets come out. But it's a lot worse when they stay hidden. I think this exhibition has been good for the town. It's been good for all of us.'

It was time to go. 'Anyway,' she added. 'I'll talk to my dad, but you have a think too, about returning the embroidery. Because Steven West won't be around forever.'

Evelyn nodded, but she wasn't looking at Alison anymore. She was gazing towards the back of the shed. 'Yes,' she said softly. 'Do you know, I think returning things could be a very good idea.'

Chapter
Thirty-Four

The time had come to tackle the boxes and bags of objects that her father had hidden away in her museum and, loath as she was to admit it, the only person she could ask to help with the job was George Rook.

For the following week, he was the sole visitor Evelyn admitted through the museum doors and she put a sign outside that said Closed for stocktake. From time to time, she heard the radio on in Della's shed and once someone knocked. She deduced it was Sariah, because afterwards she heard the two women talking next door in an animated way and then hearty laughter.

Occasionally, she checked the group chat: Della said she'd sent some financial projections to the council, although Evelyn had no idea where she'd conjured them up from. Now all they could do was wait to hear if their leases would be renewed.

Alison messaged her to say her dad was having a think about giving the embroidered sailcloth back to its rightful owner, Steven West. Already, Sariah had taken away that cracked teacup and soon Evelyn would have to return the fake painting to Jacob. Three out of the four objects she'd picked out for her poster would soon be back with their rightful owners. Only the fourth item, her lace, seemed destined to remain in the museum.

But this week, the more pressing issue was to identify the items her father had stolen over the years from the British Museum and decide what to do with them. As she or George sliced open a sealed box, it would send up puffs of dust that made them both cough. Initially, not all of it looked special – there were lots of unexciting brown pottery shards and agate beads – but they did find fragments of a Roman bas-relief carving, an ancient Egyptian funerary urn not unlike the one she'd broken all those years ago, and several opaque blown glasses.

'It's overwhelming,' she said at one point, sitting back on her heels. 'I mean, what do we do with it all? It's not like we can seal up the boxes and post them back to the British Museum.'

When she uncovered a lapis lazuli amulet that she was certain she recognised from her time in the Egyptian department, the betrayal felt complete. 'I gave up my career because of him,' she told George. 'And more.'

As if in return, George unfolded a page from the *Evening Standard* dated February 1987 and emptied two gold coins into his palm. 'Well, our fathers were in cahoots for a while. This is the sort of thing he sold lots of, so I sympathise,' he replied.

'I just want it all gone.' Evelyn got to her feet. 'As soon as possible.'

Her museum was no longer her sanctuary but a trap, sticky as low-tide mud, and the longer she stayed in it, the more danger she was in.

She'd half hoped that George might take some of the objects off her hands, but he said he was done with all that and so was his dad, who was seeing out his days in a care home. 'At this stage in my life, I'd rather sell a wonky milking stool over stolen goods, any day of the week,' he said.

As she and George continued to open scrunches of newspaper and old carrier bags, they also came across things that Evelyn had collected and, in the cold light of day, she had to admit not everything was as precious as she'd once imagined.

George suggested this was an opportunity to 'refine her collections' and he shook out two black bin bags and made two sticky labels. On one he wrote *Rubbish*; on the other he wrote *Undecided*.

'I wonder if the time has come to say goodbye to this rare artefact?' George said, holding up a faded blue jelly shoe that Evelyn remembered rescuing from the beach during the heatwave of 2021.

'Very well,' she conceded.

'And this looks a bit . . . broken?' George held up a piece of painted blue wood, part of a boat name board bearing the letters *-ORA-*.

'That stays,' she said firmly. The broken name board wasn't anything special but it felt unlucky to throw it away. Besides, it had been one of the first things she'd found on the local beach, so it had a sentimental value.

'And this?' He raised a more recent beach find, a twisted and bleached piece of driftwood.

'I thought it looked like a snake,' she said lamely.

George frowned and wiggled the stick in the air. 'No, not seeing it.'

She smiled. 'OK, it can go in the *Undecided* bag – and that's my final offer.'

As George thumbed through a box of pictures, he pulled out an abstract canvas and held it at arm's length. 'No signature, but interesting,' he said, getting out his magnifying loupe, which she'd always assumed was only for show.

'OK if I take a photo? Do a bit of research?'

Evelyn nodded. The box mostly contained her mother's botanical drawings that she had donated to the museum in its early days.

Instinctively wary of modern art (what if she hung it the wrong way up?) Evelyn had ignored the painting.

But George Rook was more au fait with that world and she was starting to wonder if she'd misjudged him. She'd avoided him for years – well, except for that New Year's Eve when she must have temporarily taken leave of her senses. Gin and loneliness, it turned out, were a lethal combination. But now George was proving to be both discreet and knowledgeable. He'd helped identify plenty of the items and then labelled the boxes with words such as *Earthenware, Tang dynasty* and stacked them by the door, although she had no idea where the boxes would go next. All she knew was that she wished they would disappear, along with Mr and Mrs Cornish Life and their cluttered diorama.

'Perhaps we could tip the whole lot into the harbour at high tide,' she remarked glumly, as George ran a length of brown sticky tape around yet another box. George gave her a look that meant he knew she wasn't serious: it went against everything Evelyn believed in. Plus, as Evelyn well knew, things cast out to sea had a habit of washing back in again.

That evening, as Evelyn settled down on her uncomfortable corner sofa, she turned on the TV. She did not often do this and soon remembered why as she skipped through the depressing news, the fake laughter of a game show and a shouty soap, but then she saw a familiar face and stopped channel hopping. It was John Thaw in his role as the fatherly Inspector Morse and she felt a wash of affection for his character who was sensitive, scrupulously honest and just a little bit lonely.

Funny, she thought, how she and Frances Parfait had shared an unspoken love for the fictional detective while they were both being deceived by the less gentlemanly Edwin Silver. On screen, Morse was deep in thought as he walked through an Oxford churchyard and Evelyn remembered her visit to Bloomsbury where a poorly Frances Parfait had told her all the ways in which she'd been wronged. Forever under a cloud of suspicion for the museum thefts, her career had never recovered. Evelyn wondered if her erstwhile landlady might like a final chance to help right some wrongs of the past.

Flicking the TV onto mute, Evelyn picked up her phone, scrolled through the short contacts list and wrote a message. *Dear Frances, I hope you are doing OK. I have a proposal. If you are able, please contact me. Yours, Evelyn Silver.*

Chapter Thirty-Five

Jacob peered into the small mirror that hung over his bathroom sink so that he could inspect the bruise under his eye. Pressing two fingers into the green-yellow skin he decided that, if anything, it looked worse not better. The last time he'd had a black eye was when he was nine. It was ten minutes into a school rugby match and he'd cried so hard that the sports master took him off the pitch and suggested he switch to badminton.

Jacob Warburn had always known he was no good as a fighter, but he wasn't entirely sure what he was good at. It used to be archaeology, but his university course and London felt like a distant life that he'd left behind. His father hadn't wanted him to go to Portheast.

'Why on earth would you want to go there? Stay with us in Chiswick. Or use the Pimlico flat – it's only a pied-à-terre, but fine as a stopgap. Or shall I transfer you some money, is that what you want?' Simon Warburn had barked down the phone.

His dad's standard response to any problem was to throw money at it. It had worked well enough with Jacob's mother, Fenella, currently ensconced in the south of France, and it seemed to suit his dad's second wife, Juniper, too. But what Jacob craved was support and maybe a bit of fatherly love.

At first, being in Portheast had been reassuring: its cobbled hill and the quay were unchanged from when he was a boy and he'd been delighted to find the museum was still there. But as time went on, Jacob started to feel like a fish out of water.

In his job at the newsagents, he made an effort to remember people's names. He always had Mrs Moran's daily newspaper set aside and he knew which brand of tobacco Leonard preferred. But no matter how many names he learned, he knew he'd never fit in.

The first time he'd met old Mrs Moran, he'd begun to introduce himself and she'd cut him off. 'Oh, I know who you are. You're a Warburn,' she said grimly. Her expression was a reminder that Warburn Hall had employed the people of Portheast for over a century, as maids, cooks, gardeners and farm workers and that legacy was hardly a basis for new friendships. His father might have sold off most of the Warburn assets, but the spa had retained the name and it served as a reminder of an inequitable past.

This was one reason why he'd pitched in to save the museum: he wanted to do something for the good of the town and, for a while, he'd felt like a part of something positive. The other reason, the one he was too shy to admit to anyone, was because of Alison. Yes, she had a baby and she was as good as married, but the truth was, Jacob couldn't get her out of his head.

In the long hours he spent in his bedsit above the newsagents, Jacob liked to replay the trip they had taken together to Fowey. He thought of Alison's easy laugh and the way she had listened to Michael and written down his story. Then she'd read it back to him to make sure he was happy with it, and the sound of her voice as she spoke of knots and fishing and a father–son love had moved Jacob in ways he couldn't explain.

Alison, so softly spoken and funny and clever. Nothing like the woman who had broken his heart the week before his finals and, if Instagram was to be believed, was now living a party life in London.

Odd, he thought, that Michael from Fowey hadn't come to the opening – perhaps he should visit him again. Would it be a mistake to ask Alison along?

Seeing her running out of her house had been an upsetting experience. He didn't know exactly what she'd been through, but it was clear Roy was bad news and didn't cherish Alison in the way she deserved.

The Save Our Museum WhatsApp group had gone strangely quiet and he missed the back-and-forth messages that made him feel like he was part of something. So when he got a direct message that morning, asking if he could come into the museum, Jacob's hopes lifted. But then Evelyn had sent a second message that read *Don't tell the others* and he felt a flicker of worry.

The door to the museum was locked, which was unusual, and there was a sign about a stocktake. Did museums do stocktakes? Surely that was the point of a catalogue. But then he remembered the state of Evelyn's desk and doubted there was any such thing for the Portheast Museum of Maritime Curiosities.

He gave a tentative knock and the door opened a crack. To his surprise, it was George Rook's face that peered out. Odd. He thought Evelyn detested the man.

'Quick, come in,' George hissed and Jacob obeyed. He had become used to the museum's slightly chaotic appearance, but inside he saw a scene of unprecedented disorder. 'Oh no, has there been a robbery?' he asked.

An indecipherable look passed between George and Evelyn, who was kneeling in front of an array of obscure-looking objects.

'Not recently,' George said darkly.

'I'm having a bit of a sort-out.' Evelyn stood and dusted off her dress.

On the floor Jacob could see a replica bust of the Roman emperor Marcus Aurelius, who seemed to stare back at him with stern disapproval. 'Remarkable,' he said, 'what they can do these days with plaster casts.'

This comment seemed to alarm Evelyn and she promptly threw an old tea towel over the emperor, like he was a canary in a cage that she wanted to keep quiet. 'Actually, Jacob, it was something else we wanted to show you. Something closer to home.'

She led him back to the Second Chances exhibition, where only last week Jacob's grandmother's painting had been on show, but he now saw that it had been taken down. 'I've decided that a number of items in the museum need to be returned to their rightful owners,' she said sadly, looking down at the painting. 'And this belonged to your family, so you are free to take it.'

Jacob gazed down at it, his mind racing.

'Wait. Does this mean it is an Alfred Wallis?'

'Unfortunately not,' Evelyn replied.

Jacob peered hard at the painting. There was no signature, but he'd read that Wallis didn't always sign his work. 'Forgive me, but are you sure? I mean, maybe we should ask a Wallis expert?'

'Well, that would be me. In a manner of speaking.' George stepped forward. 'I'm afraid this painting is a fake. I painted it in the back room of my father's shop when I was a young man. My father sold it to your grandfather in 1987 and he thought he was getting the real thing. I can only apologise.'

It must have been Jacob's imagination, but as he looked down at the picture, it suddenly looked less substantial, its colours less intense. Like it had been done by a child. 'I see,' he said, swallowing his disappointment.

'The good thing is, it still holds the same memories,' Evelyn said encouragingly.

'That's true.'

Jacob let his mind roam back to long summer days at Warburn Hall, his grandparents snoozing on the veranda, leaving the nine-year-old Jacob to explore. He'd crept along gloomy corridors and come to a dark bedroom with a four-poster bed and heavy brocade curtains that smelled of his grandfather's pipe. A shaving kit was laid out in the en suite and a plaid dressing gown was thrown over a chair.

He continued down the corridor and discovered another bedroom, this time decorated in salmon pink. It smelled of the perfumes and powder puffs on the dressing table and, hanging on the wall, he saw this painting. He sat on the bed with its frilly coverlet and looked at the jolly sailing boat being tossed around at sea, all the while taking in the fact that his grandparents slept in separate rooms.

On that day, the magic went out of holidays at Warburn Hall and he grew to mistrust its dark corridors, which whispered of unspoken secrets. He might have concluded this arrangement was because his grandfather was a snorer or his grandmother was a light sleeper, had it not been for the bluntness of his mother. When he told her about the separate bedrooms, she'd flicked her cigarette ash and said, 'But, darling, of course they do. She can't stand the man.'

Jacob carried the painting home in a tatty Lidl plastic bag, which felt appropriate for a bargain basement artwork. There were no hooks on the walls of his bedsit, so he made do with propping the painting up on the table. He ran his fingers around the frame and brushed off some dust. Turning it over, he noticed a small tear in the brown tape that secured the backing board. He ran a fingernail along the tear, widening it a little. There was something inside, wedged between the board and the painting. He wondered if it was another of George's surprises – a note that said, *Ha ha, fooled you!*

Using a cheese knife, Jacob made slits along the other three sides of the tape and prised the board away. Out dropped an envelope and on the front was written *To The New Owner*. Immediately, he recognised his grandmother's handwriting, long elegant strokes that he'd seen inside birthday cards for many years.

Jacob opened the envelope.

Chapter Thirty-Six

It was hard to believe that after fifteen years of silence, Sariah was setting off to meet her mother for the third time in as many months. Last night, her phone rang just as she got back to her room. As she kicked off her court shoes and flopped onto the bed, she barely looked at the screen before she answered it.

Her mother's voice sounded like it was playing at half speed, not slurred, but definitely slower. 'I'm sorry,' she said, after some preliminaries, 'that you don't have happier memories of your childhood. That wasn't how it was meant to be.'

'Mum?' Sariah had sat up. Was she hearing right – an apology from her mother, who never gave an inch?

The sound of Grace drawing deeply on a cigarette came down the line. 'Anyway, I just wanted to say, we loved you. But it wasn't the start to my married life I'd imagined and maybe that got in the way.'

Sariah's first thought was that this had a whiff of Step Nine of the Twelve Step Programme – to make direct amends – but that didn't fit with Grace's lazy intonation. Perhaps her mother had another reason for wanting to make her peace. 'Are you ill, Mum?' she asked.

'No more than usual.' Her mother broke into a wheezy laugh. Then she cut to the chase. 'Can we meet again? Just us this time. Now we're back in touch there are some things I should say.'

And that was how Sariah came to be driving back into Redruth on her morning off, checking her make-up in the rear-view mirror every time she stopped at a set of traffic lights. She was wearing her hotel uniform. She told herself this was because she was back on shift in a few hours, but it was also because it made her feel in charge, efficient, and she needed that illusion now more than ever.

Frankly, she couldn't face another visit to her childhood home, so they had arranged to meet at a café called the Copper Pot, where the waitresses wore fancy aprons and pinched expressions.

Grace was already sitting at a table when she walked in and it was clear she'd made an effort. Her hair looked washed and she was wearing a pretty dress, yellow with a tiny sprig pattern. Sariah thought it might even be the same one she'd worn for the fateful parents' evening, when she'd let rip at the teacher. A lump formed in Sariah's throat, remembering that misguided effort at motherly love.

Despite the café being almost empty, the tables were all uncomfortably close together and the chairs didn't fit properly underneath. In a fit of exasperation, Sariah started removing a spare chair from their table. 'Don't,' Grace whispered and Sariah had to bite her tongue, because this was her family's way, an ingrained fear of attracting attention or doing the wrong thing. But, obediently, she left the chair where it was, rammed too close to her own.

They settled on tea and scones for two and her mother began rooting around in her huge black shoulder bag for her purse. Sariah put her hand on the bag's chunky zip and said, 'Please, my treat.'

'I'd have had the carrot cake if I'd known,' Grace muttered.

Sariah counted to ten. 'So, you wanted to chat.'

Her mother didn't look at Sariah, but seemed to choose a spot in the middle distance to stare at as she said, 'Yes, I thought it was time for a proper talk. Now we're back in touch.'

Sariah resisted the urge to point out that Grace, or Sariah's brothers, could have come looking for her if they had wanted: her name and photo were right there on the Warburn Spa website. She'd left, but she was easy enough to find.

'After you were born, it was hard,' Grace began. 'Me and your dad, we thought we were grown-up, but we weren't: I was only twenty, your dad a couple of years older. There wasn't much money so at first we were still living at your grandma and grandpa's. Nobody tells you, but a tiny baby is exhausting. Non-stop. And oh, how you cried!'

Sariah crossed her arms. 'As usual, my fault then?'

'No, love,' Grace said softly. 'I'm just saying it was a shock. And so soon in our married life.'

'Again, not my fault.' The fact Sariah had been born five short months after the wedding was never spoken of. 'Not a shotgun wedding,' her dad said once. 'But we certainly got a running start.'

'Of course, your Grandma Karensa helped, but it was still a lot. And lots of people in a little house. Me and your dad in my old bedroom; Mum and Dad; then after Rose came back, it felt like there was barely enough space to turn around . . .' She took a sip of tea.

'It was simpler once we got our own place. But, like I said, it wasn't the easiest start, and your dad was useless. But I think we got stuck like that, you and me. Because life was different, once Jamie and Liam came along a few years later.'

'Quite a gap,' Sariah said. 'Before you had them.'

'True. But you can't control Mother Nature, can you?'

Sariah really didn't want to get into discussing the birds and the bees and her parents, so she steered the conversation back to the early days, when her mum and dad had felt out of their depth in Grandma Karensa's cramped house. 'So you said after Rose came back. Where had she been?'

'Oh, she was in Plymouth,' her mother said vaguely. 'But she wasn't herself for a while. Not much use.'

Sariah sensed she wasn't getting the whole truth. Had Auntie Rose been ill? Was this why everyone treated her with kid gloves?

'But where did she go?' she persisted. 'It must have been something quite bad to miss her own sister's wedding. I'm surprised Grandma Karensa allowed it, to be honest.'

A beat followed before Grace said, 'She went to stay with a lady.'

Oh. This sounded slightly different. Had this been the start of Rose learning her airs and graces, beginning to separate herself from her working-class roots? Sariah imagined elocution lessons – 'How now, brown cow' – and Auntie Rose walking around with a book balanced on her head. But, no, that didn't seem right.

'What sort of lady?' she asked.

'Someone who took girls in. Girls in trouble. Your Auntie Rose, she was only fifteen, see, and Mum didn't want her at the wedding, not like that.'

Sariah stared at her mother. Rose, pregnant? At fifteen?

'The lady was a nurse. She'd trained at the old mother and baby home over in St Agnes. Course that had long since closed down, but that didn't stop there being a need for girls who got caught out. If you were too far gone, it was easier to disappear for a few months, escape the gossip and come home once it was all sorted.' Grace dabbed her lips, as if passing on a family scandal over tea and scones in the Copper Pot was an everyday event.

'What? So Auntie Rose had a baby?' Sariah couldn't calibrate this information. She felt as if she needed to spool back all her family memories and reframe them. 'And so young, poor thing. Who was the father?'

'She never did say. I think it was either someone as young and innocent as her, because she wasn't that sort of girl, she really wasn't. Or it could have been someone older who knew exactly what they were doing. But Rose wouldn't say and Mum, your grandma, didn't like to keep asking. She wanted Rose to put it behind her, go back to school and everyone move on, like nothing had happened.'

Sariah gritted her teeth at how a fear of gossip had cowed her family. Perhaps this helped explain why Auntie Rose had left her family behind and reinvented herself as a prim and proper teacher with a cut-glass accent who lived up country and only visited at Easter and Christmas. Like Sariah, she'd found it easier to make a clean break.

'And the baby?'

'Adopted,' her mother said plainly. 'Anyway, with all that going on, it was a difficult year. Not that I'm asking for sympathy – I just thought you should know. We tried our best, but it's possible you didn't get the attention you deserved and I suppose it set a pattern.'

Grace looked at Sariah for a long time, her eyes bright. 'I'm sorry,' she said at last.

Sariah didn't know how to respond, because she barely recognised this softer version of her mother.

'Anyway, I know you're very busy, so I won't keep you.' Grace began to shoulder on her coat. She held on to her black bag tightly and, before Sariah could stop her, she stood up, gave an odd little bow and said with strained formality, 'Thank you for the cream tea.'

There was a tinkle of the old-fashioned bell as she pulled open the door and Sariah watched in confusion as her mother scurried across the road and disappeared around the corner.

It felt as if Sariah had been travelling on an escalator and missed her footing at the bottom: one minute she and her mum had been talking with refreshing honesty and the next, boom, her mother had walked out, as if she'd suddenly remembered this wasn't how they did things.

A waitress in a frilly apron that had seen better days rang up their bill and nodded her thanks when Sariah dropped a £2 coin into the tips dish. There was still over an hour left on her parking ticket, but there was nothing left for her in this town, so Sariah slowly walked back to the car park, past chicken shops, boarded-up shops and charity shops (perhaps Evelyn should have come along after all). She felt a bit silly now, all dressed up in her uniform for no good reason, and a little queasy from the scones with cream and too-sweet jam.

On the drive back the sun came out and she could smell the minibus's fake leather seats warming up. She made the mistake of taking the long way back to Portheast, along smaller, winding roads, and each time she had to pull into a passing place, she revved the engine with barely suppressed anger.

She'd gone all that way, used up her morning off and for what? Some sob story about how Grace had lived at home for too long in a too-small house with a crying baby, a scandal-dodging sister and a rubbish husband who was yet to show his true colours.

A white 4x4 appeared in the middle of the road ahead and Sariah had to give her steering wheel a sharp turn to the left, pulling into a gap just in time. She took a deep breath and turned off the ignition and then got out, suddenly desperate for air, and with one hand on the minibus's ticking bonnet she tried to make sense of the things she'd been half-told, about one teenage sister in a fix, the other just married and a family desperate to avoid gossip. She got out her phone and Grace picked up on the second ring.

'It was me, wasn't it?' she said in a rush.

She heard an intake of breath.

'Wasn't it?' Sariah repeated. 'I was Rose's baby.'

Chapter
Thirty-Seven

Eating a slice of toast while sitting on her sofa, Evelyn heard the ping of a text. She felt inside her pocket and patted a cushion before finding her phone, safe and warm, beneath Toots.

The message began: *Hello, this is Samuel. I am Frances Parfait's carer . . .*

Evelyn felt a swoop of grief, fearing she was too late. But then she scrolled down and realised there was still hope.

She finds it hard to type, so she has dictated this message: Plan sounds intriguing. Please advise. Kind regards, FP

Evelyn tapped out her reply, trying to put her proposal as succinctly as possible. Then she fed Toots, endured her customary hunch under the tepid shower, dressed and ate a second slice of toast while looking out at the Cornish mizzle.

The reply came as she was putting on her boots. It had been typed by Samuel, but the words sounded like Frances's and her meaning was clear.

Dear Evelyn, the news of this cache explains a lot. I suspect Edwin had a kleptomaniac streak. He was a small man with an over-inflated view of his own talents, so I suppose this helped him maintain that fiction. I'm sorry if I sound bitter, but it seems I am.

Your plan appeals. It is only right that the stolen goods are returned to the museum. Of course some say they should be returned to their true homes in Rome, Athens, Cairo and Beijing . . . but that is a debate I shall not live to see resolved.

Anyway, I agree to participate. You know my address. I shall ask Samuel to make the arrangements after my passing.

When you visited I was taken by surprise and I apologise for my poor manners. I should have mentioned how much I enjoyed your company, all those years ago. The museum had high hopes for you – also for your friend Asa, who left shortly after you. I'm glad he went on to thrive in his natural habitat.

Your father's betrayals were many but, as I look back from my point of no return, it wasn't all bad. There were moments of love and joy and I hope you can remember some too.

Kindest regards,
Frances Parfait

It took Evelyn a while to digest the message and she considered several versions of a reply before settling on a simple *Thank you*.

Oh, Asa. If she'd searched for him earlier and more thoroughly, would she have found him? Even if she had, would that have changed the course of her life? She considered Frances's words and tried to imagine Asa's 'natural habitat', immediately discounting London, Edinburgh and America. Then she remembered him talking passionately of the Colosseum and the Parthenon and she typed his name alongside *Rome* into her phone. Finally, she found him hidden away, like a rare treasure, on the staff list of a small Roman museum.

Except these days he went by the name of Asa Bianchi-Lingard. There was no picture on the website, just the grey outline of a head, which felt appropriate because that was how she had trained herself to think of him: indistinct as a shadow.

There and then, she resolved to go no further. She would not google his double-barrelled surname because she couldn't bear to know what other riches Asa's life had included: a handsome son, a clever daughter, a lucky wife. A whole life lived without Evelyn Silver.

Frances's ability to look back without anger was laudable, but Evelyn wasn't at that stage yet.

Shortly, as agreed with Frances, she would go to her museum and write out address labels for the boxes waiting by the door. Then she would arrange for them to be transported to Frances's flat, where their labels and any paperwork would be destroyed. The boxes would be stored in her flat 'for as long as it took' and Evelyn imagined Samuel would stack them neatly next to the dainty telephone table in Frances's hallway. Then, once Frances had passed away, Samuel would complete two final tasks. Frances trusted him and, she said, he would be rewarded for his discretion.

First, he would deliver the boxes to the gates of the British Museum with a typed letter explaining that they had been stolen over the course of several decades by a person once known to Frances Parfait, who wished to return them. The powers that be would immediately be sent into a tailspin. Naturally, they would come looking for more information, but they would find no answers because Frances was no longer available to help.

Any further investigations would also be thwarted. Frances Parfait had been confined to her bed for a long time and had not entertained any visitors. Furthermore, there were no records of phone conversations or text messages as she did not have a mobile phone (the disposal of the pay-as-you-go burner phone Samuel had bought being his second task). It was fortunate that Frances had long been in the habit of ensuring nothing in her possession linked her to a man called Edwin Silver, let alone his daughter.

The thought that her museum would soon be purged of its incriminating secrets cheered Evelyn as she set about her tasks that day. So when Sariah sent a message saying *Fancy a coffee? Could do with a chat. I'm at Della's* she accepted her offer.

◆ ◆ ◆

It was tricky when Della offered you a cup of tea or coffee or a new ice cream flavour, because there was a limit to the excuses one could make. 'Earl Grey tea, please,' Evelyn said, hoping that its milder flavour would be harder to spoil. When it arrived with a mysterious froth on the top, she realised she'd underestimated Della's abilities.

'Shortbread?' Della asked.

'Made by me,' Sariah added hastily. 'I couldn't sleep last night.' She shrugged. 'I also did coffee and walnut biscuits. And I gave the housekeeping team a Victoria sponge.'

Evelyn hadn't had Sariah down as a domestic goddess and she noticed that Sariah's hand shook when she reached for a napkin. But, she reasoned, that could be Della's silt-like coffee.

'I've always found baking quite calming,' Sariah explained.

Her shortbread was a delight: light and buttery, with just a hint of something else.

'Lavender?' Evelyn wondered aloud.

'Correct,' Sariah said. 'And a little lemon zest.'

'Good, eh?' Della wiped her hands on a tea towel. 'Ladies, I gotta pop out. Can I trust you to look after things here?'

'I think we'll cope,' Sariah said.

Della was barely out of the door before Sariah turned to Evelyn. 'I met up with Grace yesterday,' she said. 'She told me some difficult things.'

Evelyn's frothy tea grew cold as she listened to the truth of how Sariah had been brought up by Grace, but that her birth mother had been her aunt, Rose.

'Turns out I was a sort of wedding present – and one they couldn't give back,' she said bitterly. Evelyn had heard of cases like this but from further back in time. It was hard to imagine it happening thirty years ago, but then Sariah explained that the family had been deeply traditional – and Rose was only fifteen.

'Rose was taken out of school and sent away to stay in Plymouth. Mum kept calling this woman "a lady", like she was so right and proper, saving the family from disgrace. But all she did was run a private home, continuing what she'd learned to do at the old mother and baby home, over in St Agnes.'

Sariah began cutting into a slice of shortbread, dividing it into smaller and smaller pieces and then crumbs. 'I feel like something's been pulled out from under me. Like, I've been living one version of my life, but it was never true.'

Evelyn nodded, because she understood that feeling. But somehow, it was easier to give Sariah advice than it was to rationalise her own situation. 'I think it's important to remember that you are still your own person, Sariah, no matter who gave birth to you. And from what I can see, you've made a good job of it.'

Sariah used a napkin to wipe her nose. 'Thanks.'

Just then, Della bustled back in with a carton of oat milk and saw Sariah mopping her tears. 'Gee, Evelyn, thanks for lifting the mood. Must invite you in more often.'

Somehow, Della had managed to make Sariah laugh and the conversation turned to Della's latest business idea. 'Once the café is a success, I'm gonna branch out, start making my own products,' she announced.

'Cakes?' Sariah asked.

'Hmm, no, that's more your bag. I see another gap in the market.' Della set the carton she'd bought down on the counter with a thunk. 'Think oat milk, but high class.'

'Oh?' Evelyn said.

'I'm gonna call it Haut Milk.' Della looked at them expectantly. 'Good, eh?'

Evelyn got up to leave. 'Great shortbread,' she said. Then, to Sariah, 'I'm here if you want to chat more.'

All afternoon, she thought of Sariah's family, who had sent Rose away rather than have a pregnant bridesmaid at their elder daughter's wedding and how this 'lady' had taken Rose in. Remembering what Sariah had said about mother and baby homes, she set about searching for more information. Sariah was right: such homes hadn't only existed in Ireland. There had been several in Devon and Cornwall, mostly run by charitable institutions. One on the north coast had taken in women and girls until 1964, while another in Plymouth was in existence until 1969. Then she found a Facebook support group for people who had given birth or been born in these homes, and she didn't move from her chair for the next hour.

She read of pregnant girls who had to forage for firewood to keep warm, who were made to scrub, polish and sweep or do laundry at the huge boiling copper. A link took her to a radio programme, where she heard an elderly woman talk about dressing her newborn baby, knowing it would soon be taken from her. She heard how girls watched from upstairs windows as their babies were put in prams that were wheeled out and arranged on the lawn so prospective couples could pick out one they liked. This was recounted by a woman who had given birth in the home in St Agnes.

She closed her laptop and shivered because the air had turned cold. Her mind circled back to those two words: St Agnes. When Frances Parfait was told some scrap of information by Edwin, might she have only half understood his words – heard the name Agnes and assumed it was the name of a woman?

With shaking hands, she texted Frances's number and although she kept checking her phone all evening, there was no reply.

The message arrived early the next morning, as Evelyn was getting ready to leave the caravan.

It is with sadness that I have to tell you that Frances Parfait died in the early hours of this morning. I am sorry for your loss. Samuel.

A hollowness opened up inside her, a grief for a woman she wished she'd known better. In turn, this made her long for her quiet mother Elsbeth – eternally searching for the right words but never saying them. Then a more complicated grief rushed in, for the unknown woman who had given birth to her.

Chapter Thirty-Eight

There was an image Evelyn couldn't get out of her head: a circle of prams arranged on a lawn and well-dressed couples strolling from one to the next, peering inside. Was the baby pretty enough? The right colouring? The gender they wanted? It was obscene, yet this had been a practice at the mother and baby home she'd read about.

Had Evelyn been one of those babies, picked out by Edwin and Elsbeth Silver, who had made up the foundling story to conceal her true origins? Or, if the foundling story was true, had her mother given birth in St Agnes and then left her baby somewhere like a church porch?

The sun was making a slow, undramatic appearance above the line of trees when Evelyn locked up her caravan and walked out onto the main road where, instead of continuing down to the harbour, she waited for the first bus to Truro. Once there, she bought a cup of bad coffee and a surprisingly good flapjack and then, along with half a dozen schoolchildren, she got a second bus towards the north coast. By 9 a.m., Evelyn was standing in the softly falling rain in the village of St Agnes.

The bus stop was opposite the parish church and, telling herself she just wanted to get out of the rain, she walked up the path to the hefty wooden door. Church had not been a part of her childhood Sundays – science trumped religion in the Silver household – but the cool interior immediately reminded her of school carol services, harvest festivals and St Piran's Day.

She gazed up at the ceiling timbers that looked like an upturned boat, then down at the wooden parquet flooring, which had been recently polished.

This was foolish, she told herself, but just as she turned to leave, a jolly voice called out from the darker depths of the church, 'Oh, you're early.'

Looking left and right, Evelyn wondered if she could still make her escape.

'But I always think early is better than late.' The voice came again, then footsteps and a rotund woman wearing a blue V-neck sweater with a dog collar emerged from the gloom.

'Hello, I'm Carol.' The vicar held out her hand. 'Welcome to St Agnes.'

This was clearly a case of mistaken identity, but Evelyn instinctively liked Carol.

'Thank you,' she replied. 'I'm Evelyn – and probably not who you were expecting.'

'Oh.' Carol cocked her head to one side. 'Not my ten o'clock flower arranger then?'

'Sadly not.'

'Well, welcome anyway.' Carol gestured around her. 'Feel free to sit for a while.'

Succumbing to a wave of tiredness, Evelyn eased herself into a pew and let her head drop forward, a move that Carol mistook as an act of supplication and she came and knelt beside her. 'Let us pray.'

Sounds from outside drifted in: the distant peep-peep of a delivery van reversing, the gentle rustle of leaves and the chatter of birdsong. After what Evelyn hoped was a sufficiently pious interval, she cleared her throat.

'I should be getting on.'

'Of course.' There was a pause. 'Unless there's anything else?'

Oh there was more, so much more, but it was hard to know where to begin. 'I'm not from around here,' she said eventually. 'But I wonder if my mother might have stayed in the village for a while. A long time ago.'

Carol continued looking ahead and rested her hands in her lap. 'We haven't had a visitor like yourself for a while,' she said. 'Each time someone comes, I think it will be the last. Every story is different, but all of them are heart-breaking.'

There was a relief in not having to explain it all from the start. 'I'm not certain that I was born there, though,' she said. 'It's unconfirmed. It's complicated.'

'It often is,' Carol said. She had curly hair that surrounded her head in a mousy halo and dimples formed in her round cheeks when she smiled. She reached into the front pocket of her slacks, brought out a tube of extra strong mints and offered one to Evelyn.

'The church didn't run the home, but it was not blameless. The girls came every Sunday, marched through town in a crocodile and then were made to sit on their own. From what I gather, some villagers were sympathetic, but not all.' Carol popped a mint into her own mouth and Evelyn heard a dull crunching. She worried for Carol's molars.

'What year are we talking about?'

'I was born in 1964, the year it closed. I suppose I've come looking for a record of my arrival.'

Evelyn was picturing herself as a bundle of blankets, laid inside the church, but Carol misunderstood her.

'Sadly, this might not be the best place to look for baptism records. Plenty of babies were born in this village, but they were often baptised elsewhere. If the mother kept her baby, that would be back in her home parish. If the baby was adopted, it would be wherever those parents lived. Either way, that could be out of county.'

'How do you mean?'

'Lots of the girls that came to St Agnes weren't from Cornwall. If a girl in, say, Manchester or Bristol got in trouble, it was easier if she disappeared to a place where no one knew her.'

'I see.'

Carol patted her leg. 'But let's have a look, hey.'

This made Evelyn curious, so she followed Carol to a corner of the church, where she saw shelves of books and several plastic crates of toys. 'Toddler group at eleven,' Carol explained and unlocked a tall wooden cupboard. Standing on tiptoe, she talked to herself. 'OK, 1964 . . .' She ran her finger along the spines of the leather-bound books and tugged one down. 'Here we go.'

Carol opened up the ledger for 1963–5. Evelyn saw handwritten rows of names and the date of each baptism. All the records for 1964 were in the same italic script and bore the same signature. She pointed at it and looked hopefully at Carol.

'The late Father Harris, I'm afraid. His successor was Father Lane, also passed. I came here ten years ago and I expect I'll be referred to as "the new lady vicar" for another ten or more.'

There was a temptation to turn the pages more slowly, putting off the moment when there was the smallest chance her own name might appear. She saw an Edith, two Margarets, an Alice and a Nora, but no Evelyn. She had reached January 1965 when Carol looked over her shoulder.

'You'll notice that the dates of baptism are often a while after the date of birth, so don't panic if you don't see anything around your birthday. That's if you know the date?'

'The only date I have is the day when I was given up by my mother, which was in December 1964. I suppose I might have been born earlier. I was a foundling, you see.' She gave a small, embarrassed laugh. 'I almost wondered if I was left here. On the steps of this church.'

Evelyn got out her phone and showed Carol a photograph of her lace.

'This was pinned to my blanket, like an old-fashioned identifier.' Then Evelyn stopped talking because she didn't want to cry, not here in a church, with a nice lady vicar she barely knew.

'That is a very lovely piece of lacework,' Carol said thoughtfully. 'I'm not saying it's impossible, but I doubt very much that you were left in this church. If that story is true, it must have been somewhere else.'

'Why?'

'A foundling, well, it's the sort of thing that I'd have been told when I arrived. It would have been part of the church's history, plus social services would have been called in and there would have been reports. But most of all, someone in the congregation would know, because things tend to stick in locals' memories a long time,' Carol said. Then she added with a wink, 'If I tell you there remains a long-running rumour about who stole the communion wine in the Christmas of 1969, you'll get the picture.'

There was a knock at the door. 'I'm sorry, that'll be my ten o'clock. Wedding flowers.'

'It's OK, I think I'm done.' Evelyn sighed.

'Don't give up,' Carol said. 'Lots of people do DNA tests these days and find their birth family that way. I'm guessing your adoptive parents are . . .'

'Yes, gone. And they were never big sharers, anyway. The most my mother said was, "And then we were three."'

'And your father?'

'I'm learning that he lied as easily as he breathed,' she said bitterly.

Carol saw her to the door. 'I hope you find the answers you need.' She reached for Evelyn's hands. 'But whatever did happen, you can be sure that your mother loved you. It wouldn't have been her choice to give you up and she didn't forget you.'

Evelyn looked down at Carol's clean, smooth hands and thought how nice it would be to lead a life where you felt cool certainty instead of raging self-doubt.

Evelyn's business here was done. It was still possible that her mother had given birth in St Agnes, but she could have hailed from anywhere – Norwich or Swindon or London – and returned home after her baby was born. A small scrap of lace had never been enough to find her. As the bus back to Truro swerved around the tight corners and wet branches scraped against its windows, darker thoughts began to form in her mind.

Her father had spun so many tales over the years: that he was a respected academic, that the boxes in her museum contained worthless donations and that he'd never canoodled in Rules with Frances Parfait. For all Evelyn knew, he could have found that scrap of lace at an antiques fair, paid pennies for it and turned it into another tall tale for his own entertainment.

She'd treasured that fragment of lace, seeing it as a thread connecting her to her past. But now its strands were fraying, attached to nothing, and Evelyn felt as if she was coming apart too.

Chapter Thirty-Nine

Dear New Owner of Sailing Ship,
I have deliberately put this painting into a local jumble sale in the hope that someone buys it simply because they like the picture.

If you happen to be a dealer who thinks they have struck gold with an undiscovered Alfred Wallis, I advise you to calm down because I am almost certain this is not by Wallis's hand. The strokes are too tentative and the image feels flat. To my mind, Wallis's work expresses a genuine love of the sea. This painting, however, is the antithesis of that. It is a fake.

It was acquired by my husband in 1987. Did he know it was fake? Let's give him the benefit of the doubt and say no.

That was the year he'd tried to win back an old flame but she had the good sense to turn him down. To ask for my forgiveness, he bought me this 'token of love'. The irony of it being fake is not lost on me.

From the start, our marriage was one of convenience and my husband was unfaithful many times over the years. I turned a blind eye. But when he tried to go back to his first love, that hurt.

I have shared too much. But I wanted you to know that this small painting carries a story of woe. For many years it has hung on my bedroom wall and each time I gazed at it, I detested my husband a little more. Now, I am getting rid of it for good and it will be a relief never to set eyes on it or its fake sentiments ever again.

C W, October 2019, Cornwall

After reading the letter that he'd found secreted inside the frame, Jacob slid it back inside its envelope and propped it up beside the painting. Now he'd digested the information, it occurred to Jacob that his father Simon also deserved to know the contents of the letter. Jacob tried ringing him, but there was no answer and then he remembered he and Juniper were on holiday in Italy, probably drinking wine and eating arancini or whatever it was they did on those trips. A bombshell like that might spoil their appetite. But then Jacob wondered if the letter would come as such a surprise to his father.

Jacob couldn't bear to stay in his room looking at the wretched painting a moment longer. Grabbing his jacket, he bounced down the stairs two at a time and emerged onto the street, where the air was heavy with sea mist. It was the sort of day when visitors trailed from gift shops to cafés, never quite satisfied, and he felt much the same.

A couple of weeks ago, he'd have headed for the gym, but since Alison left it had lost its allure. He couldn't even while away a few hours at The Lugger because since the exhibition, he'd been quietly advised to stay away. 'Roy is a regular, so best you keep a low profile,' Arnold the landlord had told him.

For want of anything better to do, Jacob got into his souped-up Mini and set off towards Fowey. As he reached the outskirts, Jacob told himself he'd come to visit the new deli, which stocked local cheeses and sausages and those nice Spanish crackers flavoured with rosemary that he used to get from Waitrose. But as he parked in a quiet cul-de-sac, he admitted the truth: he'd come to check on Michael, the man who had told him and Alison about fishing knots but who hadn't come to the exhibition and wasn't answering his landline phone.

As Jacob retraced the steps he'd made with Alison and her baby, a visit that seemed to belong to a time when life was so much simpler, he wished more than ever that she was by his side. At Michael Bower's bungalow, the curtains were closed and his rubbish bin had been left askew on the front path, neither of which squared with the polite, punctilious man they had met several weeks ago.

Jacob rang the doorbell and looked up and down the street, suddenly self-conscious. It was strange, Jacob thought, how a bell could sound different when no one was home, emptier somehow. From inside, not even the barking of Michael's small dog disturbed the air.

He stepped back from the porch and looked up at the windows. He hoped this meant Michael had gone on holiday or was visiting family. But there was a horrible inevitability when he heard the sound of a next-door neighbour opening their front door. They too had a dog, a scampering black-furred thing on short legs that ran down their path and up Michael's until it was circling around Jacob's feet, snuffling and whining.

'Sorry, he's too quick for me.' A woman in an old-fashioned housecoat followed in his doggy wake, trying to grab his collar. 'It's the doorbell – soon as he hears it he waits by the front door and then he's off.'

'I was looking for Michael, but it doesn't look like he's in.' Jacob felt acutely embarrassed to be putting out Michael's neighbour.

'Stop, come . . .' The woman was making lunges at the dog but it was too quick for her.

Jacob reached down and took hold of its collar and waited for the woman to pick it up.

'Good boy,' she said, stroking its head, although Jacob could see no evidence this was true. 'So, you a friend of Michael? Family?'

'Neither. He helped with some information for an exhibition we had in Portheast and I wanted to update him. Tell him how it went,' Jacob said.

'Oh, I see.' At that, the woman put the errant terrier on a lead and let him sniff around the porch and the grass, as if she didn't want to say any more within the dog's hearing. 'Michael was admitted to hospital, few weeks back,' she explained.

'Is he OK?' Jacob wasn't sure he could take more bad news in one day.

'He's doing well,' the woman said. 'Fell in the park and broke his leg. Waiting to get a care package in place before they'll let him come home. Either way, he won't be walking this one for a while.'

They both watched the small dog cock a leg and mark a flowerpot as his own.

'I'm sure Michael would welcome a visit,' she added.

'Thanks, I'll do that.'

'Meanwhile, this little tyke is driving us mad. Already got three dogs of our own, see, and they don't get on. But what was I going to do – turn him away? Send him to the pound?'

An hour later, Jacob was back on the road. In the back of his car he had two feeding bowls, a bag of kibble, four tins of food and what he was told was a 'donut' bed that smelled of wet dog.

Oh, and Max, a terrier puppy of indeterminate breed. To repeat the words of Michael's frazzled neighbour: what was he going to do – turn him away?

The neighbour managed to get through to Michael on the ward telephone and explained the situation. 'But there's a nice young man here, called Jacob, from Portheast. Says he came to see you about some knots? That make any sense?'

That evening, as he and Max settled down to watch *The Dog House*, two good things occurred to Jacob. The first was that he'd barely glanced at the painting since he'd got back, because it turned out that looking after a puppy was a full-time job. The second was that he'd promised to visit Michael in hospital, which was the perfect excuse for getting back in touch with Alison.

Chapter Forty

It was 2 a.m. and Sariah couldn't sleep, because whenever she closed her eyes, she kept remembering the last time Auntie Rose had visited. It had been at Easter shortly before Sariah left home, and Rose had turned up unannounced.

Grace wasn't the sort of mum who liked surprises so the two sisters spent a good fifteen minutes shut in the front room conducting an argument in strained whispers. Sariah and her brothers listened to the high-octane hissing match from the hallway and caught a few words like 'no warning' and 'not fair'.

Finally, the two sisters emerged, tight-lipped and heads held high, and the day continued as if nothing had happened. After lunch, they all crammed into the living room to watch the film *Shark Tale* on TV, with the grown-ups on the sofa and armchair and the kids sitting on cushions on the floor.

Her mum and dad soon fell asleep, leaving their strait-laced Auntie Rose watching with them. She had thin legs and wore thick tan tights, which were at eye level with Sariah, who resisted the urge to reach out and give the material a ping, to see what it felt like.

The boys were lying spreadeagled, a tangle of shiny football shorts and smelly socks, but Sariah remained sitting up, her back against the armchair. She didn't think much of the film, so she'd been trying to put her hair into a French braid, but her hair wasn't really long enough and bits kept springing loose. As she yanked the scrunchie off in frustration for the third or fourth time, she felt a hand reach down and take it.

She sat very still as Auntie Rose, who never had a hair out of place, started over. Sariah felt gentle hands smoothing out the kinks in her hair, then dividing it into even sections. When she was almost done, Rose's fingers had accidentally brushed against the red worry spot behind Sariah's ear and just for a moment, her hand stilled. Then she'd continued like nothing was wrong before securing the scrunchie and planting a swift kiss on the top of Sariah's head.

When the film titles rolled, the boys came out of their TV trance and began wrestling each other, waking Grace up. Sariah stepped out into the hallway and dared to admire herself in the mirror, and for once her French braid looked neat and it somehow made her cheekbones look good too. When Grace passed behind her, their eyes met in the mirror but her mother's expression was unreadable.

Sariah had been wronged, that much was certain. She'd been lied to and her bond with Grace had got off to the shakiest start. But lying awake, she began to see this situation from Grace's point of view. Grace had been made to grow up and become a mother sooner than she'd wanted and, in the process, she'd also lost her relationship with her sister. They had both been forced into a silent pact that neither could find a way out of.

Grace had mentioned Rose was back in Cornwall and that they kept in touch, but Sariah wondered what those occasions were like and if they ever talked about the things that mattered.

She gave up trying to sleep and turned on her bedside light. It was 4 a.m. and the building was quiet, bar the odd creak of a floorboard or the distant flush of a loo, but it wouldn't stay like that for long. The hotel's staff quarters were in the Warburns' old servants' rooms and her suite was located above the main boiler, which would start up soon. Sometimes it was like living over a giant kettle.

She thought of her mum Grace, who had dressed up to meet her in that awful café and the way she'd held her cheap shoulder bag so tightly as she dashed out of the café. Grace was far from perfect, but she had reached out to Sariah, trying to make amends.

It was still early, but Sariah had a feeling that she wasn't the only one awake. She dialled her mother's number before working out what to say, but it was OK, because when Grace answered she said, 'Hello, love' and that was all Sariah needed to hear.

Chapter
Forty-One

There was still no word on the future of the boat sheds.

'I can't bear this waiting,' Della said, stomping into Evelyn's museum. 'Honestly, I just saw Mr Palmer at the back of the chemists and he barely acknowledged me. His face was as cold and blank as one of your precious beach stones,' she complained, gesturing at the Natural History cabinet.

Evelyn wondered if accosting a council officer in the suppositories and haemorrhoid cream aisle was the wisest move, but she suspected Mr Palmer was avoiding Della for another reason. She could feel it in her bones: their campaign was doomed.

With her resolutely upbeat outlook, Della didn't see it that way. 'Listen, once we get the council's OK, I've got big plans for my café. Ice creams are out and old-fashioned cakes are in. I'm going to rename it The Cake Shed and I've asked Sariah to come in with me. What do you reckon?'

'Sounds great.' Evelyn tried to sound positive, but her heart wasn't in it.

'Then, once my turnover improves, I'm serious about linking the two sheds. We can do a bit of a joint rebrand, hey?'

Then Della talked some more about things like increased footfall and synergy, before leaving Evelyn alone in her boat shed museum. Since George had helped her sort it out, it looked tidier than she could ever remember. It was cleaner too and the smell of briny ropes was slowly being replaced by the scent of beeswax.

The Second Chances exhibition had been taken down and the items were back in their old cabinets, except for the two that had been returned to their owners: the cracked cup and the fake boat painting. She was still waiting to hear what Alison and her dad wanted to do about the embroidered sailcloth.

The exhibition stands were stacked neatly at the back of the museum, in the spot the Cornish Life diorama once occupied. That travesty no longer existed and the best kitchenware had been transferred to the Seems Like Yesterday cabinet (George taking the opportunity to weed out a rusted egg whisk, several dirty milk bottles and those unappetising varnished pasties).

It was George, too, who suggested the mannequins might have served their time and, with relief, Evelyn had agreed. Kayla from the pub loaded them into her dad's estate car and drove them to Truro, where her cousin worked in the Cornwall Air Ambulance charity shop and wanted some dummies for the window display.

It had been a tight fit and in the end Mrs Cornish Life had to travel with her left hand sticking out of the passenger window as if giving a royal wave, while Mr Cornish Life was bent double, his rear squashed against the back window in a most undignified way. 'Got a few funny looks from other drivers,' Kayla remarked.

Kayla said her cousin had studied window dressing and wanted to go with a beach theme. She'd left her wrestling the female mannequin into a skimpy sundress, while the male one was dressed in baggy board shorts and a Rip Curl T-shirt. His wig had been ditched in favour of a green bucket hat with a logo that announced

Surf's Up. Kayla's cousin decided he had 'mean eyes', so she covered them up with a pair of gigantic mirror shades.

All this tidying and dismantling only added to Evelyn's fear that this was the beginning of the end for the Portheast Museum of Maritime Curiosities. Even if by some miracle the museum was saved, she wondered if she was the best person to look after it.

'It's too full of old memories,' she explained to Sariah, who arrived later that day bearing a Tupperware box containing a Cornish Hevva cake.

Although the future of Della's shed was still up in the air, Sariah was already trying out every recipe she knew, and Evelyn was only too happy to be her official taster.

'I know what you mean,' Sariah replied, cutting two generous slices of the currant-rich cake. 'I'm starting to think I need a fresh start, too.'

'Yes, Della mentioned you two might be teaming up. As long as the council lets her stay.'

As they ate, Evelyn told Sariah how she'd put two and two together and taken a trip to the church in St Agnes and that while it had come to nothing, she had met a very nice lady vicar called Carol.

'What about doing what the vicar said and signing up to one of those DNA websites?' Sariah asked.

Evelyn shook her head. 'No, it's time to move on,' she said firmly.

'I get that,' Sariah replied. 'But you've been curious for a long time.'

Evelyn was reconciled to never slotting her own jigsaw pieces into place and maybe that was for the best. 'My father was never to be believed,' she said. 'But I think that if my mother had wanted me to know more, she would have told me. So there's probably a reason why she didn't. Uncovering one secret can open a whole can of worms.'

'That's true,' Sariah said. 'Funnily enough, I've been in contact with my mum, Grace, a few times.'

Evelyn reached out and squeezed Sariah's hand.

'We've arranged to meet again. And she's going to ask Auntie Rose if she wants to come.'

'Well done,' she said. 'I'm proud of you.' And she was because Sariah deserved this chance to piece together her own story.

'Thanks.' Sariah fell silent and then, in a brighter voice, she asked, 'The Hevva cake. Marks out of ten?'

'Twelve,' said Evelyn. 'Best I've tasted.'

'Well, that's down to my Grandma Karensa really, because it was her recipe and not one you'll find in any book.' Sariah licked her fingers. 'That said, when I told Mum about the Cake Shed idea, she reminded me about Grandma's old 1950s cookery book. I can picture it so clearly: it was full of her scribbles in the margins, where she'd added her own ingredients. So beside the recipe for chocolate sponge, she'd written "add teaspoon coffee" and next to the one for shortbread she'd put "lemon zest".' Sariah let slip a smile. 'In fact, I've asked if she can bring the book along when we meet. It'll be a big help if this plan comes off.'

'Let's keep everything crossed,' Evelyn replied.

From beyond the open door came the sound of claws scrabbling on concrete and excited yapping and they turned to catch sight of Jacob disappearing down the quay, attached to a small, manic puppy by a lead.

'Unexpected turn of events,' said Sariah.

'Very,' agreed Evelyn, taking the opportunity to cut herself another slice of cake while Sariah was looking the other way.

The funny thing was, from a business point of view, she could see that linking the museum and the café was an excellent idea. But whether Mr Palmer and his suits would view it that way was a different matter.

Chapter
Forty-Two

Jacob could not believe how much work was involved in looking after a puppy. He'd fondly imagined a couple of leisurely walks, perhaps a spot of ball-throwing on the beach if the sun came out. Then, at the end of the day his faithful hound would sleep at the foot of his bed until morning. He didn't know about the constant demands to play, the razor-sharp teeth, the accidental wees and the way that everything from his favourite trainers to his phone charger was fair game for gnawing.

Then there was the lack of sleep. Max woke several times in the night, whimpering to be taken outside. When Jacob started his morning shift Max cried again, so loudly that Jacob brought him down and tried to settle him on a blanket behind the newsagents' counter. But every time the door opened, Max woke up, desperate to say hello and play.

By the end of his shift, Jacob was exhausted. And he still had to take Max for his proper walk. He headed down to the beach (Max had discovered digging in a big way) but there was no time to stop off at the boat sheds to say hello to Della and Evelyn, because Jacob was on a schedule. Soon, he was due to pick up Alison so that the three of them could go and visit Michael in hospital.

By the time Jacob's Mini pulled up outside Alison's dad's house, he'd changed his clothes, fluffed up his hair, brushed his teeth twice and given his armpits an extra spray of deodorant. Keith was happy to look after his grandson Will for the afternoon, so Jacob was savouring the idea of it being just him and Alison. But he hadn't bargained for Max. As soon as they set off, the pup jumped into the front and settled on Alison's lap with a satisfied yawn.

'Funny little thing, isn't he?' Alison remarked, giving his scruffy ears a scratch. 'What breed do you reckon he is?'

'Part Patterdale, part Tasmanian Devil is my guess,' Jacob replied.

'Bit of a handful then?'

Jacob blanched. 'You could say that.'

'It's all about establishing a routine.' She smiled. 'A bit like toddlers.'

'Thanks, I'll bear that in mind.'

As he drove, Jacob tried to sneak glances at Alison. She seemed different today, quieter yet more self-assured.

'I need to find a new job,' she announced. 'The sports centre let me go, but I hated it there anyway.'

'What about trying the PR company where you used to work?' he replied.

'Ah, I'm not sure they need anyone.'

'Well, you were clearly good at it and you had some great ideas for the Save Our Museum campaign.'

'Yeah. Until I stopped coming to the meetings.' Alison gave a small shiver, then stroked the tufts of hair on Max's head. 'I'm sorry for what happened – what Roy did to you at the museum.'

'Oh, all forgotten,' Jacob lied. 'I find it's best to ignore bullies.'

'But that just allows them to carry on bullying,' Alison said calmly. 'From now on, I'm going to call them out.'

Jacob felt chastened. 'You're right, but I know it's easier said than done. Especially when you're facing it every day. When it's incremental.'

Alison had turned her face away, but he heard that her breathing had changed, becoming broken, and he realised he'd said the wrong thing. 'Oh no, sorry, please don't cry.'

'I'm OK.' She found a tissue in her bag. 'Or I will be.'

'How's your dad?' Jacob thought he was changing the subject, but there was no way to avoid how Roy's actions had seeped into everyone's lives.

'He feels bad too, says he should have seen what was happening.' She rolled her shoulders and let out a breath. 'But we've had some honest chats recently, which has been good. For as long as I can remember, my dad has never been big on talking. Even after my mum died, he never spoke about his feelings. He thought he was protecting me, I suppose, by keeping it all in.'

'I'm so sorry. How old were you?' Jacob asked.

'I was eleven. Just started secondary school.' She gave a shrug. 'It was every bit as awful as you'd imagine, but we both pretended we were coping – didn't want to let the other down. But now, he's finally starting to open up.'

'My dad isn't great at talking, either,' Jacob confessed. 'Not that we went through anything as bad as that.'

'The Second Chances exhibition also threw up some family stuff,' Alison continued. 'There was a keepsake in the museum that revealed my grandpa had a secret love. So we talked about that, too.'

'Really?'

'Yes. It was the embroidered picture. The one that said *Wish we could sail away together*. It was a gift, made by my Grandpa Fred. Except it wasn't for my grandma. It was for his true love, who happened to be called Steven.'

'Gosh, that's quite a thing to find out – especially for your dad.'

'I know. The thing is, I wonder if my dad already knew, deep down. He said it always felt like his parents had come to "an accommodation" in their marriage. They were the best of friends and they were loving parents, but they weren't in love.'

'Well, that's more than many couples achieve,' Jacob said.

'True.'

'Sorry, I didn't mean you and Roy,' Jacob added, afraid he'd said the wrong thing again.

'No, I know you didn't. But you're not far wrong. A child needs to grow up seeing people being honest, don't they? Not learning fake smiles and fear.' Alison fell silent.

'And where is Roy these days?' Jacob felt he had to ask.

'He's moved in with his brother. Turns out he hadn't paid the rent on our house for months and we were about to be evicted anyway. Everything was on the verge of falling apart, but I couldn't see it. Or I didn't want to.'

At the hospital, Alison went up to the ward to find Michael, and Jacob waited outside the main entrance with Max, who was a big hit with everyone who passed by.

'Soon you'll see your real Daddy, won't you?' he told Max, realising too late that he'd become a person who talked to dogs. 'Pretend I didn't say that,' he added and Max gave an obliging wag of his tail.

Then the doors opened and Alison and Michael came out, him making steady progress with a pair of crutches. 'There's my boy,' he called out and, at the sound of Michael's voice, Max made straight for him. 'There, little lad. There, there,' Michael said and Jacob lifted the dog up so he could cover Michael's face with his licks.

As Alison remarked on the way home, 'Quite the reunion. Not a dry eye in the house.'

Jacob was driving home a different way, because Alison had asked to make a stop in St Mawes. As they got closer, her previous confidence seemed to evaporate and she grew quieter. She explained that she had brought the embroidered picture made by her grandfather.

'I thought it was best to return it to its rightful owner. It's what my Grandpa Fred would have wanted and my dad agrees.'

'That's a good thing you're doing,' Jacob told her. 'Not everyone would be so generous.'

'It just feels right,' she said as he pulled up outside the address she'd given him. 'I rang him last night and he told me how it got lost. His daughter did a big clear-out when he moved into this house and sent lots of his old clothes to charity. She managed to scoop up this picture too.'

'By accident?'

'Hmm, he didn't say. But he sounded pretty overwhelmed when I said he could have it back.' She unfurled the stiff sailcloth and gave it one last look. 'Good job Evelyn loves a charity shop rummage and has an eye for treasure.'

Then Alison closed the car door softly and walked up the path to a cottage with a neat front lawn and well-tended borders. Jacob watched as a snowy-haired man answered the door and Alison held out the roll of sailcloth. The old man seemed to sway a little, then he raised his hand to his forehead. He said something, with a questioning look in his eyes. Alison glanced back at Jacob; he gave her an encouraging nod and watched her step inside the house.

Both their grandfathers, it turned out, had led secret lives, but had left behind clues that had ended up in Evelyn's museum. Jacob hoped Evelyn knew the good she'd done in bringing those truths out – and in bringing people together.

Chapter
Forty-Three

Evelyn didn't like being told what to do. And she really didn't like it when George Rook was doing the telling.

'Your typewritten labels are all very charming, but how about we usher in the new era with some more professional-looking ones?' he suggested, setting a printer down on her desk. Evelyn gave a sniff and informed him that she'd done her best with the tools at her disposal. Then George reminded her that the council's final deadline was only five weeks away. 'What if they pay you another visit? First impressions count.'

'Fine,' she replied and set off to see if the newsagents sold white card for George's printer. All the way there she fumed. Since when was George Rook with his moth-eaten Barbour jacket and his baggy corduroy trousers an expert on making a good impression?

But once inside the shop, she didn't make it to the stationery section because there on the counter were the day's newspapers.

On the front page of *The Daily Telegraph* she read the headline: *Priceless relics returned to British Museum. Cache of rare artefacts abandoned outside museum leaves experts baffled.*

Wordlessly, she picked up a paper. This left two remaining on the counter and, in a panic, she snatched those up too, anxious no one else should see the headline. She paid Jacob and, with effort, folded all three newspapers under her arm.

'Interesting story,' Jacob remarked, tweaking his fledgling moustache like some hipster Poirot.

'What?'

'In the newspaper.'

She opened the wodge of *Telegraphs* and surveyed the back page. 'I see nothing untoward,' she said and walked briskly out of the door.

That Jacob was too sharp for his own good, she thought as she scurried back to the safety of the museum.

'George,' she hissed, locking the door behind her. 'The deed is done.'

She smoothed one of the newspapers out on her desk and together they pored over it. The story continued on page three, which showed a photograph of a baffled-looking curator looking down at several items laid out on a pristine white cloth. George got out his magnifying loupe to study it in more detail.

'Oh, please,' said Evelyn irritably. 'Do you need to be so pretentious?'

'Actually, it's quite useful,' George said and passed it to her. Annoyingly, he was right, because with the help of his magnifying glass she could make out an ancient Egyptian funerary urn, a porcelain vase and several Roman coins.

The story was short on facts, but told them all they needed to know.

In the early hours of Tuesday morning, a delivery driver double-parked outside the British Museum and unloaded several boxes onto the pavement. Barry Hotwell, 22, told detectives he believed he was dropping off cleaning supplies.

His delivery unwittingly triggered a security alert, but when the boxes were opened in a controlled environment, officers found they contained ancient artefacts from around the globe. 'This is a substantial and diverse collection,' said Sir Nicholas Alaric, Director of the museum. 'We have a promising lead regarding the source and an investigation is ongoing.'

'Promising lead indeed,' Evelyn spluttered. 'We gave them a letter spelling it out.'

It was a relief that no suspicion had fallen on the delivery driver and she guessed that, by now, the police would have discovered that Frances Parfait was not able to assist them with any enquiries.

It appeared that Samuel had done his job well and Evelyn dared to let the relief seep in.

'It's done,' she laughed. 'That stuff is out of my life.'

'It is. And now it's time for a fresh start for you and your museum,' George said.

'If they let us stay,' she cautioned.

'But they must. The museum is the best it's ever been and Della is getting her act together next door. This could be the start of something great.' He reached out and placed a hand lightly on hers. 'See it as a second chance, Evelyn. You deserve it.'

She looked down, trying not to notice how close they were standing and the way George's eyes hadn't left her face. She could smell his cologne again, that odd combination of freesias and lemon.

'But I don't deserve it, do I? I've caused so much pain,' she confessed. 'I made a poster of objects that could have stayed happily hidden. I let stolen artefacts appear on a website. I exposed at least one love affair and a family secret. And, George, let's not forget I exposed you as a fraudster – surely you can't think that was a good thing?'

She didn't say it out loud, but the only thing she hadn't managed to uncover was her own story.

George let go of her hand and she assumed he was contemplating the damage she'd wreaked. But then he started to shake his head.

'Evelyn, you can't see it, can you?'

'What?'

'The good you've done. You've brought people together, people who used to just nod at each other. Even if they did stop for a chat, they didn't always talk properly, about the things that matter.' He gave a mirthless laugh. 'Most of them certainly never gave me the time of day – or you, I'll bet.'

She supposed that much was true.

'The Save Our Museum campaign gave people a reason to work together,' he continued. 'They found out things about each other as well as themselves. Yes, some truths must have been hard to accept – Keith didn't expect to see his father's affair announced in black and white and Jacob had to be told his family heirloom was painted by yours truly. But I don't reckon any of us would want to turn back the clock.'

Could this be true? In Evelyn's experience, the truth was something people tried hard to conceal, but George was saying otherwise.

'Truths are what help us move on, Evelyn. Take me – I've wanted to leave my dad's dodgy dealings in the past for a long time now. Word of that forgery will soon spread and no one will buy a painting from Rook Antiques again, but that's fine by me.'

It was like one of those optical illusion drawings, Evelyn thought. Did you see a duck or a rabbit? A young woman or an old crone? Had the exhibition been a disaster or the beginning of something better?

'The things your dad stole are back where he found them. You've returned personal keepsakes to the right people, and the museum has a clean slate,' George told her. He walked over to the few remaining paintings that hung on the wall. 'What you need, Evelyn, is another exhibition. Something to make you fall in love with this place all over again. How about an art show?' he mused.

'Sorry, George, but even to me that sounds like the most boring exhibition ever.'

'Oh, I think you might be surprised by how many people
would come,' George added in that smug tone of his she found
particularly annoying.

'Absolutely not. Besides, the last thing I need right now is more
surprises,' she replied.

Chapter Forty-Four

It hadn't been her choice, but Sariah found herself back in her least favourite café, the Copper Pot, where she was greeted by the same frowning waitress and the words, 'We're out of scones, you know.' If that was where leaving a £2 tip got you, she wouldn't bother next time. She'd arrived early, which meant she had the chance to rearrange the chairs her way, setting three around a table, all nicely spaced out. Then she moved the vase of plastic flowers into the centre and she sat and waited.

The bell above the door and a gust of wind announced Grace's arrival. Nothing more had been said about Rose joining them but Sariah had hoped the sisters would come together, but there was Grace on her own, doing battle with a retractable umbrella.

'Sorry, am I late?' she asked, seemingly unaware of the drips of rainwater she had scattered onto the table and Sariah's sleeve.

'No, I was early.' Sariah discreetly placed a hand over her sleeve and wiped it dry. As Grace settled in, Sariah noticed that for once her mum wasn't carrying her voluminous, unattractive black bag, the one with chain handles and a chunky zip, and she felt the cold drop of disappointment: it meant she hadn't brought Grandma Karensa's cookery book.

They kept their order simple, a pot of tea, and chatted about the weather and Sariah's tentative plan to go in with Della and launch The Cake Shed together.

'If the council lets you stay,' Grace reminded her.

'Yes, Mum. If they let us stay,' she replied, biting back her irritation.

In a way, Sariah reasoned, it was better that Rose wasn't coming, because there were plenty of bridges for her and Grace to mend. One step at a time, she told herself.

'So,' Sariah said.

'Yes, so.' Grace cast a look around the still-empty tables, as if to make sure no one had crept in to listen to their conversation while she was pouring the tea. 'You must have questions.'

'Yes I do. Lots of questions.'

In that moment, Sariah felt all her patience and understanding evaporate into the stuffy café air. 'It doesn't feel very nice, you know, to be told you were passed around like an unwanted parcel. That Grandma and Grandpa were so ashamed that some story had to be concocted. I mean, it wasn't the 1950s, was it?'

Grace looked down at her lap and squeezed her eyes together tight. 'No, it wasn't, but it sometimes felt like it. You grew up here, in Redruth, but me and Rose came from somewhere much smaller, where everyone knew everyone. Your grandma had been brought up with chapel twice a day on Sunday, hymn practice on Wednesdays.' She got a scrappy tissue out of her pocket. 'Later, she admitted she'd made mistakes. She told me she shouldn't have interfered, that it had damaged Rose and made her leave. And none of it was fair on you.'

Sariah sat very still, her arms crossed. 'So, how did it happen, the switch? Did Grandma sit you and Dad down and suggest it? Did Rose ask you?'

Grace shook her head. 'No, it wasn't like that. It was more of a gradual thing. Rose stayed in Plymouth for six weeks and when she came home it was clear she couldn't cope. I mean, she was a child herself. Me and your dad were still living at Grandma's so, often as not, it was me or Grandma that got up for you in the night.'

She sighed. 'A few weeks later me and your dad got our own place and Grandma said, "Just take the baby for the weekend, give Rose a break." So we did. And then on the Sunday evening I brought you back and Rose was sitting at the kitchen table doing her homework like any other schoolgirl and I thought, no, this is all wrong. I'd always tried to look out for my little sister, but when she fell pregnant, I felt like I'd failed her. I thought, if I did this thing, it would make up for it.'

She wiped her cheek, hard. 'You came back with us and never left. Grandma was pleased as Punch, said it had all worked out for the best. First time we introduced ourselves to our new neighbours, it was with you in your pram.'

Sariah tried to imagine the logistics. 'But what about my birth certificate, all the official things?'

'Mum got the lady in Plymouth to help. She said it was an early home birth that she'd attended, as a friend of the family. She said it was just the sort of outcome she liked to hear.'

'And what did Rose think?'

'I wish I could tell you, but the fact is we didn't speak of it again, not directly. We all just got on with things. Rose did her exams and then her A levels and before long she was off to university. And each time she came home, she was more like a stranger.'

Grace swivelled round to peer out of the steamy windows, as if weighing up whether to make a dash for it, now she'd said her piece.

'It's easing off, the rain,' Sariah said tightly, but her mum wasn't paying attention.

'You'd think she'd be punctual, wouldn't you, what with her job, but she could never be anywhere on time,' Grace said.

Sariah wasn't sure she understood.

'I know she's late, but don't take offence. It's just her way,' Grace added and then the tinkle of the bell above the door rang out and they both looked up to see a tall woman in the doorway. She unbuttoned her coat in a methodical way, then untied the pink bow under her chin and removed a plastic rain hat. Beneath, her hair was fixed in a neat, dry bun.

Then Rose was sitting down at the table, reaching out a hand first to Grace and then to Sariah. 'Thank you for inviting me,' said this polite teacher, in a powder blue twinset. At her neck, a small gold crucifix glinted and Sariah noticed that her fingernails were shaped into perfect ovals.

'She's told you, then?' Rose asked, giving Sariah a long, steady look. Sariah had imagined that she'd want to study every inch of Rose's face, looking for a resemblance, but in that moment, it was too much, too soon. She found she couldn't return her gaze.

'Mum's told me the bare bones,' she replied.

Then Rose slipped her hands away and placed them on her handbag, which sat on her lap. 'Sorry, I'm a bit nervous,' she said. 'Hard to know where to begin, isn't it?'

Sariah nodded and so did Grace.

'I thought it might be easier to start with this.' Rose undid the clasp of her handbag and drew out a fat, tattered recipe book. It was Grandma Karensa's.

She pushed it towards Sariah.

'Thank you,' Sariah mumbled and opened it up. She wasn't sure if she was imagining it but it seemed that the smell of butter and sugar and spices greeted her. 'I've been trying to remember all these recipes,' she said. 'But now I can do them properly, Grandma's way. If our Cake Shed idea gets the OK, it'll be so useful.'

She turned another page and peered at the handwriting in the margin. It was a recipe for Bakewell tart and beside the pastry ingredients was written *extra ground almonds*.

She pointed to the page. 'But does she mean for the topping or the pastry? It's not clear.'

'The pastry,' Rose decided.

'Definitely,' Grace said.

'Then there's her other secret ingredient, that you won't find written down,' Rose said gently.

'Oh?'

'She always added a dash of cherry brandy to the mixture. But she never admitted it in case it set tongues wagging.'

'Hmm. It's a shame Grandma worried so much what people thought,' Sariah said. 'Would a bit of local gossip have been that bad?'

She closed the book, making it clear she was talking about more than Grandma Karensa being fond of a drop.

'I wish it had been different,' Rose said. Sariah could hear a choke in Rose's voice and she was scared to speak again in case she welled up too.

'There's a lot to talk about and it's going to take time. But if there's anything you want to ask me now . . . ?' Rose offered.

Sariah had been running her fingers back and forth over a crease on the cover of the recipe book, but at that she stopped. 'There is one thing,' she said. 'Who chose my name?'

'Me,' Rose said. 'I insisted. I thought it sounded exotic, different.' She gave a soft smile. 'What can I say – I was fifteen.'

'That's good to know,' Sariah said. 'And what can you tell me about my father?' she added. Beside her, she felt Grace stiffen.

Rose let out a sigh. 'Oh, he was just a boy, young like me. It was a mistake: kisses on the beach after dark that went further. It was the first time for both of us and I don't think he had any idea that I'd got pregnant. I was sent off to Plymouth and when I came back he'd left town. He went to work for his uncle in Canada, who was a carpenter, and he never came back.'

Sariah couldn't decide if knowing this was a relief, or another loss.

'But he was never the point, really. You were. We all just wanted the best for you.'

Grace cleared her throat. 'I'm sorry I didn't make you feel that way.'

Sariah swallowed down a dry sob. 'Well, I probably wasn't the easiest child. Especially when I was a teenager.'

'Well, the women in our family are made of strong stuff.' Grace dabbed her lips.

The waitress came and cleared away the teapot and two cups with rather more sighing and clattering of crockery than was strictly necessary and then flipped over the sign on the door.

'Time to go, I think,' Sariah said.

The three women stood up and Sariah couldn't help watching in fascination as Rose did up the buttons on her coat and retied her plastic rain bonnet. A costume of respectability that she'd put on when young and grown into, she supposed.

'What year do you teach?' she asked as they came out to the wet pavement.

'Reception,' Rose said with a sad smile. 'The littlest ones.'

And then, Grace, never one for shows of affection, surprised them all by pulling her sister in for a short, fierce hug. Next, she turned to Sariah and did the same. And finally, Sariah and Rose tentatively put their arms around each other.

All the way home, Sariah felt the ghosts of those hugs and they gave her hope.

Chapter Forty-Five

Walking up the hill towards her flimsy caravan home, Evelyn's thoughts returned to George's idea of an art exhibition and she wondered if she'd been too hasty in dismissing it. After all, she could probably squeeze in some of her mother's wildflower paintings as a tribute to her unsung talents.

As she reached the crest of the hill, she paused for breath. She heard the familiar cries of gulls and the distant crash of the sea – and then she heard a sound that made no sense at all. It was the wail of a siren. Was it her imagination, or could she smell something acrid on the wind? She looked around to see if a farmer was burning stubble, all the while panic rising because she knew it was the wrong season. She looked up towards the caravan site, then back at the jumbled houses of Portheast and then she saw it: a column of dark smoke rising into the white sky. Down in the town, something was on fire. Evelyn began to run.

From above, it had been impossible to tell where the smoke was coming from, but as she reached the narrow streets of the old town, all she needed to do was follow the people. She saw Mrs Moran gamely striding along and Jude from the pub weaving her way through. As the crowd turned into Fore Street, she felt a rush of relief because people were flowing straight ahead instead of turning left to the harbour. Her museum, at least, was safe.

The woop-woop of an ambulance parted the crowd and Evelyn watched as it came to a halt ahead. With a snap of fear, she realised it was outside Potters Newsagents, where Jacob lived. A firefighter told everyone to get back and long flaccid hoses were rolled out across the tarmac. She heard people saying the words 'engine' and 'petrol' and at last, standing on tiptoes, she could glimpse the source of the fire. It wasn't a building, but a car – Jacob's nippy, shiny Mini.

She saw helmets, a blur of yellow uniforms and then there was a whoosh of foam. A few short blasts and then it was all over, leaving a bitterness in the air. Light blobs of foam floated upwards and Evelyn watched as the wind carried them into the cool white sky.

The crowd began to disperse, disappointed that the excitement was over. She saw Nils the baker shaking his head and walking back to his shop and Mrs Moran arriving with a face like thunder because she'd missed out on the action.

Everyone knew what had happened: Roy Pinlow. As the crowd thinned out she saw Jacob's car more clearly, with its seats burned out, the paintwork blistered and its windscreen shattered. On the opposite kerb, Jacob was sitting with his head in his hands and Evelyn could see his legs were shaking. Sitting beside him was Alison, ashen-faced and staring at the car. She saw Della crouch down beside Jacob and put her chunky arm around him, and Sariah comforting Alison.

Della looked up and caught her eye. 'My place?' she mouthed. Then she held up her hand, fingers spread. 'In five?' and Evelyn nodded.

Della had invested in a brand-new, very noisy coffee machine and she insisted that everyone choose a different drink so that she could try out all the buttons. 'Right, we all need sustenance. What can I get you?' she asked, but before anyone could reply, she made executive decisions. 'Evelyn? You look in need of a latte. Alison, I prescribe a cappuccino. Sariah, I know you love an espresso. Which leaves you, Jacob, with a nice big macchiato. With extra sugar.'

If Della was like this managing a bean-to-cup machine, Evelyn could only imagine how formidable she'd have been in charge of a newsroom.

Then they fell silent as Jacob told them what had happened. He'd taken on the afternoon shift because Mrs P had a chiropodist's appointment. One minute he'd been restocking the confectionery display with Bounties and Snickers bars, the next he'd noticed a warm orange glow reflected in the shiny pull-down shutter that hid away the cigarettes, tobacco and, ironically, flammable things like matches and lighter fuel. He'd heard a snap and crackle and said that the noises had reminded him of bonfire night. 'Except, when I turned around I realised that it wasn't a bonfire – it was my car.'

They all shook their heads.

'Thankfully, Mrs P's bunions meant it was me and not her who was in the shop,' he added.

Della let out a gasp. 'Oh, no! Where's your little dog?'

'It's OK, he's with Leonard,' Jacob reassured. 'He popped in this morning, saw Max was being a bit of a handful and offered to take him out for the day.' He sipped his coffee. 'It's becoming a regular thing, actually. I think Leonard likes the company.'

'Did you see anyone hanging about earlier?' Della asked.

'Come on, let's just say his name: it was Roy,' Alison said stonily. 'But I'm sure he'll be long gone, working up some alibi. But we can't let him win.'

'The police will take statements,' Evelyn said and Jacob gave her a sceptical look.

'Like that's going to do anything,' he said.

'More coffees?' Della seemed to have finally found her catering forte: pressing a button and occasionally replenishing her gigantic machine with milk or coffee beans.

'Thanks, but I'm on the evening shift. I'd better get back,' Sariah said.

'And I'd better go and assess the damage,' Jacob said.

Alison slid off her bar stool. 'I'll come too,' she said and as they left she linked her arm into his.

'Aw, nice,' said Della.

Evelyn tended to agree. 'Every cloud has a silver lining.'

The next day, like the proverbial bad penny, George appeared in her museum again.

'You forgot to buy white card,' he said with a supercilious smile.

'What?'

'Yesterday, at the newsagents. You panic-bought several copies of *The Daily Telegraph*, but forgot card for your new labels.'

He laid a pack of white card down on her table.

'Any update in today's newspapers?' she asked, her heart thumping.

'Not that I could see.'

'Thanks.' She put his offering on top of her now very manageable to-do pile. 'Actually, I wanted to ask you a favour.'

He raised one eyebrow and she wondered how long it had taken him to perfect that particular trick.

'It's about Roy Pinlow.'

'Hmm,' said George. 'Nasty piece of work.'

'Indeed. The police have taken a statement from Jacob, but I wondered if there were any other, um . . .' She cleared her throat. 'Ways to help him reflect on his actions?'

George rubbed his chin. 'I don't know Roy, but I used to work with his older brother, Grant, back in the day. I'll pay him a visit. See what can be done.'

Evelyn didn't want to ask what line of work they had been in together, but she suspected it wasn't the sort of thing that would appear on a CV.

'Thank you,' she said and waited for George to leave. But he wasn't moving.

'Just wondered if you've given it any more thought?' he said. 'The art exhibition.'

'Actually, yes I have. And I've changed my mind,' she announced. 'I think it's a good idea, but I'd like to broaden the scope. Since our big clear-out, I've discovered more things that deserve to be seen. Come and see.'

She led George to the revised Fishing Life area and pointed out a yellow oilskin. 'Kayla and Jude remembered their grandfather wearing one of those, so it would be nice to update its label.' She brushed dust off a piece of wood with letters on it, her first ever beach find. 'Then there's this. I know you wanted to throw it out, but I feel as if it has a story, you know?'

She passed George the piece of wood, which was painted light blue with white letters that said -*ORA*- and he turned it over in his hands thoughtfully. 'Ora,' he frowned. 'I wonder if . . .' Then he turned to face her. 'Evelyn Silver, you were right and I was wrong.'

'Naturally. But did you have something specific in mind?'

George's whole demeanour changed and he turned the piece of wood over again. 'My goodness, I think it is. Yes, I do.'

'George, what are you babbling on about?'

He looked up. 'We're agreed, this looks like a boat name board, yes?'

'Indeed.'

'Well, I've got a terrible feeling that this could be from the *Cora-May*.' He fixed her with an earnest expression.

'And that would be?'

'Evelyn, think back to 1987. The fishing boat that went down in a storm. Terrible tragedy, three men lost. You must remember.'

She thought of how she'd spent most of that year in London, far away from Portheast and its news. 'I wasn't here,' she said softly. 'I was . . . away.'

'Well, as I say, it was tragic,' George continued. 'It was Gilbert Larkwood's boat – on its maiden voyage, too. He was so excited to take it out, then a big storm blew up from nowhere.' He trailed off, remembering what must have been a terrible time for the town.

'Then it should definitely go in the exhibition,' she said firmly. 'And we need to commemorate the lives lost in some way.'

'Well, Bob's the man to talk to.'

'Bob?' She recalled one of the Wise Men. 'Fisherman Bob who sits on that bench looking out to sea?'

'That's the one.'

'But never goes out on a boat because he gets seasick?'

'Gilbert Larkwood was his father. Bob was meant to go out with him that day, but didn't. Afterwards, Gilbert's family would visit the bench to pay their respects. But Bob never set foot on a boat again.'

Evelyn felt a tightening around her heart. 'Oh. Not seasickness then.'

'No. Something a bit more complicated.'

'Do you think he'd talk to me? Tell me about the boat and his father and the other men?'

'You can try. I'll ask him to pop in and see you, shall I?'

'Please.'

Still, George wasn't moving.

Evelyn resisted the urge to tut. She was keen to try out George's printer, but didn't need a witness to her technological ineptitude. 'Was there something else?'

'Yes, actually.'

He had an odd look in his eyes, one that was making her nervous.

'I'm glad you've decided to do this art exhibition,' George continued. 'Because I've got some news. It's about a painting you have.' He tried to suppress a smile.

She felt her stomach drop. 'Oh no. Not another fake.'

'No, it's not that,' George reassured. 'Quite the opposite, in fact . . .'

This sounded even worse: was he going to tell her that their clear-out had unearthed a stolen masterpiece? Did they need to start scheming all over again to return it to its rightful owner? She didn't think she could stomach any more subterfuge.

'Come,' he said and led her to one of the few remaining unsorted boxes, the one containing her mother's drawings and the abstract painting George had admired. Evelyn's private opinion, inherited from her father, was that most modern art looked childish or rushed and sometimes both.

'Don't suppose you remember where you bought this one?' George asked, lifting out the abstract canvas.

'Actually, it wasn't me, but my mother. I've no idea where she got it, but it would have been local.'

George paused. 'Well, she had a good eye.'

'Funny you say that, because there was a bit of a hullabaloo. She bought it when my father was away and he wasn't impressed. Made a joke of it, called it worthless scribbles, and eventually she hid it away.'

'Well the joke's on him, because I sent my photographs of it to an art dealer friend – a reputable one, that is. And he tells me he's certain it's a Peter Lanyon.'

Evelyn's knowledge of art did not extend beyond the 18th century, so the name meant nothing.

As George admired the painting, he explained more. 'Cornish born, mixed with Hepworth and Nicholson and Rothko, but had his own unique perspective.' He propped the painting against the wall and they both stood back to study it.

'To me, his work is rooted in the rocks and the sea, but his perspective also soars above it. He piloted a glider plane, which sadly was also why he died young.'

Looking at it afresh, Evelyn saw that of course it was of the sea.

'All of which means, he's now highly collectable.'

Evelyn squinted at the painting. She took in the sweep of sky, a curve of yellow that reminded her of Portheast's quay when the sun hit the stone. But what struck her most was the crisscrossing of strokes that captured a restless sea. Looking at it made her yearn to be outside and free, and she wondered if that was what her mother had seen in it too. Meanwhile, its fluid, fleeting beauty had gone right over the head of Edwin Silver.

It was like that optical illusion again: was a painting childish daubs of paint or a masterpiece? Was her museum a millstone or a marvel? Come to that, was George Rook a crook or rather good company?

'It creeps up on you,' she heard George say. 'Those hidden depths. But the more you spend time in her presence, the more you appreciate her.'

'Her?' she said, wondering if this was some antiquated practice, calling paintings 'she' like with boats.

'Yes,' he replied, then added, 'The painting too.'

Her face turned hot and she was grateful for the museum's dim lighting. They both continued gazing at the painting, not daring to look at each other.

'I suppose it might be worth a few bob then?' she said at last.

'Rather a lot of bob, actually. He says he already has several collectors in mind.'

'Hundreds?' she ventured.

'Thousands. Possibly six figures, with the right buyer.'

'Is that so,' she said quietly. A sum like that would be transformative and her mind ran through the things she could do to improve the museum. If she and Della were allowed to stay, they could combine their sheds, which would make her reception area larger and brighter. There would still be ample space for Della's cakes and coffees, but they could add a gift shop; maybe a crafts area for school groups to use. The museum would be unrecognisable. It would no longer feel like a relic of her past.

'So, shall I tell him you are interested?'

'Oh, yes,' she said, her heart thudding hard. 'I believe I am.'

She realised George was standing close enough to touch and she let her hand brush against his waxy jacket sleeve.

'Thank you, George.'

Slowly, they turned to face each other and Evelyn swore she could hear his heart beating almost as fast as her own.

Chapter Forty-Six

The plan to sell the Lanyon painting was moving ahead at a speed Evelyn found hard to comprehend. According to George, right now the market was 'hot' for 20th-century abstract art and a deal was on the table.

'But don't they want to come and see it first? It's an awful lot of money,' she asked George.

'Evelyn, the rich delegate jobs like that. That's why they have art dealers,' he explained. 'But the buyer is happy for the painting to stay here on loan, so it can be the star of your exhibition. I suppose it's a way to introduce the painting to the art world without being too obvious or showy.'

'Someone rich being obvious and showy? As if,' she replied with a smile.

But the more she thought about it, the more she liked the idea of an exhibition. Alongside the Lanyon, she could include other paintings and objects relating to the sea.

When George wrote down the final figure offered, she looked at it in amazement. It wasn't just the amount she found gratifying, it was more the thought that her mother, Elsbeth Silver, had found this painting and passed it on to Evelyn. It had nothing to do with

Edwin Silver or all the ways in which he'd made the museum feel tainted. Its discovery could be the start of something new.

When she told Della about the painting and how it would be the centrepiece in a new exhibition, she went into overdrive. 'Right, we're going to need a committee meeting,' she announced and started furiously typing messages in the old WhatsApp group.

'I'm going to volunteer The Cake Shed, aka myself and Sariah, to do catering.' Della paused, smoothing down her hair, which had turned from its old livid purple to an attractively faded pink. 'Don't worry, I'm strictly on drinks duty,' she added.

'How about Alison does the PR this time?' Evelyn suggested. 'It might give her a bit of a boost.'

'Good plan. We're going to need some people on security, too. This painting is very valuable. It's probably worth more than all the other stuff in your museum put together,' she said as if explaining it to a child.

'Is that so?' Evelyn replied lightly, making a silent tally of the ancient Roman busts, gold coins and the priceless Egyptian urns that had secretly languished at the back of the museum for decades. 'I'll ask around. I know someone who might know someone,' Evelyn added.

Della looked askance. 'Evelyn Silver, you are one dark horse.'

Evelyn wasn't really, but she did know that George had paid a visit to Roy Pinlow's older brother, Grant. 'I told him I had a new contact on the force and I'd happily fill them in on the Pinlows' past business interests unless Roy reined himself in. I think they got the message.'

'George – I never had you down as a grass,' Evelyn had said, shocked at such double dealing.

'Actually, I got the idea from a TV show where someone pulled a similar stunt and the criminals took him at his word.'

Evelyn wasn't up to date on all the latest crime series, but she'd asked George which one, anyway.

'Oh, an old favourite: *Inspector Morse*. I used to watch it with my dad,' George said and she'd let slip a small smile.

Evelyn left Della typing suggestions (aka instructions) into the group chat and retired to her own boat shed. If they were going to have an art exhibition, she wanted to include some items that felt meaningful to locals too – like the broken boat name board for the *Cora-May*. George said he'd mentioned the idea to Bob, but she was beginning to suspect that Bob was deliberately avoiding her.

She'd seen him a couple of times in the distance, but each time he'd swiftly disappeared. Once, he'd been walking towards the beach, but when he spotted Evelyn he did an about-turn. Then she'd seen him alone on the Three Wise Men's bench and waved, but by the time she'd made it over he was gone. She didn't blame him – she knew from experience that it felt easier to run away from grief than confront it. But she also knew that it caught up with you in the end.

It was a few days later that Bob appeared in the doorway of her museum, a dark silhouette against the sunlit harbourside.

'Come in,' she called, encouragingly. She'd been trying to get George's hulking printer to 'talk' to her laptop and introductions were not going well.

'You won't stop, will you,' Bob said, from the doorway, his voice breaking. 'You keep asking and asking.'

She hadn't realised talking about the *Cora-May* going down would be so hard for him. 'I'm sorry,' she said. 'There's really no need, if you don't want to.'

'Ah, it's only a matter of time before you work it out, so I may as well tell you myself.' He came closer and she could feel the pent-up emotion radiating off him.

'No, really . . .' She came out from behind her desk to meet him. The last thing she wanted to do was upset Gilbert Larkwood's only son.

She looked at his weatherworn face and saw pain. And then her eyes dropped down, because Bob Larkwood was holding something in his hands, something that looked both new and totally familiar.

It was a small piece of lace with a pattern of daisies and she knew without checking that its ragged edges would match hers perfectly.

Chapter Forty-Seven

Evelyn had the oddest sensation, as if she was watching the scene unfold from afar, and from this distant vantage point, she heard herself say, 'Where did you get that?' But it was a stupid question because there could only be one answer.

'She made it for you,' he said. 'It was meant to be part of something bigger: the lace trim for a matinee jacket and bonnet for your layette. But she ran out of time.'

Evelyn took a step forward, saw more clearly the familiar knots and tiny daisies.

'It was made by your mother,' Bob whispered. 'She was called Cora-May.'

'Like the boat,' Evelyn said, sensing these muddled strands might somehow join up, but she didn't yet know how.

'Yes, like the boat. Father named it after her.' Bob looked away. 'He loved her so much.'

'Was he my father too?'

Bob didn't speak, gave a brief shake of his head.

'And is she still . . . ?' A flash of hope came, like lightning over the sea, but then she saw Bob's face.

'No. Mother's gone.'

She felt a crevice of grief open up inside herself and she teetered on its edge. The woman who had given birth to her, stroked her cheek and counted her fingers and toes, had died before Evelyn had the chance to meet her.

'Couple of years ago,' Bob said soberly. 'Cancer; caught too late.'

But then the crevice in her began to fill with rage. 'Why didn't you tell me before? Why only now? I was here – I've always been here.'

Bob hung his head. 'Truth is, I only realised myself a few months ago. It was your poster that got me thinking, so I came to the museum to make sure. Your meeting was the first time I'd been in here and that's when I saw it – your lace.' He shrugged. 'After that, I started to work things out.'

Evelyn needed to rewind, get things clearer. 'Sorry, but when did she die?'

'Two years ago. It was only when she was close to the end that I learned she'd had a baby before me. Then, like I say, in February I saw your lace. And I realised that when she'd talked about losing a first child, it was you. And a lot of other things began to make sense: about Mother and the things she'd done over the years.'

'Did she ever speak of me?'

'Not until the end.'

Evelyn gestured at a chair and Bob sat down, still holding his piece of lace in one hand.

'Please. Tell me,' she said, staring at the missing half of the lace, brighter and better preserved than her own.

Bob looked down at it too. 'She kept it inside a book of poetry, in a drawer in her dressing table. After she got sick, I looked after her for as long as I could. One day, quite close to the end, she asked me for the poetry book. She opened it up and there it was.

'She told me she wanted to see it one last time. Then she said, "I made it for my daughter."' He scrunched up his face and wiped his eye with the back of his thumb.

'At first, I didn't understand – was she confused? Then I wondered if she'd suffered a miscarriage at some point, and the lace was a reminder. But then she started to talk.'

Evelyn waited for more.

'She fell pregnant when she was sixteen, long before she met Father. Her sweetheart, that's what she called him, was eighteen. But his family didn't approve and, once she was showing, she was sent away to St Agnes. She thought he'd come and fetch her and then they'd all be together. But after she had the baby, it was taken from her.'

Evelyn felt her stomach turn, as if something slick lurked inside.

'Did you say, taken?'

'Yes. Mother said his family took charge – they already had a couple lined up to adopt you: good people, well educated. They could provide her baby with a better life.'

'A better life – ha.' Evelyn couldn't keep the bitterness out of her voice. 'So, if it was all managed by this family, where did the foundling story come from?'

'No idea. Might have been to throw people off the scent. I suppose the local doctor might have confirmed the story, for a fee or a favour.' He shrugged. 'Or maybe Edwin Silver just liked the idea.'

'Maybe,' she echoed. The anger was back, rising up inside her.

'So who were they, this family who played with everyone's lives and saw fit to take babies and hand them out at will?'

Bob gave her a cool, appraising look and she felt that sense of distance return, her mind wanting to protect her from the words he was about to say.

'Her employers – and the people who once ran everything around here. The Warburns.'

Evelyn felt for her chair, lowered herself into it by touch. 'Are you sure?'

Bob continued talking. 'Mother had been in service at Warburn Hall when she fell pregnant.'

'So they sacked her and got rid of the problem, i.e. me,' Evelyn said flatly. 'I'm guessing the lad, whoever he was, didn't hang about?'

Bob shrugged. 'Well, he was sent away too, but to university.'

That didn't sound right for a lad in service and her puzzlement must have shown.

'Mother wasn't the bride they envisaged for their son and heir. Sir Jasper.'

That man she'd glimpsed from afar: at Christmas services and driving through town in his Jaguar. A tall man who opened summer fetes, cut a ribbon and wished everyone a jolly good time. Later, he was the grandfather who had stood in this very museum and laid a gentle hand on Jacob's shoulder. And then passed by Evelyn Silver without saying a word.

'Bob, are you certain about this?'

'He left for university, but promised he'd come for her. But his parents came instead. I'll never forget Mother's words. She said, "They took her and left me there, broken in two."'

Beyond the door, the tide must have come in while they were talking and Evelyn could hear the hollow boom of the waves hitting the sea wall. She gathered herself. It would take time to rebuild a wall around herself, but she'd done it before and she could do it again. She glanced down at the shattered boat name board on her desk and gave a weak laugh.

'I thought you'd come to tell me about the boat,' she said. 'This *Cora-May*.' She held the name plate in both hands. 'Not Cora-May, the woman.'

'Ah, yes,' Bob said solemnly. 'I saw that at the exhibition.' He shifted position in his chair. 'Must have washed up on the beach.'

'Yes. It was one of the first things I ever picked up.'

'Feels fitting, though. You of all people finding it.'

'I suppose so. I'm very sorry for your loss.'

'He was a good man.' Bob stood to go, but then paused. 'After we lost Father, Mother and I started coming down here,' he said. 'We lived in an estate cottage five miles away in Cowell, but four times a year we came down to the harbour and sat on that bench, whatever the weather.' He pointed out of the doorway to the bench where Bob still sat, day in, day out, sometimes with friends, sometimes alone.

'I hated those visits,' he said forcefully. 'Having to sit beside the raging sea that had taken Father, swallowed his boat whole and spat out the bits it didn't want.'

Gently, Evelyn laid down the broken name plate.

'I was afraid of the sea and I'm sure she was too, but she kept coming, as if something was drawing her back here. I didn't get it, but now it makes perfect sense. The year that Father died, I think she found out where you were and those visits weren't to see the waves, but in spite of them. She came to watch over you, Evelyn.'

Chapter Forty-Eight

In the following days, Evelyn tried to dredge her memory for an image of a woman sitting on that windswept bench with her son. They had come every three months, so logically Evelyn would have seen them or passed them by. But try as she might, she couldn't remember them and this made her feel an inexplicable shame. Instead, other imagined images filled her head: a young woman pinning a scrap of lace to her baby's blanket as she said goodbye; Elsbeth Silver reaching out for that swaddled baby, peeling the blanket back for a first look. Had Elsbeth known Evelyn's story, or had she been lied to as well?

Evelyn barely slept, but one thing helped her through her confusion and pain. Unlike other occasions when the rug of life had been pulled out from under her, this time Evelyn had people she could turn to. The first person she called was Sariah and they sat in the hotel bar and talked long into the night about lost chances and absent mothers.

'What I don't understand,' Evelyn said, 'is why she didn't come and speak to me. She could have saved me so much wondering and waiting.'

'But could she?' Sariah looked sceptical. 'She was a widow with a grieving son, living in a tied estate cottage. She'd already spent most of her life under the watchful eye of the Warburns. Also, she probably had the good sense to keep her distance from your dad, Edwin. She was in a vulnerable position.'

Evelyn mulled this over.

'I know you wish you hadn't come back to Portheast, but imagine if things had been different.' Sariah picked the cocktail umbrella from her glass. 'If you'd stayed in London, Cora-May wouldn't have had those precious glimpses of you. And if your museum had never existed, Bob wouldn't have seen your lace and my mum wouldn't have seen the teacup. None of the good things from the past few months would have happened.'

Evelyn hadn't thought of it like that.

'Besides.' Sariah signalled to the barman for another round. 'I know you weren't exactly thriving in your shed for all those years, but Cora-May didn't know that, did she? From her bench, all she saw was a bright young woman with a degree who was running a museum.'

Evelyn shrugged and weighed up the tricky issue of ordering another drink.

'Look, taking you away from Cora-May was beyond immoral and she suffered, no doubt about it. But when she caught those glimpses of you, maybe she felt proud?'

Her glass still empty, Evelyn considered this and decided, yes, she could live with that. For all its faults, the museum had been a way for her birth mother to reconnect with her child, albeit in a one-sided way. Which brought her thoughts back to Sariah's situation.

'Any plans to see Rose again?' she asked.

'Nothing definite. It's hard to know where to start.'

'How about meeting again on neutral ground? You could invite her to the art exhibition?'

'I'll ask, but I don't know if she'll come. It was quite . . . hard last time.' Sariah stood, picked up their glasses. 'Anyway, another drink? Service here is terrible.'

Evelyn smiled wanly. 'Please.'

'What was yours, porn star martini?'

Evelyn pursed her lips. 'No. The other one. The beach one.'

'Say all the words, or no drink.' Sariah grinned.

'Sex on the beach,' Evelyn whispered and covered a smile with her hand.

◆ ◆ ◆

Thanks to Sariah and her smuttily named cocktails, Evelyn woke up the next morning with a thumping hangover. It was a good job she had no plans to go into the museum, because she'd set aside the morning to do some research. At the back of her wardrobe was a box file that contained anything remotely official and she opened it up. After sifting through piles of yellowed receipts, old bills and bank statements, Evelyn found what she was looking for: the original tenancy agreement on her late parents' home.

She saw that it had been drawn up by the local solicitor, Mr Treffrey Senior, and towards the end of several pages of long-winded legalese, she found a small subclause that made for interesting reading. It stated that the tenancy would remain in force 'until such time as Edwin Silver and Elsbeth Silver are both deceased, or their daughter (unnamed as yet, born 1964) leaves home or marries, whichever occurs first.'

She refolded the thick pages. That subclause meant that for all the years that Evelyn remained living at home, declining university offers for the Open University and curtailing her future at the British Museum, Edwin and Elsbeth could happily remain in their four-bedroom house with sea views for a peppercorn rent. Presumably, they had explained away Evelyn's traineeship as a temporary arrangement, which, in the end, had turned out to be true.

Evelyn suspected that Mr Treffrey Senior had also drawn up a similar tenancy for Cora-May, who had lived in her remote estate cottage until she died. How many other people's silence, she wondered, had the Warburns bought? Certainly someone at the mother and baby home.

And yet Evelyn herself, the cause of this unfortunate hiccup in the family history, had ended up living in a run-down static caravan. Her thoughts turned to Jacob Warburn and she wondered what, if anything, he knew of his grandfather's philandering past.

In the end, her hangover forced Evelyn out in search of fresh air and, like a homing pigeon, she found herself walking down towards the beach. There was a strong easterly wind, but she kept her head down and her eyes squeezed almost shut to avoid the blasts of sand. As she neared the end of the beach, she realised she was no longer alone: there was a hunched figure sitting on the big rock and she was about to turn back when the person raised their hand. She peered harder and saw that it was Bob.

She braced herself. Hangover or not, they needed to talk. She saw him stand, then pick something up from the shoreline and slip it into the pocket of his donkey jacket.

'Bob,' she greeted him. 'We meet again.'

'Looks that way,' he said, keeping his gaze fixed on a ribbon of bladderwrack on the sand.

'What did you find?' she asked. 'I saw you pocket something.'

'It's not your beach, you know, Evelyn Silver. You don't own everything that washes up,' he said tersely.

'No, I know. I was just making conversation.'

This was going to be harder than she'd imagined. She was carrying her own pain, but she saw that Bob was hurting too: he'd lost his father when he was eighteen and his mother two years ago. And then, a few months ago, he'd joined the dots and worked out that his mother had given birth to an illegitimate child – who now seemed to think she owned the whole beach.

Relenting, Bob reached into his pocket and pulled out a piece of blue fishing rope, twisted with shreds of sea fern. It was the sort of thing she found there most mornings.

'Only this,' he said. 'Just doing my bit, tidying the beach. Like you do.'

'There's so much plastic,' she said with a sigh. 'And the tiny bits are the worst – just the right size for fish to hoover up, thinking it's food.'

'Terrible,' Bob replied.

In this way, they walked back along the beach, talking about sea pollution and fishing responsibilities and people who didn't take their rubbish home. 'We can only hope the next generation sees sense,' Bob said.

Evelyn paused, hoping she wasn't speaking out of turn. 'I wondered,' she began. 'Do you have photos of her?'

'Mother? Of course. Shall I bring them in?'

'Thank you. I would appreciate that.'

The wind was getting stronger, but she had more to say. 'And perhaps we can talk more when you're ready, because I know this is hard for you, too.'

Bob nodded. 'Sorry if I'm a disappointment. Sure I'm not the family you hoped to find.' He gave an embarrassed cough.

'Oh, Bob, it's not that at all. It's just a lot to take in.'

'I came to nothing,' he said. 'Never followed my father into fishing and never did much else.'

'What *did* you do?' she asked. 'Before you became a Wise Man.'

'Ha.' He gave a bitter laugh. 'Never claimed to be that. Well, I was a postman, that was OK for a bit. Then I worked in a warehouse, which was less good. The job I liked best was when I was a caretaker up at the primary school.'

'Well, there's a coincidence,' she said, thinking on her feet.

'How's that?'

'We're holding another exhibition soon,' Evelyn said.

'More Lost Chances or whatever you called it?'

'No, it's mostly to show off a modern painting. But I want to include things that will appeal to everyone. Including children.'

'OK,' said Bob, warily.

'My problem is, after tidying up the museum I've got lots of plastic to recycle and it's all stuff I found on the beach.'

Bob looked unsure. 'OK,' he repeated.

'I was thinking of getting the kids at the primary school to work it into some kind of display. To show the effects of sea pollution, raise awareness, I suppose.'

'Sounds good,' Bob said.

'Would you consider helping? You know, directing the kids a bit? And while it's taking shape you could talk to them about how fishing used to be done and the damage plastic nets and ropes do now.'

'The ghost nets, you mean?' said Bob. 'They're cut free of boats and left to drift in the sea. But of course, they carry on trapping fish.'

'See, you already know more than me.'

He rubbed his chin and said gruffly, 'I'll have a word with Mrs Charles, the headteacher. She'll remember me.'

They had reached the quay and came to a halt outside the museum.

'There's something else I'd like to suggest. About the *Cora-May*.'

Bob shoved his hands in his pockets and looked wary.

'I wasn't living in Portheast when she went down, but it strikes me as wrong that there's no commemorative plaque in the town,' Evelyn said.

'There was talk, but it came to nothing.'

'Well, I'd like to remedy that. How about the museum makes a tribute? Maybe rebuild the boat name, or mount the remaining piece in some way . . . I'm not sure.' She wondered if she'd gone too far, if Bob would think she was interfering.

She waited, felt a gust of sea spray. Finally, Bob spoke. 'I'll talk to Leonard, see if he can help.'

'Good, I'm glad. But why Leonard?'

'He used to be a signwriter, same as his father. They did all the boat names, so one of them would have done the *Cora-May*'s in the first place. They did shop signs too. Not that there are many left now, all replaced with plastic. Potters Newsagents' is one of the last.'

Evelyn could picture the beautiful red lettering above the shopfront and realised it had indeed remained unchanged, if slightly faded, since Mrs P weighed out pear drops for her on Sunday mornings.

Then it struck her that The Cake Shed would soon be in need of a new sign, as would she – the old museum signage painted in her father's florid hand was long overdue an update.

'While you're at it, can you ask him if he's up for some other jobs too?'

'Will do,' Bob said. As he turned to go, he added, 'I'll put some photos aside.'

'Thank you. I'd love to see them,' she said firmly. 'Come by tomorrow? I'll dig out a few photos of me when I was little, too. That's if you're interested?'

Bob nodded.

They parted and Evelyn watched him go, trying to spot some familiarity in his short stature, his sloping shoulders and round face, but she found none. And yet, that man was her half-brother.

Then her thoughts turned to another living relative and, resisting the urge to hide within the safety of her museum, she set off towards the high street for her next difficult conversation.

Chapter Forty-Nine

'I'd invite you up to my bedsit, but it's a mess and I'm due a trip to the laundrette,' Jacob explained as he stood in the shop doorway. 'Besides, there's only one chair.'

Having no desire to sit amongst a twentysomething's smelly socks and takeaway cartons, she suggested they take a walk. They decided on the coast path and as they each passed through the first kissing gate, the sun broke through, bathing the fields in a golden light. Sheep were grazing and it was an idyllic scene that even the sight of a ewe discharging an impressive stream of pee could not spoil.

'It really is a special place,' said Jacob.

'Did you ever come up here with your grandfather?' she asked, feeling slightly guilty for fishing for information.

'Not often,' he admitted.

'Was he a kind man?' she asked.

'He was to me. I think he was harder on my dad, Simon. I was his chance to make up for his mistakes, I suppose. Isn't that why all grandparents spoil their grandchildren? And he wasn't terribly pleasant to my grandmother, from what I can gather.'

Then he told Evelyn about the letter he'd found secreted within the painting's frame. 'Turns out, she hated that picture. She saw it for what it was – a fake and a reminder of his infidelity. He bought it to win her forgiveness. But for my grandmother, it was the last straw.'

'I'm sorry. That painting stirred everything up, didn't it?'

'It brought truths out into the open. But that wasn't the painting's fault, or yours.'

They came to another gate and Jacob held it open for Evelyn.

'My mum told me that my grandparents didn't marry for love. They were picked out for each other, branches of two family trees that were judged suitable for grafting. Maybe that was why my grandfather was repeatedly unfaithful – not that I'm excusing it.'

It was time for Evelyn to lay her cards on the table.

'I have something to tell you,' she forced herself to say. 'Before your grandfather was married, he got a girl pregnant, when she was sixteen and he was eighteen. The result of that relationship was a baby.'

Jacob stopped walking and his brow furrowed. 'My grandfather had another child? Like, not my dad? When?'

'It was in 1964. Before he was married.'

'That's . . . really awful,' Jacob said at last. 'To think, there's someone out there, walking around, who my dad's related to and I'm related to and we've never even met. They would be, what, in their sixties now?'

Evelyn gave a quick nod.

'Who told you this? I mean, did you meet them? Have they got in touch?' He raked his fingers through his hair, as if looking for an answer.

'Jacob, the baby went by a different family name, but she grew up in Portheast. That baby was me. It is me.' Evelyn felt as if the air was being pressed out of her lungs, but she had to continue. 'I only found out very recently myself. I knew I was adopted, but I was never told my . . .' – she gestured into the air – 'my origins.'

Jacob stared at her. 'What do you mean, it's you? How can that be?'

She thought she detected a note of outrage and wasn't sure why. Was it the same reason why his family had rejected her all those years ago, because Cora-May and her child were not Warburn material?

'Sorry,' Jacob added. 'I'm just trying to get my head around all this. Does my dad know?'

'I'm not sure,' she replied. 'I'm guessing he might have an inkling that Jasper sowed his wild oats. But, no, I don't think he knows that I exist. That I'm me.'

She felt the sad truth of her words, because for so much of her life her identity had been a malleable thing, always defined by others. First, she had been a foundling, then a quiet child who drew flowers and talked to animals rather than her classmates. Finally, she'd grown into an adult misfit – a strange bird who picked her way along the beach in a long, flapping coat.

Evelyn had long since trained herself not to cry; it was unproductive and invariably made the tip of her nose turn red, but now she felt a swell of tears demanding to be let out. She chanced a quick glance at Jacob and his expression confused her.

'But this is so cool,' he said, with a wide grin. 'It means we're related. You and me, we're family.'

And after that, it felt good to let the tears flow.

Chapter Fifty

Evelyn kept returning to the handful of photos Bob had given her. They showed a young woman smiling and holding her newborn son, Robert Gilbert Larkwood. Of course, there wasn't one of Cora-May holding her first-born baby, but they helped Evelyn imagine how such a photograph might have looked. Her mother would be younger and her baby girl would be wearing the finished matinee jacket and bonnet Cora-May had been making when her baby was taken from her.

Thanks to everyone's help, the art show was coming together with remarkable ease and on one of her morning walks, the perfect name for the exhibition came to her. She decided they should call it Horizons – not only because it would include the abstract painting of the open sea, but because it felt like a new future was within sight. Whether the council saw sense or not, the museum had left its past behind.

Already, Alison had done a brilliant job of drumming up local press stories and someone from the Tate St Ives was coming. Evelyn was nervous of meeting them because they were a 'real' curator, but George said not to worry. 'When it comes down to it, most jobs involve a bit of bluff and bluster. They know art, but you know Portheast,' had been his advice.

It was a salutary lesson that George, a self-confessed faker, was turning out to be the most genuine man she knew. It proved that you couldn't judge on appearances – and the interesting thing was, people had started to say as much to her.

'Miss Silver, I used to be scared of you, you know,' Kayla told her one afternoon, when she came to the museum to drop off some soft drinks for the Horizons show (the Warburn Spa being less keen to help since Sariah had handed in her notice). 'When me and Jude were little, we'd see you down on the beach and we thought you looked like a big black bird, pecking at the sand. We'd tell each other, "Miss Silver's going to get you!"'

'Is that so?' Evelyn wasn't sure how to take this, because she still did her morning beachcombs, although she'd recently treated herself to a nearly new smart yellow mackintosh. Perhaps, she mused, she now looked more like a yellowhammer.

'But now, it's kind of nice, seeing you down there. You're part of Portheast life,' Kayla continued.

Evelyn smiled. She would take that.

All morning, she had been deliberately avoiding the newsagents because this was the day that the local newspaper came out, and Alison was hoping for a front-page story. Evelyn was less keen: as she pointed out to Alison, it wasn't her photo that was going to be splashed across its pages.

As the hours ticked by, Evelyn was beginning to think she'd got away with it – perhaps the museum's story had been eclipsed by news of a runaway sheep or a shoplifting spree. But then, at lunchtime, Jacob burst through the door waving a paper.

'You're famous!' he said, pointing at a photograph on the front page. Thankfully, Evelyn had had the foresight to stand behind an easel displaying the Peter Lanyon painting and, when the photographer wasn't looking, she'd also bent her knees to ensure she was largely hidden from view.

A previously unknown painting by Peter Lanyon, the famous Cornish 20th century abstract painter, goes on show at Portheast Museum this weekend. The painting has long been in the museum's collections, but was not recognised until recently.

'I have always collected art and objects related to the sea,' said Ms Evelyn Silver, the museum's curator, who admitted that her collection had got a little out of control in recent years. But now her fascination has paid off handsomely.

An expert from the Tate St Ives commented: 'This is a significant and exciting discovery. Peter Lanyon was one of the most innovative artists of post-war Britain, and Cornwall was always central to his identity and inspiration.'

The untitled painting will be on show for a month, thanks to the generosity of its anonymous new owner. Other items in the Horizons exhibition include an installation about sea pollution made by the children of Portheast Primary School.

The opening will also see the unveiling of a plaque to commemorate the three Portheast fishermen lost at sea in 1987, when the vessel Cora-May went down in a storm. 'This is a long overdue tribute and it's good Evelyn has put things right,' commented Bob Larkwood, whose father Gilbert Larkwood lost his life in the disaster.

'As the museum's lease remains up for review, this may be our swansong, so everyone is invited,' added Ms Silver. Representatives from the council declined to comment.

The Horizons exhibition runs from 16 May to 20 June.

'Alison did a good job,' she said to Jacob, trying to ignore the blush creeping up her neck.

'She did. And there's more to come – a piece in *The Guardian* and two art journals. I keep telling Alison she's got a talent for this stuff.'

'Has she had any luck on the job front?'

'Well, she's invited her old boss from the PR company to the exhibition.'

'A canny move. And what about you, Jacob? Are you staying at Potters Newsagents for the foreseeable?'

'No, not forever.' He took off the green bucket hat he was wearing. 'I've told Mrs P that I'll stay until she gets a replacement, but I'd like to do something else. Something more relevant to my degree – well, uncompleted degree.'

'You could always redo your final year,' she said.

'That's a possibility,' Jacob replied. 'But, to be honest, I'd prefer to be working. I'm not sure student life suited me very well.'

'It's not for everyone,' Evelyn said.

'I'm afraid my father wouldn't agree with you. Erm, I managed to talk to him last night, actually.'

Evelyn's heart gave a small leap. 'And did you tell him? About me?'

'I did.' He looked shifty. 'It was probably a bit of a shock, so he didn't say much.'

'No, of course. Understandable.'

A silence fell.

'I'm sure once it's sunk in he'll be more receptive,' Jacob said, his voice faltering. 'It takes time for him to get used to an idea.'

'Nice hat,' she said, because this was getting uncomfortable.

'Thanks.' He grinned, smoothed out the *Surf's Up* logo and put it back on his head. 'Saw it in the window of a charity shop in Truro – it's vintage, you know.' A thought struck him. 'Hey, once this event is out of the way, we should go charity shopping together. I can show you all the good ones.'

Evelyn suspected she had a head start on Jacob when it came to rummaging, but she wasn't going to let on. 'I'd like that very much,' she said.

Chapter
Fifty-One

The day after the local newspaper's front-page story, several people popped into the museum to congratulate Evelyn. Arnold from The Lugger gruffly told her she was 'doing a great job' and Alison's dad, Keith, came in to say she'd 'done Portheast proud'. But towards the end of the day Evelyn had two unexpected visitors – and neither had come about the Horizons exhibition.

The first appeared late in the afternoon, just as the chatter from the café next door was beginning to die down. When Evelyn heard the scrabble of dog claws, she assumed it was Leonard, who was looking after Max the puppy almost full-time now. But she looked up to see old Mrs Moran and her three dachshunds fast advancing on her desk.

'I've come to apologise.' Mrs Moran's face was scrunched up, as if the words pained her.

'Oh?' Evelyn's curiosity was piqued.

'I talked to Bob, or rather he talked to me. He told me about you and Cora-May. I hope you don't mind?'

'I have nothing to be ashamed of,' Evelyn said, sitting up a little straighter.

'Thing is' – she took a deep breath – 'I knew about you being born in St Agnes and I should have told you earlier.'

'Well, you would have saved me a lot of bother,' she said quietly.

Mrs Moran sank down onto a small milking stool, her bulky bottom spreading over its circumference. 'Force of habit, I suppose. Me, my parents, my sister, we learned it was best to keep quiet about certain things. My dad worked up at Warburn Hall, you see. Any gossip and he'd have lost his job. Then, time passed – you seemed a happy enough child. You went away for a bit, didn't you? Then, you were back, just getting on with your life. You lost your mother, Elsbeth. But you seemed to cope. Kept busy here; doing your thing on the beach . . .' Mrs Moran gestured in that direction. 'Why would I want to upset you?'

'To tell me the truth?' Evelyn suggested.

'I came close, believe me. Especially once Mr Silver, rest his soul, was gone. But then I noticed that the young 'un, that Jacob Warburn, was back in town and, as I say, old habits die hard.' She shook her head. '"Don't bite the hand that feeds you. Especially when it's a Warburn" – that's what Dad told us.'

Evelyn had never been fond of Mrs Moran. She saw her as a mean-spirited woman and it was telling that her own children rarely visited. Left alone, she'd made herself feel important by being the town gossip, hoarding information and meting out scraps when she saw fit. But now Evelyn started to understand that more lay behind her decades of silence: a misplaced loyalty to the Warburn family who had expected discretion from their staff, including their families.

Damping down her anger, she asked, 'Did you know Cora-May?'

'We weren't good friends, but we were at school together.' Mrs Moran's chin shrank into a tight nugget, as if she was trying not to cry. 'Then she went straight into service and I didn't see much of her after that. But up at the Hall, my dad saw her. He heard things, about what happened.' She blew her nose.

Evelyn didn't want this woman's crocodile tears, she wanted information. 'What was she like?' she pressed.

'Oh, at school she liked to laugh and have fun. She liked animals, I remember that. Cried buckets when her dad killed the chickens. Then, in spring, she refused to eat even the smallest morsel of lamb. Said she'd rather go hungry.'

Evelyn felt a squeeze around her heart.

'Thing is, I got to know your mum Elsbeth, too. So that was another reason why I didn't want to go upsetting things. It wasn't my secret to tell.'

Evelyn remained quiet, waiting for more.

'I used to see Elsbeth up near the cliff path,' Mrs Moran continued. 'I was a mum myself by then and after dropping the kids at school I'd take the dog up there. It was my escape, just for half an hour, and that's where I'd see her. Painting or just looking out to sea. She'd show me her work if I asked, but shyly, like she didn't realise how good she was.'

'She was very talented,' Evelyn agreed.

'She was a nice woman, kind to me. But always guarded, like there were things she was keeping inside.'

It felt to Evelyn as if her mother had spent too much of her short life trying to hide things: like why she'd given up her education and future career to move to a small harbour town in Cornwall, where, overnight, she'd become a mother. Was she simply in thrall to Edwin Silver? Even if she did some digging, Evelyn sensed this was something she'd never know. Her mother had always felt unreachable and seemed destined to remain so.

'There was a point when I thought Elsbeth was going to tell you herself,' Mrs Moran said in a rush. 'It was a few years after you came back from London and I met her on the clifftop. We chatted for a bit, she asked after my kids and then she went ever so quiet. Said she was thinking of setting the record straight with you. She needed to ask your dad's permission, but I got the sense she'd made up her mind.'

'When would this have been?' Evelyn asked hesitantly.

'Oh, my Sandra had started nursing in Cardiff, so I'd say . . .' Mrs Moran looked up at the dark rafters. 'About 1992?'

That would have made Evelyn twenty-eight and, strangely enough, she had sensed a shift in her mother's mood around then. With the museum established, her father was away for long stretches, meaning she and her mother had talked more, even discussing Evelyn studying for a Master's. 'But not another correspondence course. You could go somewhere with young people and lectures and student halls and fun nights out and, oh, wouldn't that be wonderful?' Her mother's eyes were ablaze. 'Evelyn, there's a whole world out there.'

At the time, Evelyn had put Elsbeth's restless outbursts down to 'the time of life', because she was forever throwing open windows to let in the cold air and tugging at the collar of her blouse, as if unable to breathe.

It was only a few months later that Elsbeth Silver fell to her knees in a patch of sea-thrift and took her last breath, with only Edwin Silver there to comfort her.

A coldness spread through Evelyn, like a dark cloud blocking out the sun, as she wondered what might have been discussed between her parents before her mother took her last walk among the clifftop grasses.

Oblivious, Mrs Moran passed her an envelope. 'Anyway, this is for you.'

Numbly, she opened the envelope and drew out an old photograph, a school line-up of girls in drab tunics, all looking serious. Mrs Moran leaned in and Evelyn could smell the woman's breath, sour as old milk. 'That's her,' Mrs Moran said, pointing to a girl in the back row. 'And that's me.' Her finger moved to the other end of the row. 'We were thirteen.'

Evelyn had seen Bob's photographs of Cora-May as a wife and mother, but this was her before she'd set eyes on Jasper Warburn. Evelyn held the photograph a little closer. She saw a tall girl with a fine nose and dark eyes and you could tell from the shape of her lips that she was trying very hard not to smile.

'Lovely,' Evelyn said, her throat tightening. 'Thank you.'

Mrs Moran stood and the milking stool wobbled then righted itself. 'Elsbeth Silver was your mother. But Cora-May, well. As you can see, she's the spit of you.'

After she'd left, Evelyn put the photograph away. She would share it with Bob, but not the rest of Portheast. Sometimes, it was important to keep parts of yourself back, she thought. Not everything was for sharing, not even the dark suspicions that were forming in her mind about Edwin Silver and the final lengths he might have gone to, to secure his world.

When the final visitor of the day appeared, it was a relief, because Evelyn had been left with her thoughts for too long. It was just before closing time when she heard a timid knock and looked up to see a stranger: a woman who had an evangelical look about her, dressed in light blue with tan tights and sensible shoes. At her neck hung a small crucifix and her hair was fixed in a neat bun.

'Are you still open?' the woman asked.

'I can be,' Evelyn replied.

'I saw the newspaper article,' the woman said. 'About your museum.'

'Ah, well the exhibition doesn't open until Saturday, but you're welcome to come then. There will be lots to see, plus some very good cakes and tea or soft drinks.' She had learned her lesson twice over, that alcohol and museum artefacts were not a good mix.

'Actually, it's not about the show. I thought it was high time I came to say thank you.'

Evelyn breathed a sigh of relief: this sort of visitor was always welcome.

'You found something that was very precious to me.' The woman came closer. 'It might not seem important, but it was a reminder of a special day and I never thought I'd see it again.'

'What was it?'

'A cracked china cup.' The woman let out an embarrassed laugh. 'It sounds silly, doesn't it?'

Evelyn shook her head. 'Not at all. Some objects mean the world to us.'

'I think you found it in a jumble sale.'

'Yes, in Roche, about six years ago?'

'That's the one.'

Evelyn felt a final piece of the jigsaw slot into place. 'I'm curious, though, how did that pretty cup end up there?'

'I'd recently moved back to Cornwall, you see, and I was flatsharing with another teacher called Anya, who was organising the school jumble sale. I was away for the weekend when she did a sweep through our flat for the bric-a-brac stall. "Help yourself to anything old or broken," I'd said, so she took a free Sports Direct mug and that little teacup.'

'You must have been so upset.'

'Oh, I was. Funny thing was, the Sports Direct mug turned up again on Monday morning: the headteacher said it was perfect for his morning brew. I asked everyone, but that little cup seemed to have disappeared into thin air. Until a few months ago, when my sister saw it on a poster.'

Evelyn smiled and thanked the woman. Then she said, 'Will you come back on Saturday, for the opening?'

The woman didn't answer.

Evelyn added, 'She'll be here.'

'She?'

'Sariah.'

'Ah.' The woman narrowed her eyes. 'I suppose I should have guessed there are no secrets in a place like this.'

'Oh, I'd say there are plenty,' Evelyn replied. 'It's just that this museum seems to bring them to the surface.'

Before Rose left, Evelyn said she'd like to show her something and led her towards the Miscellanea cabinet.

'Found attached to a baby's blanket with a safety pin (now rusted),' Rose read aloud. 'Gosh, that's very sad.'

'It is. But there's an update, so I'll need to change the label,' Evelyn said.

'Does the story have a happy ending?' Rose asked.

Evelyn thought for a moment. 'Certainly happier,' she said finally. 'I was too late to meet my own birth mother, but in trying to find her I've met so many other good people, including your Sariah. She's been a good friend and you should be proud of her.'

Rose's reply was barely audible. 'I am.'

'So come. On Saturday.'

Rose didn't reply. Instead, she pointed at the lace. 'Yours, then?' and Evelyn nodded.

'I lost myself for a while, after I had her,' Rose said, her voice thick with emotion. 'I was so young and as soon as I could I left home. I wanted to leave that person behind.'

'We all lose ourselves at one point or another,' Evelyn said, only just realising the truth in her words. 'I was lost for years; my whole life, really.'

'I'm sorry to hear that.' Rose touched her gold chain.

'That's OK. I think I'm finding my way home now. What's that saying? Home isn't a place, it's the people. And the funny thing is, they were here all along.'

Chapter Fifty-Two

When the Horizons exhibition was only days away, a small package arrived at Potters Newsagents, addressed to Jacob. The postman's arrival coincided with a van delivery of forty-eight cans of fizzy drinks and three boxes of crisps, so it was a while before Jacob got around to opening it. The other reason for the delay was because he recognised the handwriting as his father's. Their last conversation hadn't gone well and Jacob had a feeling that this package would not be good news.

As it turned out, he was only half right.

Once the shop was quiet, Jacob ripped it open and tipped the contents onto the counter. Out slid a bundle of old letters, tied together with blue wool, and wrapped around the bundle was a typed covering letter. He read that first.

> Dear Jacob,
> Possibly you are surprised to hear from your father by old-fashioned letter. However, that seems to be the Warburn way – to hide things away but leave a paper trail to explain ourselves after the event.

Thank you for inviting me to the exhibition in Portheast. I see *The Guardian* is calling it 'A rare opportunity to see a gem of modern art'.

But the real reason you've asked me is to meet this Evelyn Silver. I will not be coming and I hope these letters will help explain why.

However, I have tried to make amends in a different way. I suspect you will accuse me of throwing money at a problem and you wouldn't be wrong.

The Lanyon painting is nice enough, but there's no way it's worth the sum I paid. Even the art dealer looked shocked, but when I explained it had a personal significance he didn't quibble. Why would he, when he was in line for a percentage?

A windfall for Evelyn Silver has been long overdue. She has been paid a stipend in perpetuity but today it's almost worthless – my father Jasper hadn't considered inflation when he set it up all those years ago. I hope this evens things out a little, at least on the financial front.

As for the moral side of things, well not all deficits can be paid off.

In his defence, my father Jasper was a callow eighteen-year-old when he met Evelyn's mother, Cora-May. Their love affair started in the summer before he went up to Oxford. She was in service at Warburn Hall and he was the son and heir, but from what I gather, their love was genuine. Given that he later tried to win her back, I suspect his ardour never waned.

He and my mother, Catherine, got engaged while he was at Oxford and the marriage was intended to draw a line underneath the business with Cora-May. Except it didn't work. And I can tell you, growing up in a loveless marriage wasn't much fun.

My father's dalliances continued: men of his class and generation saw it as their birthright, hence the family pied-à-terre in Pimlico. In all honesty, that flat still comes in handy.

When I cleared out Warburn Hall – I had no desire to take up residence in that draughty, dark place – I found these letters, written by my father to Cora-May. This was when I first learned of Evelyn's existence.

The first letter was sent in 1964 and the last in 1987. Interestingly, they were all inside a larger envelope with his name on the front, as if they had been returned as a job lot, with the final letter still sealed.

They tell one side of the story, but another side was my own unhappy childhood due to my parents' empty marriage.

For these reasons, I cannot bring myself to meet Evelyn Silver.

There are six letters in all, enclosed.

Regards, Simon Warburn

His father had always taken a perverse pride in never changing his mind, so Jacob wasn't entirely surprised by his words, but they left a deep ache in his chest. Jacob pulled on the end of the blue wool and the stack of letters came free. He read them in order.

20 September 1964
My dearest Cora-May,

I hope your stay in St Agnes is proving comfortable. The home comes recommended and my father says there are wholesome activities and a chapel for daily prayers.

I wish I were permitted to visit, but when you return with our baby in November I will be waiting for you. Father wants me to take up my place at Oxford in October, but I will talk to him again and appeal to his better side. What decent person could deny true love?

There is a pretty estate cottage in Cowell that I have my eye on for the three of us. It will be a simple but perfect life. I have a little money saved and I am writing poems and I hope to make a living from them one day.

Are you grown big? Is the baby kicking? I wish I could be with you, but Father says the mother and baby home is a better option: you will be well looked after and no local gossip will sully our future.

Just think, by Christmas, our baby will be born and we shall be married. My love, I cannot wait.

Love, Jasper

28 November 1964

My sweet Cora-May,

A baby girl! How wonderful. My heart is broken that you are not yet well enough to come home with her. Father says the home is the best place for a new mother to recover. Is the food good? Is she thriving? Let us each think of a name for her and compare notes when you are well enough to travel.

My love, stay strong. In the end, Father made it very hard for me to wait for you at Warburn, and so I write to you from Oxford. You know Father.

I feel sure that he will soon see reason. I long to return to Warburn and to you.

All my love, Jasper

2 December 1964

Dear Cora-May,

I know that by now tomorrow's arrangement has been explained to you. Please remember it is only temporary. While you remain weak and I am busy with my studies, this seems a practical solution. Besides, Father will not hear otherwise. If I go against him, we will have nothing: no home, no funds. Please, let's give this idea a go.

You may still have the cottage in Cowell. It is for you and your parents. As for the baby, I have met the perfect couple to help us out. He's a decent chap who has put his studies on hold to do some research and his fiancée is a sweet thing.

They are to be married and Father has agreed to set them up in a nice house in Portheast, where Edwin can continue his research. They will look after the baby and treat her as their own. The local doctor will collect her soon. He is a family friend and utterly trustworthy.

It is agreed, the baby will be referred to as a foundling.

With love, Jasper

12 May 1966

Dear Cora-May,

As you may have heard, I am to be married to Catherine Beaumont. Our families go way back. I hope you are keeping well and the cottage is to your liking.

The child is thriving, according to the doctor. She will be given a suitable upbringing.

Best wishes, Jasper

28 October 1987

Dear Cora-May,

I was very sorry to hear of the death of your husband, Gilbert Larkwood. Fishing is an honourable profession, but not without its dangers.

I hear you have a fine son named Robert and I hope he is some comfort to you. Catherine and I also have a son of a similar age, Simon. He's twenty-two now and a chip off the old block.

But Cora-May, there is no love in my marriage. I have only been in love once and that was with you. Please let us try again? My father is an old man and he's ruled my life for too long. I wish I had been braver all those years ago.

Our child is a young woman now and I hear she will soon take up a job locally, as curator of the new museum, so it was for the best. She had opportunities you could not have provided.

If you will consider my proposal, please write back.

Those summer days with you were the best I've known.

Jasper

12 December 1987

Dear Cora-May,

This is the last letter I shall write. I am sorry for surprising you like that, but when I saw you sitting on a bench on the quay I was compelled to come over.

It seemed you were looking out for someone, but clearly it wasn't me. I only wanted to declare my desire to be reunited, but you made your feelings clear: it was too little too late.

Unfortunately, Portheast being a small town, we were seen talking and word got back to Catherine. I have a plan to win her over, though. I've bought her a rather nice painting – a recently discovered Alfred Wallis. She's a lucky woman.

Cora-May, I accept your rebuttal, but your words wounded me and they have run around my head all week. You said, 'The day you took away my daughter, you broke me in two'.

One day, I hope those broken pieces may mend.

Yours, Jasper Warburn

While Jacob had few illusions about his father, these letters revealed a very different side to the genial grandfather he remembered fondly yet, it turned out, had barely known. Jacob reassembled the letters and retied the blue wool. It was time, he decided, to draw his own line under what his father blithely called 'the Warburn way'.

He carried the package the short distance to Portheast Antiques, where he found George Rook busy painting a pine cabinet.

'I need some advice,' he began. 'These letters tell the story of Evelyn's past.'

George set down his paintbrush and read the letters, taking his time.

'Well, they are quite the find,' he said.

'Shall I show them to her?' Jacob asked.

'Of course.'

'And what about this one?' He handed George the covering letter from his father.

'Tricky,' George pronounced. 'Not the mystery buyer we imagined.'

He resumed painting the cabinet with long, even strokes. 'It might feel kinder to hide it, but I think there have been too many secrets in Evelyn's life already.'

With the exhibition imminent, Jacob decided that the sooner Evelyn knew the truth the better and he showed her the letters that afternoon. First, he handed over the bundle written by Sir Jasper and he watched as her expression moved through joy to confusion and then pain.

'Poor Cora-May,' she said quietly. 'Alone, believing he would come.'

'I know.'

'And her words: "broke me in two".' She covered her face.

'I'm sorry,' he said after a while. 'Anyway, I think they're rightfully yours so it's up to you what you do with them.'

She gave a brief nod.

Jacob cleared his throat. 'Then there's this one, from my father.' He passed it over but this time as Evelyn read, her expression remained impenetrable. She passed it back with a weary smile. 'The mystery buyer is revealed.'

'It probably feels like you've been deceived, yet again.'

Her answer surprised him. 'Not in the least,' she said smartly. 'To be honest, it's a relief.'

'How so?'

'The Warburn family wronged Cora-May and myself. As time travel is not an option, I accept the money as compensation. In truth, I was starting to feel bad that an art lover had paid over the odds for the painting. Simon Warburn? Not so much.

'In fact,' she continued, 'everything about that painting brings me pleasure. It speaks of open skies and a yearning for freedom and, best of all, it ended up in my museum because of my mother Elsbeth. I think it spoke to her.'

Evelyn deftly secreted the old letters in a drawer of her desk and turned a key. 'Now, since you're here, you can make yourself useful,' she said, passing him a broom. 'In case you've forgotten, we've got an exhibition to put on.'

Jacob looked at his father's letter, which Evelyn had left on her desk.

'Erm, what shall I do with this?'

Evelyn, who was already polishing her cabinets with unusual force, looked round. 'I have a system now,' she said. 'Beside my desk, you'll find two bin bags. Unless you object, I suggest you put it straight into the one marked *Rubbish*.'

Chapter
Fifty-Three

A few short months ago, Alison had been in the habit of waking early. Often, she'd come to with a gasp, the adrenaline already jumping in her veins and her heart banging. All fright and no flight, she had coped with the panic-like rush by keeping still until it passed.

These days, she'd started waking early again, but it felt different: there was a sharpness to her thoughts, as if each idea was shot through with something pure. Now, the adrenaline was on her side.

She used the time to lie in her childhood bed and go over the list of things she wanted to do. It wasn't the sort of list she could write down and pin to her dad's fridge, more one that existed in her head.

At the top were:

- Find job, but something interesting
- Make Will feel safe/loved and stick to his routine
- Spend more time with Dad

Already, she realised that she'd have to be flexible about aim number one because the job market was dire, especially for part-time work. Jacob said she should get in touch with the PR company, but although it had been fun – and Alison loved promoting power tools as much as the next woman – she knew she wanted to do something more meaningful.

She realised she couldn't be too choosy, though. Every day she checked the websites and unless you were able to lay roof tiles, administer anaesthetics or flip burgers, it was slim pickings. The only remotely suitable job was as a door-to-door market researcher. But the thought of standing on doorsteps and asking people endless questions about their broadband provider or favourite dishwasher tablets made her heart sink. Plus for that position, she needed her own car.

Which brought her to the thorny issue of aim four:

- Sort car/money/access with Roy

Since Jacob's Mini had been torched, aim four had slid right down to the bottom of her list. But today she saw with fresh clarity that ignoring the Roy issue was holding her back from ticking anything off her list. He was like a bindweed that had crept into every part of her life and until she wrenched that weed out by its roots, there was no chance of her flourishing, let alone getting to the last item on her list. Which was:

- Spend more time with Jacob

After dropping Will at nursery, Alison kept walking until she found herself at the oily forecourt of the Pinlow brothers' repair garage. When she smelled the engine grease and heard the blare of rock music, she almost lost her nerve and then she thought of Will, her gentle, kind boy, and she took a deep breath.

In her mind, she'd imagined Roy might be lying under a car on a creeper trolley with his legs sticking out, which would give her a handy advantage as she stood over him and said her piece. But instead she came face to face with him as he emerged from the garage toilet (a grim cubicle she'd resorted to once, when pregnant and desperate). He was wiping his hands on his overalls and she wondered if that meant he'd washed them or that he hadn't.

For a fleeting moment, Roy looked alarmed.

'Alison,' he said stupidly. Then, 'Has something happened to Will?'

'No, he's fine,' she said quickly. 'But I thought it was time for us to talk.'

Roy gave a dismissive snort. 'Babe, I'm at work. If you've come to apologise, you know when I finish.'

It was then she realised Roy would never understand or admit to what he'd done and the best she could hope for was civility. She felt her heart speed up and her mouth grew dry. She had to be strong.

'I need my car back, Roy. And if you want to see Will that's fine, but we'll need to agree a regular time and place.'

Roy was making a show of laughing and shaking his head. 'You are a piece of work, Alison, you know that?' He walked towards her and instinctively she stepped back because she could tell the switch was about to flip.

But then the atmosphere changed. Someone snapped off the radio and suddenly Roy had lost his macho soundtrack. It was Roy's older brother, Grant, and she wondered how long he'd been listening.

He nodded at Alison. 'You and Will doing alright?'

'He's fine. We're both fine.'

Grant kept his eyes on Alison as he spoke very calmly to his brother. 'Roy, give her the car keys.'

'But I need it. It's mine now.'

'Give them to her.'

To reach into his jeans pocket, Roy had to peel down the top half of his overalls and as he stood there with his sleeves turned inside-out and hanging down from his waist, Alison saw him for what he was: a big toddler who was prone to tantrums. Dangerous ones that she'd been right to be scared of, but tantrums nonetheless.

'I can help with any visits with the little 'un if you like,' Grant said. 'Be a bit of a go-between.'

'Thanks,' she said. Her eyes flicked back to Roy and only just in time because she saw a glint in the air as he pitched the key fob towards her. She caught it, one-handed.

'I'll be in touch,' she said and walked as calmly as she could towards her little red car. Once she was behind the wheel, the familiarity somehow gave her the last bit of courage she needed. She wound down the windows because the inside of her car reeked of sweat and old beer and she was already looking forward to getting it cleaned.

Alison Blake put her foot on the accelerator and didn't look back.

Chapter
Fifty-Four

Once more, Evelyn was being herded by an overenthusiastic Alison, but this time she felt like she was in good hands. Each of the museum committee members had been given timetables for the launch of the Horizons exhibition and Evelyn read hers out loud to Della. '10 a.m. Evelyn arrives in chosen outfit. 11 a.m. Evelyn has make-up done by Jude. 12 p.m. Evelyn gives speech (two minutes).'

She put the piece of paper down. 'I'm a grown woman, does she think I need this level of intervention?'

'Don't be offended, she took me in hand too. Said my clothes were either traveller hippy or power-dressing and I needed to find a comfortable middle ground.'

Evelyn had to admit the result was good because Della's hair had been trimmed and treated with a toner that had turned it a soft pinky-blond. She was wearing a jumpsuit, but it wasn't like the low-cut electric blue number she'd sported for Second Chances; it was navy and belted and said 'efficient' rather than 'Disco Inferno'.

For Evelyn's outfit, Alison had taken the extreme measure of a home visit. 'Hmm, style-wise, let's take a break from browns and greys as we head into spring,' she'd said breezily as she scanned Evelyn's meagre wardrobe. She'd flicked through the hangers until she came across the sailor-collar dress Evelyn had bought in Topshop in Oxford Circus all those years ago. 'Vintage nautical chic – very fitting for the occasion, no?' Once it was on, Evelyn had to agree it was a good choice and she'd always liked its square collar and satin ribbon tie.

Now, on the day of the exhibition, it was almost 12 p.m. and Evelyn was ready to step onto the podium (aka the faithful tea chest covered in a white sheet).

'Hello, everyone,' she began. 'It gives me great pleasure to welcome you to our Horizons exhibition, where we celebrate a painting by Peter Lanyon, which captures the extraordinary light of the Cornish coast.' She paused. 'Three months ago, certain people expressed the wish to "put Portheast on the map" and I hope this fits the bill.' Looking out, she spotted Mr Palmer at the back of the small crowd, thanks to the way Cornwall's extraordinary light highlighted his bald patch.

'You may notice that Portheast Museum's name has been short-ened – thank you, Leonard, for your sign-writing skills – and I hope that this simpler name will cement the connection between us and the town. I would like to thank the museum's committee – Della, Sariah, Alison and Jacob – for their hard work.

'Please also take the time to admire our other new exhibits. First, the children of Portheast Primary School have created a dis-play about the damage plastic is wreaking on our marine life.' She gestured over towards the entrance, where a large fishing net was suspended from the rafters and shimmered with shards of plastic. Ice cream wrappers and sandwich bags fluttered between plastic shoes, a broken diving fin, toys and tangles of fishing rope. It had a sobering sort of beauty.

'Secondly, there are some lovely paintings by the late Elsbeth Silver, which depict our native flora and fauna, some of which are now endangered species.

'Finally, if you progress to the Fishing Life area, you will see the recently restored boat name board for the *Cora-May*. She went down in 1987 with her crew, men who were husbands, fathers and sons, all missed but not forgotten. The restored boat name board and a plaque commemorate those lives lost.'

Instinctively, those wearing hats removed them and a moment's silence was observed.

'Please enjoy the exhibition and sample some truly excellent refreshments provided by The Cake Shed. Thank you.'

There was a ripple of applause as Evelyn stepped down and she spotted Alison mouthing, 'Well done'. Except then came the sound of one person clapping in an overly long and loud way and Mr Palmer walked towards the front. As he gave Evelyn an oily smile, she feared the worst. This wasn't fair – not to her and not to the community that had come together to make this happen.

Regardless, Mr Palmer stepped onto the podium. 'Ladies and gentlemen,' he said and waited for a hush to settle.

'I know that many are waiting to hear about the future of these historic sheds.' He beamed out at the crowd, his gaze skimming past Evelyn and Della. 'Officially, our decision is due next week, but I am minded to announce it now.'

Beside her, Evelyn sensed Alison and Jacob's excitement and, over by the food table, Sariah was standing on tiptoes. Only she and Della remained poker-faced.

'Due to the groundswell of support and the council's commit-ment to preserving local history, we are happy to extend the leases on both sheds.'

'Yes!' Della punched the air and a cheer rose up from the crowd, but Evelyn knew there was more to come.

'However,' Mr Palmer continued. 'We will be increasing the rent, in line with the market.' Well, that was to be expected, Evelyn supposed.

But Mr Palmer wasn't quite finished. 'And as a gesture of commitment, we ask that the first five years' rent be paid up front.'

'What the actual?' Della advanced, hands on hips. 'So we just rummage around in our pockets to find, what, a spare fifteen grand a year?'

'Closer to twenty thousand,' Mr Palmer clarified. 'Each. Multiplied by five.' He shrugged. 'It's what Rufus Rowan Holdings offered.'

'You can't do that,' Della protested. 'It's immoral.'

Mr Palmer inclined his head, as if to indicate that he could and would.

Della caught Evelyn's eye. 'Come on: you're not going to take this, are you?' she said.

So Evelyn walked the short distance back to the sheet-covered podium. 'May I?' she asked and, sensing a win, Mr Palmer stepped down.

She drew breath. Dignity at all times, she reminded herself and, looking Mr Palmer in the eye, she said, 'Thank you. This is marvellous news.'

'What?' Della gasped and Evelyn tried not to notice that Alison was frowning and Sariah had turned away in disgust.

'I totally understand. Business is business.' She brought her hands together and gave a serene smile. 'It's. All. Fine.'

She made as if to step down then paused, one finger in the air. 'Just send the paperwork to my lawyer and I'll authorise her to pay the rent up front for both sheds. Not a problem.'

It wasn't often that Evelyn Silver experienced elation but in that moment, she embraced every fizzy, head-spinning, heart-pumping molecule of it and she committed the image of Mr Palmer's face — his mouth opening and shutting like a fish's — to memory.

Della wasted no time in catching up with her. 'Mate, you can't just make up things like that. You're getting people's hopes up and then you'll disappoint them. What are you playing at?'

It felt good to lay a reassuring hand on Della's arm. 'Really, don't worry,' she said. 'I'll explain later.'

First, she wanted to see people's responses to the newest exhibit: the restored boat name board of the *Cora-May*. Leonard had taken the rescued fragment that spelled out *-ORA-* and set it in a rectangle of white plaster. Then, on either side of the blue wood, he had built up the plaster to recreate the missing sections of the name board and etched the rest of the boat's name in ghostly white-on-white letters. It was a work of art that conveyed both absence and presence, indicating that those who were missing had not been forgotten.

A voice beside her said, 'Perfect, isn't it?'

It was George, doing his usual thing of creeping up on her, but also saying exactly what was on her mind.

'Perfect,' she agreed.

'I take it you've decided what to do with your windfall, then,' he said.

'I think so. It feels right,' she replied.

They continued looking at the reworked name board.

'What about asking Leonard to do something similar for a few other museum items? I'm thinking specifically of your piece of lace,' said George.

Evelyn thought of her lonely scrap of lace that had been overlooked for so long and how it might look. If Bob agreed, the two halves of the lace could be pressed into wet plaster: one with its rusted safety pin, the other half more pristine because it had been kept hidden inside a book of poetry. The two ragged edges would lie side by side, almost joined but with a distance between them, representing the years apart. It would convey the pain of that gap remaining forever unbreached.

'Yes,' she said slowly. 'I like that idea.'

She looked around to say thank you to Leonard, but he was busy talking dogs with Jacob, who in turn was making a fuss of Max the puppy.

Closer by, two big blokes, the muscle that George had hired as 'security', flanked the Lanyon painting. Burly though they were, they were also connoisseurs of fine art and one was deep in conversation with Bob, explaining modernism and the rise of multiple perspectives.

On the other side of the room, Sariah confidently made her way through the crowd with a tray, handing out napkins and slices of cake. She was in her element. Then Evelyn spotted Grace and, to her delight, saw she was talking to her sister Rose: one was holding a piece of carrot cake, the other a slice of lemon drizzle and Evelyn watched as each sister took a bite, then gave a long serious nod before swapping cakes.

Before long, the hubbub began to die down. Teacups were left on tables and all the cake had disappeared. 'Not even a crumb left,' Della remarked with satisfaction. Evelyn hadn't had a chance to catch up with Alison, who was talking to a man in a baseball cap and she had a hunch he was from the PR company.

Alison's dad, Keith, was easy to spot because he had his grandson, Will, on his shoulders. Evelyn wasn't the sort of person who got dewy-eyed about children, but even she had to admit he was a very bonny boy. Alison must have called out to her dad because he turned around and Evelyn glimpsed who Keith had been talking to: a sprightly gentleman with snowy white hair and bright eyes and she wondered if it was Steven West, the owner of the embroidered sailcloth.

Three months ago, she had randomly selected four items for her poster. Of course her lace held a personal meaning, but the other pieces had intrigued her and it had turned out that the embroidered sailcloth, the cracked teacup and the fake Alfred Wallis had all held hidden stories. Yes, each had brought difficult secrets to the surface, including her own, but, as George had once told her, 'Truths are what help us move on'.

Looking around, she felt proud of the museum, now so different from the damp, dingy shed she'd hidden herself away in for so long. Somehow it didn't feel like 'her' museum anymore and that was down to Della, Jacob, Sariah, Alison and George.

Epilogue

THREE MONTHS LATER

Bob had promised to be there on time and she didn't doubt him. But the others: a beach clean at dawn? She wasn't holding her breath.

So at first it was just Bob and herself standing together in the blue darkness, listening to the familiar rush and drag of the waves. The horizon was starting to lighten as the next person arrived. It was George and he strolled across the sand like this was no big deal, when Evelyn knew for a fact that he rarely opened his eyes before 9 a.m.

Next came Sariah and Della, who could be heard grumbling loudly. 'I mean, why does it have to be at dawn? The rubbish is still going to be there at lunchtime.' But as they got closer, Della stopped in her tracks.

Even Evelyn, who had seen many a Portheast sunrise, was impressed by this morning's display, with clouds of orange and pink haloed in gold against a lilac sky. Della let out a low whistle. 'OK, now I get it. Totally worth it.'

Last to arrive were Jacob, Alison and Will, who was definitely the most lively of the three. 'Sorry, took us ages to get out of the door,' Alison said, trying to wrestle her son into a jacket. Jacob set about handing out yellow fabric tote bags and litter pickers made from recycled marine plastic – the sort that Evelyn wanted to sell in the museum shop, once it was up and running.

Taking on both leases for the boatsheds had been surprisingly straightforward. The last Evelyn had heard, Rufus Rowan Holdings had been sniffing around a former bank building in Fowey, which lacked the harbourside views but still had 'wonderful high ceilings'.

After a bit of stretching and yawning (and a flat refusal from Will to wear his jacket), the group set off to comb the beach. Instinctively, they spread across the sand in a line, Jacob and Alison closest to the incoming tide so that Will could splash through the waves in his new wellington boots.

The yellow tote bags had been Alison's idea and had *Pick for Portheast* printed on one side and the logo of a local PR company on the other. The fact that she'd persuaded her old boss to sponsor the bags even after she'd turned down his job offer was testament to her negotiation skills. 'I want to move forward, not back,' she'd explained to Evelyn, who understood completely.

They worked in companionable silence and now and then Evelyn glanced right and left, to see what the others had found. Bob had already given up on his litter picker, preferring to do the job by hand because he was concentrating on tiny bits of sea-smoothed plastic. In contrast, Della proudly pincered and held up each of her finds, which included a clump of orange netting, a dented beer can and a pair of red boxer shorts, which she waved at George: 'You missing anything, mate?'

Evelyn had to admit it was a good system – already, they had covered half the beach – but it felt very different to her lone beach scours. Back then, she'd been free to take whatever meandering route along the shore she liked, drawn by a glint of metal, the shine of cellophane or an unusual shape. But hers had been a lonely route and now, when she came across something curious, she had people to share it with – friends and family.

When they had finished, the sky was a milky blue and the sand had lost its early-morning cool. It wouldn't be long before holidaymakers started to arrive, but for now they still had the beach to themselves and they gathered around the big rock to compare their finds.

George had the best haul, which included a piece of green sea glass and a dangly beaded earring. 'That might be special to someone,' Evelyn said and George dutifully put it in his pocket for safekeeping. Bob held out a fistful of tiny plastic fragments and Sariah opened a tote bag containing plastic bottles, a shredded tennis ball and a beach spade.

Then, with a flourish, Della produced two flasks of coffee and handed round enamel mugs. Evelyn spotted a handy nook in the rock where she could set down her mug, but Sariah reached out and tapped her wrist. 'Careful. Mind it doesn't fall,' she murmured.

Secretly, Evelyn had been hoping for a few slices of Sariah's cake, but she knew there were rarely any leftovers. Sariah baked fresh each day, sending the glorious smell of fruit tarts, fluffy sponges or salted caramel cookies drifting into the museum.

The sun was getting higher and Evelyn knew she was running out of time.

'I have an announcement,' she said.

Beside her, George moved a little closer, because he alone knew what she was going to say.

'As you all know, I have used some of my windfall to secure the museum's future.'

'Hurray!' said Alison, raising her enamel mug.

'Go, Evelyn!' Della added.

She looked over her shoulder towards the quay. 'The thing is, the museum has been my world for so long. At times, it was my anchor, but it also weighed me down.' She looked at each person in turn and smiled. 'It has kept secrets and it's revealed a fair few. More importantly, it has brought all of us together.'

'Hear, hear,' said Sariah, lifting her mug into the air. 'To friendship.'

Evelyn continued: 'To me, the best thing is that it doesn't feel like "my" museum anymore. It represents Portheast and everyone who lives here. Which is why it's time for me to leave and let someone fresh take over.'

'What do you mean?' Della protested.

'I shall be passing the day-to-day running of Portheast Museum to two highly capable people. If he's willing, I would like Jacob to be the new curator. And Alison, I would love you to take charge of publicity and community links.'

'Seriously?' Jacob asked.

'I'm very serious,' she replied. 'I can see you two building on the link with the school that Bob started and taking the museum to new heights.'

'That would be amazing. I can't believe it.' Alison beamed. 'We'll do you proud, I promise.' She lifted her son into a huge hug – 'What do you think of that? Your mum's got a new job!' – and Jacob slipped his arm around Alison's shoulders.

But on the edge of the group, Bob wouldn't look her in the eye and she knew she needed to explain more. 'I'd also like to set in place another museum initiative. Each summer, we will charter a Portheast Museum boat to take visitors around the harbour and along the coast. It will only run when the sea is calm and the skipper will tell visitors about the old fishing ways. If you are willing, Bob, I would like you to be the skipper.'

Bob looked up. 'Calm days only, you say?'

'Definitely. We don't want seasick tourists, do we?'

'Then I would be glad to,' he replied solemnly.

'There's also the small matter of a black cat called Toots who will need looking after,' she added.

Bob frowned and rubbed his chin. 'Hmm. Does he like fish?'

'He does.'

'Then we have a deal.'

'Sariah and Della, the council has agreed to the plan to join the two sheds, but I think you two can see the project through. I'm not really a building site sort of person.'

'Not a problem,' said Della. 'We're both good at keeping a crew in line and, personally, I think I would rock a hard hat.'

'But I don't get it.' Sariah got to her feet. 'Where are you going? Why are you leaving? All the things that we shared – don't they mean anything to you?'

Evelyn felt her throat swell.

'I'm not going forever,' she said more gently. 'I just need to spread my wings a bit.'

Sariah still looked upset.

'So much of my life has been about looking back,' Evelyn explained. 'Now I need to look forward. And to answer your question, yes. You all mean the world to me.'

No one said anything for a moment and Bob had to turn away and vigorously rub his eye, muttering something about the sand and the wind.

'So where are you going?' Della asked. 'London?'

'No, further afield,' Evelyn said. 'I thought I'd travel.'

'Excellent, mate! I can give you some tips: beach bars in Bali, shopping in Bangkok.'

'I was thinking more museum-based locations.'

'Right,' Della said warily.

'For Evelyn, it's a way of making up for lost time,' George added.

'Years ago I worked at the British Museum, but that journey was cut short. Now, I'd like to see it through, by seeing artefacts in their home countries,' Evelyn explained. 'I was thinking of starting with the Museum of Oriental Ceramics in Osaka. But geographically, the Egyptian Museum in Cairo makes more sense.' Shyly, she turned to George. 'What do you think?'

'How about we start in Athens?' he mused.

Alison caught Sariah's eye and mouthed, 'We?'

'That's great,' Della said warmly. 'Imagine, Evelyn – you'll see pagodas and pyramids and temples. What an adventure.'

'I know.' Evelyn was giddy with excitement. 'I'm going to take some art materials too and try drawing the things we see.' She looked down. 'I used to love drawing.' Then she nodded at George. 'It might encourage someone else to rediscover his artistic side as well.'

'About time he found his own style,' Jacob added with a wry smile.

'But before we go, I do have a final favour to ask,' Evelyn said. 'It would be great if someone could keep the beach clean going. Not every day – that was probably a bit over-zealous on my part – but maybe once a week?'

'I'd be happy to step up,' Bob said, having mostly recovered from the whole sand-in-the-eyes problem. Evelyn pretended not to notice that the affliction had spread to Jacob and Alison, and even Sariah was doing some rapid blinking.

Having said her piece, Evelyn felt her shoulders relax and she turned to gaze out at the sea, which was glittering prettily under a clearer sky. It was turning into the sort of day when she wouldn't want to be anywhere else but Portheast, yet at the same time, she was itching to venture beyond that horizon. As her mother had said, there was a whole world out there.

Almost to herself, Evelyn began to speak again. 'The good thing about doing a beachcomb is that you slow down. You start to spot the little things that go unnoticed.' She kept her eyes fixed straight ahead. 'Then, even if something is broken, with the right people around to help, it can be mended and made whole again.'

Nobody said another word because there was no need and, after a while, as if by mutual agreement, the group of friends began to collect their things and walk up the beach, the incoming tide chasing at their heels and the seagulls wheeling above them.

ACKNOWLEDGEMENTS

First, a huge thank you to you, the reader, for choosing *The Museum of Second Chances*. As soon as I started writing about Evelyn and the people of Portheast, I felt immersed in her world and I hope it was the same for you.

As always, my thanks to Alastair, my first reader and my greatest supporter. Thank you for cheering me on (and the tea and toast every morning).

I am also grateful to:

SOME SPECIAL PLACES

For this book, I delved into my memories of visiting weird and wonderful little museums around the UK. As a child, I remember an agricultural museum in Dorset that was full of rusty tools, old apple sacks and cider flagons. Then, when my son was little, my friend Caroline and I used to take our boys to a place called The Hop Farm. There was a soft play area, but also a museum, with dioramas featuring endearingly wonky mannequins and displays of old sweet wrappers.

I also visited a place called Kent Life on a trip with my daughter's school, with room sets from yesteryear. I don't think the kids were very impressed by the recreated 1960s kitchen or the hop-pickers' cabin, but I longed to step into those frozen-in-time worlds and linger a while, just like Evelyn.

More recently (ironically, after I'd almost finished writing this book) I visited the Mevagissey Museum in Cornwall. It's a treasure trove with a similar feel, full of interesting objects and recordings of locals' experiences. A special mention goes out to the RNLI volunteer staff there, who are lovely.

Then there's a slightly bigger institution called the British Museum. Fresh out of university, I worked at the British Library, which back then was housed at the centre of the museum in London's Bloomsbury. It was an archaic world and the memory of its galleries and warrens of corridors, not to mention a cast of true eccentrics, has remained with me.

However, the place that has been the biggest inspiration for this book is the south coast of Cornwall, and much of it was written there. *Meur ras* to its people, who welcome visitors and share this beautiful place and its history. Please note, the councillors in this book – and the council's processes – are all figments of my imagination. The same goes for the vicar at St Agnes and its record-keeping, and while some places named in this book are real, others are imaginary.

A big thank you to Cornish history and heritage expert Michael Bunney for checking some of the details. Any errors are mine alone and the events are fictional.

My Parents

Like Evelyn, I have a lifelong love of rummaging in jumble sales and charity shops, where a faded photograph, a piece of hand-worked lace or a lone teacup can conjure up a sense of past lives.

I inherited this habit from my late mother, Maureen (along with being a voracious reader).

As a child I'd tag along on her weekly trips to the nearby Portobello Road market on a Friday, where she'd somehow winkle out gems from piles of old clothes or a tabletop of tarnished trinkets.

In turn, I dragged my daughter around charity shops from a young age and she's now continuing the family tradition. In fact, it's come full circle with her being the one who spots all the best stuff and me saying, 'Can we go home soon?'

My father, Philip, has passed on an appreciation of art and this helped me visualise how the paintings in this book might look. In recent years, my father's dementia has meant that he can't access many memories, but he will always ask me, 'How's the writing going?' and I really appreciate that.

Publishing People

I'm indebted to my agent, the amazing Hayley Steed, for supporting my writing journey. She has invaluable insights and is the best champion I could hope for. My thanks also to her assistant Mina Yakinya and the wider team at Janklow & Nesbit for their enthusiasm for *The Museum of Second Chances*.

At Amazon Publishing, I loved working with my editor Victoria Pepe, and I learned a lot from her about creating stories that tap into your emotions but ultimately make you feel more hopeful about life, community and friends. My great thanks to my new editor Bekah Pickering, who also has a passion for great stories and is a pleasure to work with.

A book is brought to life by editing and I had the best team, with Mike Jones (who also came up with the perfect artist for the Horizons painting), Rebecca Baker and Ian Howe.

Thank you to designer Emma Rogers, who created the gorgeous book cover. I love how the longer you look at it, the more details you notice. I feel sure Evelyn would approve.

I am very grateful to the fellow writers who have read my books and provided such lovely quotes; your support is so appreciated.

Great Friends

A big thank you to the perfect group of Bristol and Bath writers that I am lucky enough to meet up with: Charlotte Packer, Zoe Somerville and Lucy Barker. Our chats have kept me going through all the ups and downs of this unpredictable publishing process. The same goes for the Lake Union writers – what a lovely bunch of people you are.

A special thank you to my lovely friend who let me use her first name for one of the characters. She has nothing whatsoever in common with that character; I just thought the name was a good fit!

Finally, I discovered the Museo degli Innocenti in Florence, thanks to reading *Wet Paint* by Chloë Ashby. Like the Foundling Museum in London, it has a collection of love tokens, left as identifiers with babies that had to be given up. Each scrap of cloth, amulet or hairpin in that museum felt heartbreaking.

I posted a story on Instagram saying, 'I wish I could write a foundling's story, but I'm not a historical novelist.' A woman I used to work with messaged back: 'I'm sure you could find a way.' The idea lodged in my mind and when I later found out about Cornwall's mother and baby homes, a story began to take shape. Thank you, Harriet Paterson, for saying the right thing at the right time.

Lovely Readers

I want to say a very sincere thank you to the many readers around the world who sent me messages after reading my debut, *Tell Me How This Ends*, saying how it had helped them understand their own experiences of grief.

Somehow, readers' messages always seem to arrive in my inbox just as I'm wrangling with some writing problem and they buoy me up at just the right moment. Similarly, I am grateful for the messages and reviews for *The Last Time I Saw You*. We writers really appreciate readers' and bloggers' reviews and they help our books get seen by more readers.

Second Chance Moments

In October 2024, we lost our dog Lottie, who was the inspiration for Dave, the equally beloved dog of my first book. We missed her dreadfully and couldn't contemplate getting another dog.

But then in the spring of 2025, shortly after I'd started writing this book, I saw a Facebook post about a dog needing a new home. We met Jack the Whippet and we fell for him.

Thank you, Jennifer, who gave Jack his second chance, and Norfolk Greyhound Rescue, who put us in touch. Jack brings us joy every day.

I'm a big believer in second chances and my life has taken several unexpected swerves. In my thirties, I gave up a great job on a UK magazine to travel to Papua New Guinea and work on a community newspaper. It was an experience that opened up new horizons and it has stayed with me and my family.

In my forties, I was back in the UK working as a subeditor on an interiors magazine. Again, it was an enviable job, but I found myself hankering for something different. I handed in my notice and slowly built up to writing features for magazines and newspapers. It was a gamble that paid off.

Then, in my fifties, I began writing fiction. At first, I did this quite secretively, unwilling to admit it was a lifetime ambition. I'd never studied creative writing and I knew it was a long shot. But I also knew that if I didn't try, I'd never know if I could.

Today, I can't quite believe I get to do this as my job.

Like Evelyn and her friends, we all deserve second – and third and fourth – chances in life. If you are wondering about taking a chance, maybe this is your sign to do so.

If you're contemplating a change, or have already made one, I'd love to hear from you. Why not message me via Instagram, Substack or Facebook? I'd love to keep this conversation going.

More Information

There is a very moving BBC Devon radio documentary called *The Crying Shame*, about the Rosemundy mother and baby home that existed in St Agnes. It is by Dr Phil Frampton, who has worked tirelessly to uncover truths, and his research provided me with valuable information. His website is philframpton.co.uk.

In Cornwall, the RNLI plays a life-saving role. I found their website (rnli.org) useful and one of their rescue stories inspired the one Carl Brown tells Evelyn.

British Divers Marine Life Rescue (bdmlr.org.uk) rescues stranded animals and raises awareness about the accidental entanglement of seals, dolphins and other species due to fishing gear and plastic waste.

Many coastal villages carry out informal beach cleans and welcome help. Surfers Against Sewage (sas.org.uk) is one of several charities working to reduce plastic pollution.

SUGGESTED QUESTIONS FOR YOUR BOOK CLUB

1. Four objects hold clues to four characters' stories. If you were asked to submit a special object to a museum, what would it be?

2. Alison tells Evelyn, 'It's hard when secrets come out. But it's a lot worse when they stay hidden.' Is this true for everyone in the book – or should some secrets have stayed buried?

3. Evelyn tells Rose, 'Home isn't a place, it's the people'. Does this reflect your own experiences of community?

4. Adoption and fostering are integral to many families, now and in the past. Did Evelyn and Sariah's experiences make you reflect on what makes 'a family'?

5. Evelyn's relationship with Asa ended very suddenly. Could she have handled this differently?

6. How did Alison's storyline affect you? Could she have left Roy sooner?

7. How do you imagine Evelyn and George's global adventures will pan out? Will they thrive outside Portheast – or look forward to returning to the town they call home?

If you loved *The Museum of Second Chances*, why not read Jo Leevers' debut novel, *Tell Me How This Ends*.

Chapter One

Henrietta

The bench Henrietta Lockwood chooses to sit on is at the junction of three main roads. It could not be considered a peaceful spot, but it is convenient. She estimates it to be one minute's walk from this bench to the Rosendale Drop-In Centre, where she has a job interview in twenty-two minutes. She will leave the bench in twelve minutes, just to be sure.

Being late October, it is a little cold out here, but she does not wish to pay for the privilege of sitting inside a café. She can see one from her vantage point. It is called Plant Life, which she thinks is a very ill-advised name and, if she didn't have an appointment at 2 p.m., she would explain this mistake to the proprietor.

Despite the weather, Henrietta can feel a sweaty patch collecting on her back, so she leans forward to ensure it doesn't seep into her blouse. It is a result of her keeping her backpack firmly on. Granted, the only person who has even glanced at her was a sad-looking woman walking two chihuahuas, but muggings are on the rise. Henrietta knows this is true because she reads about them on a daily basis in the city's free newspaper.

The drop-in centre (why don't they just call it the I've Got Cancer Centre, she thinks) is located in the west wing of a hospital in an exclusive part of London, all Victorian squares, private gardens and tall plane trees. Henrietta can see it from her bench: a handsome double-fronted building with fluted pillars either side of glass front doors.

The building may be elegant but the people who come and go are all sorts. A rake-thin woman in a Puffa jacket and a billowing skirt is making slow progress up the ramp: she keeps a firm hold on the handrail and her body is oddly tilted. As she reaches the doors, an elderly man in a camel coat is on his way out. Wordlessly, he steps aside to let her pass, his face ashen, fingers fumbling for his buttons. The Rosendale Drop-In Centre does not, Henrietta has to admit, look like the jolliest of workplaces.

The advertisement for this job had been buried in the back pages of the *London Review of Books*. Since she inadvertently became a lady of leisure, Henrietta rather enjoys her fortnightly read of the classified section, tut-tutting at the frivolity on display. Yoga and writing retreats in Greece. People seeking a mate to share interests in poetry, hillwalking 'and possibly more'. But then she spotted this:

The Life Stories Project

Interviewer and transcriber required three days a week, including Saturdays.

Typing, copy-editing skills and empathetic manner essential. Six-month contract with possibility of renewal, funding pending.

A short-term job is far from ideal, but with a CV peppered with unexplained gaps and abrupt terminations, Henrietta can't be too picky. The 'empathetic manner' bit of the advertisement is also slightly concerning, so for the past week Henrietta has been practising facial expressions in front of a mirror.

In the privacy of her bathroom, she tried out a wide smile. This would be her 'hello' face. Then she tilted her head to one side, to show empathy. Even to Henrietta, the results looked alarming. There is a reason, she realised, why monkeys bare their teeth as an act of aggression.

Luckily, Henrietta's teeth are pleasingly even. Her face is round and her hair is cut to shoulder length, a style bestowed upon her at the age of eleven that she has never felt the urge to change. She does not indulge in make-up. Even at the age of thirty-two, her efforts always look like those of a child let loose with a set of crayons.

However, she knows that clothes make a good impression, so she spent an entire evening removing the lint from some navy British Home Stores trousers that served her well in her old job. A blue blouse ordered from an advertisement in the *Radio Times* some years ago is, she judges, formal and yet casual.

The hands of her Timex watch (a sixteenth-birthday present, still going strong) tell her it is time to leave her bench. Swallowing down a familiar knot of dread, Henrietta puts on her 'hello' face and strides towards the Rosendale Centre.

'So . . .' The woman in the pink sweater is shuffling pages around her desk in a random manner that indicates she is rather ill prepared. Finally, Pink Sweater looks up at her. 'Aha. Henrietta Lockwood. Why do you think you would be suited to this job?'

Henrietta clears her throat and begins. 'I believe I am suited to this post on several counts. One: I am not prone to outbursts of emotion or sentimentality. Two: I possess excellent editorial skills, so I am well equipped to transcribe and then type up people's life stories before they die. Three: I like a deadline.'

It is almost word for word what Henrietta had written in her application letter. But Pink Sweater – 'Call me Audrey' – doesn't seem to notice. Audrey looks across the desk through thick glasses that magnify her eyes into two huge fish-like orbs.

'It's not always that simple,' she sighs, bringing her hands together. 'But, yes, here at the Life Stories Project, detachment can be an advantage.'

She swivels the computer screen around to face Henrietta. 'The final part of your interview is a proofreading test. This is Kenton's Life Story, which I wrote up myself. We lost him last week, but I got most of it down. His family would like copies in time for the funeral. That's often what happens. Unless we are caught unawares . . .' She trails off. 'Anyway, you have forty-five minutes. Are you familiar with "track changes"?'

She needn't have worried because track changes is Henrietta's very favourite thing to do. She is happiest when she can correct punctuation, spelling and facts, and highlight her superior knowledge in red. As Audrey leaves the room, Henrietta is already tapping away, scoring through words, frowning at the shockingly poor grasp of grammar.

When Audrey shows her out, she points to where Henrietta will conduct the Life Story interviews if she gets the job. Momentarily, Henrietta is confused because she had pictured herself in a private office, rather like Audrey's but with a window. And a pot plant. Perhaps one of those scent diffusers, too. But it seems that Audrey is gesturing towards a corner table in the centre's coffee bar, just by the main entrance foyer.

'People prefer the informal atmosphere. They like to talk over a cuppa,' Audrey says, as Henrietta hovers by the automatic doors. The glass panes judder, trying to open and shut, leaving Henrietta unsure whether to step outside or move back into the warmth, because Audrey is still talking.

'Officially it's called the Reith Café – after a generous donor. But all the staff call it the Grief Café!' Audrey delivers this as if it is a punchline to a joke, but Henrietta thinks it best to ignore this. Jokes, in her experience, feel like a ball thrown at great speed: hard to catch; even trickier to keep a rally going. And Henrietta has never been a games person.

'I can see how the coffee bar setting would facilitate conversation,' she replies levelly, stepping out on to the stone steps.

'I look forward to hearing from you presently,' she adds, as the glass doors snap shut.

It feels good to walk away from the fug of hand sanitiser, old, unwashed clothes and old, unwashed people. Henrietta admits she is a little disappointed by the Rosendale's down-at-heel ambiance. Having done her research thoroughly, Henrietta knows that this centre is the first to pioneer the Life Stories Project, an initiative funded by Ryan Brooks, a 1980s pop star who lost his wife to ovarian cancer. She's watched the video where Ryan does a walkabout at the Rosendale Centre, high-fiving his way round a TV lounge, then looking more serious as he talks about his wife, Skye, who had died swiftly and too young. 'If someone had helped Skye to write her life story, our little girl could read it when she's older,' says Ryan, jiggling his bald, scrunch-faced baby. 'Everybody has a story – and these life stories should be heard.'

Having so much time these days to listen to the radio and watch daytime TV, Henrietta is not surprised that Ryan's idea has hit a nerve. There are grief podcasts, cancer blogs about good days, bad days and chemo days, and vlogs on dying well and making bucket lists. Henrietta finds it all rather unseemly, but she's clearly in a minority because other people are falling over themselves to talk about grief or their own imminent death and Ryan's hashtags – #last-words, #lifestories and #grievingwithryan – went viral for a while.

As a reward for getting through her interview, Henrietta treats herself to a scone from the Plant Life café. There is some confusion over the price, but it seems £4 is deemed perfectly reasonable for an artisan baked product in this neighbourhood. Vegan, apparently.

She carries the paper bag to what she now considers to be 'her' bench and eats her scone in small chunks, chewing and swallowing each morsel before picking off the next. It's a little dry, in her opinion. A pigeon is making its jerky, circuitous way towards her, looking at her sideways with one orange-ringed eye. Henrietta quickly drops the last of her scone back in the bag and folds over the top. She's wary of these bold, unpredictable birds, but will try not to let the incursion spoil her moment: the sun has come out and she might have a new job.

In fact, there is already a voicemail from Audrey on her phone, but she will wait until she gets home before listening to it, with Dave by her side. Dave likes to share her news, good or bad, and has seen her through some difficult times.

Henrietta is about to place her paper bag in the bin when she has a change of heart. Making sure no one is looking, she tips the remaining crumbs into a small pile on the pavement. Being a resident of Chelsea, that pigeon probably has more of an appetite for vegan scones than Henrietta.

Back in her flat, she sits on the sofa and listens to Audrey's message several times. After the third time, Henrietta allows the smallest bubble of pleasure to rise up inside her. Dave, however, has already lost interest and is busy making a burrow in the cushions next to her, leaving a scattering of coarse black and tan hairs in his wake.

He's panting slightly, waiting for her toast crusts, and his breath leaves something to be desired. She loves Dave dearly, but it would be nice to have someone else to share her news with. She could ring her parents, she supposes, but she's not ready to have her bubble burst just yet.

Henrietta pads into the kitchen, drops two more slices of white bread into the toaster and, after they pop up, slathers them with dairy spread. She eats standing by the window, looking out at the street. After a while, Upstairs Woman comes out of their shared front door and sets off at a clip to the bus stop. She's wearing her blue coat, which Henrietta worries will be far too flimsy for this time of year. Henrietta steps back behind her curtain, just in case her neighbour looks back, but she never does. She's always in such a hurry.

All communication between Henrietta and Upstairs Woman is done via notes or texts. Henrietta prefers the former, which she writes in neat cursive letters and slides under her neighbour's door. Then Upstairs Woman replies by text. Their messages say things like 'Your food waste caddy is on pavement. Unsightly. Please remove ASAP' (from Henrietta). Or 'Your dog sounded lonely. Used spare key to let him into courtyard. Hope was OK' (from Upstairs Woman).

On cue, Dave saunters in, hoping for more crusts. He's starting to smell again and Henrietta isn't sure if it's his ears or his glands. She sighs. Either way, it's time to take him out for his constitutional. Pushing her feet into her Crocs, Henrietta bends down to clip on his lead. It's a special orange one that has RESCUE DOG printed along its length. This gets them a few sympathetic looks when Dave lunges, barks and snaps his way around the streets because Dave hates, in no particular order, cyclists, pedestrians, buggies, skateboards, cats, Labradors and German shepherds. Well, most dogs really. Next, Henrietta puts a fluorescent dog coat over

Dave's head and fastens the Velcro. This time, its lettering reads IGNORE ME.

'Right, walkies!' she chirrups, without conviction. Already Dave's claws are scrabbling on the laminate flooring and a low growl is building at the back of his throat. As she opens the front door, Dave's furious barking begins, a sound that is surely now familiar to every one of her neighbours. His barking reaches a crescendo as they head off down the street, one woman and her dog against the world.

Henrietta's new position might not be everyone's dream job, but it will suit her just fine. There will be no team targets or bonding sessions and at least the dead can't file official complaints about 'dangerous and intimidating behaviour' from beyond the grave. The people she'll meet won't be around for long – all she will have to do is transcribe their rambling, probably quite tedious memories, sort them into chronological order and turn them into Life Story books. The drop-in centre may be in the business of death, but Henrietta is only too glad that business is booming.

ABOUT THE AUTHOR

Photo © Charlotte Gray 2022

Jo Leevers grew up in London and began writing fiction after a career in magazine journalism. Her Kindle No.1 bestselling debut, *Tell Me How This Ends*, was a BBC Radio 2 Book Club choice. Whether writing fiction or interviewing people for articles, she is fascinated by the stories and secrets that we all carry with us. She has two grown-up children and lives with her husband and their rescue whippet, Jack, in Bristol. She is on Instagram as @joleevers

Follow the Author on Amazon

If you enjoyed this book, follow Jo Leevers on Amazon to be notified when the author releases a new book!
To do this, please follow these instructions:

Desktop:

1) Search for the author's name on Amazon or in the Amazon App.
2) Click on the author's name to arrive on their Amazon page.
3) Click the 'Follow' button.

Mobile and Tablet:

1) Search for the author's name on Amazon or in the Amazon App.
2) Click on one of the author's books.
3) Click on the author's name to arrive on their Amazon page.
4) Click the "Follow" button.

Kindle eReader and Kindle App:

If you enjoyed this book on a Kindle eReader or in the Kindle App, you will find the author 'Follow' button after the last page.